"*Only on Gameday* has all the good stuff. Slow burn, banter, fake relationship, so much pining! Classic Callihan. Loved it!"

—**MOLLY FADER**, *USA TODAY* bestselling author

"*Only on Gameday* is a five-alarm fire of a romance. The chemistry between Pen and August will grab you by the throat. Absolutely delicious!"

—**XIO AXELROD**, *USA TODAY* bestselling author

More praise for Kristen Callihan's Game On series

"*The Game Plan* has pulse pounding sex and stomach twisting emotion. I fell in love with the hero by chapter one, straight into all-out lust by chapter two."

—**TESSA BAILEY**, #1 *New York Times* bestselling author

"*The Friend Zone* is an exquisite, delicious cupcake of a book. You will gobble it down and hunger for more."

—**SARINA BOWEN**, *USA TODAY* bestselling author

"I've fallen for another Drew . . . Drew Baylor is that delicious mixture of sweet and hot in Kristen Callihan's sexy new adult book *The Hook Up*. I dare you not to fall in love with him too."

—**MONICA MURPHY**, *New York Times* bestselling author

"Smart, sharp, and wonderfully romantic; a hero to die for and a heroine so endearing you'll want her for a friend; I fell hard for this book and Kristen Callihan's incredible writing!"

—**KATY EVANS**, *New York Times* bestselling author

Also by Kristen Callihan

Game On series

The Hook Up
The Friend Zone
The Game Plan
The Hot Shot
Only on Gameday

VIP series

Idol
Managed
Fall
Exposed

For additional books by Kristen Callihan,
visit her website, kristencallihan.com.

KRISTEN CALLIHAN

ONLY ON GAMEDAY

MIRA

/// MIRA™

ISBN-13: 978-1-335-66128-9

Only on Gameday

Copyright © 2026 by Kristen Callihan

All rights reserved. No part of this book may be used or reproduced in any manner whatsoever without written permission.

Without limiting the exclusive rights of any author, contributor or the publisher of this publication, any unauthorized use of this publication to train generative artificial intelligence (AI) technologies is expressly prohibited. Harlequin also exercises their rights under Article 4(3) of the Digital Single Market Directive 2019/790 and expressly reserve this publication from the text and data mining exception.

This is a work of fiction. Names, characters, places and incidents are either the product of the author's imagination or are used fictitiously. Any resemblance to actual persons, living or dead, businesses, companies, events or locales is entirely coincidental.

For questions and comments about the quality of this book, please contact us at CustomerService@Harlequin.com.

TM is a trademark of Harlequin Enterprises ULC.

MIRA
22 Adelaide St. West, 41st Floor
Toronto, Ontario M5H 4E3, Canada
MIRABooks.com

HarperCollins Publishers
Macken House, 39/40 Mayor Street Upper,
Dublin 1, D01 C9W8, Ireland
www.HarperCollins.com

Recycling programs for this product may not exist in your area.

Printed in U.S.A.

For Kimberly and Cat. Without them, there would be no book.
And for the readers, always.

PROLOGUE

AUGUST

YOU SEE THAT guy? The one standing precariously on the four-top, wearing tuxedo pants, a—God, is that a purple faux fur coat—and nothing else? The one yelling, "Are you not entertained?" with arms spread wide as a crowd of drunken onlookers cheer.

No, fucko. No, I am not.

I am embarrassed as hell. Heat-flushing, "please make it stop," "why won't it stop" humiliation. The problem is?

That wannabe gladiator fucko is me. And I can't seem to shut him up. I am outside myself, looking on in horror as I decide to gild the lily and dance . . . Oh, God, is that . . . No, no, no.

It's the Funky Chicken.

I am dancing the funky chicken. At a black-tie fundraiser, crawling with media. There's got to be a hundred phones lifted high and facing me. All those little palm-sized rectangles, like eyes of hell, recording every second.

It might not have been so bad if Coach hadn't given me a "lock it up and concentrate on your game" speech a few short hours earlier. My agent had done the same the day before. They're both here now, standing on opposite sides of the room, sporting surprisingly similar stances: arms crossed over chests, legs braced shoulder width apart. Angry sentinels itching to take me down.

My pulse kicks up. Horror courses through my veins. This

is not the way to celebrate our second game win. I know I'm fucking up. Inside I'm shouting: *Stop, this isn't me. I'm never like this. I'm a rock, the cool head both on and off the field.* Yet what do I do? I wink at Coach before gyrating my hips. I'm woefully out of sync with the music. I mean, if you're going to go down in flames, it should at least be skillfully done, with a certain panache. But I'm a hot mess.

Before you ask, I'll answer: No. There is absolutely no reason for me to be acting like a clown right now. I have the world at my feet—good looks, good health, went number one in the draft, an outrageous contract, multiple corporate sponsorships, starting quarterback for a team that has a ton of potential . . .

Everything I've ever wanted is mine for the taking.

Maybe that's the problem. When you've reached the top the only place to go is down.

Isn't that what they say?

I think I'm about to find out. I take a wrong step, the table wobbles, the room spins. My stomach roils. What was once up is now down. I go down, down, down.

My first thought is, *Not the arm!*

My second?

Well done, fucko. Are you not entertained?

ONE

PEN

"ARE YOU NOT entertained?" I mutter, as I squint into the void that has become my view and try to pinpoint when it all went wrong. I'm not lost; I know exactly where I'm going. But that's just geography. My life however, is another story.

I push back on the swell of worry that threatens, and concentrate on the music throbbing all around the cocoon of my little car.

If you grew up in my house, you would have heard my mom listening to Nirvana. She'd blast it on those rare occasions she cooked dinner, and our town house would pulse with frenetic guitar licks, Kurt Cobain's biting sarcasm slicing air thick with the heat of the stove and redolent with *soffritto* and garlic. To this day, if I catch a whiff of ragù, I want to shout out, *Entertain us*.

Mom says that, despite her generation's demand to be entertained, they never expected it from anyone and made their own fun. My generation, on the other hand, has entertainment at the ready, 24/7 at the tap of a screen.

Given the utter glut of sensory riches we have, you'd think we'd grow tired of it all. But no, we thirst for more. Always more. Maybe that's why some people act out the way they do; a desperate need to provide us with more.

I think of this. Of my mother. Of inebriated chicken-dancing yahoos and . . . other things, as I wind my way down a road that is too narrow and too dark for comfort. It's my fault for taking an alternate route out of Boston to beat the traffic that flows into the suburbs. I've never been this way before. Darkness and the heavy rain are disorienting me.

My stomach has a nice little clench-and-unclench rhythm going that's picking up speed.

With a huff, I forward "Smells Like Teen Spirit" in search of something a little calmer. U2's "Bad" fills the small space of the car for about twenty seconds before it's interrupted by the shrill sound of my phone ringing.

Despite white knuckling it through the night, my lips quirk. I hit the answer button on my steering wheel. "Speak of the devil."

"And she shall appear," my mom finishes happily, her voice coming at me through the car's speakers. "Were you thinking of me, Penny Lane?"

"Hard not to when someone loaded a 'Don't Forget to Call Your Mother' playlist on my phone."

She chuckles, and the clenching in my stomach eases a bit at the familiar sound. "And yet here I am calling *you*."

"I was too busy listening to ancient Complaint Rock."

"Horrible child!"

I snicker then turn on my windshield wipers. What was once a light mist has gone full-on rain. Great. "What's up?"

"What's that noise?" Mom says over me.

"Mother Nature's wrath. It's raining like hellfire now."

"Maybe you should get off the road."

"I'm in the middle of nowhere. I'm not getting off until I'm there."

"Why on earth are you in the middle of nowhere? The house is in the suburbs."

"Yeah, well, tell that to my map app. I've been sent a weird-ass circuitous route to avoid an accident backup."

Mom's voice grows tight. "Now I'll worry about you until you're there."

"I'm fine."

"Are you?" By the quiet concern in her voice, I know she's not asking about my driving anymore.

My hands tighten on the wheel. "I'm fine, Mom. There's nothing more to talk about."

We'd said all there was to say without totally devolving into a full-on fight. And I'm not eager to continue.

The windshield wipers squeak-squawk as tension stretches between us. But then she sighs in resignation.

"At least tell me you're close."

I glance at the little map on my car's screen. I might not have my own place at the moment, but thanks to my mom, I've had a nice car to drive while visiting her in Boston for the week before my final semester of college begins. I am not even a little ashamed. It's keeping me safe and dry right now. "About five minutes out. What's up?"

"Oh, nothing." Mom sounds way too casual.

"Uh-huh."

"I was just wondering if you saw the news about Luck."

That clenching in my stomach? It returns full force. I glare into the dark blur of the night. "Luck?"

Mom's not fooled for an instant. She's my mom, after all. "Little Augie Luck?"

He's not so little now. And he's never been "Augie" to me.

Sweat-slicked skin, ripped muscles framed by that ridiculous purple faux fur coat. *Are you not entertained?*

Jackass.

My fingers flex on the wheel. When had they grown so sweaty? Ick. "No, I haven't seen the news."

There's a beat in which Mom absorbs my lie and lets it pass.

I shoot a defiant glare in the direction of the phone. I do not need to talk about August Jackass Luck and his increasing list of frankly baffling tom-fuckery moves. It's hard enough to get away from it in normal life. And given where I'm headed? My mother bringing up "Augie" is just too much.

"I only ask because—"

"Mom, I'm driving in a rainstorm on some spooky haunted house lane. The last thing I want to talk about is August. The guy gets enough attention as it is. I don't care enough to know, honestly, and—"

"Penelope."

Just that. In *that* tone. My mother and I may be friends but she's still my mother. Sassing is not allowed. Evasion, on the other hand?

"Where's your compassion?" she asks in that famous dramatic, hand-wringing fashion of hers that has theater attendees at the edge of their seats. As for me? I'm immune to it; she is my mother, after all.

Scoffing, I flick on my turn signal and make a right. "Ma, you've got to be kidding. August Luck has the world in the palm of his hand."

"He's falling apart, Pen."

My mind's eye sees that perfectly formed chest glistening under hot lights, tight abs moving in exertion. Dark hair falling over wild silver eyes, diamond bright smile. Disgrace looks good on August.

Frowning, I push the image away. *And stay there, damn it.*

"He'll be fine." Will he? Something is definitely wrong there. He's only two games into his rookie season and is acting like an attention seeking fool. Does it matter? I've never been involved in his life, never will be. "He always is."

"That's my point. This isn't like the boy." (I scoff here at the term "boy.") "He's the levelheaded one. When he was little, he used to separate his Froot Loops by color."

No, I will not smile. Luck is charming enough as it is without adding onto it.

"He saves the instructions to everything, did you know? Who does that?"

"Total rebels."

"Smart-ass."

Luckily, she can't see me rolling my eyes. "Look, Mom. This August retrospective has been great and all, but maybe you should call him if you're so worried."

"*Ooh*, I knew you were still mad. You're being smarmy."

How well she knows me.

"I just don't understand why we have to talk about him."

Yes, she knows me well, and yet she's never picked up that I shy away from August as a topic of discussion. Even now, she digs in.

"It's important—" She pauses when I make a contrary noise. Then speaks louder. "You should empathize with him because—"

"It's getting a little dicey here. I'm gonna have to let you go and call back when I get there."

"Pen." It's a sigh that says I'm being childish.

Like I don't know that. Frankly, I feel a bit like a child at the moment. Then again, I'm twenty-two; it's not as though she can revoke my car privileges . . .

"Okay, Mom?" I say as though fighting with a faulty phone connection. "Call you later, bye!"

"Penelope Jane—"

I cut her off before she can finish. "Kisses and hugs. Love you!"

And then I hang up.

Oh, that's going to come back to haunt me.

"I don't care," I mutter, then stick my tongue out at my phone. The fact that she hasn't immediately called me back means I'm not in total trouble. Friction is to be expected at any rate.

Mom and I are dancing around a very awkward place right now. Neither of us has budged our stance on Pegs and Pops's house, and okay, I *might* still be a little salty about it.

"Shit." I need to concentrate better because there's the turn. I switch on my blinker, even though there's no one behind me; one does not ignore the rules just because they can get away with it.

Oh, but how I wish I could.

TWO

PEN

THE LUCK HOUSE sits at the end of a semicircular drive. Or should I say it looms, because the white clapboard center hall colonial is huge. Thankfully, it also has a nice wide portico. I park as close as I can to the front step and, holding my coat overhead, make a mad dash to the door.

I'm fairly dry when I reach it. But outside is cold as hell. It creeps up my bones and shivers along my flesh. The narrow windows that frame the front door reveal a slice of the warmly lit big hall with its worn and well-loved Persian runner, rectory red walls, the antique sideboard that May dented when riding her scooter indoors.

Another shiver goes through me, this one of longing. I want to be in there where it's warm and familiar. It's as simple as knocking on the door, but it doesn't feel that way at all. It's as though it won't matter; I can get inside but I'll still be all alone.

Shrugging off self-pity, I ring the bell. There's absolutely no need to be maudlin right now. Everything is fine, and . . .

A man strides to the door. Holy hell is that . . . ?

I'm transfixed, frozen with my hand halfway up in the act of ringing again. No. It can't be . . .

The door swings open with a soft woosh, and we stare at each other, this man and I. Only, he's no mere man. He never was. It shouldn't be a surprise that he's here; this is his family home. But, in my heart of hearts, I didn't expect him to be visiting tonight. It's Saturday. I thought he'd head straight back to LA after Thursday night's game. I *thought* it would just be Margo, the girls, and *maybe* March. Mom *said* it would only be them!

Yet here he is in vivid, stunning color. All six foot four of him.

I guess that's what Mom had been trying to tell me. *That'll teach you to hang up on her.* I tell myself to shut it and stare up at August.

It's been a few years since we've been face-to-face. Sure, I've seen him in recent pictures, *in the freaking news*, and in this week's latest viral videos. But, in person, these differences are shocking and, frankly, overwhelming.

He looks exactly the same. And totally different. How can that be? There's not an angle or line of his face that I hadn't covertly studied throughout our childhood. I would recognize August Luck anywhere.

And yet . . . He's grown into himself. Hard where he used to be somewhat soft. From age fifteen on, he'd towered over me. I'm used to feeling small around him. But now he's huge. A veritable wall of honed muscle.

He's so attractive it hurts—deep in the center of my chest. I feel like I've been kicked. Maybe that's why I can do nothing more than gape at him and blurt out, "August?"

There's an awkward beat and then, "Penelope." As if my name is the answer.

Most people who know me either use Pen or, if we're close, Penny. I don't know how it started or why, but August usually calls me Penelope—in that stilted, disapproving way of his that makes it sound more like a dismissal than a greeting.

And we're stuck on a loop because I blurt out his name again. "August?"

The corner of his lip twitches, except it looks more like agitation than amusement. "Penelope."

That mellow voice rolls over me with the force of a wave.

Okay, this has to stop. But I can't seem to refrain from staring. Why does he have to be so appealing to me? It would be easier if I could simply write him off as another hot guy. But, no. August Luck has the singular ability to turn my brain to mush and my knees to jelly.

I tell myself that this reaction is nothing special; almost everyone who encounters August takes pause. He's always been beautiful. Glossy hair so dark it's nearly black, straight yet strong nose, firm lips, an almost aggressively stern square jawline: all of it lies in perfect symmetry.

Before the draft last spring, videos of August running drills at the NFL scouting combine went viral. Slow-motion shots of him sprinting were everywhere, prompting sports commentators to laughingly refer to August as a Roman god or runway model.

However, his eyes are the real kicker. I often wondered if anyone looked August Luck in the eye without feeling a little hitch of wonder. Deep set, under sweeping dark brows and framed by long black lashes, his blue-gray eyes are so pale and luminous, they appear sliver.

Lucky Eyes was what the Lucks were called in school. Neil Luck, their father, has grass-green eyes; Margo, their mother, sky blue. Combined, all their children have some shade of vivid green-through-icy-gray eyes that contrast so well with their dark hair.

With those quicksilver eyes alone, August can stop traffic. The whole package? He's too beautiful for words. It has intimidated me my whole childhood. Whenever August Luck walked into a room, I'd soon leave it. Either that or suffer the humiliation of gawking at him, tongue-tied and red-faced.

Great green grapes, woman. Control yourself this time. Back the truck up and be cool.

"August?" I say again. For no reason whatsoever. And distinctly *not* cool. I have, unfortunately, lost the ability to formulate proper thoughts or actions. And it's all his fault.

My interactions with him might have been bearable if August treated me with the same effortless charm he oozes on others, but he never has. When it's between us, he's stoic and distant, and I feel reduced to nothing more than a commercial interrupting his favorite game.

Only something strange is happening. He's gawking too. As if I'm an alien that's just landed and he's not quite sure if he should wave a white flag or run for weapons.

Even more odd? His reaction makes something snap deep inside of me. Suddenly, I don't feel tongue-tied anymore.

"Something wrong?" I ask.

August swallows hard, the line of his brows drawing together. "No. Uh . . . No."

"Okay, then." I gesture toward the entrance hall. "May I come in?"

He starts as though pinched. "What? Yeah. Sure. Sorry."

Maybe I turned my car in the wrong direction a ways back and somehow unknowingly entered a parallel universe. That's the only reason I can account for Mr. Rizz himself stumbling over his words and jerking back like he's lost coordination. Hell, did he have a bad hit and get a concussion?

Craning my neck so I can study his eyes for dilated pupils, I ask him, "Are you all right?"

At that, August scowls, looking a bit more like himself. "Of course." Then, as if it occurs to him that he's acting strange, he sighs expansively and shakes his head. "Rough week. Sorry, Penelope."

The image of him gyrating on a wobbly table fills my head. I bite my lip and glance away. Not before I see him flush again. He takes a bigger step back, and, when I ease past him, closes the door with a little more force than necessary.

"So . . . Penelope." That's all he says.

I nod gravely. "August."

"Penelope."

We're back to that again?

As though reading my mind, he huffs, the corner of his mouth starts to curl.

"Augie? Did I hear the door . . ." Margo walks into the hall by way of the kitchen. She sees me and breaks into a beaming smile. "Penny!"

Before I can say a word, I'm enveloped in a wall of cool silk, warm bosom, and strong arms. Margo squeezes me tight and rocks a bit. It's like being a kid again, but I don't mind.

"It's been so long," she says, still hugging me.

I saw Margo at Mom's place a few months ago, but I smile against her breasts—it's a miracle I can breathe—and manage a muffled, "Missed you too. Happy birthday, Auntie Margo." Her birthday was yesterday, but I didn't want to intrude on the family then. Mom, however, ordered me to "get my butt over there" and wish her well, "pronto!"

Apparently, Mom's insistence was valid because Margo squeezes me tighter and utters a weepy sounding, "Thank you!"

Aunt Margo isn't really my aunt. She's Mom's best friend and college roommate. But we kids gave our mom's friend the honorific of aunt. She's also half a foot taller than me and loves hugs that last forever.

"You're gonna make her tinkle," says a deep voice.

I pull back, and Margo and I glare at August's brother, March, as he saunters into the hallway. A year younger than August, he might as well be his twin. Except, where August is sternly handsome, March has a sunnier expression. Which is kind of odd, given that August, until this bizarre hall incident, has always been just as charismatic.

The main difference—and it's a huge one—is that March never treated me like I was invisible. Something I appreciated so much in my youth that I *might* have had a bit of a crush on him during high school—well, for about a week, anyway.

"Stop teasing Pen," Margo chides. "You know she doesn't like it."

"Pretty sure she loves it, Ma."

I punch his arm right before he gives me a bear hug as well.

"I'll tease *you*," is my very witty threat, also muffled against yet another chest. This one broad and solid as a brick wall.

He laughs and sets me back. There's a twinkle in his eye that I don't entirely trust. "Promise?"

When I give him a repressive glare, March rests his arm around my shoulders and turns to a stone-faced August. "How long has it been since we've seen Penny, Gus-Gus?"

"Since your high school graduation," August answers woodenly.

March and I are the same age, and we graduated together. Has it been that long? I suddenly feel ashamed that I've been neglectful in visiting the Lucks. Well, not all of them, just the males. Then I note the blank stare August is still subjecting me to. There's a good reason I've stayed away from him.

March doesn't seem to notice our weird tension. He pulls me more securely against him. It's strange. Once, I might have swooned if he'd done that, but now it feels more nostalgic and comfortable than anything.

"Doesn't Penny look great?" he asks August.

Okay, now I'm uncomfortable. I resist the urge to pinch March.

August blinks down at me. "She looks nice."

The compliment sounds like it's been dragged from him, delivered in such a deadpan, disingenuous manner that I give him an overly bright smile. *How's that for nice, mister?*

As if reading my mind, he frowns and tries again. "You have nice teeth."

What!

"What?" March manages through a snort.

August blinks again, then turns heel and strides into the kitchen.

Margo shakes her head softly, watching him go.

"Is he okay?" I ask. "I mean, he didn't get a concussion or anything lately?"

This sets March completely off and he's doubling over. I'd been serious in my query, but I guess that sounded bad. I wait for the floor to grant my wish and swallow me whole.

Sadly, the floor remains solid.

Margo, however, huffs in exasperated humor and gives her son an affectionate punch on the shoulder. "Quiet you." To me, she simply shrugs. "Augie's had a rough week."

So I've heard.

THREE

AUGUST

YOU HAVE NICE teeth. Holy shit. What the hell was that? Nice teeth?? Why the great fuck did I say that? Grimacing, I run my hands through my hair and plop down on the old leather couch in the study. My head hurts as though I've had my bell rung.

Might as well have, what with that absolutely nonsensical exchange out there. I still don't exactly know what happened. I'd opened the front door and there she was, Penelope Morrow.

I'd recognize her anywhere—we've known each other our entire lives, of course I would. Except, she's also completely different. She's grown up. Grown up *well*.

How is it that a mere five years can change a sweet little elfin face into . . . art?

I'd majored in art history, much to the amusement of both the press and some of my teammates. Not that I care—art and beauty soothe me in a way that is necessary given the stresses of playing at the top of my chosen sport.

Regardless, when I looked at grown-up Penelope Morrow, with her creamy oval of a face, framed by flowing chocolate-brown hair, and wide brown eyes that seemed both innocent and wise, all I could think was that she resembled the John William Waterhouse painting, *Destiny*.

All the little hairs on my arms had lifted at the thought. Destiny. It had felt . . . portentous. Which is plain ridiculous. I'm clearly on edge with this whole Funky Chicken Gate.

I blow out a breath to dispel that horrible memory. But it doesn't dismiss the image of Pen's face floating around in my head. Her lips are rose pink and pouty. The kind of mouth that needs kissing. And often.

Pinching the bridge of my nose, I let out an expansive sigh. I don't need to be thinking about Pen. I've got enough problems as it is. One huge fucking problem in particular. My insides roil when I think about today's meeting with public relations, my coaches, manager, and my agent—specifically, about how to handle the mess I've made of my image.

"Jesus, Mary, and Joseph," I mutter under my breath. I don't have to toe the line like a criminal let out early on parole. It is, of course, up to me. Laughable, because we all know I either show up as a team player willing to do what it takes to make amends, or I dig in and look uncooperative. Doesn't matter that I am their number one pick, shiny new toy; image is everything, and I've done too much to tarnish it already.

Sinking into the couch, I press the heels of my hands over my eyes.

The door bursts open with enough force to make me flinch. I give a silent groan when March saunters in grinning like a little shit.

"Nice teeth?" He snorts out a laugh. "Seriously?"

"Apparently so." I rub my hands over my face. "Fuck."

March closes the door behind him, then wanders over to Dad's collection of the Luck family footballs lining one of the wall-to-wall bookcases. "That was—"

"Horrific. Yes, I know."

Plucking one of the footballs from the display, he drawls, "I was going to say—"

"Hilarious?" I glare. "You're wrong. It was definitely not hilarious."

March tosses the football between his hands, his grin growing by leaps and bounds. "Oh, I don't know. Seemed pretty fucking funny to me."

"Who the hell comments on a person's teeth?"

"Our orthodontist loves to. Maybe you went into the wrong career."

I grimace. "She's probably wondering if I took one too many blows to the head."

"In fact, she did ask—" He puts a hand up when I give him a death look. "Merely reporting the facts."

"Go away."

March takes a seat on the big wing chair by the fireplace, crossing one leg over the other like he's a professor. "You don't mean that."

"Yes, I do."

"No, you don't. You need me here." He tosses the football again. "For moral support."

I stare him down.

His grin breaks out again. "One doesn't bounce back from 'you have nice teeth' without some sort of game plan."

"Here's my game plan—I kick you out on your ass."

"Like you could." He blows a raspberry through his lips. "Tight end takes quarterback any day."

Cheeky bastard spins the ball on the tip of his finger.

"Dad sees you playing with that, it won't matter. You'll be dead anyway."

"Hey, this is *my* high school championship ball."

"If it's on The Shelf, it's Dad's."

Those are the rules. We don't make them, we merely obey them. He's the best dad I know, but he's also obsessively covetous about his kids' memorabilia. And his own. A Hall of Fame wide receiver, Dad was the start of a football dynasty with his sons following in his wake. He's hella proud.

With a sigh, March returns the ball to its stand. "Stop deflecting. What *was* that?"

"Man, I don't know. Rough week, I guess."

"Bullshit."

I wince and look away.

"I've seen you limp off the field like a lump of pounded meat and give better game than that."

Apparently not anymore.

"Penny's grown up very nice, hasn't she?" He's way too smug.

I deliberately do *not* think of the luminous quality of her skin, as though she held some inner light that the rest of us didn't. She looked soft as a petal. I'd wanted to touch her, to see if the sweetheart shape of her face fit within the rough palm of my hand.

Said hand curls into a fist. There will be no touching of Penelope. While Penelope Morrow has always gotten along well with the rest of my family, I am the outlier. Anytime I'd walk into a room her buoyant mood would deflate like a lead balloon. For whatever reason, Pen does not like me. I'd say I rate at tolerable, but only because she has to.

"Hey, dickhead." March's voice penetrates the fog.

I manage a glare. "What?"

"I said Penny looks pretty good, doesn't she?"

"She looks all right."

"All right? That why you were gaping at her like someone dangled a Super Bowl ring in front of your face?"

"Those rings are ugly. Penelope is—"

"Ha!"

Bastard.

"We both saw her," I say blandly. "I don't need to state the obvious."

March stares at me for a long moment. I stare back as if I've got all the time in the world.

Then he smiles. I know that fucking smile . . .

"That's not the only way she's grown up. Her ti—"

"Do not disrespect Penelope."

"So you did notice!"

How could I not? Pen is stacked. Those curves, the way they

dipped and swelled like a lazy river . . . Honestly, I'd tried not to stare—Mom had taught us better—but it had been touch and go. She'd gone from barely noticeable to more than a handful for me; and I can palm a football with ease. Matched with a tiny waist and those breasts? I'd nearly swallowed my tongue.

"It's Penelope." I force a shrug. "We don't discuss things like that about her."

"I don't know . . ." He taps a beat on the armrest. "She had a huge crush on me in high school. Maybe it's time to reassess."

There's a paperback resting on the coffee table in front of me. I mentally calculate how fast I can ping it at March's forehead; accuracy won't be a problem. It's doing it before he ducks that's the issue.

March glances at the book and then raises a brow at me. "I dare you."

"Think I won't?"

"I think you'll miss."

"I think my sixty-four-million-dollar arm says differently."

March will be eligible for the draft next spring, and I know he'll make as much, if not more. And I'll be proud as shit of him. But until then, I'll dig in the blade.

Predictably, his eyes narrow. "Sixty-three-point-three million."

"Look who's paying attention."

"I have my moments. Still say you miss, Rocket Man."

Okay, that was low. I'd been singing "Rocket Man," a cappella, before I'd moved on to the Funky Chicken. That's it. He's going down.

Before I can make my move, the door opens again. I experience a moment of frozen fear that it might be Pen, but Mom pokes her head in instead. Her gaze darts between March and me with well-deserved suspicion.

But she doesn't address the guilty tension in the room. "Dinner is ready in ten. Come help set the table."

"Okay, Mom," March and I say as one.

Her smile is faint but pleased. Then her laser gaze focuses on me. "And mind your p's and q's, Dr. Teeth."

March bursts out laughing, while I groan. This is going to be worse than meeting the press after a bad game.

PEN

I STILL HAVE a bit of the "stuck in an alternate reality" feeling clinging to me as Margo leads me into the Luck family living room, patting my hand as though I need sympathy.

I suppose I do. It's not every day a girl smiles at a boy and gets told she has nice teeth.

She leaves me in the capable hands of her daughter June before bustling off to finish dinner. June takes one look at me and squeals a happy hello.

"Sorry, I didn't answer the door," June says when we're alone. "I had to dress the chickens. Mom says it makes her sick when she does it. Personally, I think she found a great way to get out of doing the messy work."

"Probably," I say with a laugh. "Not that I blame her."

Despite her claim of "messy work," not a strand of June's sleek black hair is out of place. Tall and willowy, June somehow manages to maintain an image of cool elegance whatever the occasion.

Although June went to college in Boston and I went to California, we text and call each other frequently. Only a little over a year apart in age, we've always been close. Along with her twin sister, May, we were an unstoppable trio of mayhem as kids.

Yes, the Luck kids are all named after a month—usually the one in which they were born. January, the eldest son, was born on New Year's Day. March was born on the twelfth of. Twins, June and May fit that rule, since May came out at 11:55 on May 31 and June arrived ten minutes later; there's big-time family speculation that Margo somehow engineered this spectacular feat.

August, however, is actually a July baby, but Margo thought

"July" sounded silly. Ironic, given the fact that her kids were all pretty much aggrieved by her naming practices. She didn't care, maintaining that it was adorable, especially when they were younger.

I can only be thankful that my parents were not like-minded when it came to choosing for me. I have an old family name and am ambivalent about it.

"Did I hear Augie getting the door for you?" June asks. "That boy . . . He's a disaster lately."

You have nice teeth.

I'm not sure if I should laugh or cry. I really want to reach into my purse and find my compact to study my smile. I've never paid attention to it before. Is it some pained Chandler Bing grimace? Or maybe it's more horsey?

Suddenly, my teeth feel huge, as though they take up all the space in my face. Gah.

Giving myself a mental shake, I take a seat on the sprawling couch, sinking in deep. It's one of a set, and each couch can easily hold four people. June nestles into a huge cream armchair kitty-corner to the couch.

"Yes, August answered. That was the extent of it." *And so say I.*

Instead of meeting June's eyes, I look around, refamiliarizing myself with the place. My grandmother, Pegs, had been a set designer. Even though I majored in film history, some of her passion for interiors must have rubbed off because, whenever I enter a space, I find myself either redecorating it in my head or soaking in the style.

I've spent many good times here. Done in soothing shades of dusty blue and cream, the rectangular-shaped room is divided into three seating areas: the main one before the fireplace where we're sitting, the large nook by the bay window, and another cozy space at the far end that is flanked by bookshelves.

Everything in the Luck house is on a grand scale. There are seven of them and they're all over five foot nine, with the Luck men averaging over six foot four. Add in friends or extended family, and you are left with a house almost bursting at the seams.

I love this house. Almost as much as I love Pegs and Pops's house. Longing, sharp and clear, pierces my chest so deeply that my breath hitches. God, it *hurt*.

"You're not even going to ask me why Augie's a mess?" June's dark brow lifts in clear disbelief.

"Oh, I know why. It's hard to escape, unless you're living abroad." I shrug. "If *he* wants to talk about it, I'll listen."

June's eyes soften. "You know, you're the only friend I have that has never expressed any interest in my brothers."

Practice makes perfect. And I'm a good actress when I want to be.

"I don't think you realize how refreshing that is," she continues.

"Maybe that's why I don't go there."

June pulls her long legs up onto the big chair and tucks them under her. "I shouldn't have tried to gossip. I'm more worried than anything."

I'm saved from having to answer by the sound of the front door slamming, followed by the feminine bellow of "I'm home!"

May. No one else announces her arrival with such authority.

From somewhere in the bowels of the house, come equally loud replies of:

"Baby girl!"—this from Margo.

"Loudmouth!"—from March, and finally,

"We know, Chuckles!" from August.

"Aw, you missed me," May shouts back.

There's some muffled exchange, May stomping around, then she comes dance-walking into the room, waving her hands in the air, as she sing-songs, "is our sista from another mista here for a visit?"

Curvy, where June is lean, May is and always was, a whirlwind. Even her inky hair, flying wildly around her heart-shaped face, resists any attempts at calm.

"Mom probably needs help setting the table," June deadpans.

"Nope." May flops dramatically down on the couch next to me. "Got the boys doing that, as those little pampered punks should. Hey there, Pennywise."

I get a quick kiss on the cheek.

"May Day."

"I hate when you call Penny that," June says to May with a shudder. "Gives me nightmares about creepy-ass clowns all week."

I leer at June, and she makes a sound of horror, swatting her hand in my direction.

Struggling not to laugh anymore, I turn to May. "We really shouldn't. Coulrophobia is real and horrible."

"Right?" June scowls at May—and me.

What did I do? Oh, right. I leered. That was bad of me. I wrinkle my nose in apology. June sniffs, but all is forgiven in a look.

May, however, makes an indignant face. "I'll remember to respect her clown phobia the next time she puts a fake spider in my shower stall, shall I?"

"It wasn't fake. That sucker was real. And, for the last time, I didn't put it in there!"

"Lies!"

"And, anyway, you're the one going around calling me Bug."

"If the name fits . . ."

"I'll fit you!"

"What does that even mean? Fit this!"

They stick their tongues out at each other, both trying not to laugh. I love their antics and boisterousness; I've always wanted to be as free. Sometimes I am, but the fact remains: while May and June have had to make themselves heard in their family of seven, I am an only child and silence comes naturally.

May takes her own corner of the couch to curl up on before pinning me with a look. "Not that I don't love that you've *finally* come back home to dinner—"

"Hey, I was in California." I still have one semester to finish up.

"And apparently, she's forgotten about the use of *aeroplanes*."

I roll my eyes at her use of the old-fashioned word.

"You had all summer free," May complains. "And you wait until the middle of freaking *September* to show up."

Unlike May, June, and March, who started class on the first, my academic year begins on the final week of September.

Guilt twists as I rest my head on the sofa back cushion, but then I think about my last conversation with Mom. "I'm beginning to think I should have stayed away."

They both know why. May goes quiet. We all do.

"Things didn't go so well?" June asks softly.

March leans in from the kitchen entryway. "Enough yapping. Get your chatty butts to the table, 'cause I'm not waiting to eat."

"When my butt is being chatty," May shoots back, "you will know it, bro."

On that note, we go in to dinner.

FOUR

PEN

SINCE THE WHOLE family isn't here, Margo sets up dinner at the big round table in the kitchen nook rather than their large dining room.

I've often wondered how long it took her to figure out how much to make to satisfy her very hungry brood. Not that the kids live at home anymore. A car accident last winter left January unable to properly throw and forced him into early retirement. He lives in Austin's Lake District now, near the University of Texas where March goes to school. With May and June in school at Boston University, and August in LA, it's just her and Neil.

Tonight, however, Neil is visiting an old teammate in Denver. Even so, she sets down a platter of roasted potatoes large enough to feed a dance hall. May follows, carrying a bowl piled high with pillowy biscuits. There's three roast chickens and a bowl of caramelized Brussels sprouts already on the table.

At Margo's urging, I take a seat just as August enters bringing yet another bowl—buttered carrots, by the look of it. I fuss with my water glass so that our gazes don't inadvertently collide. The teeth thing still looms in my mind. It's all I can do not to cover my mouth with my hand. Or grin at him like the Joker just to see him sweat. It's a toss-up at the moment.

Unfortunately, he decides to take the seat across from me,

which means I'll have to look at him at least a little or make it obvious that I'm avoiding him. Damn it.

I've managed not to be in a room with August since my high school graduation. Yet, in a little less than an hour, it's like he's suddenly become unavoidable. Glancing at the windows where the rainstorm still rages on, I wonder again if I've entered an alternate universe.

When I move to set a napkin on my lap, I find him watching me, a moue of discontent marring his perfect lips. *Yeah, well, too bad. I'm more uncomfortable, buddy.*

As if he hears my inner monologue, those pretty lips quirk and the corners of his eyes crinkle. He gives me a look that's not quite apologetic but definitely self-deprecating. The longer I stare, the more his smile grows. A flush works its way under my knit top and up my thighs. Despite my current anti-smile stance, I want to grin and laugh with him. It's weird. Aside from when we were little kids, we've never held meaningful eye contact this long before. He's never smiled at me like this before.

I would remember that. Mainly because that would have been the day I melted into a puddle of incoherent goo. Events like that tend to get marked in my mental calendar.

"Wine, Penny?"

Margo's question jerks me back into present company. I blink for a second before accepting a glass of Chardonnay. This time, I do not look August's way.

Soon, I forget to be flustered. It's impossible when eating with the Lucks; they're too boisterous, happily chatting about anything and everything. While Margo's kids love and respect her, they talk to her in the same way I do with my mom: like a good friend. I wonder if it's because Margo and Mom are best friends and raised all of us similarly.

March tells us stories about his teammates and how they covered some linebacker named George in red body paint when he was foolish enough to pass out during a party. George had retaliated by slowly replacing all their underwear with a size too small.

"I'm going to miss those guys next year," he finishes with a sigh.

June and I exchange a look and suppress our snickers.

"I don't know how you stand it," May says, spearing a potato with her fork. "Not knowing where you'll end up after the draft. What if you hate your city?"

March shrugs. "The fuck-load of money they pay me will ease my pain."

"Language," Margo murmurs half-heartedly. That's one difference between her and my mother. Mom is theater folk. Cussing is an art form as far as she's concerned.

March gives his mother an innocent smile.

June shakes her head. "I swear, I should have been born a boy. These twaddle heads are all going to be loaded just for tossing balls around all day."

August makes a noise of amusement. Up until now, he's been fairly quiet; something I'm far more used to from him. "But we'll be limping around like old men by the time we're forty."

"Yeah, yeah," she grumps, waving an idle hand. "And you can cry yourself to sleep on a two-thousand-dollar eiderdown pillow."

"There's pillows that cost that much?" March asks, intrigued. "Why? And what must that feel like?"

"It better make me weep with joy." August reaches for his wine. "Or sleep like the dead."

"You do that anyway."

"Tell you what," May says. "You crack open that fat wallet, Augie, and buy me one. I'll give a full report."

"Or I could buy myself one and make my own report."

"That's no good. You fall asleep anywhere. Which means your pillow choice won't factor. No, no, what you need is a fussy sleeper. I'll be your huckleberry."

August gives her a dry side-eye.

"You know," Margo says, leaning back to survey us. "It just

occurred to me that you and August live in the same city now, Penny."

I jolt, glancing at August then away. "I hadn't thought of that."

Liar, liar.

I remember the exact moment I learned he'd been drafted to LA. And exactly how I felt.

I feel his gaze. Heat prickles come back to torment my skin.

"You should have looked her up by now, August," Margo goes on, in that motherly way, which is apparently oblivious to any embarrassment she might be bestowing on others.

August clears his throat. "I've only been in town for a little while."

Translation: *Get off my case, Mom.*

"Well, you're settled in now." She helps herself to more carrots. "You two should go out some time when you get back."

Kill me now.

Unfortunately, in my attempt to look anywhere other than at August, I catch March's eyes. His glint with quiet humor, fully aware of how awkward his mother is making things and even a bit sympathetic to my plight.

"Ma," he says, grabbing her attention. "I've been meaning to ask. What the hell is up with that sweater you sent me?"

Margo's expression becomes all innocence. "What's wrong with it?"

"Oh, I don't know. Maybe it's the knitted toy soldiers draped around the shoulders?"

May perks up. "You got one of those too? Mine has teddy bears!"

June and August join in. Apparently, they've all received "absolutely darling"—Margo's words—sweaters.

She scowls at their outbreak of outrage. "Come on now, you all know perfectly well they're for our holiday calendar photoshoot."

"No!"

"No way!"

"Over my dead body, lady!"

"That can be arranged, March." She cuts him a look.

August leans in, giving her what I'm going to assume is his version of puppy eyes. "Mom, we stopped looking cute a decade ago. Now it's just creepy. Like those photos you see on true crime shows. Where the family ends up having a human meat farm in their basement."

"Seriously," June grumps.

Margo colors, then taps a manicured red nail on the table. "I don't care. I want a family photo. You're all getting older and these times are precious."

May makes a face. Discreetly, of course.

"But why does it have to be a staged one?" March demands. "We look like total boobs. Just get us all together and do a candid."

"Oh, yes, a candid," Margo huffs. "You try and corral this family into getting close enough to take one."

June toys with the stem of her glass. "Doesn't matter. Either way, I'll look like an angry chipmunk."

"August is the worst," May says. "His eyes are always closed."

"That's me trying to will away the pain of picture taking."

Margo shakes her head. "I don't know what you all are complaining about. I look terrible in every picture. But I still want them."

Until now, I'd been quietly watching them, enjoying the show. But the way they all start to complain about bad photo angles has me speaking without thought. "Oh, come on. You all are ridiculously attractive."

A pause thumps into the room, and they all stare at me with varying levels of amused surprise.

My fork stops midway to my mouth as I look around at them. "Don't tell me you didn't know because I won't believe it."

August frowns at me like he can't tell if he's been somehow insulted. That wasn't my intention. If I'm honest, it kind of slipped out. But it is the total truth: they're the most attractive family I've ever come across.

Margo purses her lips as if she's trying to figure out how to answer that and still appear humble, which makes me want to laugh just a little.

March, however, has no such humbleness and grins wide. "Well, of course we know. We got mirrors and everything."

"Yeah," May adds with a snort, "and we all know who preens in front of them."

"You?"

"Not as much as you." She waves her empty fork in his direction. "I'm surprised you don't put gilded frames around your mirrors and ask them the eternal question—"

"How to successfully toss my little sister out the window without actually hurting her?"

"Ha. No, but you're hilarious."

March winks at her, grinning and unrepentant.

"March won't ask who's the fairest of them all," June deadpans. "He already thinks he is."

He shrugs. "Facts don't lie."

"Taste is subjective, brother."

Margo watches them much as I do, slightly smiling and enjoying it. Then she shakes her head. "June is right. Attractiveness is in the eye of the beholder."

"All right, then," March says, turning his gaze on me. A sinking feeling opens in the pit of my stomach. There's a gleam in his eye that I don't like. "Since our dear Penny is the one who said we were all so hot—"

"Attractive." It comes out gravelly. As for hot? That would be my cheeks.

"Attractive," he amends. "She can tell us who's the most attractive of us all."

August grips his glass with a muttered, "Jesus."

It's so soft, I almost miss it. As I'm right across from him, I can't escape the look of annoyance on his face. To be sure, he's been annoyed since I opened my mouth. And, honestly, I'd love to end this whole conversation right now. But there's something about his attitude that irks. Suddenly, I feel buoyant, impish. Maybe this is how March feels when he stirs things up. If so, I can forgive him.

I take a long look around. "Oh, that's easy."

Despite themselves, everyone seems to lean in. Everyone but August, who doesn't even meet my eye, his indifferent expression and languid body language suggesting he's bored by the whole thing. *Game on, Luck.*

"It's August."

August chokes on his water. Badly.

He covers his mouth and coughs as March bellows an outraged, "What!"

I shrug and neatly cut a slice of roasted potato. "August is the most attractive to me. No offense, ladies. You're more beautiful by far. But if I'm going for flat-out attractiveness, then it's got to be August."

May and June start to laugh. Margo sits back, looking pleased. While August turns an interesting shade of red. He finally lifts his head. That ice-blue gaze of his cuts like a knife when it slashes into mine. He doesn't say anything. He simply stares at me like I've grown another nose. I smile at August. With teeth.

"Oh, come off it," March protests. "My jawline is definitely superior—"

"Nope," I say. "It's not."

"It so is," March says. "And my eyes are definitely prettier."

"Sorry, Hairball—" an old nickname he hates "—but you asked, and I answered."

March sits back in a huff muttering about fixed games and unfair judges.

Still August stares at me. Flummoxed.

I stare back. Nice teeth indeed. Victory bubbles through my veins like champagne. For the first time in my life, I haven't been reduced to a bumbling, blushing mess when put on the spot. It feels so nice, I don't know how to fully process it.

It all crashes down when August's mouth curls in a soft, slight smile. His voice, when he finally speaks, is a low rumble that touches my skin like a hot finger. "For what it's worth, Penelope, I think you're the most attractive person here as well."

All that fuzzy, fizzy champagne victory explodes in a riot of blushing butterflies. August Luck just said I was the most attractive person in the room. Me. Pen. I'm the most— Wait. I'm the *only* person in the room he's not related to.

I deflate with as much grace as an untied ballon let loose.

AUGUST

"HOW COULD YOU hurt Pen's feelings like that?"

May's irate question and hard poke at my ribs has me yelping. Can't a man do the dishes in peace without his little sister popping up at his side like a Whac-A-Mole to attack him? I swear, the girl can get the jump on me better than any linebacker.

My heartbeat returns to normal, and her words sink in.

"Wait. What?" I set down a soapy platter before it drops. "What the hell are you talking about?"

May glances back toward the great room before answering in a hissing undertone. "That crack about finding her the most attractive person in the room? Not cool."

My skin feels too tight and too hot. It has since dinner and that unfortunate round of Mirror, Mirror. Fucking March. He always goes too far. But me?

I blink down at a glaring May.

"What the hell are you talking about? What's 'not cool' about saying I find her attractive?"

Let's be real. It was a hell of a lot more sincere than her answer, which I can guess was to put March in his place. Not that I don't approve; anytime someone can accomplish taking his huge ego down a peg, I'm all for it. But I don't want to be the weapon used to do it. Just remembering Penelope's little statement of "fact" made me twitchy.

May huffs in exasperation. "August, she's the only person in the room not related to you! It would be full-on weird if you said anyone else."

What?

Oh.

Right.

Shit.

Was that why she seemed to wilt? Put that forced smile in place? I couldn't figure it out at the time. But now?

I rub a hand over my face and then flinch when I realize it's wet and soapy. Scowling I accept the dish towel May tosses me. "I didn't mean it like that. I was trying to be nice."

"Patronizing is what it was."

Turning back, I concentrate on scrubbing the platter. But my guts feel like lead. "Honestly, May. That wasn't my intention."

"Well, then . . ." She peers at me with cool eyes. "If you say so, then I guess . . ."

"I should apologize to her."

"No!"

"Jesus, woman. My ears."

She sets a fluttering hand on my arm, as if to forestall any attempt I might make to leave the room, and her voice goes back to the stage whisper she's been using since sneak attacking me. "Just. No. That would make it even more awkward."

"I don't see how. You just told me I've made her feel like crap. I can't let that go."

"I shouldn't have said anything to you."

I give her a speaking look, then hand her the clean platter to dry off. "But you did."

"Just forget it."

"Not likely."

"Damn it, Augie." She huffs, glances back to make sure we're still alone. "I wasn't thinking, okay? If you hunt her down to say sorry it will embarrass her even more."

"Why? I'm the one who'd be apologizing." I wouldn't exactly call that an embarrassing endeavor, but uncomfortable sure. How would I even go about it? *Sorry, Penelope, but I really do think you're gorgeous. You're so pretty it hurts to look at you, which pisses me off in ways I don't understand. So can you kindly leave before I do something to make it even more awkward?*

Beside me, May takes her frustration out on the dishrag. "Because . . . I don't know. Somehow, you'd bumble it and make things worse, I guess."

Probably. I'm apparently on a roll tonight.

She rubs her forehead like there's a headache blooming. "Just, let it go, okay?"

"I don't understand you at all sometimes, May."

"Well, right back at you." Her nose wrinkles. "Usually it's March we have to lecture. But you've been acting clueless all night. What gives, anyway?"

I stare down at the sink where dying bubbles circle the drain. The panic that's been trying to hitch a ride on my back since I signed my contract comes swooping back. I follow one stubborn soap bubble with my eyes and try to breathe. Part of me feels like I'll go right down that drain with the soap if I'm not careful.

The tips of my fingers tingle. May is saying something, but my ears are ringing too loudly to make out the words.

"Augie?"

Fingertips touch my arm. It's as though I'm wearing my gear, too swaddled up in padding to truly feel it.

"August."

A firm shake.

May's big eyes peer up at me, worried and slightly scared. I swallow hard. *Just put on a smile and she'll go away.*

But I can't move. The moment stretches. And I know May is going to panic soon. Shit, *I'm* panicking. What the fuck is wrong with me? I'm not like this. I don't panic. I don't bug out for nothing. All I've been doing since being drafted is panicking. And I hate it. I fucking *hate it*.

"May." Mom's voice breaks through the fog. "Go on into the den."

May's eyes stay on me for a second longer, then she nods. "Sure."

I don't watch her go. I look for that damn soap bubble, but it's gone.

Mom comes up alongside me. "August."

I swallow hard. And then she's turning me toward her. I go along with it like a zombie. But when her arms go around me, I give in, bending down so she can properly reach me. I'm a grown man, but it feels ridiculously good to have her hug.

A sigh gusts out of me, and I hug her back. Warmth blooms through my middle, and I'm no longer unsteady.

"I'm okay, Ma." A lie muttered into her hair.

"I know," she says, rubbing my back gently. "But I needed a hug and here you were."

Our family hugs. It's what we do. When we're happy, sad, scared, or sometimes just for the hell of it. Before we were born, Mom had read that frequent hugging was essential to a person's emotional and physical well-being. She made certain we were never without them. That she knew I needed one now has a lump welling within my throat. I pull back to meet her eyes.

Cupping my cheeks, she studies me. "Baby boy, you want to tell me what's going on with you?"

"If I could I would."

"All right." She steps away and picks up a bowl. "Why don't you go in with the rest of the kids and watch a movie."

I'm convinced that, in her mind, we'll all be ten years old forever. I smile but it feels heavy. "I'm thinking of heading out and getting a hotel room in the city."

Her brows lift in outrage. "To spend the night alone instead of in your home? I think not."

I haven't lived here since I entered college, but this is my home in all the ways that count. I tell myself this, even as panic has me straining toward the front door. I'm headed back to LA, and reality, in the morning. It would be more convenient to stay closer to the airport.

Mom's voice gets slightly muffled as she bends to put away the bowl. "Is it so wrong to want you here? March is staying until Sunday. Even Pen is spending the night here with the girls."

Penelope's staying here? I'd thought she'd go back to her mom's house in the city. I glance toward the arched entrance to the family room where it's darkened with only the glowing light of the TV screen flickering and the occasional sound effect blaring out. Someone laughs. It sounds light and feminine. I know it's not either of my sisters.

My insides do a weird sort of flip.

"All right, I'll stay."

FIVE

PEN

THE GREAT THING about visiting the Luck home after all these years is that, for this brief moment in time, I get to feel like a kid again. Once we'd cleaned up after dinner, we'd all gone back to our rooms, changed into our pj's, and then met back up in the family den. June, May, and I curl up like kittens in the corner of the massive sectional couch, while March sprawls like a king on the other end. August has gone missing. Which is for the best, really. If I don't have to look at him, I don't have to remember being utterly embarrassed by him. It's been my go-to game plan when dealing with him for years.

"What are we watching?" March asks, picking up the remote.

An impassioned argument ensues. As usual, no one can agree on anything. We never could when it came to movies. Except that one summer when, inexplicably, we'd all decided, as though by magic, that it was the perfect time to watch *The Lord of the Rings* trilogy. The sun had shone, the pool had been open, and we'd all hunkered down, bleary-eyed and pale, stuck on the drama of Frodo, the intensity of Aragorn, and beauty of Legolas tossing his golden locks. It had become a quest: must finish, no matter how sore our butts had been. Even August, who usually eschewed such group get-togethers, had been sucked in.

Today, however, is not that day. March insists on a smashup

car chase. May and June want a fantasy series—truly, the power of Legolas remains an influence to this day.

"You're going to have to break the tie," March says to me. "Or we'll get nowhere."

"What tie?" June says with heat. "May and I agree. That's two to one. We win."

"A," March holds up a finger. "You two are a freak hive mind when it comes to movie choices so that counts as one vote. And B . . ." He holds up another finger. "Pen gets a say. You never know, she might want my pick."

"As much as I enjoy cars," I deadpan, "I don't think I'm up for another showing of *Fast and Furious Fifty—The Furiouser*."

"Hey! It's *Ten*. The tenth one."

"Which is, like, nine too many," May says.

"Try ten too many," June mutters.

March's brows lift in outrage. "Did I say anything last Christmas when you two insisted we watch *The Devil Wears Prada*? Yet again?"

"Yes. Frequently." May sniffs, crossing her arms over her chest. "We could hardly hear the dialog over your commentary."

"It added much-needed depth to the plot." March shakes his head in disgust. "That chick wouldn't even eat the grilled cheese sandwich. I'd have killed for that sandwich!"

"Why don't you go make a sandwich now?"

March lobs a pillow in the direction of June's head. Unfortunately, his aim is not as good or as fast as August's. May ducks, and I get a face full of pillow.

"Ack!"

"Sorry, Penny."

"March, you bonehead!"

"I said I was sorry. You all right, Penny?"

"All right? You nearly killed her. I'm telling Mom."

Holy hell. We really have reverted to children.

"I feel like we've entered a bizarre time warp," I tell them darkly. "Next thing you know, May is going to stomp her feet and March will wet his pants."

"I never!"

A rumbling chuckle cuts through the chaos. August stands in the doorway to the den and shakes his head. "I leave you kids alone for twenty minutes and look at all this squabbling."

Quicksilver eyes find me. The impact of meeting his gaze does funny things to my insides. Maybe he knows this because his mouth quirks with humor. "I must say, Penelope. I didn't know you'd had it in you to bring up The Pants Incident. Nice hit."

Hot shame colors my cheeks and swarms along my skin. God, that was a low blow. I glance at March, but he grins back like he's proud.

"We'll corrupt her thoroughly by the time she leaves."

"It's already too much." I cover my face with my hands. "I'm sorry, March."

"Don't back down now," March says. "That was a wicked bad hit."

I shake my head, refusing to look up. I could say it was shame making me hide, but that would be a lie. My heart beats fast and light. My skin has gone tight and sensitive. It's as though I've been shocked into full wakefulness. And it's all because of August. I don't want this awareness. It's uncomfortable and inconvenient. At the very least, when we were younger, my discomfort came from the way he ignored me.

He's not ignoring me now. And it's unsettling. I can actually feel him enter the room. It's like a useless superpower.

August sits in the big swivel armchair at the far side of the room. Which is good because he didn't sit next to me. And it's bad because the position gives me a direct sight line to him.

He's still watching me with a faintly amused expression. I refuse to twitch.

"Augie," May says. "Help us pick out a movie."

His attention is unwavering. "You never gave your choice, Penelope."

This is for the very simple reason that no one here will accept my choice. I like classic Hollywood movies from the 1930s and '40s. Movies my great-grandparents would have worked on when they were young. I watch them and feel connected. But those movies are best watched alone, when I can really sink into them. Here?

"I don't think it much matters in this crowd. May and June will talk throughout—"

"Hey!"

"—and March will fill in all other silences with jokes."

"True." March salutes me.

"And you'll fall asleep halfway through it anyway," August says to me with a small smile.

I blink, a punch of surprise hitting me. "I don't fall asleep."

"Yes, you do." This from everyone. In unison.

"It's this couch," I protest. "It's always been too comfortable."

No one seems convinced.

"Why don't you pick, August?" I counter.

Leaning back in the chair, he sets his hands on his flat stomach and appears to think about it. The lamps are on low, and the only other light source comes from the flickering glare of the TV. Everything is muted and soft around the edges. Except for August. Finely delineated and sharp against the soft curved back of the chair, the colors of him—espresso dark hair against cognac leather, crisp white T-shirt pulled tight against golden-brown arms—is more vivid than anything else.

I've often wondered why it is some people shine and others don't. But perhaps it's the ones doing the looking that make it so. Perhaps, I only see August's shine because I've been trying my whole life to ignore it.

Oblivious of my turmoil, August squeezes the back of his neck and squints into the distance. "How about," he finally says, "*The Fellowship of the Ring*?"

At March's groan, August grins but then glances my way. "We watched it last time we were all together."

That he remembers is a shock. August barely paid attention to the movie at the time and spent most of it looking at his phone, "studying plays" he'd claimed. Regardless, his choice is accepted. Or rather, March shrugs with indifference, June immediately cues it up, as May does a *Legolas dance*, which mainly consists of wiggling in her seat and singing "Legolas" over and over.

June spreads a throw over our laps. My fingers curl into the caramel-colored chenille. The blanket is worn, buttery soft, and likely as old as I am. Everything in this room has a patina of age and care. Framed family photos and well-loved books grace the shelves. The papier-mâché carnival mask January made in elementary school hangs on the wall, battered but miraculously still whole. There is history here. Maybe that's why we revert to children in this room, in this house: because we can. Here, in these walls, with these people, we're safe and loved. I want that feeling in my life. More than I've realized.

"And all was right with the world again," I say as the movie starts.

August's grin is quick but wide. "If you fall asleep, Penelope, I'll make sure these yahoos don't mess with you."

Sweet but . . . "I'm not going to fall asleep."

I FALL ASLEEP.

I come to this unfortunate conclusion when a gentle touch on my shoulder eases through warm layers of slumber.

"Pen." Another touch. "Penelope."

That voice. I know that voice. It's like Pops's favorite bourbon: rich, smooth, a hint of bite. I jump fully awake with a gasp and nearly knock heads with August, who's leaning over me.

He lurches back just in time with an apologetic sound. "Jesus. I didn't mean to scare you." Something almost smug glints in his eyes. "But you weren't waking up."

Stiff with sleep, I fumble my way into sitting, surreptitiously wiping at my face to make sure I haven't drooled. "No, no. It's okay. I was just surprised because I . . ." The words trail off.

August crouches beside me, his expression perfectly composed. The truth of the situation hangs between us, and I know he's laughing on the inside.

"I did *not* fall asleep," I tell him.

"Uh-huh."

"I was resting my eyes."

"And snoring."

Horror pricks my skin. "I do *not* snore!"

A tiny dimple forms near the left corner of his mouth. "Fine, we'll call it a snuffle."

I glare.

His smile blooms until he's showing his teeth. His perfect, toothpaste commercial–worthy teeth. "An adorable little snuffle. Like a chipmunk."

My brow rises.

He frowns but amusement lingers in his eyes. "Aw, come on. Not one little smile at that?"

"After you've likened me to a chipmunk? I'd rather not risk further tooth-related comments."

August winces and rubs the back of his neck. "I'm sorry about the teeth thing earlier. That was . . . ah—"

"Traumatizing?" No, I will not smile. Not ever again in front of him.

But *he* does. It's wry with a self-deprecating tilt. "Yeah. It was definitely that."

A small huff of laughter escapes despite my best effort. "I meant for me."

A look of regret pinches his features. "Shit, Penelope. I didn't mean to traumatize you."

"I may never smile again." But I feel it tugging on the edges of my lips.

He sees it. Of course he does. I don't think anything escapes August. His eyes narrow, his own lips quirking. "You so want to, don't you?"

"I don't know what you're talking about."

"Yes, you do." God, that voice, all deep, teasing, coaxing. "Come on, Penelope. Smile for me."

I bite my lip, try to hold it in. It's nearly impossible. What with August grinning at me that way.

"I see it trying to break free," he says, laughing now. "Give in, Penelope. For me? Just one little smile."

It's a struggle. I give my head a quick shake.

He holds up his fingers in a small pinching motion. "One itty-bitty smile? Just for me?"

Then he waggles his brows.

I'm lost.

A smile breaks free, wide and uncontrollable.

"There it is." Satisfaction warms his tone as his gaze moves over me. "Like sunlight on water."

If I hadn't already been sitting down, I might have stumbled. As it is, my breath hitches in a little hiccup of pleasured surprise, and the wide smile pulling at my mouth gives way to parted lips unable to draw a breath.

August's answering smile fades as well, a slow setting sun as his brows draw together. I have seen his eyes countless times, but until this moment, I've never truly looked into them. Striations of the palest frost mix and swirl with summer blue. It's like staring at the cross section of a blue lace agate stone. Against his dark lashes and slashing brows, the effect is startling. And though I've often thought of August having icy eyes, they aren't cold now.

No, not cold at all. Not when they send heat washing over me. Not when I feel myself softening, going pliable as warm wax. It dawns on me how close we are to each other—him half crouched on the floor, me half sprawled on the pillows and leaning his way.

Awareness has me pulling back, breaking the moment. His easy manner becomes stiff as he retreats into himself as well. Silence follows, heavy and awkward. I look around, searching for something to say.

"Where is everyone else?"

August rises to his feet. "They left when the movie ended. I said I'd wake you up."

Why him? Why not June or May?

My questions must show.

"I volunteered," he says. "After all, you promised me you wouldn't fall asleep. How could I not be here for the 'I told you so'?"

Wrinkling my nose, I haul myself up with all the grace I can muster, which is to say none. My shirt is twisted around my torso like a green snake. I pull it into place as August stands back to give me room.

"I think your mother drugged the potatoes."

He nods like it's an entirely reasonable accusation. "Only one problem with that, Sweets. We all ate the potatoes."

"That's true— 'Sweets'? I am not sweet."

"Yeah, I'll give you that." He bites his bottom lip. "But you look it."

"Listen—" I'm cut off by a loud, insistent stomach gurgle. The kind that demands: *Feed me!*

August and I blink at each other, then he grimaces. "Sorry. I need constant refueling."

I can only thank the gods that it wasn't my stomach yelling at the room. "You didn't eat much at dinner," I say, and realize it's the truth. August had picked at his food when he usually packs it in like his stomach is going on vacation.

His easy expression blanks. "Better make up for that now. You want to join me for a sandwich?"

My knee-jerk reaction is to decline, but it hits me that I'm hungry too. Because I hadn't eaten much at dinner either. "Okay."

He hides his surprise quickly, but I still see it. August inclines his head toward the kitchen and then leads the way. The house feels bigger in the quiet of the night, the old wood floors creaking underfoot. The kitchen, however, is warm and cozy, with its creamy Shaker cabinets and brushed steel appliances. Someone left the under-cabinet lights on and they glow upon the walnut wood countertops.

"All right, then," he says, all business now. "How hungry are you?"

"I could eat an average-size sandwich, but nothing like the massive ones you guys tackle."

"Okay. One regular sandwich and one tiny sandwich coming up." He rubs his hands together, then pauses. "You trust me to make you something good?"

"Sure. Do you want help?"

"Nah. Relax, and I'll get you fed."

I take a seat at the wide island counter and watch August pull supplies out of the fridge before heading to the bread box. He moves with the grace and confidence of the professional athlete that he is, deftly cutting two soft onion rolls in half and slathering them with Thousand Island dressing. Next comes thinly shaved roast beef—piled like a mountain on one and hill on the other—and then slices of white cheddar. I rest my chin on my hand and watch.

"I had no idea you could cook," I tell him.

"Making a sandwich is more an exercise in architecture and creativity." He grabs a large carrot and begins to grate it onto a plate. "But Mom made sure we could all do the basics." August looks up at me from under the mop of hair that has fallen over his brow. "You won't starve when you're with me, Sweets."

"Keep calling me that, and I'm going to come up with an equally ridiculous nickname for you."

"You say that like it's a threat."

"It was."

"Not to me." With flourish, August piles the grated carrot

onto the sandwich and adds a dab of chili crisp oil. He grabs another jar but stops. "Pickles?"

"No thank you." My nose wrinkles. "I've tried multiple times to like pickles because they look delicious, you know with that snap crunch sound they make when you eat them? But they've never grown on me. They're too overpoweringly sour."

"Maybe you haven't found the right one."

"At this point, I don't think I ever will."

"I get it." He adds a couple of slices of pickle on his, and then puts the tops on the sandwiches before deftly cutting each one in half. "I'm the same with olives. People pop them in their mouths like candy but, blech. No. Horrible." He shudders.

Laughing, I hop off the stool and head for the fridge. "What do you want to drink?"

"I think there's some lemonade."

I pour us each a glass, and we meet in the middle, setting our late-night meal on the counter. Sitting side by side, we're silent as we take our first bites. I close my eyes and enjoy before looking over at him. He's turned my way, clearly waiting on a verdict.

"You make a mean sandwich, Pickle."

He huffs a breath. "Pickle? Harsh, Sweets. Harsh."

"Why's that?"

"You just told me you didn't like pickles." He takes a huge bite and chews while giving me the stink eye.

"But it sounds cute, doesn't it? And it's not as though I'm going to be eating you—" I cringe, blushing hot. "Oh, stop. No, that was too easy."

August's chuckle is warm and smooth. "Amateur hour. Don't worry, Sweets, I'm not gonna tease you for being easy."

I pick up my sandwich half again. "I see what you did there."

"I always knew you were a quick learner."

"Did you?"

He pauses midway from taking another bite. "Why are you looking at me like that?"

I dab at a little crumb that's fallen on the counter. "Like what?"

"Like I have two heads."

"Well . . ."

August chokes on his bite, then thumps his chest as he laughs. Cheeks ruddy, he looks over at me in shock. "They have no idea what a little devil you are, do they?"

I'm not sure who "they" are but it doesn't matter. Few people see that side of me. I suspect that's my fault; I hide away as much as I can. It's a reflex now, something I mentally have to fight against. But the fact that August knows it is unsettling.

I take a sip of lemonade. "You're different tonight. That's why I was looking at you."

"How?"

"I don't know . . . teasing, funny. More like March—" As soon as the words leave me, I know they're a mistake. The problem with words spoken is that they can't be taken back.

"Like March." August studies his sandwich. "I guess that's true."

"I only meant that you're usually stiff and reserved with me."

"And March isn't," he adds with an absent nod.

I feel terrible. Because it clearly insulted him to be compared to his brother this way. I don't know how to fix my flub.

The cozy air of the kitchen chills and thickens with awkwardness. I miss how it was before, eating and joking in the dark of night. I miss it so much I blurt out the first thing that comes to mind.

"You usually make me nervous is all I meant."

August bolts straight on his stool. "I'm sorry? I make *you* nervous?" Brows high, he rubs a hand over his mouth.

"What are you muttering about?"

"I'm working through a moment of irony is all."

"Okay . . ."

A long finger points at me as his brows lower. "You haven't had a nervous moment since you got here."

"I'm having an off night."

"Welcome to the club." He lifts his glass in cheers.

I want to reciprocate, but my shoulders slump. I'm needling him because I'm edgy and it isn't his fault. "I'm sorry."

August waves a hand as if to bat the apology away. "It is what it is—I can't believe I make you nervous!"

Oh, the irony. His outrage is cute, though.

I sip my drink before continuing. "You can get . . . broody."

His broody expression appears as if on cue. "I'm thoughtful, not broody."

"If you say so."

"I do."

My smile threatens to break free. We sit in silence for a moment, August brooding and eating his sandwich as I toy with a piece of mine. I like it here with him in this kitchen I've known forever.

In the far corner on the counter sits Mr. Cocky, an old, chipped, ceramic rooster that often holds cookies. School pictures of the Luck kids cover the double wide stainless steel fridge in a checkerboard pattern of gap-toothed smiles, bad haircuts, and questionable fashion choices.

Someday, August will bring his kids into this room and they'll see his growing years. Or maybe space will be cleared for their pictures. Whatever the case, his story will continue here.

The heavy weight of sorrow becomes too much, and the truth pours out of me. "I didn't want to come here tonight. Not because I didn't want to see any of you but because my heart hurts. But I couldn't disappoint Margo, so I did. It wasn't enough, though. I can't shake my blue heart. You see, I came back to ask my mom for a loan and she said no."

My word eruption seems to bounce around the room before settling between us. August blinks, mouth stern. "Why do you need a loan?"

My shoulders slump. The half-eaten sandwich in front of me no longer looks appetizing. "Pops and Pegs left me their house."

"That's a good thing, right?"

"It's . . . great." My voice breaks a little, and I clear my throat. "I love their house. It's a second home. No, not even that. Mom and I moved around so much over the years, it's my only home now."

I risk a glance his way and find him watching me intently. It's too much to take, and I turn back to staring at the plate in front of me. "Losing Pops and Pegs so soon was . . . hard."

"Yeah." It's a soft affirmative that has the lump in my throat growing.

"Finding out they left the house to me was both painful and wonderful. I'd lost them but they left me a home. *My* home." I trace a gray swirl in the granite counter. "Dad was, well, he was pissed."

There's a pause before understanding hits August. "They didn't leave it to him."

Shaking my head, I grimace. "He got nothing. It shouldn't have been a surprise to him. He'd ditched his family and cut ties with his parents years ago."

"Penelope—"

At his pitying tone, I hold up a hand. "No, no. I came to terms with who my dad is a while ago." Okay, a few years ago, but progress is progress. I consider mine hard-won. It wasn't an easy thing to learn that my dad had left not only my mom, but me in the process, in favor of my nanny. I was ten when they ran off to France to live it up in a villa—yes, a freaking villa—he'd purchased without Mom's knowledge.

Thing is, I can accept what he did. But I still don't like him very much for it. Or Nanny Cathy. Ugh. I can't think of either of them without a bad taste filling my mouth. They never had kids. I still can't decide if that makes it better or worse. Maybe, just maybe, if Cathy had been pregnant, then I could see how he'd leave Mom. And me. Because, in truth, from that moment on, my dad had zero interest in my life or seeing me. The one time I went to France to visit him during summer break had been a soul crushing disaster.

No. I will not spiral over him anymore.

"Anyway," I force out. "He was clearly expecting the house when they died."

"Asshole," August mumbles. He catches my eye. "Sorry, it's the first thing I think whenever anyone mentions him."

"Me too." We share a look, and then I shake my head. "The house is mine. No matter how much he complains."

"So, the loan?" August lifts a hand in confusion. "Is he trying to contest the will or something? Is that why you need the funds?"

God. The mere thought has my stomach clenching. "No. That is, I don't think so. I know he argued with the estate lawyer. But he was advised that the will, actually it's a trust, was well drawn and he'd have a tough time contesting. Not to mention, he'd need a lot of money to continue down that road." My nose wrinkles. "Dad is short on funds as well."

"Then why the loan?"

For a moment, I'm lost in the ugly sludge of feeling Dad leaves on me. Then I blink and clear my head. "It's the house."

"The house?"

"August," I say sadly. "My great-grandparents may have bought the house for ten thousand dollars way back in the 1940s, but it's now worth about ten million."

August spits out his lemonade and proceeds to cough violently.

"Sorry." I pat him on the back and hand him a napkin.

"Jesus," he says, still sputtering. He wipes his mouth and huffs out a laugh. "Holy shit!"

"Yeah."

Silver eyes alight on me with shock. "No, really? Ten million?"

"The house is a Cliff May original, sitting on an acre in

Brentwood. The land alone would be worth a ton, but the fact that it was designed by the man credited for inventing the California ranch house?" I shrug. "It's highly desirable."

To me it's home. But I don't underestimate its worth.

"The property tax would be a lot," August says, finally understanding.

"To say the least." My fingers clench. "Approximately one-hundred and twenty-five thousand dollars a year."

August whistles low and long.

I snort in agreement. "More than this college student can afford anytime soon."

"And your mom wouldn't loan you the money."

"Nope."

"Maybe it's too much for her."

"That's not it." A sigh escapes. "I mean, yes, it's a lot but she won't even entertain giving me a small part of it until I can figure out what to do. She wants me to sell. Says it's ridiculous to sit on that much money and not take it."

"Well . . ." August scratches the back of his neck. "She's not wrong to want that for you. Not entirely," he amends at my dark look. "You'd be set for life."

"My life is just beginning." I throw my arms wide, nearly hitting him in the process. "She doesn't know what I'm capable of. I could do . . . things!"

I have no clue how to make that much money a year.

"Of course you can."

"Don't patronize me, Luck."

"I'm not!"

My lips purse, but I accept his word. "She wants me to take the money, invest in my future. But that house?" Tears well in my eyes. "It's been in my family since it was built. Oscar-winning screenplays were written there."

My great-grandparents had been screenwriters in Hollywood's Golden Age.

"It's the only true and safe home I've known. Is it so wrong that I want to keep it?"

August's voice turns gentle. "No, Penelope. It's not wrong at all."

"Just hopeless. God." I set my head in my hands and sigh. "You want to know what's really messed up?"

"Lay it on me, Sweets."

"I *am* ridiculous! I have a problem most people would kill for."

August hums, and then takes a massive bite of his sandwich, frowning as he chews. He wipes his mouth with a napkin before talking. "Thing is, Pen, there's always someone who has it better and worse than you. Doesn't make what you're feeling any less real or any less true. You love something that's in danger of being taken from you. Don't shame yourself for that."

My eyes burn, and I blink rapidly before taking a bite of my sandwich, if only to do something other than cry. I don't know what I expected of August, maybe for him to placate me, or tell me to buck up. But his simple understanding squeezes my heart in a way that has me wanting to turn and ask for a hug, and maybe bawl on his shoulder for an hour.

"Well," I say when I finish chewing. "That's my confessional for the night. What about you?" I turn his way. "Anything got you in a mood? Other than failing basic balance while attempting the Funky Chicken, that is."

"Fucking hell." He winces and ducks his head before tilting it back to scowl up at the ceiling. "Has anyone *not* seen those forsaken clips?"

"If they haven't, they probably will eventually."

"Oh, thank you. No really, your sympathy overwhelms me." He's fighting a smile, however.

I fight one as well. "I figured you'd resent sympathy."

He studies me with those silver eyes. "Yeah, I would." Then he brightens and nudges my shoulder with his. "But you can still offer to kiss my hurts and make it better."

"I'm not going to fall for that one."

"Damn it."

Grinning, I wipe my hands on my napkin. "Seriously, August. You okay?"

"Of course." He waves his hand idly as if to bat the question away. There's something going on with him, but I can't see past the barriers he's put up.

When I don't respond, he quirks a brow. "What would you do," he asks, "if I said I wasn't?"

It's my turn to frown; it's not a question I expected. I don't like to think I'm ill prepared to truly help someone who really needs it. But how? It's one thing to want to; it's another to actually succeed.

"I suppose, I'd just listen. I don't know if that's the right thing, but I would, you know. I'd listen for as long as you like."

Straight brows draw together. His mouth opens then abruptly shuts. August turns more fully my way. His hand lifts as though he might reach out but then falls to this thigh and grips it.

For a second he simply stares down at his hand, clutching his thigh tightly. Then he smiles, a small, gentle thing that has me flushing under my shirt. "I'm okay now, Penelope."

"Okay . . . good." It stutters out because, for a moment, I got the feeling he wanted to say something else. "So long as you're sure."

His smile grows, morphing into the one I've seen him give during interviews.

"Nothing like a good late-night sandwich to change one's perspective," he says with cheek. "Right?"

Oddly disappointed, I smile back, with my very nice teeth. "Right."

And that is that.

SIX

PEN

STRANGELY, I FEEL hungover when I arrive at the airport. I hadn't had much to drink at the Lucks' house, and I went to bed right after my sandwich with August. Even so, my head is muzzy and my body sluggish as I pull my carry-on toward the check-in kiosk. The airport is fairly empty, and I'm hoping for an equally empty flight so I can sleep off whatever this crappy feeling is.

My mood sinks a little lower. I can deny it no longer: the sticky itch of failure is upon me. My grandparents' house will go on sale and be lost to me.

Worse things have happened. Much worse. If viewed from the outside, I'm complaining for no reason. I'll benefit financially in ways most people never dreamed of. I tell myself this regularly. Eventually it has to sink in.

I'm staring blindly at a row of kiosks when there's a voice at my ear. "Hey."

As though zapped, I whip around.

"August!" It comes out in an unfortunate squeak of surprise.

"Hi." That gorgeous smile of his unfurls slow but sure. It does funny things to my insides. Worse, though, is the way his sudden appearance has somehow brightened everything and happiness flows through me like liquid light.

Stranger still? He seems happily surprised as well.

His gaze travels over my face like he can't believe I'm here. "I didn't know you were on this flight."

"Why would you? We never exchanged travel plans."

"I don't remember you being this sassy." He peers at me in mock suspicion. "Did you grow into it or something?"

"No, I take sassy supplements at bedtime. I mean, 'if you haven't got your health—'"

"'—you haven't got anything.'" He inclines his head toward mine. "I was subjected to *The Princess Bride* too."

"One is not subjected to *The Princess Bride*. One watches with glee or one hates it and is resigned to a lifetime of wallowing in freakish misery."

"Cute. The way you keep sliding in those quotes."

"It's a gift. And a curse."

"You did it again," he points out.

"Did I?" *I so did.*

August nods. "That was from *Monk*."

"Hmm . . . Are you sure?"

"Yes. Mom loves that show. She watches it every time she does a deep housecleaning. Says it 'channels' her sanitation energies." He studies me for a beat, and a little line forms between his brows. "You don't seem pleased to see me."

"What? No!" I wave my hand. "I'm totally fine with it."

If he only knew.

"Faint praise."

"Well, I'm not going to gush, if that's what you're looking for."

"No." August straightens. "No . . . I don't want that."

"But?"

"Not a 'but' exactly. More a why? As in, why do you keep looking at me like I'm a bad stink caught in the wind? Because I'll have you know, I shower every day. Twice when I'm working. Which makes me a fairly clean individual."

It's cute the way he's rambling, as though he's nervous. I've never actually seen August nervous. Maybe he's not. Maybe he's feeling chatty. But I enjoy it regardless.

"And," he concludes with a proud lift of the chin, "I've been told I smell pretty damn good."

Truth? He smells great. Always has. Pure delicious pheromones. But that little taunt does something to me. Something wicked that's not like me at all.

I tilt my head, considering. "Oh, really?"

"Yes, really. Women love the way I smell—" He lets out a strangled sound as I rise to my toes until the tip of my nose touches the warm curve of his neck to draw in his scent.

I'd acted on pure impulse, wanting to be *that* girl: the fun one who disarms men with her charm. But I'm an amateur, way out of my depth. My body tightens like a clenched fist, hot and quick. All rational thought falls by the wayside.

He's warm and solid, and the scent of his skin makes me dizzy. My eyes flutter closed as I swallow hard and try not to fall into him. Because I want that. I want to lean against August's long, hard body and just burrow.

The moment stretches, both of us sort of swaying. My heart beats so hard and fast—he must hear it. Panic follows. He's going to know what he does to me, and I'll never live it down. Worse, if I don't move I'm going to kiss his neck, and where would that leave me? Total humiliation.

My breath gusts out, and he shivers, little goose bumps rising on his skin. For a second, I swear he's turning his head, lowering it to get closer. I can't breathe. Maybe I'll faint and end up in an inelegant sprawl right here on the airport floor.

The horror of that image has me falling back on my heels with an audible thud. We stare at each other, August with his brow knit as though he can't believe my cheek, me with what I'm going to assume is red-faced awkwardness.

I clear my throat. "You smell . . . ah, great. But for the record. I never thought you smelled bad. And I don't find you annoying. That expression is just my face doing its thing."

His brow clears. "For the record, it's a great face."

"I . . . oh." What???

"I know you thought I wasn't serious when I said you were attractive last night. But I was. You're very pretty, Penelope."

I'm in very real danger of giggling. Or swallowing my tongue. *Focus, woman. Be* that *girl again.*

"Is this a come-on?"

"Do you want it to be?"

"Cut it out, August."

A frown flits across his face. He's going to argue. But he retreats like a pro. "All right. I'll behave. Besides, I have something I want to talk to you about, so stop distracting me with your cuteness."

I have no idea how to respond. I simply nod.

August turns to an unoccupied kiosk. "You got a QR code to check in?"

"Uh . . . Oh. Yes."

"Let me see."

Not thinking, I hand him my phone with the code at the ready. He deftly signs me in, and before I can blink, he's upgrading me to first class.

"Hey—"

"Don't worry. I'm paying for it." He slips his card into the machine while I flail around trying to stop him. "I want to talk to you, and we'll have more privacy this way."

"That's all great, August. But you still need to ask me if it's okay."

The little frown wrinkle between his brows returns. "In what world would anyone prefer coach over first class?"

"You got me there. But it costs money—"

"I'm paying for it—"

"And some people—me in this particular instance—don't want to feel beholden, especially over something they can't afford."

"Okay, I get that. And I know this will sound a bit—" he waves his hand "—whatever. But I have money. A lot. For me, in this particular instance, it's the equivalent of buying you coffee. It ain't fair, but it's the truth."

He hands me my boarding pass.

I blow out a breath. "Okay. But I'm buying you a drink on the plane."

"Thank you. I appreciate the reciprocation." His fingers lightly touch my elbow to move me along. "But the drinks are free in first class."

"I knew that."

"Uh-huh."

"I'll buy you a coffee when we land."

"I look forward to it."

AUGUST

THE FIRST-CLASS SEATS on the flight from Boston to Los Angeles aren't enormous private pods, but they are extra wide and lie flat if you prefer. More importantly, they are still arranged in two by two formation, so I can talk to Pen in relative privacy and comfort.

As someone who was six foot four by age eighteen, I've been shelling out the cash for upgrades since my first endorsement check came in. I thank my paycheck every time I fly. The fact that anyone, regardless of size, has to cram into the medieval torture chamber known as coach is a social injustice that needs to be remedied. How we as a society continue to stand for it is a mystery to me.

I digress.

Last night, we'd left things at a somewhat awkward place. She'd offered me comfort: something I wanted more than I'd been prepared to acknowledge, and I'd hedged, withdrawn. It disappointed her. I'd disappointed myself as well. But it made certain things clear. First, I am through avoiding some truths in my life. Second, I have found a solution for my problem. It's a huge risk that will most likely blow up in my face. I can live with that; my life revolves around calculated risk. This current risk all comes down to Penelope Morrow.

It's adorable watching Pen quietly inspect her area. She opens and shuts her seat cubby. Then opens it again to pull out the bottle of water provided, puts the water back, takes out the headset, looks it over, puts it away. Next up is messing with the seat controls. But only a little. Just enough to see how they work.

She catches me watching and discreetly tucks the quilted blanket back into the footbed in front of her. "I hate how much I like this."

"Fucking sucks, doesn't it?"

Shining brown eyes flash in indignation. "Right? Everyone should have this."

"They should."

"I should thank you, but I'm not sure I will. Because now I truly know what I'm missing."

I'd put her in first class for the rest of her life if she'd let me, just for the simple pleasure of knowing she'd glow with this quiet happiness once there. But I know she wouldn't allow it. Which is a downer.

She inhales sharply as though bracing herself. "I'll just enjoy the moment."

I certainly am.

We don't get a chance to talk before takeoff. Honestly, now that I have her here, I find myself hedging again. Why the hell did I pick a plane trip to ask her? I know why. My devious lizard brain figured it would be best to ask where she couldn't walk out on me. I never really considered the fact that I wouldn't be able to escape either. And she's going to say no. Of course she'll decline. Despite her claims to the contrary, Penelope doesn't like me very much. Given that I've just maneuvered her here to spring an awkward as hell proposal on her, I wouldn't blame her.

I adjust in my seat, accept the glass of champagne the flight attendant hands out . . . do anything but make eye contact with Pen. She's already put her feet up and turned on her e-reader. All right, then. I pull out my phone and scroll through sports news.

The first article is about the chicken dance.

Fuck.

Champagne turns sour in my mouth. I set my phone down and rub at my sternum. A hard knot formed there weeks ago and won't go away.

"Are you going to tell me what was so important that you paid for my upgrade?" Pen doesn't look up from her book, but I know all her attention is on me.

"For the record, I would have upgraded you regardless. What kind of . . ." Friend? No, we're not friends. Childhood relations? That sounds horrible. ". . . person would I be if I let you sit back there when I'm up here?"

A small smile curls her pink lips. With her oval face and shining brown hair shot with red-gold flowing around it, she's a Botticelli. "You're stalling. Sweet, but stalling."

Sweet? I never.

"I decided I don't want to talk about it now. We've got nearly six hours together."

Pen sets the reader face down on her lap and turns toward me. "Thought that far ahead, did you?"

"Obviously."

"It can't be that bad."

"Maybe it's worse." I pull at my collar. It's a T-shirt but it smothers all the same.

Pen simply stares. She's always done this. Looked at me with solemn brown eyes, so glossy and big, and fucking serene. I'd never been able to stand it, knowing that if I ever truly looked back, I would be lost.

I pick up my glass and swallow the dregs.

"You know," she says, "this past day and a half is the most we've ever spoken to each other since we were little kids."

"What? No." I mentally try to recount all our past conversations. "It can't . . . well, hell. It is, isn't it?"

She nods, and a lock of hair slides along her cheek. My fingers twitch.

"That's kind of shit, Penelope."

Pen shrugs. The tiniest movement of her shoulders.

I clench my hand. "We've known each other our whole lives. We should have talked more than this."

"Well, we know each other, but we were always going different directions, I suppose."

And why was that?

I clear my throat. "Still."

Her gaze lifts and collides with mine. I feel it in my solar plexus. As strong as any blindside hit. A soft flush colors her cheeks. Penelope is *shy*. I've known this in a vague way, but I didn't truly *know* until now that being at ease with others doesn't come naturally to her. Pair that with my instinct to retreat anytime I encountered her disapproving expression, and you have one big, uncomfortable void.

"We didn't really have any reason to talk," she adds.

Another hit. I resist the urge to rub my chest again.

Glancing at her book, I take a breath and start. "I hate reading books. My mind wanders two sentences in. But I love audiobooks. I don't know why it's different, but I can let go and dive into the story when it's audio."

Her brow knits for a fraction of a second, then clears. "I'm the opposite. I read every chance I get but if I try to listen to audio or a podcast? Poof! I'm already gone."

My grin is wide. "What's your favorite book?"

Her nose wrinkles. "That's like asking your mother who her favorite child is."

"I know that's me, so . . ."

"Whatever gets you through the day, August."

I ignore the dramatic eye roll, even though it's cute as hell.

"Okay, then. Favorite genre?"

"I like romance, fantasy, thrillers, mysteries . . . Depends on the story."

"Huh. Me too."

"Even romance?" She sounds highly dubious.

"Would you like me to discuss details?"

A sweet blush rises over her cheeks. "No."

I chuckle at her quick reply. I like that blush and want to see more of it. "You sure? Because a man can learn a lot from—"

"La, la, laaa." She puts her hands over her ears. "Not listening."

With an exaggerated sigh, I move my seat back to get in line with hers. "Okay, okay. On to the big question. Anime?"

"Of course."

"Dub or no dub?"

"No dub. Dubs are awful."

"Agreed."

She wings a brow. "I'd have thought you'd like the dub since you hate reading."

I shrug. "My loathing of the dubbed voices overrides having to read the subtitles."

"You are both cultured and reasonable."

Laughing, we take it from there, talking about everything and nothing until the captain comes on the speakers to announce landing preparations. Pen, who has become totally relaxed, smiles over at me. It's like sunlight at the end of a long tunnel.

"You never said what you wanted to ask me."

"Oh, that." I buckle my seat belt. "I wanted to know if you'd marry me."

SEVEN

PEN

I DON'T REMEMBER landing. I'm not even sure how I got from the plane to baggage claim. My brain is stuck on pause. A screeching freaking halt. Because, what the fuck? How dare he? We were getting along so great. I had been feeling good—like I was floating, basking in the sunlight of his regard. August was funny, engaging—the guy I'd seen glimpses of my whole life but never really met. And suddenly there he was, just as I'd dreamed he'd be.

And then this. This fucking joke. Marry him? *Har.* Just hardy-har-*har.* So funny, August. Really.

"You're fuming." He sounds concerned. Worried. He should be. I have drawing pens in my bag and I'm not afraid to stick them in painful places.

"I'm not." I don't know how I manage to get the words out so calmly. But I'm proud of my aplomb.

"You so are. You sound like a constipated robot."

Well, then.

"And you sound like a . . . a . . . big penis spew!"

A woman walking past does a double take.

August chokes on a laugh, his stride tripping. "A what?"

He laughs again, all amused insouciance, but I see the tightness around his icy eyes.

"You heard me. Whatever. I'm trying not to curse in public."

"And *penis spew* is acceptable?"

Oh, he's loving this. I want to stomp on his big size thirteens.

"Shut up." There's no heat to my demand; I'm too embarrassed to form words with any force.

He bites his lower lip. "Look, I'm sorry. I shouldn't have sprung it on you like that."

"You shouldn't have said it at all. That was mean."

"Mean?" He stops mid-stride, taking me by the elbow so I have to halt too. Foot traffic breaks and flows around us like we're rocks in a stream. "No, Penelope. It was an honest proposal."

What? *What?*

"What!" Apparently, I'm stuck on the word.

His handsome face twists in a grimace. "Shit. I am so fucking this up."

"You think?"

He runs a hand through his hair, making the ends stick up wildly. "Look, I'm parked in the lot. Can we talk while I drive you home?"

His expression earnest, and my curiosity is running wild. I wilt.

"Okay, but if you pull any more wack shit, if you haul off and ask me to have your baby, or say you have twenty-four hours to live and need a kidney, I'm going to be very put out."

"I kind of like angry Penelope."

"Shut. Up."

"On it." He does the zipped-lip gesture, but it doesn't hide the twinkle in his eyes.

"It's lucky for you that you're so cute."

August's brows lift high. "Cute, huh?"

"I didn't mean to say that out loud." I turn and continue walking, ignoring the wide, delighted grin on his jerk face.

WE MAINTAIN A strained silence as August leads us to his parked car. When we exit the terminal, he takes a ratty Bass Pro

Shops cap the color of hot dog mustard from his bag and pulls it on low. A pair of mirrored aviator glasses follow. His entire demeanor changes, from his confident stride to a soft shuffling. It takes me a moment to realize he is adopting a disguise.

I had forgotten: August Luck is famous.

Famous enough that his hat, glasses, and unassuming walk doesn't stop a schluby-looking guy hanging out by the arrivals gate from turning his massive camera our way and taking a couple of shots.

"Ignore him," August says. Now that he's been caught, he straightens his shoulders and walks in his usual loose-hipped stride. "Or try to. I know it's hard—hell."

His lips pinch as he glances at me. "I forgot to warn you. There might be pictures of us on the plane."

"On the plane," I parrot.

"Yeah. People take sneak shots. There was one of me sleeping on the flight to Boston."

"They do that?" I know I sound naive when, in actuality, I'm pissed.

But he seems to get that. His smile is wry. "I'm in public, thus I am public domain in their eyes."

"I bet it's a lot easier to say that when pointing the camera rather than being pinned under its lens."

"True. But you'll never get people to admit it." He holds the door to the parking garage stairs for me. "I'm sorry, though. I should have warned you so you had the choice to back out of flying with me."

I stop short. "I'd never do that, August. Not for that reason."

He stares at me for a beat, then we keep walking. Looking at him from under my lashes, I remember how long he's been famous. The Luck Boys, as the press calls them, have been in the public eye since they were just kids. But it got really intense when they started college. How could a needy press ignore model handsome, incredibly talented siblings who were already part of a football dynasty? Impossible.

The garage smells of garbage, jet fumes wafting and the slow, hot baking of asphalt. But the light is dim, and my head filled with possible ways to comfort August, so I don't initially see where he's leading me. When he pulls out his keys, my fog clears, and I snap to attention.

"Is that . . ." I stare at the ancient SUV hulking in the parking space.

August glances over and a pleased expression spreads over his face. "The Grouch? Yeah."

Blood whooshes to my feet, and I become a little lightheaded. The Grouch is a duck green, 1989 Jeep Wagoneer, complete with wood-paneled sides. Its formal name is Oscar the Grouch. Legend has it, my dad called it that as a kid because the big truck was always growling.

"You have Pops's truck?" It comes out as a squeak. I hadn't seen the old SUV for years. My grandfather had stopped driving it after a time, preferring the heated seats of a newer Volvo in his later years. Even so, too many memories were tied to the Grouch for me not to think of Pops.

A lump of emotion swells in my throat, as August watches me.

"Pops left it to me. I thought you knew."

"No. I—ah, no. I didn't think about what happened to it." I pull myself together and give him a smile. "I'm happy you have it. I just didn't think . . ."

In all honesty, when I'd been told about the trust and what it entailed, I'd assumed Pops had simply sold it off before he died.

August unlocks the trunk and deftly puts our suitcases inside. Tan carpeting lines the trunk. Shag carpeting in a trunk. It had always struck me as patently ridiculous. My eyes smart. Suddenly, I'm a blink away from crying.

"When I was in tenth grade," he says, "I went to that football camp at USC." Dark brows knit over stormy eyes. "Pegs and Pops let me and March stay with them for the rest of summer."

"I went to visit Mom's relatives in Italy that summer."

"I remember. I was just a wee bit jealous of you going there."

I hold back a laugh. If he only knew how much I'd wanted to come home when I'd learned August and March would be visiting the one year I was away the whole time. Upon reflection, I'm fairly certain that was arranged on purpose. Likely, my parents and grandparents had reservations about me sharing a house with the youngest Luck brothers all summer long. I'm still a little bitter about it, though.

August closes the trunk and guides me to the passenger door. He unlocks it. "Anyway, while I was there, Pops taught me to drive on this beast."

"He did?" I grin at that. "Talk about a trial by fire."

"I loved it." He huffs out a small laugh. "Even if I was terrified the first few times I got behind the wheel. Felt like I was racing down the road in an out-of-control barge." Glossy hair falls over his brow when he ducks his head. "Shocked the hell out of me when I got word that Pops had left it to me."

"I'm glad you got it," I say, fighting the urge to touch his arm. "I love the beast, but I never liked driving it. Clearly Pops knew you'd love it more."

Raw emotion makes his voice thick. "I do. It means the world to me."

I swear the ground tilts as if trying to push me into August, or into doing something ridiculous like hugging him close.

Flustered, I slide onto the worn leather seat and close my eyes for a moment. Gently, August closes the door, the familiar solid clunk of the metal ringing out in the quiet cabin. I open my eyes again when he lets himself into the driver's side.

"It used to smell of wet dog, pipe smoke, and—"

"A whiff of old fish?" August supplies with a knowing look. Pops loved to fish off the Santa Monica Pier and bring home his catch, despite the fact that my grandmother, who everyone called Pegs, hated fish. "I had the car fully restored. Sorry to say that particular miasma of Grouch is no more."

"I can't say as I'll miss the funk." Although I do a little.

I think he knows that, because his expression gentles, then he starts the truck. It trembles and growls, my seat vibrating. I run my hand along the leather captain's seat armrest as August takes us out into the California sun.

It's always striking to me how different the light is here. In Boston, there is a bluish-gray tint to the world, a coldness even in the heat. Here, everything is softly golden. That gilded soft patina is beautiful to look at, but I am of quiet, dark libraries, cozy sitting rooms with roaring fires. Flirty skirts, sunbaked skin that gleams, and hair fluttering in the breeze aren't me. But I still love LA.

August fits. Even with his winter-sky eyes, he fits. He's a bit grim now, however. Frowning at the road as he easily maneuvers the Grouch through the snarls of LA traffic. The silence between us is a living thing breathing down my neck.

I can't take it. "Are you ever going to tell me what the hell you meant by that ridiculous declaration?"

"Ridiculous." It's a mutter as he winces then changes lanes. "Way to kick a guy when he's down."

"I wasn't aware you ever got down."

Hot silver eyes shoot my way. "Why the hell would you think that?"

"And anyway, it isn't an insult to call that . . . " my voice gets a bit high and panicked, "marriage proposal—if that's what it really was—'ridiculous.' Any nondrunk or drug-free person would agree."

"Okay, okay." He lifts a big hand in surrender. "Given the way I blurted it out, the whole thing sounds ridiculous."

"I don't think it would matter how you delivered that bomb. It would still blow up in our faces."

"Ha." He turns off the expressway, heading toward Santa Monica Boulevard. An expansive sigh escapes him. "I don't know how to begin."

The confession comes out so hopeless that I soften.

"Try the beginning."

I get a sidelong glare.

Then his shoulders sag. "Let's start at the fucking infamous chicken dance."

"That was . . . interesting."

"Wasn't it just," he mutters darkly. "Never living that one down."

"I admit, I was a little shocked. Drunken dancing on tables doesn't seem like you."

"It isn't." August rubs the back of his neck with his free hand before putting it back on the steering wheel. His fingers drum an impatient rhythm. "I'll be honest, Penelope. I don't know what the hell got into me. It was like I was outside of myself, looking down in horror, begging myself to just stop. But I didn't. I couldn't."

"Sometimes anxiety can lead to acting out of character. It isn't always about hiding in your room."

"Are you saying it can also be acting like a complete goober asshole?"

"Maybe. You have a lot on your plate."

"I should be used to it by now." The frown is back and darker. "Regardless. I did the deed—deeds. And now I look like an unhinged, undedicated player."

"Okay." I'm starting to get the picture, but I can't quite believe it. I must be wrong. I have to be.

"We had a meeting. My agent, manager, PR, team staff, all that fun stuff." August swallows audibly. "The consensus was that I need to clean up my newly tarnished image."

"By getting married?" It comes out in an undignified sort of squeal.

"Well . . ."

"They can't make you do *that*!"

"No. It's more a matter of optics. I buckle down, don't party, get a nice fiancée so that it appears I'm focused on work and family. That sort of thing."

"But to get married."

He holds up a finger. "Engaged. We don't actually have to marry."

"Well, at least there's that." I spread my hands wide and roll my eyes. When he simply gives me a deadpan look, I forge on. "Why on earth would you ask me of all people?"

His brow quirks. "Why not? What's wrong with you?"

The man can't be this obtuse. Honestly, I know he's smart. Damn it. "Aside from the fact that no one would believe it?"

"You're kidding, right?" He says this with a hint of laughter in his voice.

"No, that would be you."

"I don't understand."

Must not tackle the quarterback.

"Don't make me spell it out for you, August."

"I'm afraid you're going to have to because I'm not getting it."

With a sigh, I close my eyes. "I'm not a model, or an actress. Nor, do I look like one."

"Penelope." His voice comes out of the darkness, soft and easy. "I've said it before. You're beautiful."

One eye opens despite my best effort to remain aloof. "I don't believe you said 'beautiful.'"

As though he knows it will be too much for me if he makes any sort of eye contact, his focus remains firmly on the road before us. "So I'll say it now. You're beautiful. Besides, I need someone real. Or, should I say, someone who doesn't have her own public drama."

"I'll give you that bit." I'm allergic to drama. If there's a hint of it, I run for the hills.

"And I need someone who . . . ah . . . at the risk of sounding vain—"

"Which means you're going to sound incredibly vain."

"Cute. But that risk aside, I need someone who won't fall in love with me or expect forever."

Silence ticks out.

"Hence, me."

His big shoulder lifts in a half shrug. "We both know you have never liked me that way. Hell, March and I are similar in looks and you had a huge crush on him but regarded me as . . . a worm."

"I never—"

"Oh, come on." At this, he glances my way. "You never liked me."

I sigh dramatically, if only to distract from any chance that I might be blushing. "I said I like you fine."

"Yeah, that faint praise is burned on my brain."

"If you're fishing for compliments, I suggest you go to the Pier."

"I really had no idea you were so saucy." He doesn't appear to find this a fault.

"Neither did I. Maybe this is a nightmare, and I'll wake up, plain old quiet Pen."

"I can pinch you, if you'd like." He waggles his fingers.

"Not if you want to live."

"Just a suggestion . . . Where were we?"

"You were complaining about how I liked March better."

"Right. That. Which means you're perfect for this. You won't fall for me. Plus, and this is huge, I trust you. We've known each other forever. I know you won't tell. Or sell your story later down the road."

"Thank you for that."

August nods as if I'm not being sarcastic, and then we fall quiet, the sound of the road humming along. He hasn't put on the radio. I don't know if it's because he wanted to talk or if he's one of those rare birds who doesn't like listening to music while driving. Because I love listening to music while driving.

And because it's now way too quiet, I break it. "I have a question."

"Just one?" Amusement crinkles his eyes.

"Okay, this is the first in a line of many."

"Ask away."

"What if you fall in love with me?"

Silence slams down upon the car. Rolling to a stop sign, August stares at me, before a soft huff of laughter escapes him and the corner of his lip quirks.

"What?" I ask. "Is it so comical, then?"

I know it is. Honestly, I do. I also have a perverse, inexplicable and highly ill-advised need to mess with him. But, still, he doesn't need to laugh so quickly.

August is smart enough to understand the minefield he's been thrust onto. He shifts in his seat like he's dying to escape. I picture him flinging open the door and sprinting down the street, leaving behind nothing more than an August-shaped dust cloud.

I'm about to tell him not to bother with an answer, that it was a joke. But then he looks my way with a wry expression.

"I won't lie," he says. "This blunt and sassy version of you surprises the hell out of me. But you don't have to worry about me suddenly falling in love with you."

I reach for nonchalance. "No?"

The muscle in his jaw bunches.

"I can't," he says, almost apologetically. "I found my true love years ago."

Oh.

Something hard and dull thuds in my chest. I didn't expect that. Not at all.

"Then why don't you ask her to do this—"

"It's football I love," he cuts in with an awkward laugh. "God. That was cheesy."

That hard, dull *something* inside me softens and flips. "No. It's . . . I don't know—"

"Cheesy."

"Lovely," I insist. "Truly. To know what you want to do and love it so much."

Absently, he nods, as he drives on. "Yeah. But I'm not just

trying to wax poetic here. Football is my wife, my child, my boss, it's everything. I have to give it my all, you know?"

I don't truly know because I don't love something that much. But I can understand a little. And it feels kind of lonely.

His voice is soft but tinged with something bittersweet. "How fair would it be for anyone to have to compete with that? I don't know much about love, but I know that a relationship needs the players to be fully present."

I think of my dad. Was he ever fully there? Or did he always mentally have one foot out the door?

"I agree." I give August what I hope is a reassuring look. "It's good you know that already. A lot of people never really do."

"My parents were good role models there."

"They certainly were."

A frown wrinkles between his brows, and I know he's remembering my not-so-great role models. "Oh, hey. I didn't mean—"

"It's okay, August." I move to touch his arm but fall short, feeling shy. "Really. Your parents are my role models for relationships too. I love watching the way they are together."

"Let's not go too far now. I could do without catching them making out when I walk into rooms unannounced." His mouth flattens with distaste. "Too many images are burned into my brain."

Laughter bubbles out of me. "It's cute!"

"I'll be sure to tell my eventual therapist just that."

My laughter increases, and he sends me a reproachful glare. But his lips are twitching. He turns at a cross street and then pulls up to a driveway. Until then, all my attention had been on August. Only this street is too familiar to ignore. I sit up straight.

"This is Pops and Pegs's house."

It's not the actual house, but the gates of it. Yes, my grandparents' house sits behind gates. In Brentwood. Which might as well be the moon to a college girl living on a severely limited budget. Given that it's an enormously expensive enclave of Los

Angeles, I had figured we were headed toward wherever it is August lives. But, no, the sneaky rat took me here. He might as well have cut me open and poured salt in my wound.

I turn toward him and let the hurt show. August frowns.

"You're not living here?" The surprise in his voice is real.

Slowly, I shake my head; it feels like a lump of lead. "No. I'm in an apartment with a roommate who barely tolerates me. I could have moved in but . . . I don't know. I didn't want to get even more attached, you know?"

"I get it."

"I come here from time to time. Clean and make sure the grounds aren't falling into disrepair. But there's only so much I can do on my budget."

"Can we go in?" he asks gently. "I'd like to see it, if that's okay."

"Sure."

The big gate is made of weathered reclaimed barn doors, hung on thick cut stone pillars with antiqued bronze lanterns on the tops. Flanked by lacy olive trees and thickets of twenty-foot-high evergreen trees, it completely hides away the house inside.

"What's the code?" August drives up to the gate and makes as if to leave the car.

"I have a remote opener on my phone," I tell him, inexplicably shaky. I love this house. Every last inch of it. The estate is my heritage, the place I visited time and again for comfort, for sanctuary. But, in this moment, I feel like an intruder, as though I'll never fully belong here again.

The big wood gates slide back, and we enter another world, far removed from the sun and heat and noise of LA. Here is grace and beauty, an age long gone by.

An allée of jacaranda trees in full bloom line the crushed limestone drive, creating a tunnel of purple. Sunlight spills through the fluttering blooms and dapples the windshield in violet light.

The end of the drive opens to a wide circular limestone paved car park and the house itself. The one-story ranch would be right at home in Provence with its dusky stone and stucco siding, weathered wooden shutters, and climbing vines. The roof extends out on one side to create an open porch that follows the length of the house.

And all I can think is I'm home. But home isn't supposed to hurt like this, is it?

EIGHT

AUGUST

I'VE VISITED THIS house several times, even stayed here that one summer. It's never failed to impress me.

Pen's quiet as we leave the truck and step under the shade of the porch, heading for the front door. Much like my own house, there's a security panel in place of a lock. She punches in the code and lets us in.

The house is cool and still like it's been waiting. Again, I'm struck by how beautiful the place is. White stucco walls reflect the light pouring in from oversize iron-framed windows.

Quietly, like she's a visitor, Pen sets her bag on the wide plank floors and then walks farther in. The house is a U shape branching out on each side from the main living room. Like an old barn, the roof and ceilings are pitched, with a massive weathered beam running along the center line and smaller beams branching out like ribs on a whale all along its length.

We wander past the den with overstuffed bookshelves lining the walls, and then a pretty sitting room that reminds me of Pegs and how she'd invite me to sit on those deep cream-colored couches and tell her about my games.

The kitchen has been redone since I was here. Instead of being dark and brown, it now has white cabinets, marble counters, and a walnut wood island. A huge carved limestone mantelpiece that looks like it came out of a French château surrounds the stove area. Skylights let light spill down on the counters.

"It's slightly different than I remember," I tell a silent Pen. "But I can still picture your grandmother here making those sweet orange breakfast rolls that she loved."

"I can too. God, I'd eat so many, my stomach would ache. No regrets, though."

"Not when it comes to those rolls."

Along the back of the house runs a long hallway with iron framed French doors that lead out to the pool and central courtyard. We head for the main bedroom.

Pen stops just inside the big square room. There's an adobe fireplace curving out of one corner and a set of stairs along the wall closest to us that leads to a loft room. This is the only area in the house that's two stories and the ceiling is double height because of it.

"I left most of their things in the other rooms but cleaned out everything here," she says.

"I've never been up there," I confess, glancing at the loft.

"Feels weird, doesn't it? Like we might get in trouble for snooping in their room."

"I'm betting they'll love it if we do." With a waggle of my brows, I take her hand and lead her up. The loft is an office, probably Pops's, given the big ash wood desk and leather executive chair. But the shelves have been cleaned out of books. A set of double doors leads to a Juliet balcony and a view of the garden. It's a nice spot, sunny, away from everything.

"You could study in here," I tell Pen. "Write your papers."

She stands at the threshold of the room, just at the top of the stairs, hands clasped before her. There's a look of such longing in her big brown eyes that my chest clenches.

"Penelope?"

She shakes herself out of wherever she went and blinks back at me before answering with exaggerated gravity, "August."

"Cute." A smile blooms but then fades to seriousness. "You should be here. This house is your place."

She fits in here. Just as beautiful. Just as graceful. I see her growing old here. I want that for her.

"Sometimes we don't get what we want," she says, as if hearing my thoughts.

"And sometimes you can get help from your friend."

Her nose wrinkles in confusion.

"That would be me. I'm the friend," I add helpfully. We've been avoiding each other for years. Of course she doesn't see me as a friend. That changes today.

"You want to help me." She draws the words out as if she's dubious.

"Yes." And because I know she's got more pride than she's ever let on, I expand on my offer. "If you recall, I did propose earlier."

Pink washes over her pale cheeks. Her full lips flatten. "Are we still on that?"

"Yes."

"Bah."

"Not the answer I'm looking for, Sweets."

"I am aware."

I lean a hip against the high pony wall that looks down on the bedroom below. "Being my fake fiancée is no cakewalk. If you do this, it's going to be a huge hassle for you. Press can be ugly. So can some fans. I won't ask without offering something."

"August." She sighs wearily. "What are you saying?"

"You pretend to be my fiancée, and I'll give you the money to pay the taxes."

Instantly her back is up. "You can't— That is, it's too much."

"I can. I want to. How else will you get it?"

"I can't do that. Not for that much money. If you want my help, I'll help you. But I can't take money for it."

"Pen. I don't want to see this house torn down by some

money-hungry developer who will slap in another concrete-and-glass horror."

"Then buy the house for yourself."

"It's your house, Penelope. You love it so much you were willing to beg your mom for it. I want to do this. Please."

Even white teeth worry the plump curve of her bottom lip. Her gaze darts over the room. I can all but hear her working it over in her head. "The thought of taking money . . . It's not something I can do just like that. It would eat at me . . ."

Guilt rushes in. I want her to accept, but not if it pains her this much. "Damn it. This was bad of me."

"Bad?"

"My help shouldn't be transactional. It's ugly." Sighing, I run a hand through my hair. A headache threatens around the edges of my sight. "Penelope, take the money. Forget about my proposal. Just take the money free and clear."

For some reason, this makes her smile softly. "I know you mean well, August, but that's not any better. I can't accept that much from you for nothing."

"So what you're saying is we're in a catch-22."

"Not precisely. If we pretend this conversation never took place, then—"

"Too late. The knowledge is there. It's going to prick at me. I want to help you, Sweets. More than I want to save my own ass." I'm surprised to find it's the complete truth. Maybe there's hope for me, after all.

"August . . . that means a lot to me. And I want to help you too. I just don't think I can. No one will believe it."

For a second I just stare. She's standing in a puddle of golden sunlight that gilds the delicate curves of her face and shines in her waving hair. Botticelli couldn't have done better. If I had even half the talent for painting that I did for football, I would have painted her just as she is now.

"If you could only see yourself the way I do."

A scowl twists her pink lips. "Don't—"

"No, let me say it. No, you're not a supermodel or an actress. And, no, I don't care. You worry that people won't believe it. But you're missing the main point."

"Which is?"

"If we make it believable, it will be."

"H-how do we do that?"

Oh, sweet Pen, that will be the easy part. Not a single person around us will doubt how into you I am.

"We look like a real couple—don't worry. It would only be on game days and a few public appearances."

"Oh, well . . ." She puffs out a breath. "August. I don't know . . ."

But she's thinking about it now. Which is a huge step in the right direction. I have to play this right.

"I know it's a lot to ask."

The stiffness eases from her shoulders just a bit. "Fine. I'll think about it. But I'm not promising anything."

"Okay. Good. Thank you." I should feel relief, but that weird relentless *yearning* seems to increase. "And while you're thinking about that, please let me help you with the house. We can come up with a payment plan or whatever. But let me help you, Penelope. Please."

"I guess I have a lot of thinking to do."

There's literally nothing I can do now. It's all up to her. Releasing control isn't something that comes easily. Football is a competitive sport; it's in my nature to do whatever it takes to win. But this isn't a game. It's something much more.

Swallowing hard, I will myself to look relaxed and non-threatening.

"I'll leave you to it, then."

NINE

AUGUST

I'LL THINK ABOUT IT.

Pen's subdued response to my plan runs through my head as I drive home. I messed up, fumbled the ball, what have you. I felt it with every word I'd uttered since blurting out that marriage proposal. I'm lucky she didn't punch me in the nose.

My mouth twitches despite my worry. There were moments Pen definitely looked like she wanted to give me a good slap.

Turning onto Laurel Canyon, it hits me that I don't like driving away. I haven't seen Penelope in years, and already I'm missing her voice, her eyes, the way she suddenly felt comfortable enough to tease me. My hands twitch with the urge to turn the wheel and go right back to her.

"Great," I mutter, and increase the volume on the radio. Unfortunately, the next song cues up to the Rolling Stones' "Satisfaction."

Ordinarily, I love the classics, especially the Stones, but having Mick Jagger sneer about not getting any satisfaction isn't helping my mood. Stabbing the forward button gives me a slight bit of satisfaction, thank you very much, Mick.

Until the radio blasts out the horrifying harmonizing of "Take a Chance on Me" by ABBA.

"What the fuck?" Now, I know that's not on my playlist.

And I know exactly who could figure out my password to add it. "That little shit."

I hit the hands-free call button on my phone. March answers on the third ring. Since I haven't turned down the radio, he hears the music immediately and laughs.

"Excellent," he says.

"Fucker." I'm trying hard not to laugh.

"Please tell me Pen is in the car with you."

Scowling, I turn the volume down. "Why would Pen be in the car with me?"

I can almost hear him shrug. "You had the same flight out. Logic dictates that you'd offer her a ride home."

"How the hell did you know we had the same flight— You know what? Never mind. I don't know why I even ask."

"You choose futility. I know everything."

"Sure you do." I make a right onto my street. "Just remember payback is a bitch."

"Bro, you are on a different coast from me for months. I feel pretty safe."

"Famous last words, squirt."

He snorts. "I'm bigger than you."

"Only in height."

"And muscle."

"Please. I can toss you like a bag of cookies."

Outrage colors his laugh. "Like hell."

"Hell is what's going to rain down on you when I get my revenge."

Again he snorts, long and exaggerated. Then his voice brightens. "So . . . How was the flight with Pen?"

It's scary how well he knows me. And annoying. "Fine."

"Fine, huh? You two crazy kids get along all right?"

"Sure." I eye the call button. Maybe I can hang up on him and blame it on bad LA reception.

"Uh-huh. Did you ask her out?"

"What?" The car swerves, and I glare at the road. Fucking March.

"Don't give me that." He sounds bored. "There were definite vibes between you two—finally. You need to get off your ass and ask her out."

If he only knew what I'd asked of her.

"What's with you trying to put me and Pen together, anyway?" It comes out far more annoyed than I want, and any sign of weakness will make March dig in.

"Truth? Because you were looking at her the way you used to look before an upcoming football game. And I'm thinking if something gives you that feeling you go after it. But what do I know?"

The ancient SUV feels too close and too hot. I should never have asked March a question I didn't want the answer to. Lesson learned.

"The flight was fine. I drove her home. End of story." For now. *Please don't let it be the end of our story.* Shit, I'm in so much trouble.

March, for once, doesn't push. "If you say so."

"I do."

"Welp." He sighs expansively. "If that's all, I'm gonna text Pen and ask her what's up."

What! And, wait. That little . . . How the fuck does he have her number?

"Don't you dare—"

He's already gone.

"Shit!" Banging the wheel, I'm halfway to calling him back, maybe calling Pen and begging her not to say anything to March. But then I take a breath. March is bluffing. I know it. And if, on the off chance, he's not, I trust Pen not to talk.

Even so, my head starts to throb.

"I need a fucking nap."

Pulling up to my gate, I'm reminded of Pen all over. While

her house, and its gate, are old Hollywood class, my place is new construction ostentation.

Since the new rules for college athletes went in place, I've been making money on endorsements for years. Not the obscene amount of the NFL deal, but a lot, as have both my brothers. My father immediately found us a money manager, and my savings were nice and plump long before the draft. It's a comfort given that the career of a professional athlete is short and brutal. I invested in some properties, but I didn't buy a home until I'd signed.

Punching in my code, I wait for the brushed steel gate to slide open and make my way down the small incline to my house. Pen's place—and it is her place no matter what she says—has old graceful trees and flowering plants, ripe with maturity, that lead you like a secret map toward the house. My spot has a few saplings dotted here and there, opening to a flat expanse of new sod lawn that hugs the mountainside with downtown Los Angeles shimmering in the distance.

The house itself is a series of three interconnected and staggered flat squares made up of whitewashed concrete and steel windows. Yes, I bought a soulless, overpriced, modern pop-up mansion that was slapped over the remains of someone's previous home. It seemed like a good idea at the time; I'd wanted a home not a rental, and the agent, who I'm not going to lie was smoking hot with a sweet smile, persuaded me that this was just the place to settle down in—at least for the next year or so. Here, it isn't uncommon for the wealthy to move around on a whim.

Looking at it now, with its twenty-foot maple-and-glass front door that opens on a whisper and the endless expanse of gray stone floor, it feels . . . ridiculous. Why do I need a ten-thousand-square-foot house with two owner's suites—upstairs and downstairs—an indoor *and* outdoor home theater, and three party bars. I don't even drink that much.

A headache blooms as I park in my empty five-car garage and head into the house via my catering kitchen. Two kitchens and all I can do is make sandwiches. Honestly, what the hell was I thinking?

I wasn't.

I was more interested in scoring with Jessie the real estate seductress.

Only, and here's the kicker, I hadn't. Oh, she'd been willing, I'd been wanting, and there'd been opportunity. And when it all came to a head? I couldn't.

Everything in me had just withered like a fallen leaf in the sun. I might have felt humiliated if I hadn't been so terrified. Nothing was right anymore. Not my sex drive, not my behavior, or my love of the game. I don't feel like me anymore.

You did when you were with Pen.

The thought doesn't help.

Sighing, I toss my keys in the little wooden bowl on the counter by the door and head into the main living area. Hot blocks of sunlight fall through the wall of windows and onto the floor. It might be impersonal here but at least it's light filled—that's what my mother said when she'd visited.

Evidence of her ensuing attempt to make it "homey" are in the thick cream-colored throw draped over the end of the low-slung sectional, and the various vases dotted around the bookshelves that flank my granite fireplace.

I know how it hurts Pen to worry about losing her grandparents' house. I understand it better than she realizes. There's nothing of me here. My mother's house is still my home. Not this place. I remember doing the dishes back in Massachusetts, and suddenly I miss Mom with a yawning emptiness in my belly.

Hefting my overnight bag onto my shoulder, I head toward my bedroom when I spot someone lying out by the pool. The bag plops on the floor, and I stride to the patio.

Trent Gellis, aka Jelly, my main tight end, doesn't acknowledge me as I approach. Sprawled out on one of my loungers, he's oiled up, wearing a damn banana hammock that's way too small, oversize mirrored aviators, and nothing else. Coupled with his spiked bleached blond hair, I can't tell if he's going for an Iceman from *Top Gun* look or just trying to give me nightmares.

I step closer, and he deigns to lift his glasses to squint at me.

"You're in my sun, Rook." Jelly reaches for the glass of lemonade sitting on the side table next to him. Ice cubes clink as he sips through a pink flamingo curly straw—I'm going to guess he brought that with him.

"Is there a reason you're lounging by my pool and not your own?" I ask conversationally. Jelly returned to LA with the rest of the team. After getting my ass chewed out by Coach, I was given two days "grace" to get my act together.

"You asked me to water your plants before you went to visit your ma." He waves an idle hand in the direction of my house.

"I was being sarcastic. I don't have any plants."

"That's why I'm sunning instead of watering." Again his glasses come up. I'm treated to a dark-eyed squint worthy of old Clint Eastwood. "And sarcasm is unbecoming in a rookie."

"Is this another hazing attempt?" I take a seat on the neighboring lounger. "Terrorize the rookie by sunbathing in a bikini bottom?"

"Nah. If I was terrorizing, I'd put *you* in the suit."

"You could try. But you'd be limping back home."

"That's the fighting spirit. Even if it is deluded." He threads his hands behind his head and settles in. "I'm working on my tan."

His face, arms, and calves are ruddy brown. The rest of him, where his uniform usually covers, is pale ivory. I don't fault him for trying to even out; I'd just as rather not have to witness the process.

"Would have gone in the buff," he adds, with a rolling drawl, "but I didn't want to rub sunscreen on my junk. That's my girl's job, and she wouldn't come over with me. Said I was invading your privacy."

"Smart girl."

"Isn't she just? And it ain't a bikini. It's a . . ." He frowns before his expression clears. "Mankini."

I grab his drink and take a gulp. "The leopard print is a nice touch, really."

"Monica says leopard print is in now. She knows these things."

"I guess we'll take Monica's word on that."

With a grunt, Jelly sits up and swings his legs over the side of the seat. He's a good six foot six and his long legs fold up toward his chest before he parts his thighs. I avert my eyes. Honestly, nightmares about this for months are in my future.

"Tell you the truth, son—" (he's only four years older than me) "—I'm here to discuss your poultry party proclivities."

"Nice alliteration."

"You want to throw SAT words at each other all day or are you gonna explain why you danced on a table like an inebriated chicken?"

Grimacing, I attempt to take another drink of lemonade. He snatches the glass and raises his brow in warning before sipping through the straw. Jelly's my first true friend on the team, and despite his unfortunate attire, he's a straight shooter who works hard and doesn't fuck around. His disappointment in me stings.

"Won't happen again." I hold his gaze before looking out at the pool. Its opaline blue surface ripples faintly in the breeze.

"No it won't. We don't have time for fuckups. We got the tools, and we got the talent. I want a ring on this, son." He holds up his massive hand. It's hard and scarred, and ring-free at the moment. "And I ain't talking about getting one from my girl neither."

A laugh sputters out of me. "Fuck's sake, Jelly. I'm a rookie. And you want a ring this year?"

He simply looks at me with those steady, squinty eyes the color of new football leather. "You can do it."

My insides twist tight. God, I want to dive in the pool, sink down in its cool quiet waters, and rest on the bottom.

"You can," he says again.

Of course Jelly expects a ring. He should. It's what the team paid top dollar for. A superstar. The QB who could become a legend. Thing with being a legend is that it isn't easy or common; if it were, we wouldn't revere them. My team can be the best in the world but if it isn't in me to shine, then nothing will change that.

It's a struggle to breathe, but I suck in a deep breath and look back at him. His broad face is placid now. He knows the struggle too. We all do.

"I won't fuck up again, Jells." My hand spreads wide over my thigh. "I don't know if I can lead us there, but I'll try my hardest."

"That's all any of us can do."

I wish that were true.

TEN

PEN

MONDAY MORNING STARTS with bossa nova. Astrud Gilberto's "Summer Samba" to be precise. Her honey-cream voice combined with the up-tempo Moog synthesizer makes me think of pretty ladies with lacquered beehive hair and A-line silk brocade dresses socializing at a cocktail party, swinging elaborately long cigarette holders while making their point and sloshing pink ladies onto the toes of their pointy kitten heels.

Snuggling down in my bed, I smile at the image. I'd like to have a cocktail party one day, hand out colorful little hors d'oeuvres that look like art but taste even better. I'd put on a flirty dress and laugh with friends while sipping martinis out of etched glasses. In theory, I'd like that very much. In practice? I don't have enough friends to fill a room, and I'd probably hide in the corner or play waitress in an effort to avoid talking to anyone.

How . . . unsatisfactory. I turn to my side and pull the covers up high. August wants me to play at being his fiancée. I'd have to socialize on a public stage. I'd have to make conversation, to laugh and smile, and be . . . something that I'm not. He doesn't understand that because, for a brief but brilliant time with him, I'd been someone different. I'd been open in a way I never am. He fails to remember clearly how quiet and withdrawn I usually am.

Or maybe he doesn't care.

But he will. When I'm at his side, in public, he will. Someone like August needs a fake fiancée who will shine like a diamond. He needs polish and poise. Most days, I can barely tolerate talking to strangers. As much as I'd like to help him, I'm going to have to decline.

The thought of not seeing him anymore depresses me. Without this deal between us, what reason would he have to continue?

My stomach grumbles. As much as I'd like to stay in bed all day, I'm awake now, which means I need my coffee. But given that bossa nova is blasting throughout the apartment, my roommate, Sarah, is definitely up and about, and she's a bit much to take today when I want nothing more than to be quiet with my own worries.

Another grumble from my stomach has me sighing and throwing back the covers. Glancing at my phone, I'm surprised to find it's already ten. It isn't like me to sleep in this long. The last thing I need is to spiral into a depressive episode. I have classes to attend, money to find, and a fake marriage proposal to contemplate. I'm swamped.

Laughing at my own cheesy joke, I pull on some clothes then head out to find my coffee.

Sarah is in the center of the living room, now bopping around to "The Girl from Ipanema." While it's not quite a beehive, she's teased the top of her orange hair into a smooth dome before sweeping it up into a high ponytail. She's wearing bubblegum-pink pedal pusher pants and a purple mock turtleneck tunic.

She twirls around and spots me. "You're back."

It isn't a particularly happy announcement; Sarah finds me too quiet for her tastes. But I pay my half of the rent on time and am clean. Cleanliness and financial solvency in a roommate has become increasingly hard to find.

"I am." I head to the small galley kitchen. The cabinets are vintage tin, painted in bright teal. Salmon-pink walls and yellow

Formica countertops and vintage avocado-green appliances complete the look. In the full light of the midday sun, it's bright enough to give me a headache, and I squint as I reach for an *I Love Lucy* mug and pour myself some much-needed coffee.

"You don't look great," Sarah says from the doorway. Her pet, Edward, eyes me with distaste from his perch on her shoulder. As usual, they are in complete agreement.

"Thank you." I add a dollop of half-and-half to my coffee and stir. "I'm grumpy."

"Well, it can't be from Astrud." She takes another step into the room. "No one can resist the happiness of her voice."

"I always thought she sounded melancholy." In all honesty, I'd heard a bit of Astrud Gilberto and bossa nova, but never really listened to it before living here. But the point remains.

Sarah laughs shortly. "I guess she does. But her voice makes me happy, so." She shrugs and Edward shifts to get more comfortable.

Sipping my coffee, I root around in the fridge for the eggs and butter. I'm going to fix myself a nice scramble with toast and then go for a long walk. I don't want to make small talk with the headache I'm currently blooming, but Sarah stays and watches me cook.

"Where'd you go again?"

"Boston to visit my mom." I crack an egg and watch it plop into the bowl. "It was all right."

The eggs start to firm up in the pan. Plating my food, I grab a fork and head out to the little dining nook. I take a seat at the round teak dining table, and Sarah remains leaning against the doorway, watching.

A sense of smallness and failure crawls over my skin. Sometimes I feel like there's something wrong with me for wanting my solitude. I like being social. But I *need* my alone time. I need to be able to eat my breakfast without having to talk. Not every day. But today, it pricks at my chest.

When I don't say anything, Sarah sighs and shakes her head

as if to say I've failed her yet again. "Edward is a better conversationalist than you."

"No doubt." I'm tempted to say she's free to talk to Edward and leave me to my breakfast.

Maybe she sees it in my face; she huffs in a mix of annoyance and amusement, then strolls over to the turntable and selects another album from the library of records stuffed onto the built-in shelves lining one wall.

The room fills with the melodic sounds of Charlie Byrd's classical jazz guitar, as Sarah sprawls on a chartreuse velvet armchair and Edward settles on her chest.

Digging into my eggs, I plan my hiking route when the door buzzes.

"I'll get it," Sarah says with a watery sigh.

She disappears into the front hall. I hear the rattle of the door opening and then the deep, smooth sound of August asking for me. My fork clatters to the table. It irritates me how quickly my heartbeat kicks up.

Before I can do anything more than sit straight, Sarah rounds the corner and enters the main living room with August in tow. He spots me immediately.

He smiles with his eyes. The thought hits me in the solar plexus. How had I never noticed this before? Oh, there's a small curl to his lips, polite and reserved, the kind I've seen on August's face many times before. But his eyes? They're lit with a glow of pleasure that makes me want to beam with happiness, and spreads a glowing warmth through my belly.

I think I've waited my whole life for August Luck to look at me like this, and now that he is, I don't know what to do with myself. My hands flutter about like butterfly wings before I shove them in my lap and give him a dignified "Hello, August."

It only makes the smile spread over his whole face. God, he's like the sun breaking over bleak hills.

"Hello, Penelope." He uses the same proper tone, but I hear the humor in his voice all the same. It's as though we're sharing a private joke, only I've forgotten the punch line. All the same, I feel like smiling wide. I don't, of course. Sarah is hovering, mouth agape as she stares at August. As if feeling her gaze, he glances back at her, and his "dealing with the public" expression returns.

I shove back my chair and stand. "Sarah, this is August. He's ah . . . an old friend. August, Sarah is my roommate."

At that moment, as if to voice his protest in being ignored, Edward perks up and lets out a loud croak.

August nearly jumps out of his skin. His wide-eyed gaze zeroes in on Edward and he turns decidedly pale. Despite this, he clearly makes an effort not to react further. No, August Luck, King of Control, merely bows his head. "Good day to you too, sir."

In less than five minutes he's made my whole day better. I'm in big trouble.

AUGUST

PEN'S ROOMMATE LOOKS like she's cosplaying Daphne from *Scooby-Doo*, right down to the orange hair. I do mean orange, not red. She's been eyeing me from the moment she opened the door. And frankly, I'd been too distracted by those long, gawking looks to notice her companion. Until he croaked.

He's all I notice now. Because sitting on the roommate's shoulder, is a fucking enormous frog, wearing a jaunty purple top hat. A top hat just like the Mad Hatter's from *Alice in Wonderland*. There's even a tiny "10/6" ticket tucked into the hatband.

I blink again, wondering if I tripped up somewhere and fell down a rabbit hole.

"Where are my manners," Sarah says, shooting a glare at Pen before picking up the frog and presenting him to me on the palm of her hand. "This is Edward."

Years ago, I came across my parents laughing their asses off while watching an old '50s cartoon of a frog in a top hat who would sing and dance for his owner, but only when no one else was looking. I wouldn't be surprised in the least if Edward here does the same.

"Ah . . . good to meet you, Edward." I am *not* shaking hands. It's all I can do to keep from diving over the red lip-shaped coffee table and hide behind Pen. I'm not ashamed to admit: Frogs give me the creeps. I'm not going to admit this out loud, however. I have the feeling Sarah would brain me if I did.

Edward, perhaps sensing weakness, croaks again and twitches. Like he'll leap onto my face at the slightest provocation. My body tenses. Flight or fight. It's fifty-fifty at the moment. I try to hide my terror with a stern warning look. His glassy half-lidded stare tells me he's unimpressed.

"Edward, dearest." At this Sarah gives his frog ass a little kiss. "Meet August Luck, our team's new quarterback."

So she knows who I am. Wonderful. She'll probably record it if Edward tries to get personal.

"Edward?" I ask, one eye still on the frog. "Like from *Twilight*?" Honestly, my sisters plague me with those damn movies whenever they can.

Sarah, however, sniffs as though she's smelled something foul. "Certainly not." She gives the frog a loving smile and sets him back on her shoulder. "Edward, as in Edward Hopper."

"Ah. Because of the hopping. Cute."

They both give me a look of disdain.

"Because he's an artist." She motions toward a framed painting. It's a white canvas covered in a rainbow of squiggly smudges, presumably made by a paint-covered Edward hopping around with glee. But what do I know? Maybe he holds a paintbrush too.

Swallowing hard, I nod with due gravity. "You must be very proud."

A snuffle, like a laugh quickly smothered, sounds to my right where Pen sits. I don't look that way. If I make eye contact with her, I'm going to lose it. I doubt Sarah's mood will improve if I crack up laughing in her living room.

I shift my weight on my feet, edging just a little bit away. But I'm ready to spring if shifty-eyed Edward does. It's a game of chicken now. Sweat breaks out on my lower back.

Sarah doesn't fill the silence but looks at me expectantly. Okay, then.

"So, how does his little hat stay on?" I push a smile. "Let me guess. Magic?"

Her upper lip curls. "Another comedian." She shoots an accusatory glance at Pen, then thankfully moves away, heading for the back hall. "His hat stays on with a little elastic band, of course." The orange of her ponytail swings with her stride. "Maybe try being less of a funny guy and concentrate more on playing football."

At that, she stops and glares at me from over her shoulder. Edward does too. "True fans are counting on you, *Luck*."

Unable to help myself, I give her a quick salute. Her eyes narrow, but she leaves without saying anything other than, "Turn off the record player when it's done, Pen."

As soon as she's gone, I let out a breath and finally look at Pen. "She seems nice."

"She has her moods but she's okay."

"I admit, I was not expecting the frog."

Her laughter sounds so good and warm, my lingering tension vanishes. "No one does. I think she gets off on disarming people with him."

She picks up her dishes, and I follow her into the kitchen. "I can't believe it keeps the hat on."

Pen grins wide, her brown eyes alight as she puts her plate and fork in the dishwasher. "I couldn't either at first. But she's got dozens of them."

"Frogs?" The horror.

"Hats." Pen laughs. "Cowboy hats, baseball caps, boaters, derbys, newsboy caps . . . you name it."

"Dear God."

"It's cute."

"If you say so." I suppress a shudder.

"You don't like the hats?"

"Frogs. They give me the willies. But don't tell your roommate."

"Oh, really?" The question is filled with glee. I would expect no less.

"Jan hid one in my football kit when I was thirteen. And I didn't find it until I got dressed." My skin crawls at the memory of that clammy frog wriggling over my torso in a desperate bid for freedom. "I don't know who was more upset, me or the frog. But the fear remains."

She makes a sound of sympathy. "I'd be scarred for life too. Don't worry, your secret's safe with me."

Stuffing my hands in my jeans pockets, I lean against the counter. "Why did Sarah say 'another comedian'? Have other guys said the same?"

I'd like to think I'm subtle here, but I doubt it. Then again, Pen simply shakes her head, clearly not getting my query into the topic of any guys she may or may not have dated.

"No. She meant me." Her eyes light up again with humor. "When I met Edward, I asked if it was magic that made his hat stay on."

This pleases me more than it probably should. "It's a perfectly logical conclusion. Anyone who can get a frog to dress in hats and stay put has to be practicing some sort of magic."

"Exactly!"

We share a grin but then I shoot a wary glance toward the way Sarah exited. "He stays put, right?"

Pen pats my arm kindly. "Don't worry, Pickle. If he hops out here to have a word, I'll protect you."

"Ah, Sweets, I knew I could count on you to save me."

I thought it would make her smile some more, but her happy expression dims.

"Speaking of that," she begins in a tone that sets off alarm bells in my head.

She's going to turn me down. I know it. Before she can get another word out, I take her hand. "Let's go for a walk and talk."

When her brows draw together, I give her hand a gentle tug. "Come on. I need to be far away from Frogville. And I'm in the mood for a hike."

"Huh."

"What is it?" I ask.

"Nothing, really. I was planning to go on a hike today, is all."

"Perfect. Let's go." I take her hand again. My fingers curl over hers and something deep inside of me seems to click into place. And for one thick moment, I just want to stay right here and hold on. The feel of her hand in mine centers me. I like it. A lot.

Oblivious to my turmoil, Pen makes a sound of amused exasperation. "Wait, wait. I've got to change first."

For the first time since I got here, I notice her clothes. She's wearing an oversize ivory T-shirt with *Murder, She Wrote* printed in gold across her chest and tiny frayed jean shorts. I swallow hard. Pen's legs are slim and pale with ankles so delicately thin, I could easily wrap my thumb and forefinger around them. Lust tightens my core with unexpected speed and strength. It's far too easy to imagine sliding my hands up those smooth legs and wrapping them around my waist.

My breath punches out in a gust. "You look perfect."

It's clear she doesn't believe me. But I don't give her too much time to think about it. Instead, I hustle her out of the kitchen and ask where her shoes are. Trained or not, there's a Mad Hatter frog on the loose in this place and we need to get out of it as soon as humanly possible.

"Stop rushing me," she grouches. "I know you're doing it so I won't argue with you on my choice of attire."

Choice of attire. She's too adorable for words.

"You caught me. Now my dastardly plan is foiled." I glance around. "You got a purse or something?"

"I have a bag, which I'm going to get ready," she corrects, one delicate eyebrow raised in affront. "And you can hold your horses."

"I love it when you talk grandma to me."

"Being cute won't help your case either."

"But you love it when I'm cute."

God, I hope she does; I need all the help I can get.

Thankfully, Pen huffs with a smile and heads for her room. A lack of denial means she agrees with me. That's what I'm sticking to, at any rate. I watch her go. Her posture is prim straight and correct, but her peachy butt sways like a pendulum. I want to take a bite out of it, out of *her*. I settle for stopping the record and putting it back in its sleeve. I have no idea if the massive collection of records is Pen's or her roommate's, but I'm guessing the latter.

Hovering by the front door in case I need to escape a sneak frog attack, I try to see anything of Pen here. I can't. Pen's true place is back at her grandparents' house. Not that there's any of her things there either, but she can make it her own. I want that for her, and I want to be there to witness the whole thing.

The trick is convincing her to let it happen.

ELEVEN

PEN

AUGUST AND I debate where to go the whole walk down to the car and while I buckle up. But finally, we settle on heading for the Santa Monica beach bike path. Mainly because it's a perfect day, and we'd both like a bit of fresh sea air.

It feels good, though, to drive along with the windows down in Pops's old Wagoneer and the radio playing. August chose The Doors *Greatest Hits*, something my grandfather loved listening to as well, and I'm reminded of going fishing off the Pier with Pops. We'd end the day with a ride on the Ferris wheel, after which, he'd buy me a custard shake. Maybe I can convince August to get one with me later.

Speaking of August . . .

"Keep your eyes on the road, mister."

August lifts his brows in a parody of innocence. "I am!"

He most certainly was sneaking looks at me slathering sunscreen over my arms and legs.

"You act like you've never seen anyone take proper precaution against sun damage before."

"There you go with the grandma talk again." He switches lanes, the corner of his lips curling upward. "It only turns me on, you know."

"Glad to know you have a thing for grandmas."

"Try again, Sweets." He risks a glance, quick but hot. "And

I should be lecturing you on distracting the driver. Can't you rub that on your legs when we get there? I vote for a slow and thorough application."

"Ha. And no. Sunscreen needs to absorb twenty minutes before going out for maximum efficacy."

He groans and takes a deep breath. "Killing me here."

This flirty side of August is something I'd witnessed from afar but had never been subjected to. It's surprisingly fun, and addicting. But he doesn't need to know that. His ego is healthy enough.

Rolling my eyes, I cap the sunscreen but stick it in the bin between the seats instead of my bag. "If it wasn't a safety risk, I'd say you should put some on now too. We'll have to wait until we get there."

White teeth flash in a grin. "You gonna rub it on me, Sweets?"

"Nice try, buddy."

"Can't blame a guy."

With a dubious hum, I lean back and close my eyes, letting the wind hit my face. "LA Woman" ends, and The Raconteurs' "Old Enough" starts playing, the bluegrass-rock version with Ashley Monroe harmonizing alongside Jack White. I know this because I played the song multiple times one year in high school. I have no idea where I discovered it, but it's a nice surprise to know August likes it too.

As it usually happens when I hear the song, I start to sing along, taking the contralto notes. It doesn't occur to me to feel self-conscious, even though I never sing around other people. Maybe it's because August is strumming his thumb on the steering wheel in time to the beat and eyes bright with pleasure. But I'm not sure that's it. Maybe it's just him. Somewhere between him telling me I had nice teeth, eating sandwiches in the night, and me hearing out his wild false marriage proposal, I fell into *trust* with him.

"Okay," I say when the song ends. "I'll do it."

The car swerves a little when his attention swings my way. "What?"

"Road!" I point, scrambling upright.

But he's already corrected. "Focus, Penelope—" as if *I'm* the one driving all over the place "—you'll do what exactly?"

It's clear he understood me perfectly fine because he's beaming, his smile so wide, he's dimpling. But he's not letting it go, his insistent gaze darting between me and the road, waiting for my answer.

Brushing an errant strand of hair away from my eyes, I repeat myself with a calm I don't exactly feel. "I'll go along with your crazy-ass scheme."

"Just like that?" He sounds dubious.

"Just like that." I frown. "Why are you questioning?"

He lifts a shoulder in a half shrug. "I don't know. Back at your apartment, it sounded like you were going to turn me down."

I so was.

"Shows what you know." In truth, *I* didn't know until the words tripped out of me.

"Okay," he says with a happy slap on the wheel. "Okay! Let's do this, Sweets."

We don't say much more until he pulls into the massive beachfront parking lot that flanks the pier. It's fairly empty and the SUV stands on its lonesome as we get out. I'm making an attempt to grab the sunscreen bottle when August hops out of the truck and rounds it with quick strides. He opens my door and captures my hand.

"Come here for a second." That's all the warning I get before he lifts me high and spins me around. I squeal both in surprise and pleasure. No one has swung me like this since childhood.

That August is doing it, smiling at me like I've made his year, his firm body pressed against mine, has my breath hitching. His neck is warm where I wrap my arms around for stability, and he smells so good, all I want to do is nuzzle in close and breathe. The whole thing flusters me so much, I get hot.

"Put me down, *pazzo*!" It comes out by rote because I don't know how to be this publicly free. Unfortunately, August immediately sets me down.

But he doesn't let me go. His big hands rest on my waist as he grins down at me. "*Pazzo?*"

"'Crazy' in Italian." The wind blows my hair in my face, and I swat it back. "*Tu sei pazzo.* You're crazy."

August groans and tips his head forward. "God, that sounds sexy."

Flushed, I avoid his gaze and try to ignore the heat of his hands seeping through my shirt. "And here I thought you had a thing for grandma talk."

He bites his bottom lip as his eyes light up. "Maybe you could combine them?" The suggestion sounds far too hopeful. "We can get you one of those long-ass pins they use to roll out pasta dough, and you can wave it at me while lecturing in Italian."

"Maybe you should go to Bologna and spend some time with my *nonna*."

"Will she make me pasta and those little almond cookies your mom always has at Christmas?"

"For you? Probably."

"I am very charming when I try." This is offered with a perfectly straight face. It makes me laugh, despite my best efforts.

"Yes, you are."

His snicker is unrepentant, but, after giving my waist a squeeze, he lets it go. "Why'd you change your mind, because I know you did."

Before I can answer, he holds up a hand. "Doesn't matter. You said yes." Again, that light comes in his silver eyes that makes my insides flutter and float. "That's enough for me."

"Okay." It's all I can come up with under the brilliance of his joy. But relief has me breathing a bit easier. Telling him why I'd said okay to his *pazzo* idea is a bit more than I'm ready to reveal.

He hasn't moved away and doesn't look as if he's planning to.

Whatever is going on behind those eyes has his brows drawing together in concentration. "Right, then." That sharp focus shifts to me. "Let's do this."

"Okay but . . ." I reach into the open truck and grab the sunscreen that I'd dropped on the seat when August decided to have a celebratory whirl. "Lather up first."

He blinks at me as though not understanding.

I shake the bottle enticingly. "Protection is key."

The corner of his mouth quirks. "Usually when I hear this, I'm being offered a condom instead."

"I'd like to think you wouldn't need reminding of that," I say primly. No, I am not going to picture him in that situation. No, thank you.

He takes the bottle. "Joking, sweet Penelope. I am a safety guy through and through."

"Then you won't forget to use sunscreen religiously as well."

With a grunt that may or may not be agreement, he squirts out a good dollop, hands me the bottle to hold, then proceeds to rub it on his arms. Up until now, I've managed not to look too closely at his body. No sense in risking being caught gaping. But I can't ignore it now.

His arms are works of art: baked brown by the sun, corded and defined, with rocklike biceps that bunch and shift when he moves. August is leaner than March; he doesn't need the bulk that his younger brother does. But the Lucks have the genetics of the gods, as far as I can tell. Every one of them has strong, well-toned bodies that would take me hours of working out a day to achieve. August is no exception. There's a reason images of his torso went viral leading up to his draft.

Thankfully, he leaves his T-shirt on and only focuses on his arms and neck. He catches me looking, and waggles his brows. "You sure you wouldn't want to put this on for me—"

"Nope."

"I might miss a spot or two."

"Your hands are big enough to catch all outlying territory."

A soft laugh rumbles in his chest. "Cut it with the sexy talk, Pen. I can't take much more of it."

Sternly, I hand him the bottle again so he can get some sunscreen for his face. He does an admirable job of covering himself, but there's a white streak on each side of his nose where it rises up to his eyes. Since he's rubbing his face hard with frowning determination, I know he doesn't realize this. Something in me softens.

Tossing the capped sunscreen back in the truck, I step up to him. Immediately, August stills, his hands falling to his sides as he watches me with quiet eyes. So still, as though I might bolt if he makes a sudden move. I just might.

My voice comes out too breathy. "Here." Not entirely steady, I cup his face between my hands. Instantly, his lids lower, his head falling forward so I can reach him easier. With the blunt edge of my thumbs, I smooth out the sunscreen.

A gull cries overhead. In the distance comes the faint crash and rush of the waves, and the bright quick laugh of a child. But here, standing in the lee of August's long body, it's so quiet the agitated rhythm of our exhalations sound like thunder. My belly quivers as I stroke my thumbs over the high crests of his cheekbones.

Somehow, I've migrated closer, into the warm circle of his arms. Somehow, his hands have drifted back to my waist, settling there heavy and secure. We share a breath, and my knees weaken. I want to rest on his wide chest, melt into him.

August's grip tightens ever so slightly. A whip of heat licks along the backs of my thighs, and tightens my lower belly. His forehead rests against mine.

Control. I need to regain it. My hands fist, and I lower them against my chest where my heart pounds out of control. He sees the withdrawal and takes a deep breath before raising his gaze to mine; pewter skies outlined with inky lashes.

"I didn't expect you to be this potent, Pen. It's doing my head in."

The whispered confession has my breath hitching. Potent? He's looking at me with those storm cloud eyes, as if he's halfway to angry, halfway to . . . what? It can't be lust. It can't be. Not from him. Teasing is one thing.

My fists tighten. "I'm just . . . me."

"Yeah, you are," he says, a smile in his voice. When I gape up at him in *slight* panic, he gives me a small squeeze with the tips of his fingers then sets me back. "Eventually you'll see it, Penelope Morrow."

"See what?"

With a wry shake of his head, he locks up the car. "See yourself the way I do."

I'm too chicken to ask for further clarification. Besides, I have a feeling he wouldn't give me a straight answer anyway.

"Come on, then." He holds out a hand. "Let's take a walk and plan our strategy."

AUGUST

I ALMOST KISSED her. It was a near thing. And it would have been a mistake. Pen isn't ready for that from me. She'll bolt or explain it away—it was the heat of the moment, I didn't realize what I was doing, or some similar nonsense.

Fact is, yes, the heat of the moment was almost too much to restrain me. But no, I'd have known exactly what I was doing. I've been trying to keep from kissing Penelope since I saw her in my parents' doorway, outlined by the pouring rain and gaping up at me like I was a mirage.

Maybe this is a dream: frogs in top hats, chicken dances on tables, and Penelope Morrow calling me Pickle with a wide smile on her perfect lips.

Maybe I took a hard hit and I'm in a coma.

The thought slides down my spine like wet ice. I take a short breath and blow it out hard. But I'm still unsettled. Somehow, my hand finds Pen's. She takes a misstep like she's surprised, but doesn't pull away, and our fingers thread.

This is real. Nothing in my imagination would come up with the sense of calm and rightness that holding Pen's hand gives me. I wouldn't have thought it possible. Not to this extent. I'm holding hands with a woman—something I've always considered a cliché and an unnecessary activity—and it feels *good*. In direct opposition of my earlier stance, it feels *necessary*.

Pen glances up at me. Her rounded cheeks are slightly flushed, and I know she's preoccupied with the hand holding. This amuses me. Despite her shyness, Pen wouldn't hold my hand if she didn't want to. That much I know. The same way I know she's nervous because some part of her must like this too. No, I'm not a mind reader, but I know her. A lot more than she realizes. It would never occur to Pen that I've made a study of her all of our lives. She'd probably faint dead away—right after insisting that it wasn't true.

"Why are you smiling," she asks, suspicious.

I give our linked hands a little swing. "Sun's shining, weather's perfect, and I got a pretty girl walking with me along the beach. What's not to smile about?"

"You know, I had no idea you were such a smooth talker."

"Should have talked to me more."

Her lips purse with a wry expression. "I don't think my teenage self could have taken it."

"Sure you could've. I've recently been told I'm very charming."

"I have regrets."

A laugh bursts out of me, causing an elderly couple sitting on a bench to glance our way. The woman smiles indulgently as the man nods. Pen flushes a nice shade of rosy pink, then hurries us past as if we've been caught doing something naughty. Hell, I'd love to be caught doing something naughty with her.

I keep a straight face as we wind our way down the beach

path. A couple of people on bikes are out and a few joggers trot by. I'd be happy to walk for miles. Except for one thing . . . "You want to grab some lunch?"

"I just ate breakfast!"

"That was at least twenty minutes ago."

"It amazes me how much food you can pack in and still look like that."

I rub my belly; it's beginning to grumble. "Like a god? Yes, yes, I know. But even gods need to be fed."

Pen doesn't appear impressed. "And here I thought March was the one with the overinflated ego."

Again with March. Every time she mentions him, I get a swift kick in the balls from the little green man. I don't want to be jealous of my brother. I don't like the feeling. Unfortunately, when it comes to Pen and March, that ugly, petty emotion has a way of worming in.

"March absolutely has an overinflated ego," I deadpan. "My ego, on the other hand, is within perfectly acceptable limits."

"Sure." She tugs my hand. "Let's go to the Pier. I haven't been there forever."

"Uh," is my witty reply. Looming above us in the distance is the massive pier with its Ferris wheel and roller coaster. The rides mainly appeal to families with kids, teens on the prowl, and young couples wanting to cuddle up for a small thrill. Lights and noise and fried food. I'm not against any of it in theory.

My step slows. "Thing is . . . I might be recognized. And I'm not saying that in a hopeful manner, by the way."

Her expression is both soft and amused. "Or you might not."

"Your roommate did."

"She's a football fan. Has season tickets."

"I'll get her a box seat. She can bring Edward." I feel a moment's glee picturing everyone's reaction to that.

Happiness lights Pen's gaze. "She'll love you forever."

"Obviously, my plan all along."

"August. You're dragging your feet."

Am I? I glance down. Yep, not really moving forward. With a sigh, I adjust my hold on Pen's hand and trudge forward. "I don't have my hat."

"It's not the disguise you think it is, big guy."

My free hand twitches with the urge to tug on a brim that isn't there. "It's a good disguise," I mutter.

Pen pats my hand and leads me into chaos. It's more crowded here, people heading in different directions, looking for fun. Over the thunder of the coaster, Pen and I go in search of food.

I settle for a double cheeseburger, fries, and a peanut butter custard shake. I talk Pen into a vanilla shake. Not that she needs much persuading. Her resistance seems to be more about me buying it for her.

"You can pay for dinner," I tell her as we sit down at a little picnic table with an umbrella for shade.

"Or I could have simply bought my own drink."

"Nope." I shake my head. "Mom taught me better. I insisted on eating. Ergo, I pay for said meal."

"Sounds like grandpa talk to me."

"Ha. Ha. No more sass from you, young lady." I take a nice, satisfactory bite of my burger.

Pen frowns from across the table. "As an athlete, you should eat better."

I dab a bunch of fries in ketchup. "It's nice that you worry about my health."

"Somebody should."

"See?" I smile and shove the fries in my mouth. "It's like we're already a married couple."

"Then I feel safe in telling you not to talk while eating."

I salute her with my burger before taking a big bite. Pen uses the moment to steal a couple of fries. Duly chastised, I finish my mouthful before speaking.

"You're telling me to eat better yet here you are snarfing my fries."

"Well, I'm not an athlete so . . ." She shrugs and takes a long pull of her shake. The cheeky smile has me laughing again. I might know a lot about Pen, the girl from my youth, but the way she effortlessly makes me laugh is a surprise. A nice one. Tenderness squeezes low in my chest as I look at her.

It's probably a good shot: me and Pen grinning at each other from across a table. The sunlight shining on Pen's hair, catching the glints of copper and gold among the nut brown. Part of me would love to see it. But that's not what goes through my mind when I notice the young woman pointing her phone our way. I've been the subject of sneak shots long enough to instinctively know when someone's taking a picture of me.

I'm used to the invasion of privacy. Pen isn't. My mood plummets as my back stiffens. I want to yank down the umbrella fluttering overhead and use it as a shield between the two of us and the world. I want . . .

"Hey." Pen's hand settles over my clenched fist. Chocolate-brown eyes look at me with warmth and sympathy. "It's okay."

"You saw that too?" An icy rod has fused to my spine. "I'm sorry about—"

"August." Another gentle squeeze. "You wanted to have a public relationship with me. I guess it starts here."

My mouth opens to argue, to tell her that I don't want our relationship public, that it's nobody's business but ours. Then I catch myself. What the hell am I thinking? This is exactly what I asked of her.

Swallowing past a lump in my throat, I nod shortly. "Yeah, I guess it does."

But the ease in our conversation has died. We're both too aware of our surroundings as we finish up our meal and toss the trash. Pen takes the shake with her and sips at it as we walk down the pier.

"You want to go for a ride on anything?" My question is subdued, even though I'm earnest in the offer; I'll take her anywhere she wants to go.

"Maybe another time." She sidesteps a stroller. "How about we go back on the beach path?"

"I'm down for that."

Once on the beach, I walk a bit easier. We're more exposed but, for once, that feels like a boon. I can see everyone around me.

Pen sips her shake and focuses on the ocean. "How long do you expect our engagement to last?"

"For the season should do it. Football gods willing, that would be until February and the Super Bowl. Otherwise, in January." I roll my stiff shoulders. "Attention on us will drop dramatically after that, and we can orchestrate a quiet breakup announcement in the spring."

"Seems reasonable. It will be my final semester of college." She squints as a gust of wind blows past. "But I'm basically coasting along at this point. Everything dire has already been done."

"What's your class schedule?" I ask.

Pen spots a trash bin and tosses the empty cup. "Class starts next Thursday on the twenty-fifth. I'm in class Mondays through Thursdays, but only until around three in the afternoon."

"You up for a couple of dates when I'm free during the week, and attending home game days?"

"Of course."

"I don't expect you at my beck and call or anything. It's more that my schedule is pretty full with training, practice, and games. Wash, rinse, repeat."

She touches my hand. "August, it's fine. This is what you asked of me."

"Yeah." I'm already regretting it. But I push it aside. Focus on the ultimate goal. It's what I do best. "I talked to the guy who did the settlement on my house. Sean says he can set you up with a payment schedule so you don't have to pay the taxes in lump sums."

At this, Pen halts and blinks up at me. "You did?"

"I said I'd help."

"I know . . . it's just . . . thank you, August."

"Don't thank me just yet. It's still a lot of money each month." I peer down at her. "Do you have a job right now?"

Her cheeks pinken, and she nibbles on her bottom lip. "There was enough in the trust for me to set up a rental-living expense account. I could have used it for the taxes, but it wouldn't have been enough, and I figured, double up on classes, focus on graduating so I can devote all my time to earning would be a good thing."

"All right. Then I'll pay off this year's taxes—it'll give you some room to figure things out," I add when she stiffens.

"How about this. If I can't figure out how to pay for it myself by tax time, you can help."

"It's your choice."

"It is."

"Okay, then. But the offer is always going to be open."

"And I appreciate it. Truly, August. I do."

We walk a bit in silence.

Her expression turns resolute. "If you do end up helping me, it will be just the one time. I'll either sell the place or find another way to pay you back."

"Okay." It's all I can say. Pen sees this as charity, which couldn't be farther from the truth. It's an attempt to give something back in gratitude for the public pressures I'm about to subject her to. That part, I don't like. Only, I can't back down now. I just *can't*.

I'm an intelligent guy. There are other ways I could go about fixing my tarnished image. But somewhere between finding her on my parents' doorstep and hunting her down at the airport, I'd realized with absolute clarity that this is the play I *need*. Not only to help my career. But to get closer to Pen, something I could never do before, given that she'd flee any time I was around.

Our new ease together tentative at best. I need more time with her. I need to play this right. It's a gamble. Anything worth having is. All that is required is a good strategy.

I take her hand in mine—friendly-like. "Meet me on Wednesday for breakfast?"

TWELVE

PEN

ONE OF THE great things about LA is the classic Americana diner. There's something comforting in knowing you can get a plain cup of coffee, bacon and eggs, waffles, a fluffy stack of golden pancakes, crisp hash browns, a tuna melt, whatever floats your boat, and it will always be served up the same. Hangover food, a family breakfast, works well either way.

When I was a kid out visiting Pops and Pegs, we'd go to the 101 Coffee Shop, a '60s-style diner, with a chunky rock stone wall, hanging milk glass globe pendant lights, and faux wood-paneled counters. Amidst the scents of drip coffee, grease, and pancakes, we'd slide into one of the tan booths, the backs of my bare legs squeaking along the pleather, and settle down to calorie-laden fry-cooked paradise.

During the pandemic, the 101 closed. And with it, a slice of Hollywood history. I'd gotten a huge kick out of watching *Swingers* one night, in my freshman year, and seeing the 101 featured, and knowing I'd often sat in that very spot, eating a short stack with a side of bacon. But time moves on.

Thankfully, it was saved and reopened under the new name of Clark Street Diner. It's no longer a late-night drunken haven, but, seeing as I'd never been here after midnight, I'm okay with that.

I haven't been back since my grandparents passed, but the

sensation of sliding my bum across the tan booth remains the same as I meet August for breakfast two days later because he wants to settle "some things" before we go public.

He smiles at me from across the table—that happy, gorgeous true smile of his that crinkles his eyes and brackets his mouth with little dimples. Dressed in faded jeans, a gray T that stretches tight across his shoulders but hangs lose on his trim waist, and a trucker hat worn backward, he looks like a walking ad for casual wear. Honestly, as my mom would say, the man could sell ice to penguins, and they'd walk away happy. Given that this is LA, where hot men abound, he doesn't stick out. But he's still the only man I notice.

"I'm starved," he says, glancing at the menu with ravenous intensity. Oh, to be a menu. "I met with my trainer at six in the fucking morning and was tortured for hours."

"Poor baby."

His eyes twinkle with good humor. "It was hell, I tell you. Pure hell."

"I can imagine." No, honestly, I can. And I'm glad I wasn't subjected to it.

"And all I could think was, soon I'd be with you."

My breath puffs out in a little "oh" of surprise. Damn the man, he's too good with words. How did I not know this? I'm saved from having to respond when our server arrives. I order my usual pancakes and bacon. August goes for the gold, getting a protein omelet and hash browns.

"No shakes?" I ask, amused.

"Maybe later." He winks as our server comes back to pour us coffee. "Today's a build and bulk day."

August is more lean than bulk. But his build is well honed.

I must have been caught looking, because he gets cheeky.

"Mostly the legs," he says casually, that gleam still in his eyes. "Strength equals stability and protection. Did so many squat thrusts today, my thighs burn like hell. If you're interested."

"Fascinating," I say weakly. I will not think of August's thick, strong thighs.

"I also train for flexibility." He watches me from under his lashes, lips twitching. "If you're too stiff, things can get hurt."

"Things . . . ?" I blink and then narrow my eyes. "You're messing with me."

He chuckles, a carefree, far too delighted sound. "No, I'm completely serious." Leaning in, August braces forearms corded with muscle against the Formica. "You started to look a little flushed there, though. You all right?"

The jerk.

I lean in too, resting my breasts at the edge of the table. It's gratifying to see his attention flick there and remain. "August?"

Caught, his gaze darts up to my face, studying me with interest. "Yes, Penelope?"

I lick my lips, and he follows the motion, his own parting.

"Bite me."

There's a pause, and then his smile erupts. "Where do you want it, Sweets?"

Gah.

Tight with heat and pulsing embarrassment, I'm tempted to tell him he can start on my neck and work his way down. Oh, how I want to, but this isn't that type of relationship, no matter how good he is at flirting.

Giving him a repressive look as he chuckles in victory, I wonder if he always flirts as easy as breathing. I know March does. August, however, is a different story. My view of his personal relationships has been a bit skewed. I'd watch from afar, seeing only rare glimpses, and hoarding those times in the vault of my memory. Whenever August was around other women—girls really, back then—I'd leave. It hurt to watch, so why do it?

Our server arrives, food plates running up his thin arms. "Here we go."

We're soon tucked into our food. August, true to his claim of rabid hunger, practically inhales half his omelet before taking a sip of coffee. Only then does he slow his pace. "God, I needed that."

Cutting a pillowy square of pancake, I take a bite and make a sound of agreement.

"Good?" He looks at me with a fascinated intensity that sends an agitated wave of heat over my skin.

"Delicious."

His nostrils flair with an indrawn breath. "Give me a bite?"

I don't hesitate, cutting a huge piece and offering my fork. Bracing his forearms on the table, he leans over the plates and snags the bite, firm lips sliding over my fork. Slowly he chews. There's a glint of something in his eyes—teasing, definitely, but the other thing . . . His gaze lowers to my lips, and everything slows down, the clatter and chatter of the diner fading.

August's eyes meet mine. My heartbeat sounds overloud in my ears. Base desire flows like liquid gold through my veins, hot and languid. Beneath the table, I press my thighs together to ease the ache between them. How the hell does he do this to me so easily?

This is why I avoided August so vehemently all these years. I can't control my response to him, and I can't hide it.

Maybe my agitation shows, because he blinks as if coming out of a fog and then flashes me a sweet smile. "You're right. It's delicious."

My response is a supremely smooth, "Guh-huh."

The bracket dimples around August's mouth deepen. He stabs a golden portion of hash browns and offers it to me.

"Oh, I . . ."

"Don't be shy." He gives the fork an enticing wiggle. "I know you love hash browns. Especially the crispy bits."

Surprise has my lips parting, and he gently feeds me the bite.

"How did you know that?" I ask, when I'm finished chewing.

"Pen, come on. We grew up together."

"You were almost never around."

August concentrates on his omelet. "I guess just enough."

Is that why I know he hates mushrooms but love. Or how he gets car sick if he has to sit behind the dri\ collected these pieces of him because I paid attention o. sidelines. Had he been doing the same? Or was it more like mosis based on a sometimes shared childhood?

"I used to come here with my grandparents," I say, to fill the silence that's descended between us.

"Me too." His expression grows fond. "When I visited them, we'd go here, or out for hot dogs, burgers . . ." He huffs a laugh. "They loved 'Americana food,' as they called it."

"Yes, they did." It's useless to regret things that will never be, but my chest squeezes. Part of me mourns that August and I never went here together with them. That we grew up together yet somehow completely apart.

"The year Jan won the Heisman, March and I joined him out here. We drove along the coast, went surfing, and Jan met with his agent and some PR people." August stabs a thick, golden, lump of omelet. "All that stuff. Anyway, we got together with Pops and Pegs. They took us to Sushi Park. Do you know the place?"

It's an extremely expensive yet traditional sushi restaurant inexplicably located on the second floor of an innocuous strip mall. It's also a known celebrity magnet, pulling in A-listers on the regular.

"They took you there?" I can't contain the surprise in my voice. While Pops and Pegs loved sushi, I didn't think that would be their go-to.

August nods shortly. His hands, once loose with relaxation, fist. "They said to Jan . . ." He clears his throat. "He was soon to be a famous sports legend, and that one day, March and I would be too, so they might as well take us where top celebrities hung out."

He looks down at his plate. "God, they thought that was a hoot, you know?"

I can see it." For a second, my breath goes short; I miss my grandparents so much.

"I still remember Pegs beaming. Said she was showing the world the Luck Boys, and the world better be ready for us."

My smile is watery. "They were right."

He holds my gaze with his. "I loved them too, Pen."

"I know."

It sits between us for a quiet moment. Then he exhales long and slow. "So many people I might let down."

"August . . . no. You're not going to let anyone down."

He looks away, staring out of the window where the traffic flows by. When he turns back, it's as if he's shrugged off the dark mood cloaking him, and his expression lightens. "No, not anymore. I've got you now."

"Ha."

"Ha ha!" he answers goofily. Then reaches into his pocket and pulls something out. He slides his fisted hand across the table toward mine. I automatically reach out to meet him. His big hand engulfs me and suddenly, I'm holding a small box.

My pulse skips a beat then starts up hard and fast.

"To seal the deal." August's expression is enigmatic as he slowly withdraws his hand. "Maybe open that up discreetly."

Is he kidding me? I swear I must be red as a hothouse rose right now. All I want to do is look down at the ring-sized box burning a hole in my palm. Or chuck it away and run.

I settle for slowly sitting back and bringing my hands down to my lap. Now and then, during my teen years, I envisioned receiving an engagement ring one day. Those passing fantasies were vaguely romantic and the giver a nebulous stranger. I never thought I'd be given one by August Luck. And never under false pretenses. Yet here we are.

Blood rushes in my ears as I fumble with the hinged top. It flips back with a crack that I swear is loud as a gunshot, but probably no one hears but me.

A huge part of me doesn't want to look. Not here, with August watching. It feels too exposed, vulnerable. I don't know why I'm freaking out. If we're going to do this, I need a ring—people will wonder if I don't have one. Only I expected . . . I don't know, maybe he'd give me a "faking it" welcome packet and the ring would be in there, along with detailed instructions and a schedule of upcoming events.

The silence between us stretches. Taking a breath, I flick a glance down. And my heart trips.

Nestled in a bed of black velvet is a platinum ring with an intensely saturated and velvety royal-blue sapphire the size of my thumbnail as the center stone. Narrow, emerald cut diamonds flank it like mirrored shutters on a tranquil window.

The deco design holds the patina of age, and I know it's an antique rather than new. My head jerks up, and I frown at him.

He shifts in his seat, his brow knitting. "No good?"

"No . . . I mean, yes . . ." I huff a bemused laugh. "It's beautiful. Exquisite, really. But August, this is . . ." I shake my head to clear it. "Where did you get it?"

A flush darkens his skin. He shrugs a shoulder and busies himself with pouring out more coffee from the table carafe. "You need an engagement ring. I liked that one." His gaze collides with mine for a moment. "I thought it suited you."

Oh, he did, did he?

"If I had to pick one myself, I'd choose this ring."

His shoulders loosen. "Well, good. That's good."

I guess that's all I'm going to get out of him about his choice of ring. This perfect fucking ring that makes me want to cry. Makes me want to crawl over this food-laden table and kiss the hell out of his lush mouth.

My hand fists around the still-open box. "Isn't it risky to give this to me in public?"

"No one's looking," he says diffidently. "People are more into their breakfasts than people watching."

"Still . . ." I look around. He's right. No one has noticed us at all.

"Besides," he mutters, spearing some hash browns. "Seemed safer."

"Safer?"

At that, he pauses, freezing as though he's going over what he just said and regrets it. He eyes me carefully. "Ah, well, if you're going to give a girl a ring for a fake engagement, it seems safer to do it in public."

Disappointment is a sucker punch to the chest. This *is* a fake engagement. August is smart to remember that. I need to be too. With that in mind, I slide the ring on—perfect freaking fit!—and snap the box closed, stowing it in my bag.

"Well, there's that done." I reach out, my hand now weighing a thousand pounds, and take a sip of my coffee. Somehow I manage not to look at the gleaming ring on my finger—I'll do that later—and pretend like it belongs there. Casual-like.

August, however, stares at my hand for a long moment, his expression flummoxed, like maybe he has regrets. But he doesn't reach out and snatch it back, only copies my movements and drinks his coffee. Casual-like. "After breakfast, I'm meeting with my agent and the team head office to discuss 'the plan.' I'll tell them I found my fiancée."

It should feel impersonal, like I'm nothing more than a body to fill a job. But it doesn't stop the weird little thrill that zips through me. I struggle to keep my expression neutral as he continues.

"I'll most likely announce the engagement during the presser at the away-game this weekend. I have one more away. The next home game will be on the fourth." His gaze collides with mine, steady and just a bit concerned. "That's when you start attending and publicly be my girl."

Oh, hell. Awkward, shy heat invades my cheeks. A blush he clearly sees.

His tone becomes gentle. "Are you ready for this, Penelope?"

I can handle this. I *can*. "As I'll ever be, August."

AUGUST

"JUST SO WE'RE clear," Coach Harper says evenly. "You're engaged?"

I sit back in my seat with a nonchalant air, though inside I'm anything but; I keep seeing that ring on Pen's finger, and it's doing weird things to my mind. But appearances matter here in my coach's office where I'm meeting with the team. "Team" being the highest up people who want to make sure I don't do another drunken chicken dance and focus on winning for them.

The fact that I'm even here is degrading and surreal. I'm not a clown or a fuckup. Only I *have* been. So now I've got to present myself as a reformed man.

"I am," I say. "To Penelope Morrow. She's a childhood friend and we reconnected over the summer."

"And you were so in love, you decided to party with a bunch of women all over the place at the same time?" Bud Lester, the GM, gives me a "get real" look. "Yeah, sure, that'll work."

"Okay." I lift an idle hand for show. "So we tell them we had a breakup and it sent me over the edge, but now we're back together."

Nala, the team's PR manager, taps a hot-pink nail against the bright blue binder with the team logo emblazoned over it resting in her lap. I know my files are in there, containing everything I've probably done since birth. "Could work. Heartbroken, you lashed out with a bit of reckless behavior, but now true love has healed all wounds."

Inwardly, I roll my eyes and cringe. If anyone buys that . . .

"We can have you announce it at the post-game presser this Sunday," she says, as expected.

"We'll need a couple of good shots of the happy couple

doing happy things," her assistant, Troy, adds, furiously tapping away, his phone screen reflected in his gold cat-eye glasses.

Nala's cool brown eyes pin me with a no-nonsense stare. "I'm assuming this is the girl you were eating with at the Santa Monica Pier?" She turns the binder to show a print of Pen and me smiling goofily at each other.

As I said, she's got everything in that binder.

"It is."

"She's cute." Troy studies his screen where he now has the picture up. "In a wholesome sort of way. A classic beauty."

Personally, I think Pen's fucking hot in an "I want to peel off her shirt every time I see her and press my face between the bounty that are her breasts" way. But I'm not saying that here. And if anyone *else* says something like that, I'll probably pop them one. Which wouldn't be good for my new tame image.

"It's not the angle I was workshopping," Nala muses, "but I think this might be better. Childhood sweethearts? What could be cuter?"

I'd said childhood friend, not sweetheart. I'm not even sure anyone who knew me or Pen throughout our childhood will believe that.

"Well . . ." I trail off, not wanting to stop her now that she seems to be going with my pick of Pen.

At my side, my agent, James Perry, crosses one leg over the other in a total *Godfather* move. "What we need to focus on here is that August's behavior *was* an aberration that has passed. As we said before, August is, and always was, a levelheaded team player."

"All appearances to the contrary this past summer," Bud drawls, unimpressed.

Harper's executive chair creaks as he leans forward and rests his linked hands on his desk. "Look, Luck's buckled down and is doing the work on the field and off. He's signed up for a bunch of charities . . ." At this he glances at James and I for confirmation, to which we both duly nod, not bothering to mention I've *always* worked with charities.

"He's got himself a sweet-faced fiancée and has stopped with the foolishness. As far as I'm concerned, he's doing what we asked of him, now let's focus on the important things. Like winning."

Weathered blue eyes, deeply set under bushy gray brows stare me down. "I've said it before, and I'll say it again. There is greatness in you. That's why we signed you."

Bud Lester nods in agreement but says nothing as Harper goes on.

"You're the top pick in a competitive sport. That's never going to be easy. But you're more than ready to rise to the challenge."

"Yes, Coach."

He tips his chin. "Management and PR, they focus on image. That's fine. They got their spin now. Let 'em at it. But you and me? We go to work to win."

"Yes, Coach." I've learned this is the best response to almost all interactions when being lectured by one.

"Integrity, work ethic, and focus. That's what matter to me."

"To me as well, Coach."

With that, I'm free. Once in the parking lot, I blow out a breath and roll my neck. I feel sticky with my lie. Worse? I pulled Penelope into it.

Again come the images of her sliding on the ring. The way she looked at it the first time, shocked but then her eyes went soft and shining. Like she loved it, wanted it. Seeing that had been a kick to the gut.

It's all wrong. But what can I do? It's too late to end it.

"It's all bullshit." James unwraps a small mint gum and pops it into his mouth, chewing like it's his mission in life. Six foot one, deep brown skin, hair precision cut close and tight, with a gray bespoke suit probably worth twenty thousand, he's intimidating to most. But I hired him because he's honest, and I feel comfortable with him. And he's a killer negotiator.

To that end, he glares back at the headquarters building we just left. "With the amount they paid for you, they should be licking your balls."

I laugh shortly. "Shouldn't that be the other way around?"

"Please. Number one never licks balls. You afford others the privilege—for a hefty fee."

"How about we stop with all the 'ball licking for profit' talk?"

James chuckles and tucks his hands into his pockets as he chews his gum. I'm not sure if he's an ex-smoker or just has an oral fixation—ball licking debate notwithstanding—but he's never without something to chew on.

I once heard another agent call him Jaws because James will tear into an unprepared offer and leave a bloody trail. Fine by me.

"So . . ." James looks me over with those killer eyes. "You got yourself a fiancée."

"Seems like it." I put my hands low on my hips, absolutely refusing to pull at my collar. Even if it is like five thousand degrees outside.

"Childhood sweetheart, was it?" His eyes are now narrow slits of a predator stalking prey.

"Friends. Childhood friends."

"I suppose congratulations are in order?"

I study the distant mountains. "A bottle of Pappy Van Winkle wouldn't go unappreciated."

He snorts eloquently. "That all?"

"I heard The Macallan 1926 is pretty good."

"A two-and-a-half-million-dollar whiskey for getting engaged?" He tilts his head. "You know what? For you, I just might."

We share a laugh, but then it fades and he's back to giving me the hard stare.

"When do I get to meet the lady who is so special you up and proposed to her in the space of a month?" His snark is clear and biting, but I know it's not directed at me. While I might be the one who fucked up by acting like a fool, I'm the client and he'll always be on my side against PR and management.

I also know it's imperative that he and Pen do not meet. It would be a disaster for many reasons. And I do not want to play referee between them. I'd pick Pen and piss off James.

I turn toward my truck. "At the wedding."

"The wedding!"

I enjoy his shock. "Yeah. We'll be accepting gifts then too."

"Asshole."

Grinning, I wave him goodbye. But once inside the Grouch, my smile fades. I think of Pen wearing the ring and I break out in a cold sweat. Something few people really appreciate is how good actors quarterbacks are. We need to be. I'll need to be an excellent one for the next few months.

THIRTEEN

AUGUST

SOME THINGS CAN'T be texted. Or they *shouldn't be*. Not when it's your brother who also happens to be your best friend. Discussion is needed, and truth? I don't want a written record of this anywhere. I can just see it being pulled out at some future family meetup and being shoved in my face to much hilarity—for my brat siblings.

A call is in order.

March answers quickly. "Bro. Nice game. The way you lock-armed that tackle?" He starts laughing. "Fucking classic. I'll never admit it at family dinner, but that shit was badass."

From my end of things, all I'd seen was a brick-house defensive tackle charging my way, his helmet an enormous red ball. I could have run around in the pocket and hoped he didn't flatten me before I'd thrown. But he'd been too close. So I simply put my hand on his helmet, locked my arm, and danced back, while I took the opportunity to throw.

Watching it on our playback assessment, it *had* looked like I'd been Super Quarterback, able to hold tackles at bay with ease. In truth, my ability to ward off a three-hundred-pound lineman with one arm, while appearing badass, was more about physics than anything else. But I appreciate the sentiment.

Huffing out a laugh, I turn on my truck and start the air. "What choice did I have? Not trying to get my bell rung."

"The guys were impressed."

March often watches my games with his teammates. When I was in college, I did the same for him and Jan as well. I still watch March play, though it's often recorded these days.

"I have to tell you something," I say.

"Oh, hell. I know that tone. It says, *I'm guilty as all fuck and please won't you help me out of it, oh awesome March?*"

"Never have I ever said that." I *might* have said something similar, but I'm not copping to the "awesome March" bit.

"Spit it out because we both know the truth."

Sighing, I confess. "I asked Penelope to be my fake fiancée to improve my image for the team."

Silence follows. Thick and judgy.

"Come again?"

"I'm not repeating myself."

"Yeah . . . What the actual fuck were you thinking?"

"That she'd make a great fiancée."

"She would. She's very loyal and can keep a secret."

"Exactly." I knew he'd get it.

Another sigh comes through the line, this one irritated.

"Broseph, who the fuck are you trying to fool? More importantly, how are you going to keep your hands off her? Or is this a fake relationship with benefits, because somehow, I can't see Pen going for that."

"Now you're just being insulting."

"I'm speaking the truth. Sucks, doesn't it?"

Scowling, I turn the air on high and glare out the windshield. "We're getting along. This will work."

"You're going to get hurt."

"Me?" An itch starts on my spine and crawls up my back. Of all my family, no one knows better than March how much I can get hurt. I'm fucking excellent at hiding pain.

"Yeah. Because you like her too much to fake this."

There's a downside to someone knowing you almost as much as you know yourself. I can lie to myself, but it's a lot harder to lie to him.

I put the truck in Drive and head out. I hate when the little shit is right. Especially when he digs into my misery. His drawl turns downright lazy, which means he's enjoying the hell out of himself.

"I mean, from the moment we hit puberty, anytime Pen came near you'd clam up tighter than a defensive line on fourth and goal." He snickers. "Or flee the room like you had the rips."

"Funny." And sadly, true. Damn it. I couldn't help myself; Pen would get that flat "oh it's *him*" stare, and it was such a kick to the gut that I'd . . . shut down. Pride: You can try to reason with it, but it doesn't always listen. "I was . . . working through some things."

"Took your time about it, bro. Frankly, I'm amazed as fuck you're even talking to her now."

"Well, obviously I am—"

"Yeah. Jumped right on into the deep end, didn't you?"

"Are you through?"

"I'm not going to change your mind, am I?"

"No."

"Then why the fuck are you calling?" he asks.

"I have no fucking idea." Maybe part of me wanted him to talk me out of this. But it was never really in the cards; the idea of walking away from Pen now has my back up. I'd rather get the shit knocked out of me by a defensive tackle.

Since the draft, I've been in a panic, messing up and acting out. When I'm with Pen, all the expectation and pressure just fade, and I feel like me again. Happy. Excited about life.

"I'm supposed to announce the engagement during my presser," I say. "Pictures of Pen and me are out, and the question will be asked."

Fed to the press by PR more like it. They have a way of controlling those things. Like sneaky information elves.

"You giving me a heads-up, is that it?"

"Yeah."

I can almost see March meditatively nodding.

"What are you going to say to the family?"

"I don't know yet. I've got time. None of them watch the pressers. Mom and Dad are on that trip to Mexico." My parents are enjoying their early retirement by traveling everywhere. I want to do the same one day. Right now, I'm glad they're away. I know I have to tell them, but I'm choosing avoidance at the moment. "It'll be fine."

"If you say so."

I don't trust his tone. He had that same tone when we were six and five, and I announced it would be a great idea if we went trick-or-treating for a second night. I got halfway down the block before Mom came to hunt me down, with March in tow.

"Do not rat me out."

"Are you kidding? I would rather be kicked in the balls than tell them."

At this moment, I really don't know why I called him.

"I'm hanging up."

"Fine. Go."

"Going."

"Augie?"

"What?"

"Congratulations. You make a beautiful fake couple."

He hangs up before I can tell him off.

PEN

IT IS A surreal thing to sit on my sad little sagging twin bed—the same bed I've had throughout college—on Sunday night and watch August John Luck tell the world that he's engaged to Penelope Jane Morrow.

I mean, I see it just fine. Broad shoulders relaxed, firm chin raised, silver eyes clear, he sits front and center at his team's press table surveying the room with the confidence of a king knowing they're hanging on his every word. And tells them he's marrying me. *Me!*

It's the believing I have a hard time with. This has to be a weird episodic dream. The kind you wake up from and are immediately sorry you did, then think about it all day as the smaller details slowly fade away.

I once heard a story about a man who was in a coma for twenty years. He spent it lucid dreaming about his awesome job, his loving wife, children, and all the wonderful things he did with them . . . only to wake up one day and discover it wasn't real. He didn't have any family; he never had that great job. He was all alone.

A chill dances over my shoulders at the thought. *Please don't let me be in a coma right now.*

On my phone screen, August is fielding questions. Apparently, some people are shocked to learn he's now engaged. You know, when he'd been dancing on tables and making out with multiple women, with varying degrees of enthusiasm, for the past few months.

I cringe.

August doesn't. He merely shrugs and looks slightly sheepish as if he'd been a naughty boy caught in the act but they all know he's not really like that, which is technically true, but still amazing to watch.

"Penelope is the love of my life," he tells them—and holy hell, that makes my cheeks burn hotly even though I know it's a lie. "I've known her since we were kids. To protect our relationship, we did our best to keep it out of the spotlight."

Did we ever. One might even say it was nonexistent until now. I snort and curl up tighter in my pillow nest.

"Unfortunately, we hit a rough spot this summer and broke

up. I didn't take it well." His gaze goes straight to the camera, silver blue under strong dark brows. And for a breathless second, it's as if he's speaking directly to me. "It's a difficult thing trying to live without the person who completes you."

I'm waiting for them to call him Jerry Maguire. But they don't.

Instead, one person yells out, "Are you saying your play is directly affected by your personal life?"

Ah, caught. I fidget, worrying what he'll do now.

August flashes the Luck "aw, come on now" smile I know very well. "I don't recall my play being affected. From what I remember, we've won every game so far. Or do I have that wrong, Kirby?"

"Ah, no. That's right."

"We were addressing the fallout from certain dancing videos I'd rather forget. Since y'all not gonna let me, till we talk it out, I'll just say this. I got my girl. I got the best team I could ask for. And from here on in, we're going to focus on football. We gotta keep up our practice intensity, find out what needs to be adjusted and expanded on. I'm pumped for this season and looking forward to what we can accomplish."

While August continues to give them cliché answers straight from the sports-press Q&A handbook, I let the phone fall to the bed and stare up at the ceiling. Holy wow, I'm *engaged*.

Though I'm alone in my room, I feel oddly exposed, as though I've been stripped bare and set down on Hollywood Boulevard. I can almost feel the speculation going on right now. People wondering who the hell I am and why her? Did August Luck really love this girl so much that he fell apart without her?

I can't see anyone believing it. Probably because I can't believe it myself.

To calm down, I hold up my hand and look at the ring upon my finger. The sapphire is so intensely deep blue, it's almost like the complete combustion of a gas. Yet it's also cool and tranquil, the royal blue velvet of a twilight sky. I could look at it forever.

My phone buzzes.

> **Pickle:** It's done. Hold on to your butts.

Despite the unsettled state of my nerves, I instantly feel lighter, bubbly even. August Luck: the original champagne high. Settling in more comfortably, I tap out a reply.

> **Pen:** Jurassic Park remains superior in the franchise

> **Pickle:** IDK, I kind of liked Jurassic World too

> **Pen:** Eh. I kept wanting that velociraptor to bite off Chris Pratt's hand

> **Pickle:** blood thirsty Pen. I like it.

> (. . .)

> **Pickle:** You got that I meant I told everyone about us?

About us. Like we were a thing. In some ways we are. Partners in crime.

> **Pen:** Yes. I'm in avoidance mode. That was the first time I'd heard my name on national TV

> **Pickle:** You watched it?

> **Pen:** Of course. It's not every day a guy says I'm his true love and that I kicked his heart in, causing him to do the chicken dance. I had to soak it in, you know?

> **Pickle:** And there's salty Pen. Can we not talk about the dance anymore. Like ever?

> **Pen:** So that shot I got blown up and framed of you gyrating while wearing a purple fur is a no-go for over my bed?

The phone vibrates with a silent ring. Uh-oh. I'm in trouble. Fighting a grin, I answer. "Penelope Morrow, first-time fiancée, longtime man-killer, speaking."

August's warmly amused voice tickles my ear. "Keep teasing, see what happens."

"Now I'm intrigued. What dance can I expect next? The Macarena, perhaps?"

"Ha ha. I'll have you know I took ballroom dancing with all the Luck kids for two miserable summers. I can waltz you so good you'll think you're on air."

"Stop. 'You had me at hello.'" I giggle—a sexy giggle, damn it. "'You had me at *hello*.'"

"It's a good thing you're marrying me, then," he drawls.

Yep. Still makes my insides sway. I grip my phone with a hand that's gone clammy.

"In all seriousness," I say. "You did good."

"Thank you." There's a beeping like he's opened a car door, then the rumble of an engine turning over. "Got PR training in freshman year. And another round when I was drafted. It's annoying but part of the job."

"And your PR is okay with this? Truly?"

"It was their idea to say I was acting out over a broken heart."

I'm still not sure how I feel about that. But I adopt a light tone. "Smart of them."

A dubious grunt is his response.

"You okay with this?" he asks. "I know it hits different once it's out there."

"Pickle, I'm fine."

"Penelope . . ." He trails off to heavy silence.

"Yes?"

There's a pause before he speaks. "Thank you for this. Now that it's real, I can't help but think it's fucking heroic of you."

My heart skips and stumbles in my tight chest. "Hardly that."

"You put yourself out there in a public light that can be cruel. For me. I didn't expect—" He exhales audibly. "Whatever happens, I will always be there for you, Pen. You understand that, right?"

A lump swells within my throat, and I swallow past it. "I do. And me too. We're partners now."

When August answers, his voice is deeper. "Partners."

FOURTEEN

AUGUST

ONE OF THE benefits of playing for my team is that they charter private planes. Not every team does. Some have their own, some simply go with a commercial carrier, but it's nice not to have to go through TSA or cram myself into a regular airline seat—often only the top players get first class, and definitely not college players.

A hired car takes me from the hotel straight to the tarmac. I grab my bag and head up the boarding stairs. None of the other guys are around, which feels off, and I'm starting to worry I got the times wrong. Jan has been on me to hire an assistant, and I've dragged my feet about it. I had one in college, but he was doing it for credit, and it felt weird as hell at the time. Sure, I needed the help, but part of me always felt two steps removed from other students as it was; having an assistant made it more so. But this is my job now. I already have Gracie, my nutritionist, Hakeem, my trainer, and a fleet of team staff on hand. Might as well take the next step.

Such thoughts distract me enough that I don't initially notice the plane is full when I walk into the cabin. Someone snickers. I stop short.

"What the fuck?"

Laughter erupts, giddy and gleeful as a plane full of big-ass man-children double over in their hilarity. The fuckos have veils on. Glittery tiaras that barely fit their big heads.

"The groom has arrived!" Jelly calls out.

Everyone cheers, or catcalls—it's dead even. In the center of their chaos, Rhodes clutches a human-sized stuffed chicken dressed up like a bride. He wiggles enticingly as he does a little gyration of his hips.

"You're all nuts," I tell them, trying not to laugh.

Our coaching staff are hovering along the edges of the mayhem, snickering into their hands. Jay, my offensive coordinator, has a row of pink pearls draped over his thick neck.

I glance at Coach and arch my brow. "What, no crown for you?"

"Nah, son, that's for you." He looks downright evil as he holds out an oversize gold crown with fake jewels on the ends that looks like he raided from a Burger King.

"Oh, hell no."

Jelly jogs over, a glass of champagne in his hand. "Damn, Rook, why didn't you tell me you were getting hitched?"

"Because I don't live in the 1890s?"

He slaps my shoulder fondly and thrusts the glass into my hand. "If I had known, I'd have given you some tips. Monica says—"

"Monica says," everyone intones at once.

He doesn't even look back as he flips them the bird. "As I was saying—"

"Jells," I interrupt. "You getting married too?"

He blanches. "Hell no. Marriage terrifies me."

"Then you can't give me advice. Neither," I say over him, "can Monica, as I know she's never been."

"Spoilsport."

In truth, my pulse has kicked up in a powerful rhythm of sheer guilt. I'm lying to my guys. But someone might talk, and I can't risk it. Still sucks balls. They did this for me, albeit to torture me as much as to celebrate.

Inadvertently, I catch Coach's eye. I don't know what he sees in mine, but he lifts his glass.

"To the groom-to-be and his lovely fiancée."

Everyone cheers.

My insides clench, but I raise my glass as well and do a silent salute to Pen for sticking with me.

One corner of Coach's lips curls and he raises his glass higher. "May this chicken be the last one you dance with."

At that, Rhodes tosses me my feathered bride. I catch it with one arm while the guys cackle and "Rocket Man" starts playing on the speakers. Jelly produces a purple fur coat from somewhere and drapes it over my shoulders. Up until now, they haven't fully razzed me about the incident, and I suppose I'm due.

So I laugh. Because it *is* funny. It's also expected of me. I can't let them see the panic stirring in my chest. I didn't fully consider this end of my arrangement with Pen. March is completely right on one account: When it comes to Penelope, I stop thinking clearly. My focus has become her—being with her, getting to know these new facets of her personality. She makes me forget my worries and responsibilities.

Even now, when I'm shepherded to a seat and plied with pink cupcakes—honestly who did this??—and treated with slaps on the shoulders, and good-natured jokes, some part of me is still thinking about Pen. I'll tell her about this, show her the selfies I'm taking with my crew—ridiculous crown tilted on my head—just to watch her smile, hear her laugh. I want that. I want that as much as I want to win the title.

Even as we take off, the force of it pushing me back in my seat, soaring up and heading home, part of me is already on the ground in LA. With her.

Logic tells me that should be concerning. But the only thing floating around in my head is: *I can't wait.*

I can't fucking wait.

PEN

EXPECT THE UNEXPECTED. Isn't that what they say? The phrase never made much sense to me, since how are we supposed to suspect something that never enters our minds? Or maybe it's that we should always be on the lookout for surprises?

Either way, I *should* have expected attention after August's postgame presser. He warned me my life would change. Tempting fate, I shooed that concern away as though it were a fantasy, something that would happen to other girls. Certainly not me.

Fate must be having a good laugh right about now.

It takes me a bit to notice. Ordinarily a walk across the quad on my way to class soothes me. The Romanesque architecture of UCLA's four original buildings are all a little different in style but share a similar fairy-tale beauty, with their soft pinkish bricks, mullioned windows, Moorish and Gothic touches. I could be anywhere—a merchant's stronghold in Milan, an ancient library in Spain, a basilica in Florence. It stirs my imagination every time.

It does today too. Only, while I'm strolling along, mentally prepping for my first day of class, others are turning their heads and watching me pass. At first, I only notice on the edges of my consciousness, little prickles of warning that something isn't right. It takes accidental eye contact with a guy lifting his phone in my direction to take a picture for me to truly feel the change.

The first thought: *What am I doing that warrants a photo?*

Surreptitiously, I glance down at myself, the horror that I might have forgotten to put on pants making my heart thud. But, the pants are on—soft drapey gray trousers paired with a burgundy knit sweater T because I like to dress professionally for class. Maybe that's it? I'm too dressed? But no, I always dress like this. Why take a snapshot now? I can't check my face, but I desperately want to.

Picturing a gargantuan zit on my forehead or perhaps lipstick that somehow migrated all over my face, I duck my head and hurry to class.

This is my final semester and I've taken it easy on myself, saving interesting classes to fill out my requirements for last. This class, History of Classic Film, should be fun.

Should be.

Only . . . as soon as I make my way to an empty seat, everyone—except a girl in back who hasn't lifted her face from her phone—looks my way. Eyes follow me as I walk. I feel like Tippi Freaking Hedren creeping past a murder of crows in *The Birds*.

Holy crap, what *is* the issue?

August's warning turns over in my head even as I sit and have a quick glance at my face using my phone's camera. Face clear and the same as always, I know with the certainty of a rock sinking to the bottom of a lake that he'd been right.

A guy takes the desk directly in front of me and promptly turns in his seat to gape. "You're her, aren't you?"

"Her?" *Playing ignorant will work, right?*

"August Luck's girl."

Man, that sounds so strange.

"It's her," another guy says, holding up his phone like he has proof. I guess he does. I can see the flickers of August and me holding hands in the clip he's been watching. He gives me a triumphant look. "I recognized you as soon as he said your name."

This class is made up of seniors and juniors all in similar majors. I recognize most of them too. But I'm ashamed to admit, I don't know their names. I've always simply attended class, listened to the professor, done the work, and left.

Phone guy, with his mop of brown curls and oversize Rams sweatshirt might be Brian or Brad. Definitely a *B* name. Doesn't really matter. Mr. B and his friend . . . Dwight? Dwayne?—look at me expectantly.

"I . . . ah . . . I'm Penelope."

"Ah, yeah, we know." An eye roll of exasperation followed by another searching look. "So? Is Luck gonna buckle down now?"

"How's he feeling physically?"

"More like mentally." Dwight/Dwayne mocks a chicken, arms flapping.

I glare at him, but don't answer.

"He's not gonna do shit. First picks always fizzle out," says a guy at the window with a small sneer.

"No, that's what the ladies say about you," Brian—it's totally Brian!—snaps back.

"Not what your mamma said last night."

"Boys." A cute blonde, way more likely to be dating a star quarterback, scoffs at them then leans toward me with wide eyes. "God, August Luck! I can't believe you . . . I mean, is he, like . . ." She makes a rolling motion with her hand. "You know? Is he?"

I have no earthly idea what the hell she's talking about. Surely, she's not asking me about . . . ?

"I mean those eyes! That body just . . . slaps." She sighs expansively. "He must be *transcendent*."

I guess she is. My face flames. I'm part horrified and part outraged.

Thankfully, I don't have to answer. The professor enters, saving me from further questioning. I like Professor Jackson. He's always been professional and informative. Dressed in a rumpled brown suit and an argyle sweater vest, he plays the part well.

Rubbing his mop of gray hair, the professor sets down his leather bag, adjusts his wire rim glasses, and immediately starts class. I fall into the familiar comfort of reading lists, expectations, and upcoming assignments. And if the other students keep glancing back at me? I can handle it.

I'm fairly certain the blonde—who I learn via roll call is Jessica—has been texting her friend about me the entire lecture. Her thumbs are tapping away like mad, only paused by intermittent looks my way. Our gazes clash at one point, and she flashes a quick apologetic smile before going back to her phone.

It's fine. I *can* handle this.

Class ends, and I tuck away my writing pad. Call it old-fashioned, but if I don't physically write notes down, I forget them as soon as I'm done. I'll go back and type them into my laptop, which adds an extra layer of memorization.

As I pass Jackson's desk, he stops me.

"A word, Ms. Morrow."

I halt, perplexed. Out of everyone today, I know I actually paid attention.

The chair Professor Jackson sits on creaks as he leans back and surveys me with a stern expression. "Are we going to have a problem here?"

"A problem?" My heart thuds hard and fast within my chest.

Jackson pulls off his glasses and rubs the bridge of his nose before setting them back on. "Is Mr. Luck going to be a problem?"

"You mean is he going to pop up in class and offer to sign autographs?"

Watery blue eyes narrow in warning. "Don't get smarmy with me, Ms. Morrow."

Heat races over my skin and pulls it tight. My mouth goes dry. I hate confrontation. But, on the heels of that comes another thought. How dare he? Drawing in a sharp breath, I steel my spine.

"I was aiming for baffled, Professor Jackson. Because I truly am."

"I fail to see how, when your mere presence disrupted the entire class."

"I would say the entire class has a concentration problem, given that I didn't utter a word during the lecture."

"You know perfectly well it's your connection to Mr. Luck that has them distracted."

"With respect, Professor, this is UCLA. We've had Oscar-winning guest lectures, legends of film. Most of us have interned at studios and interacted with huge stars." Well, at least *seen* them walk past. But still.

An incredulous scoff escapes him. "You speak of industry professionals. Not some . . . overpaid athlete."

I'm so shocked my skin prickles. I can only stare as he goes on with scathing vehemence.

"The next thing you know, they'll be arguing about who's going to win what game and spitting out inconsequential stats, when they should be concentrating on film." He slaps his palms on his desk. "No, I won't have it."

There're many things I could say. I'm not sure where to begin. Or if it even matters. He's not rational here. Prejudice rarely is.

Hauling my bag higher on my shoulder, I strive for calm when I'm anything but. "Are you asking me to drop this class, Professor?"

He pauses, mouth open, then snaps it closed with a befuddled frown. "That would be extreme."

I nod in agreement. "I've taken three other courses with you in the past. Have you found me to be a disruptive student?"

"No . . ."

"A poor student, then?"

"That's hardly the point."

When I stare him down, he sits up straighter in his chair and links his hands on his desk.

"You are an excellent student, Ms. Morrow."

I nod again. "I *am* an excellent student. Which means your line of questioning is not only unwarranted, it is inappropriate."

It's his turn to color. Before he can say a word, I forge on.

"I'm going to leave now and pretend this never happened. I look forward to your lectures, as I've enjoyed them in the past. Good day, Professor."

I stride out, head held high. But on the inside I'm shaking. August had warned me. I hadn't taken him seriously. It's time I do.

FIFTEEN

PEN

SO FAR, BEING a fiancée is lonely. I haven't seen August for over a week and a half. He's been busy with game prep, practice, and travel, and I've been settling into my new semester, each class basically starting like the first—lots of gawking, a few brave questions, then subtle stares. Thankfully, no other professor seems to care about my personal life or makes inappropriate remarks about August. We text a lot. And have fallen into an easy friendship. Still, I miss his face. His voice. *Him*.

"You're going to have to move out."

Sarah's announcement catches me mid-sip of my morning coffee. I bobble the cup but thankfully don't spill.

"I'm sorry?"

"Yeah," she drawls, before sucking her teeth. "Me too."

"No, I meant, what?"

With an impatient sigh, she perches on the end of the sofa. In a rare instance, Edward is not around. Maybe she thought I'd go into tantrums and throw things. Hardly. But I guess it's nice to imagine her at least having enough self-awareness to know she might deserve a little anger coming her way.

"It's like this," she says. "Daniel and Priti are moving back in."

The news is shocking for many reasons. "Okay. But there's three bedrooms." Not that sharing living space with all of them would be remotely pleasant.

"You know very well they're not a couple anymore."

And just who's fault is that? I think darkly. Unfortunately, I have the worst poker face ever.

Sarah bristles. "We're going to attempt to give it another go. However, to maintain a healthy relationship standard, we figured we'd each have our own room."

"And you all figured, why not take mine?" I nod slowly like this is perfectly okay. Which it's not.

"You can't say you didn't see it coming."

I take a sip of coffee and cross my feet at my ankles. I'm weirdly calm. Yes, this is a shit thing to spring on me but, as I'd been trying to figure out how to kindly tell Sarah I was leaving, her news is really a boon. I don't need to let her know that, though. Up and kicking out a roommate to make way for two new ones isn't cool.

"How on earth would I see this coming, Sarah?"

She raises her hands in exasperation. "Since your *news*—" At this she gives me a repressive glare. It's been a bone of contention that I didn't tell her August wasn't just a friend but my fiancée "—there have been people hanging around, taking pictures, trying to follow me upstairs."

My ire fizzles. I'd encountered the occasional photographer or gawker since August's press conference, but I hadn't thought it would bleed into her life too. "I didn't know. I'm so sorry. Truly. I never wanted that to happen."

Sarah softens as well. "It's not your fault people are nosy dicks. And no one in their right mind would blame you for landing August Luck. The man is gorgeous and a legend in the making."

I'm certain August would cringe right now.

"I mean, well done you," Sarah says with heart.

"Ah, thank you."

"But you can't stay." She leans in, all business now. "You never signed a lease."

"It's the first of October. I just paid this month's rent!"

"I'll give you a refund."

"That's nice. But I'm pretty sure giving me no notice is illegal, lease signing or no, so I'm going to take my time moving things." Call me petty. I don't care.

Though I can practically hear her teeth grind, she wisely refrains from complaining. "Very well. Though I'd have thought you'd move in with August by now. He's got to have a great spot."

"I'm not moving into August's house." Let her make of that what she will. I'm feeling salty.

Her brows lower. "You're not one of those 'wait until you're married' types, are you?"

Her question doesn't dignify an answer. I decide then and there to start today. I leave Sarah hovering in the kitchen—God knows why since she's delivered her news; maybe she really wanted more of a struggle. Even if I hadn't any place to go, I wouldn't have given her one. Filling a duffel with some clothes and a fair bit of toiletries, I head for home.

Home. That feels good to say.

The house is still and quiet when I let myself in. It's the gentle calm of sanctuary. The wide plank floorboards, honed to a silky soft finish, give off the faint scent of old wood. Sunbeams stream in wide blocks and warm the air.

I toe off my shoes and pad down the back hall to Pops and Pegs's bedroom. It's mine now. Initially, I'd been hesitant about claiming this room as my own. One did not simply take over one's grandparents' private space. But they'd left this home, and everything in it, to me, which means they'd wanted me to have it fully. Earlier, after they'd died, I'd cleaned out their personal effects, picking what could be donated and what to save in storage. Mom helped me do it, but it had still been awful.

The bed is stripped clean, as are the clothes closets and dresser drawers. I find fresh bedding in the cedar linen closet off the main room. White, fine-spun cottons, softly worn pure linen, fluffy comforters, these are the things my grandmother loved.

Lavender and sage sachets, tucked among the sheets to keep their freshness, scent the air when I snap out the top sheet. It billows like a cloud before gently settling into place. With each layer put on, I feel myself settle a little more. A toss of a snowy down comforter, fluffing plump pillows, the simple tasks done here in this room remind me of watching Pegs do the same.

Once they're done, I smooth a hand over the cool cover and then head to the bathroom with my toiletries. Pops and Pegs expanded the main bath some years back, breaking through a wall and claiming some of the space from an unused bedroom. It's far bigger than I need. A long double sink topped with softly honed marble takes up one wall. On the other is a big soaking tub, shower stall, and two toilet rooms. Two, because, as Pegs once said, *I love my husband dearly but some things should be kept very separate. Toilets are definitely one of them.*

I smile at the memory.

As in the rest of the house, the walls are soft white stucco with no sharp edges. Pale distressed oak trims the windows and runs in beams along the ceiling. Late Deco period bronze sconces in the shape of little hands holding frosted glass flower shades are set between the mirrors and over the tub. In the corner, by a wall of windows, is a built-in vanity table original to the house. I used to watch Pegs put her makeup on there. I'd sit on the edge of the tub, while she brushed out her hair or spritzed her perfume. She once told me she'd done the same, watching her mother "glamor up."

The ghost of her laughter lingers in my memory as I set out my own makeup, brush, and one bottle of perfume I've brought along. The act makes the space feel a little less empty. On impulse, I take a small potted jade plant from the veranda hall and set it on the vanity top. A framed picture of me and my grandparents leaning in close and smiling while at the beach is found in the den. I set it next to the jade.

Pleased, I head for the kitchen. Unfortunately, aside from

some condiments and spices, there's no food. That will have to change. I'm not bringing anything with me from Sarah's place. Biting the bullet, I place a huge order for the basics. It's too much for me to carry, so I have it delivered and add a big tip. The extravagance makes me squirm, but I'll be saving on cooking at home. Besides, the vegetable garden is miraculously still going, surviving my amateur gardening attempts.

I'd looked up methods and tried my best to figure it all out, but I'm not a natural green thumb. Even so, when I let myself into the small greenhouse, it's satisfying to see beds of lettuces and herbs thriving rich and green. There's squash, red and green peppers, some sort of chili, and what appears to be carrots? I'm not experienced enough to know by sight and don't want to go yanking things out. More study is clearly needed. The tomatoes, however, hang heavy and ripe with promise. I pick several plump ones and add them to my basket of butter lettuce and herbs. I bring them into the house and make myself a small salad while I wait for my groceries.

After years of dorm rooms then the chaos of Sarah's place, I relish the silence. It's not lonely but soothing. Maybe later I'll want people around me, but for now, I eat my salad and pull out my laptop to start a few assignments.

When the groceries arrive, I put them away, fussing over where everything should go and what the best places would be for my liking.

It's only then that I feel the sudden urge to be able to look over at someone and squeal in delight, to say, *Look at me! I'm making a home.*

My phone pings, and a secret rush of hope goes through me. That fragile flame is dashed when I see Sarah's message.

> **FrogLvr:** Priti is going to move in now. She suggested we create a bathroom schedule. Since you weren't here, you got last pick.

She adds the schedule in the next message. For fuck's sake, even Edward has a bath hour. My gaze narrows as I tap out a brisk reply.

> **Pen:** Have at it. I'll only be coming and going to pack and move my things.

She responds with a thumbs-up. I don't know why but it *feels* aggressive. Shoving the phone away, I clean the dishes and go back to studying. My mood isn't precisely soured but little prickles of irritation remain.

When the phone pings again, I eye it warily. But I've never been able to successfully ignore messages. A smile blooms over my face.

> **Pickle:** What you up to?

> **Pen:** Not much. I'm at the house. Cleaned and studied a bit

> **Pickle:** what's wrong?

A bolt of shock goes through me, and I sit straight, reading the message again. How did he . . . The phone pings with another text.

> **Pickle:** Talk to me

Nibbling my lip, I ponder the question. Where to begin? I'd have to write a whole book in response.

The phone rings, and August's face—the goofy selfie he took when putting his number into my phone—shines up at me from the screen. He's got one brow raised high, his mouth curled in a half smile, half smirk. He'd called it his Flynn Rider smolder. Which is eerily accurate. Now, however, it appears as if

August is prompting me to answer the phone or else. Oh, how I've missed him.

"There's nothing wrong," I say by way of greeting.

He doesn't miss a beat.

"Yes, there is," he says patiently. I love his voice. Smooth and rich like whiskey cream, it never fails to flow through my body, leaving me all flushed yet oddly comforted.

He's not quite so soothing now, however. "Pen, I can tell. You might as well spill it."

"You can tell there's something wrong with me from one text?"

A pause thrums through the phone. I can almost picture him frowning, maybe rubbing the back of his neck the way he does when pondering something. "Yes," he says, sounding quietly surprised by this, but very certain. "Yes, I can."

With a sigh, I curl my legs up on the chair. "I've had a weird morning. Too much to go over on a text, though."

"Which is why I *called*."

Warmth billows soft and fluffy within my chest. He did call. The thoughtfulness of it has me almost weepy. But before I can answer him, August speaks again.

"Why don't you come over?"

He's been home for a few days. I'm trying hard not to look too much like an eager puppy, knowing I'll see him this weekend on game day. Still . . .

"Come over?" I repeat, because, apparently, I'm smooth like that.

"Sure. I'm home now. And you haven't seen it. Unless you're still busy?"

"No, I'm not . . . I can come over."

"Great." He sends me his address then hangs up with a final, "Get your sweet butt over here, Penelope."

Well, then.

SIXTEEN

PEN

HE DOESN'T LIVE far, and I'm there in less than ten minutes. Punching in the code he gave me—*Balderdash!*, seriously—I wait as the massive brushed steel gates silently glide back. They reveal a wide drive that curves sharply to the left. As soon as I make the turn, the house looms into view. My immediate impression is of glass and steel garment boxes piled haphazardly and punctuated here and there with enormous wood panels. It's beautiful in the modern way of glossy airport terminals. It hugs the cliffside as though a giant plunked those boxes into the earth before moving on.

August is already coming out of the gigantically tall wood door as I pull up. He skids to a stop and wavers there as I cut my engine.

"Holy shit," he exclaims, holding a hand to his chest in dramatic fashion.

Taking off my helmet, I look up at him in confusion. "What's wrong?"

Shaking his head slightly, his eyes are wide and on me. "Give me a second here, Sweets. I gotta . . . You just . . ." His hand lifts, weakly gesturing in my direction. "Seriously, Pen?"

With a roll of my eyes, I press down the kickstand and step off my bike. "Have you been drinking? Because I don't think that's wise."

August waves my question away with a distracted hand. He's still staring at me like I have two heads as he trots down the front walk. "You're riding a motorcycle!"

"Ah, yeah." I glance at my bike, then back to him. "You have a problem with that?"

"Pen . . ." He sounds a bit weepy. "A motorcycle!"

In two strides, he's before me. He clasps my waist, and, with a soft growl, tugs me close. My hands land on his chest to steady myself. Against my palms, his heart thuds quick and strong. It's so sudden, he's so big and solid, I struggle to breathe properly.

With another sound of frustrated distress, he rests his forehead on mine. "Do you have any idea how incredibly sexy that was to see?"

"Oh, for Pete's sake." I'm so flustered, I don't know whether to laugh or wrap my arms around him.

"I don't know who Pete is," he murmurs. "But I empathize with his plight. I'm gonna need a minute."

He's gently rubbing up and down my waist, going a little farther down my hips with each pass. It feels good. Far too good. Heat swirls in lazy circles deep in my core, weakening my knees and urging me to drift closer to August, to lean against his firm length. I resist, but only just.

"Don't tell me you're turned on by this?" I say weakly.

"Okay, I won't." He's kneading the dip of my waist now, his breath escaping in deep gusts that make my skin shiver.

"August . . ." It comes out a little desperate. Whether it's for him to act or to back off, I'm not sure. He's done my head in. This is August, the boy who ignored me our entire childhood.

A fine shudder wracks his body, the grip on me going tight. He expels a breath and steps back. When his eyes meet mine, they're strained around the edges, his smile brittle. "Not cool, Penelope."

"What!"

One brow lifts high. "You gotta warn me before you up and

do hella sexy things like pull into my driveway on a motorcycle—and wearing a tight leather jacket too!"

"Oh, for crying out . . . I can't tell if you're joking or not."

He nods once, shortly. "I know. It's very annoying."

"To me," I correct. "Annoying to me."

"Uh-huh." No longer listening, he steps around me to study the bike.

My ride is a 2019 Triumph Street Twin in a matte ironstone finish, which gives it a nice vintage styling.

"God, the way you look on this . . ." Quicksilver eyes flash with interest. "When did you start riding motorcycles?"

"Last spring. I needed a cheap mode of transportation. The seller was motivated, and I got it for under six thousand, which is much cheaper than a car. This is LA. I rarely have to worry about the weather. I can get around quick and easy. And . . ." I shrug. "It's fun."

"I fucking bet." He runs his fingers over the leather tooled seat. "She's very pretty, and a good size for you. Fast?"

"She can be." I flash a smile. "But I'm a responsible driver."

August grabs my backpack and straightens to his full height. "I must say, Pen. You keep surprising me."

"Lots of people ride motorcycles."

His look is admonishing. "Penelope Morrow, don't try to play this off with that insouciant tone. You go around all sweet and shy, wearing those cute little good girl sweaters—" I bristle and he grins "—and then come roaring down my drive like Lara Croft—"

"Lara Croft! I hardly—"

"Just like her! And it makes my head spin."

"Are you going to stand out here all day talking crazy or are you going to show me your house?"

August takes my hand in his. "I'm done for now. Come inside. I think I need a lie-down after all this."

"Goof."

The inside of August's home is cavernous and cleanly beautiful. Our footsteps click along the polished limestone floors and echo in the empty space. Huge abstract art canvases hang here and there bringing splashes of color, while twisty-shaped alabaster glass chandeliers glow overhead.

"It's very serene," I tell him as he leads me into a great room that's punctuated by a towering stone slab fireplace.

"It's totally void of personality," he says offhandedly and sets my pack on the couch.

"You could say that about a lot of houses." A glass wall that must be at least fifteen feet wide exposes a picture-perfect view of the valley below and skyscrapers of downtown in the distance. I turn back to August. "What would you add to make it a home?"

Frowning in thought, he looks around and rubs the back of his neck. "I don't think there's anything to be done that could make this homey. It's just too big."

"Why did you buy this place if you didn't like it?"

He keeps his gaze firmly on the room, but a slight flush crosses the bridge of his nose. "Let's just say I was still riding the high of being drafted, and mistakes were made."

"Okay."

My simple acceptance has his mouth pursing. He gives himself a shake as if stirring out of deeper thoughts and finally meets my eyes. A gleam of self-deprecation enters his. "Truth, Pen? I think what I really wanted was to get something the polar opposite of my parents' place. That doing so would somehow cement my adult status, and I'd make a definitive statement."

"Well, you definitely accomplished that."

"Problem is, once I actually moved in, I realized I vastly prefer the house I grew up in." A quick glance around has him sighing. "Whenever I'm here, all I feel is weirdly exposed and ridiculously alone."

My heart squeezes at the thought. It must show, because he pushes a smile and cants his head. "I mainly hang in the outdoor living area. Let's go out there."

Under the shady overhang of the main house, there are two seating areas: one facing a giant TV, and the other a black stone fireplace. A bar stands between them.

But the real gem of the outside is the infinity pool that runs the entire length of the house. It shines like a mirror, reflecting the California sun and the blue sky above.

"I do laps here," August says with a fond look at the pool. "It's great for endurance training and gives my joints a break."

"I try to get some laps in at Pops and Pegs's when I can."

His smile is soft when he turns my way. "Eventually, you'll have to call it your house, Pen. Because it is now."

"You're right, I know. Eventually, I'll get there."

"Have a seat at the bar. I'll makes smoothies while you tell me about your weird morning."

I slide onto a barstool as August rummages in the outdoor fridge for ingredients.

"Sarah kicked me out."

He pauses in the act of pulling out the blender from under the bar. "The fuck?"

I recap my conversation with Sarah. And August makes us blueberry yogurt smoothies that are thick and delicious. He serves them in tall glasses with aluminum straws.

"You're an artist with this," I tell him after taking a long taste. "What makes it so thick?"

"Chia seeds. They have a variety of health benefits." He gives me a knowing look. "Smashburgers and diners aside, I actually follow a pretty strict diet our team nutritionist set up. Now, back to your roommate situation. This Daniel and Priti lived there before?"

He leads me to a long U-shaped lounge couch, and I take a seat on one of the chaise sections. "Daniel and Priti were a couple and they lived there with Sarah. But then Sarah slept with Daniel—"

"Awkward."

"Not yet." I take another pull from my smoothie then set the glass aside. "Priti didn't mind. The trouble started when she slept with Sarah too."

"And that Daniel minded?"

"He minded that he wasn't included. That pissed him off. Then Priti called him a hypocrite."

"Where's the lie?"

I grin. "Exactly. They fought a lot and eventually, Priti moved out. Daniel stayed. In came Becca."

August's eyes are alight with interest. "Don't tell me. Becca and Sarah?"

"Yes, but then Daniel wanted in on the action. He figured Becca would be into it. But she only liked women. She left, and apparently said the atmosphere was unhealthily predatory." I stop and raise a shoulder. "I learned this from Daniel, so the source is spotty at best."

August stretches his long legs before him at an angle to avoid the coffee table. "I've got to say, this makes my college years look boring. And I was a star athlete."

"No instances of 'ring around the frat house' sex for you?"

"My roommates were football players, so no. Even if I'd been so inclined, sleeping around isn't my thing."

"No?" I strive for nonchalance. I don't really want to picture him with flocks of bed partners. But his comment has me wondering.

The corners of his mouth curl up slightly as though he sees right through me. "No. Mom taught us that both the act and our partners deserve respect. I never felt comfortable going all out like that. Besides, when it's offered from every corner at every turn, it kind of takes the thrill out of things."

If he says so.

"Don't look so surprised," he says. "I thought you knew March was the biggest player in the family. Not me."

Part of me wants to say that's like comparing red apples to green apples. Despite his words, I'd never seen August Luck without a companion hanging on his arm. Until now. But I guess now he has me. Which is a ruse. Ugh. I don't want to think about it anymore.

Resting my head on the back of the sofa, I blink up at the sky just beyond the roofline. "Where was I?"

"Sarah and Daniel had either banged or run off every other roommate with offers to bang?"

"Right. By this point, Sarah was tired of Daniel and didn't want to hook up with him anymore. Apparently, this was fine by him, as he had an entire city of hot chicks to choose from. His words."

August's brow clouds. "He didn't try anything with you, did he?"

A stray leaf drifts onto the cream fabric of the lounger. I flick it off. "He asked if I swung his way, and I said only with my fist if he tried anything. That was that. Anyway, he moved out a month after I got there, and I was glad for it."

"And Sarah?"

"And Sarah what?"

He gives me a speaking look and patiently waits for my answer.

"There were a few feelers put out, but when I didn't bite, she left it alone. Despite all the roommate shenanigans, she's not actually pushy that way."

August reaches down and picks up a football that had been under the coffee table. It looks downright small when he palms it in thought. His expression clouds. "Okay, you're out of the revolving-bed-partner house, and will avoid what's probably going to be another ugly blowup You'd already planned to move out anyway. So why are you upset?"

"She didn't know that!" I lift my hands in irritation. "For all she knows, I'm a struggling college student with no place to go, and yet she just . . . booted me!" I deflate with a sigh. "I found it callous and hurtful, is all."

Somehow, we've drifted until August's shoulder rests against mine, our heads nearly touching. As if he's done it all his life, August takes my hand in his. The connection is instant. Warmth flows through him and into me.

Thoughtfully, he spreads my palm and fingers out over the larger expanse of his own and studies the difference in sizes. Mine looks tiny in comparison, though thankfully not childlike. We both have long fingers, narrow palms. His is rough with calluses, taut with strength, while mine is soft and smooth.

Our breathing slows, each inhale, exhale matching. We aren't doing anything more than pressing our palms together, and yet it's as if he's stroking along my neck, down the small of my back, up the inner edge of my thighs. My head lolls, the fall of my hair puddling on his shoulder.

His voice becomes low and warm. "It was shitty of her, Pen."

Okay, maybe I'm not totally calm, because I still hear Sarah bluntly telling me I had to go play over in my mind.

"And here I was agonizing over how to leave the place."

His hum is noncommittal. But I hear the way he's struggling not to point out the irony all the same. Taking my hand back, I shoot him a repressive look. "I repeat, she had no idea I had another place to live. And—" I lift a finger for punctuation "—she rents because she likes the company not because she needs the money."

August shifts around so that he's resting on his side and facing me. His eyes glint with humor. But his tone is conspiratorial. "Do you want me to hold back the box seat pass I was going to give her?"

My heart trips. "You were going to do that?"

"Sure." His gaze searches mine. "She's your roommate and a huge fan. I thought it might ease the way when you announced your departure."

Oh, God. Oh, God. Do not get misty-eyed.

I bite the corner of my lip. "No, no. Don't do that. She's not a bad person, really. Just . . . complicated."

"I don't like that she hurt your feelings." August scowls down at the football and picks it back up. "I'll give her the tickets, but she's not getting the team hat."

"You got her a hat?"

The bridge of his nose pinks again. He spins the ball in his palm. "Ah, no. The hat was . . . ah . . . for Edward."

A beat of silence pulses between us. One in which August tries valiantly not to squirm or look my way, and I try not to melt into a puddle of goo next to him.

"August," I breathe. "That's so . . . sweet."

"God, not the dreaded 'so sweet.'"

"What's wrong with being sweet?"

He shoots me a repressive glare. "I don't know. Maybe it's latent trauma we little dudes experienced whenever one of our female relatives would cry out that word while pinching our cheeks or smothering us with kisses."

"Oh, the horror."

"Talk to me about 'horror' after you're thrust in front of fifty relatives at the annual family picnic and are made to sing 'Food, Glorious Food' from *Oliver Twist*," he says darkly.

I try to smother a laugh with my hand but fail spectacularly. "I had no idea you even knew the words to that song."

"They played the musical on TV, didn't they? And I was only singing it in ode to the buffet I was about to attack. Then Aunt Edna swooped in and outed me." His voice dips to singsong. "'Oh, isn't that so sweet? Margo, you simply *must* hear this!'"

I laugh harder. "How have I never heard this story? How old were you?"

"Six," he mutters, then lifts a lofty brow. "You finished?"

"Almost. It's just so sweet—ack!"

One second I'm laughing, the next I'm on my back with August half sprawled on me. He rests his weight on his elbows at either side of my head, a satisfied grin spreading over his face. "That's enough out of you, Miss Morrow."

Breathless, I stare up at him. He's been touching me more

and more since that rainy night we reconnected. The entire Luck family is physically affectionate. But August has never been with me before. That alone would have me disoriented by this new closeness.

But the truth is more concerning. Because I had no idea how good it would feel to be held snug beneath his body. Good lord, he just does it for me. Base lust swirls alongside drowsy pleasure. I don't know what I want to do more: push against him and feel that prime body or simply melt into the furniture with a sigh.

I settle for narrowing my eyes up at him and pretending my heart isn't trying to thump its way free of my chest. He must feel it, though. God knows, I feel *him*—hard and pulsing with restrained energy. I don't *think* I make a greedy noise of want, but I *might* have.

August adjusts his position just enough to slide his thick thigh in between my splayed ones. The move sends little devils of heat dancing in my core. He grunts, a soft rumble of sound, and his gaze moves over my face. Everything slows and tightens.

"You know," he says almost conversationally. "We could practice kissing."

"Practice?" My head's gone all floaty.

The tone of his voice deepens. "So it seems natural when we do it in public. Your first game day appearance is this Sunday."

Is it? I can't think. He's so close now, all I see is him. The diamond-bright beauty of his sculpted features, the hot gleam in his eyes. His lips look both firm and soft. I want to know which. He smells delicious, of berries and August.

Kiss him?

He dips his head closer. A lock of his hair brushes the crest of my cheek. The light touch might as well be a brand. I feel it all along my skin, in the sensitive nerves of my lips.

The blunt tip of his thumb skims along the underside of my wrist as though to soothe. It sends tiny shivers of pleasure along my skin.

Kiss him.
For practice.

That last bit catches hold just before his mouth brushes mine. My breath hitches. Instinctively, I press deeper into the couch cushion, away from him. He feels the change and halts, lifting his head enough to meet me gaze.

"I . . . ah . . ." My voice croaks, and I clear it. "I don't think that would be a good idea."

Lies! Take it back!

But I can't. He's already easing away. I scramble to get out from under him. A frown mars his face as he watches me fumble my way to standing, and then gracefully stands himself.

"I'm sorry, Pen," he says slowly, troubled. "I didn't mean to make it awkward for you."

"You didn't. I mean . . . I can see the . . . ah, merit of the idea." I run a shaking hand through the tumbled mess of my hair. "I just think it might confuse things, and perhaps it's best to keep our . . . performance to only on game day." I swallow hard. "So to speak."

There. That wasn't an awkward word salad at *all*.

Hands loosely braced low on his hips, August stares at me for a second like he's deliberating what to say. But then he takes a breath and offers a relaxed smile. "Of course, Pen. Whatever you want."

SEVENTEEN

PEN

WHATEVER YOU WANT.

Ha! As if I have the mental capacity to know what I want when I'm around *him*. Because I don't. I really freaking don't.

Case in point? I've had a whole night to erase it and still can't get that near kiss out of my mind. Or refrain from kicking my own ass for halting it. What a noob I'd been. I had August sprawled over my body, ready to kiss the hell out of me—and I know enough to realize that he would have; the man does everything well. And I said no!

Because you wouldn't have been able to fake it.

With a sigh, I sit on my bed and bite at a ragged nail. If he'd kissed me then, I'd have lost the tenuous hold I have on pretending I don't want August in all ways. I'm not that good an actor. If he had just kissed me, I'd have yielded without pause. But he said it himself: It was for practice. And, no, August, that's not what I want. I cannot kiss him in private while knowing that it isn't real.

Shoving to my feet, I will myself to forget about kissing under false pretenses and focus on packing my stuff.

I have more clothes than I realized, and sorting through them is draining. Mainly because I have the urge to try on everything just to be sure I want it, and then end up depressed, as most of it looks dowdy and plain.

Why have I hidden myself away? I like clothes and pretty

things. And it's not about being able to afford them. Plenty of people on a small income manage to creatively dress themselves with style. It was about me feeling as though I shouldn't be seen. Or perhaps it's more not wanting to be seen. I'm not certain. What I do know is that I don't like it. I need to find Me in all this mess.

Mood spiraling, I toss aside a pair of lumpy jeans that I never liked wearing. The door buzzer distracts me from my project. I shove on the first bottoms I find and hurry out to answer it. Earlier, I'd ordered a bunch of garment bags; hopefully they're here now.

But it isn't a delivery person on the other side. It's much worse.

"What the hell?" I say as June and May take advantage of the open door and stride past me, twin expressions of murder on their faces, carry-on cases rolling behind them.

"'What the hell,' she says." June snorts and crosses her arms over her chest.

"What the hell indeed," May parrots. Her nostrils flair. "That's our line, Pennywise McSneaky."

I shut the door with a sigh. "I meant . . . Why are you—*how*—did you two get here? You're supposed to be in school. On the *East Coast*."

"Oh, she's a funny one." May puts her hands on her hips and taps her toe.

"It won't save her," June adds.

"Look." I cross toward the living room. "Can we skip the Tweedledee act? I'm not in the mood."

"Defensive too."

"Guys!"

My outburst catches their attention.

June wrinkles her nose, but answers calmly. "We can attend classes online for a week. We traveled by plane. January paid for the tickets. As to why—"

"You're freaking engaged to our brother—to *August*—and

we have to hear about it on the freaking news!" May shouts in outrage. "I repeat. You're engaged to August!"

"August!" June echoes.

"You keep saying his name like I don't know who he is."

June points a finger at me. "Don't get cute, Pen."

"You've never indicated even a passing interest in him," May says. "Now you're marrying him! August!"

"Yes, August," I snap, then sag against the side of the sofa. "I know, I know. It's . . . unexpected."

"No shit, Shirley."

Okay, I've . . . erred. I didn't consider the fallout of our news, which is just plain sloppy—of both August and me. We should have planned for this. In my defense, I didn't consider it would spread so fast— No. I just didn't want to face my friends and lie.

"So what gives?" May flings her arms out in exasperation.

"I . . . ah . . ."

Sarah strides out into the living room with brows raised. Her sharp gaze darts around. "What is going on out here? Your yelling woke Edward!"

It's clear May is about to tell my roommate to mind her business, but then May's lips part in a gasp and she squeals. "Oh, my God! It's that a real frog?" She all but leaps over to Sarah—and Edward, who is on her shoulder. "Oh, he is! Oh, isn't he the cutest?"

Edward preens.

June joins them, making happy noises of appreciation. "Oh, look at his little hat. Isn't it darling?"

Today, Edward is sporting a silver glitter cowboy hat. He looks appropriately jaunty.

Irritation dissipating in the face of my friends' obvious love of Edward, Sarah beams like a proud mama and introduces them to her frog.

"He is adorable!"

"I want one!"

"You'd lose it in a week, May."

"Would not."

They bicker and gush over Edward, and I take the moment to text August an SOS.

> **Pen:** Your sisters are here. HERE! They know! HALP!

He doesn't answer. It's not entirely unexpected. August warned me he'd have his phone silenced at various times throughout his working days. And it became a little . . . strained between us after the Incident. When he walked me to my bike last night, he reverted to the formality I've received from him our whole lives. Okay, not *that* formal. But echoes of it returned, and with it, a sense of awkward uncertainty. I responded in kind, determined not to push or cling. I'm the one who drew the boundary lines and this is a job of sorts, after all. If he's busy with other things, then it's his right.

But this is different. I'm not going to face this particular fire alone.

May and June have remembered I'm here. Quickly, I pocket my phone. June narrows her eyes but doesn't mention it. Instead, she smiles with clenched teeth.

"Has August met Edward?"

I narrow my gaze right back at her. "He has."

"He was very cordial to Edward," Sarah says, somewhat primly.

"Now, that's a surprise." June snickers. "He hates frogs."

Little traitor.

Sarah scowls. "He does a good job of hiding it."

"Childhood trauma," I explain. "It isn't against Edward personally."

"Look at her, defending Augie. Isn't it sweet?"

I refrain from pinching May's side. Barely. "I was just heading out. Why don't you two come with me."

"Where do we put our luggage?"

At June's query, Sarah's attention darts to their suitcases. "They can't stay here! Edward doesn't like strangers sleeping over."

Sure, blame Edward. He doesn't seem to mind when she's hosting a "friend" for the night. In the entire time I've rented here I've "hosted" exactly zero guests. Toeing on my sneakers, I grab my purse, and a bag of things I'd stored by the door.

May and June raise their brows at that but remain silent and follow me out.

"Did you rent a car or should I call one?" I ask briskly. Unlike August, they know all about my bike.

"Rental." June pulls out a set of keys. She hands them to me, stating that I know where to go so it's better if I just drive.

We don't say anything else until we've stowed our things in the trunk and are headed west on Sunset Boulevard. Golden sunlight streams through the windshield and catches on my ring where I'm holding the wheel. The square-shaped sapphire ring glows in an almost unearthly shade of deep tranquil blue, while the flanking diamonds glitter and gleam. I'm still not used to seeing the ring on my finger, or how utterly beautiful it is.

I'm not the only one who notices. There's a quiet gasp from the back seat, while June, at my side, makes a strangled noise.

"Holy shit," she gets out. "You really are engaged."

"Isn't that why you're here?" I hedge, because she's looking at the ring as though she's seen a ghost.

"That there is Nanna Linda's ring," June states in awe.

A pulse of shock slams through my body, and I glance at the ring then at June's wide-eyed expression. "No," I say. "No, August said he picked it up in a shop."

He did, right? I can't remember now.

"No way," May says emphatically. "That's Nanna's ring!"

"Why would he—" I bite my lip. I can't ask. Not them, at any rate. I amend my denial. "He would have said it was hers."

"Hmm." June tilts her head, peering at me as though trying to crack open my mind and read it.

Good thing she can't. All she'd hear right now is: *What the fuck!?!* Over and over.

"He'd definitely tell you," she agrees.

"Well, why the fuck didn't he?" May argues. "Because that's the ring!"

"We might be wrong," June says. "It's been years since I've seen it."

"I think I'd remember a stone that big." May huffs. "Thing must be eight carats. An authentic Kashmir sapphire. It was Nanna's pride and joy."

The ring seems to wink at me, as if to say, *How you like me now?* I don't know, to be honest. I'm obviously giving it back after all this. But if it's his grandmother's? God, what if I lost it? I *won't*. I'm never taking it off. But if I *did*, an heirloom isn't easily replaceable by an insurance check.

"We were eight when she last wore it," June says sternly. "All I remember is it being big and pretty."

"Well, I—" May shuts up when June glances back at her.

I don't know if it's for my benefit or what. I'm too busy wondering if May is right and, if so, why would he give me something irreplaceable? The worst part is I don't want to ask him. How humiliating would it be if he laughed and said, *Now, come on, Pen, would I really give you a family heirloom?* in that way of his. Awful.

"You're probably right," May grumbles. "It has been a while."

Awkward silence swells, threatening to burst. I turn into my grandparents' neighborhood.

"You're finally moving into Pops and Pegs's house?" June asks. The thoughtful tone makes it sound more like a statement than a question, but I answer it anyway.

"Yeah."

May leans forward, holding on to the seat back in front of her so her face hovers between me and June. "But you didn't have the money— Oh, August is paying it, isn't he?"

It's the truth in the simplest sense. Even so, it's as though I've been kicked. My hand tightens on the wheel. I don't miss the way June shoots May a repressive glare.

"You don't . . ." The words get caught up on my tongue. "You don't think I'd use August that way, do you?"

They're silent.

"Do you?" I ask again, sharper with hurt.

June touches my hand. "No! *No*, we don't." She gives May a warning look. "Do we."

It isn't a question so much as a directive.

May colors. "No, no, of course not. We know that's not you—what are we supposed to think?" she wails. "I'm so confused. Last time we were together, you could barely look at him—"

"There were definite sparks between them," June murmurs. "Despite all protests to the contrary."

Were there? I know I felt them. But had August? I shake myself out of speculation. Now isn't the time. My friends are still on a tear.

"And you never, ever made eyes at August," May rolls on. "March, I could understand. But August? Most of the time you two act like strangers to each other."

"Well, we don't anymore," I mutter.

"I should certainly hope not," June intones.

May slaps the back of my seat. "I'm serious! I don't believe for one minute that August would up and propose to you out of the blue like this. Now you're wearing what might be Nanna's ring. And moving into a super expensive house. All I know is something funny is going on."

The dark accusation in her gaze has my hackles rising. Being upset is one thing, but looking at me like I'm trying to put one over on them is another.

"Well, gee, Velma, are you and Daphne on the case now?"

"I'm not trying to accuse you of anything. It's not like you're some gold digger—"

"Oh, thanks for that."

June cuts in, "—I . . . that is, *we*, want to understand."

Gritting my teeth, I make the turn up to Brentwood. "I know it looks . . . odd."

May snorts. I push on.

"We just . . . got caught up in the moment—" they both scoff loudly "—and forgot to call. I know it was bad of us to not say anything to family first. But I'm sorry, I can't tell you the rest right now."

"What?" they yell in unison.

Calm. Strive for calm. "I promised August that we'd talk about it with everyone together."

"But it's *us*."

Yeah, and it's me. Don't I rate being given the benefit of the doubt? Hurt twists my heart, but I hold it close to me and focus on the road. "A promise is a promise."

May huffs in annoyance and sits back in her seat. "Fine, but he better get his butt to the house because we're not waiting forever."

AUGUST

THERE ARE TIMES I regret not falling to cliché and buying myself a badass supercar. Right now, for example, I'd love to have something that corners like it's on rails. The Grouch can haul ass but it's a rocking barge on the curves. I need high performance. I need to get to Pen. Right the fuck now.

I halt at a red light and curse, my fingers tapping in agitation on the steering wheel. I also don't need to get pulled over for reckless driving—wouldn't that just be the cherry on the fuckcake? A balance of speed and caution is needed. Speed is winning out, though.

I've left Pen alone with monsters. Okay, I love my sisters. They're cool most of the time, but they absolutely can be little monsters when they so choose, and I know without doubt that they're in Monster Mode right now. I break out in a cold sweat.

Shit. Why hadn't we told them? *What* will we tell them?

I don't think any of my well-intentioned yet incredibly nosy family members are going to appreciate: *You see, I begged Penelope to be my fake fiancée and she hesitantly agreed.* Nor will they go for: *Ah, well, we fell in love over a flight to LA and I just had to make her mine forever.*

"Fucking, fuck." How did I get here? I'm supposed to be the steady one. Sensible August. The voice of reason. Okay, that's pushing it. But not by much. I'm not this impulsive, shenanigan-having . . . liar.

Yes, a liar. I'm lying too much to too many people I care about. But what to do? Once it's in motion, a lie becomes a sticky ball of tape, rolling and twisting until you have no clue how to get out of it. Not without cutting in deep.

Earlier today, a group of boys had cheered me as I left the practice facility. I'd signed autographs and told them to follow their dreams. If they could see me now. I make a noise of self-disgust, as my phone rings.

Fearing it's Pen, I punch on the speaker immediately. Unfortunately . . .

"Bro, are *you* in trouble."

March. Perfect.

"Did you rat me out?"

"Me?" he squawks in outrage. "I would never!"

"Yes, you fucking would."

"Okay, I would. But, sadly, not this time." He tuts. "You told the world and didn't think to inform your family—"

"Yes, yes, it was very thoughtless."

"More like boneheaded but . . . You said you'd tell them!"

"I thought I had more time!"

"You forgot, didn't you?"

"Shit." It really was more a "pretend I don't have to and it will go away" thing, but . . . details.

"Mom and Dad are hella pissed. I'm surprised they haven't called you."

Note to self: Don't answer the phone again without looking at who's calling.

"So . . ." March drawls with far too much glee. "Whatcha doing?"

"Driving to rescue Pen. She's already in the clutches of the Wonder Twins."

"Jaysus, no. She's doomed."

Fucking hell. "I know!"

"How the fuck did they get to LA so fast?"

"Man, I don't know." I had assumed they were safely in Boston attending classes. Shows what I know about my sisters.

"Doesn't matter. They've invaded your territory."

"Not helping, March."

"The real question is, why are you wasting time talking to me? Go save your girl, asshat."

"On it." I hit End and punch the gas.

At the next stop sign, a slow-moving delivery robot toddles along. The thing takes forever to get back up on the sidewalk. As soon as it does, I'm off again, hunching forward as if the action can somehow get me there faster.

Finally—finally—the turn into Pen's driveway appears. Thankfully she already gave me the code and a key.

Now that I'm here, I approach with caution, parking the Grouch on the far side of the carport instead of in a garage. Stealth is needed. I want to find Pen before my sisters find me.

Anxiety for Pen has my fingers twitching and heart pumping. Sneaking around the side path, I send her a text.

LuvGod: I'm here. Where do you want to meet?

It takes a second, then she answers.

Sweets: Bedroom

Now is not the time to make innuendo. Oh, but I want to. Anything other than contemplating my upcoming conversation with The Sisters. Fuck, but they're terrifying. The only thing worse would be my mother. *Don't tempt fate that way, asshole.* Quickly, I cross myself.

> **LuvGod:** I'll be there in a sec. Sneaking in now

A couple of dots spring up on the screen but then disappear. I'm going to guess she'd rather ream me out in person. Silently, I move past the side yard and toward the pool where I can sneak into the bedroom via the back door. The sound of feminine laughter has me halting. Okay, they're by the pool.

I switch course and return to the front door. Inside, it's cool and quiet. The house already smells of Pen—a faint smokey sweetness. Her perfume? Scented body lotion? I want to find out.

Later. Focus, Luck.

Getting to her bedroom is tricky, given that the entire back of the house is a wall of windowed doors that open to the veranda and the pool just beyond. On stealthy feet I move, low and quiet. A quick glance has me relaxing a little. From what I can tell, they're sitting under the stone pergola at the far end of the pool, which takes me out of their direct sight line. With that in mind, I book it down the hall.

On my heels comes the sound of Pen's voice. "Anyone want anything?"

"Chips!" May cries.

"And dip!" from June.

I roll my eyes and slip into the bedroom, slowly pulling the drapes across the set of French doors facing the patio and pool.

Pen scrambles in a second later, closing the door and leaning against it like she's been chased by wild dogs. "August!"

I close the distance between us in two steps and wrap my arms around her. Pen jolts as though surprised but then relaxes against me with a sigh. For a moment, I don't think about anything other than how good she feels: soft and warm and delicate. The back of her neck, where I cup it, is hot and damp, and I know she's been stressing.

"Pen," I murmur, pressing my lips to the top of her head, and smell the sunlight in her silky hair. "I'm sorry."

At that, she gently but firmly steps from my hold. I mourn the loss but let my arms drop and run a hand through my hair to keep from reaching for her. If I touch her again, I'm going to be angling for a kiss. She was very clear about how that will be received.

More to the point, she deserves to be treated with honest intentions. I'd been sending mixed messages and leaving her uncertain how to act. That isn't cool. Maybe later I'll think about how bad this is for my heart. For now, I take the moment to fully look at Pen, because it's been a whole day and, sisters or not, I've missed her.

God, but she's cute. She's wearing a retro white-and-yellow flower print bathing suit. With her swerving curves and slim legs, she could be a classic pinup girl. My head goes a little muzzy at the way her breasts swell upward as if fighting to break free of the suit. They look so plump and soft. I could rest my head there and . . .

"We're both guilty here," she's saying. "I feel like such a jerk."

I give myself a mental shake and focus on a spot just above her head. "No, it was my idea. This one is on me."

"I'm going around pretending to be your fiancée. I think I'm a little in it." The dryness of her tone is unmistakable.

My skin feels too tight, my fingers itching to breach the distance between us. "I put you here. I only thought of the moment." *Of being close to you.* "It was stupid. I should have thought of how they'd react."

Her nose wrinkles in that cute way that makes me want to kiss it. "We both forgot."

I know why I forgot, but for a fleeting instant, I want to ask her why she did too. Was it for the same reasons? But I bat that aside and blow out a long breath. "Okay, tell me what's happened so far."

Pen wrings her hands. "Where to begin? Okay, let's see. They showed up at my apartment. Jan paid for their tickets as soon as they found out the news. According to them, he wants to know what's up too."

I wince. "I guess we should be thankful he didn't come with them."

"There's that." The way she gives me a sidelong look makes it clear Jan is the least of her worries. Then again, Jan wouldn't kick *her* ass the way he would mine. Pen leans back against the door. "When they found out I'm moving back into Pops and Pegs's house, it was suggested that the reason we're doing this is so you can pay my debts—"

"What the fuck!" I cut in sharply.

Her expression turns so dry, I feel it in my throat.

"What are they supposed to think?" She lifts a hand in exasperation. "This is exactly why I didn't want your help— What are you doing?"

Obviously, I've taken her hand in mine, so I don't answer. Yanking back the drapes, I head for the patio through the French doors, a protesting Pen in tow. My fingers link with hers, securing my grip but keeping it gentle when I'm feeling anything but.

My sisters, lounging by the pool in bikinis, see me almost immediately.

"Oh, look, the happy couple is holding hands!"

"They don't look happy to me."

"True, June. True. Trouble in paradise—"

"Enough!" The use of my field voice has them shutting up. "Not another fucking snide word out of you two."

At my side, Pen grimaces like she wants the ground to eat her up. I did this. They did this too. The Lucks strike again. Guilt crawls over my skin, but I ignore it in favor of staring down my sisters. We don't usually fight—bicker, sure. But they don't see me angry often. It's enough to make them squirm now.

"Let's get some things clear. We are aware this news wasn't handled well, but that is the last time you talk shit. You're hurting Pen. Your *friend*."

"August." Pen tugs my hand. "It's okay."

I keep my glare on my sisters. "No, Pen. It isn't."

June has the grace to look away, her cheeks coloring with guilt. May, however, grits her teeth and attempts to take control. "Listen, buddy, you—"

"No, you listen. Who paid your way to LA?"

She blinks in confused surprise. "Jan did. Because he—"

"Your brother paid your way. Not you."

"Because he's our *brother*."

"Yeah, and Pen's family. She's been with us our whole lives, so if I offer to help her out with whatever I choose, don't you dare suggest she's taking advantage."

Pen groans and thumps her head against my arm. "They didn't really suggest that."

"Oh, yes they did. I could see it in your face. And it hurt you."

She lifts her head then and gives me the beady eye. "When I texted to get your butt here, it was to figure out what to tell them, not for you to go charging in and yell at them on my behalf."

My ire bursts like a stuck balloon. Shit. I've been managing her. The dark look she sends me makes it clear she knows I've just realized this. "I made it worse, didn't I?"

A glint lights her eyes. "I wouldn't go that far. They were being kind of snide."

"Hey!"

Pen ignores May. "Just don't go all QB mode on me and start barking out commands like you're the only one in charge." Her smile becomes sly but somehow brilliant like she's turned on a light inside her. "We can tell them off together."

For a second, I swear my knees go a little weak. May and

June are scoffing, and we'll get to them in a second. Right now, it's all I can do not to pull her close and kiss the hell out of that smiling mouth. She solidified us as a team. I'll follow her anywhere she wants to go. She has to know that.

"I told you before, I don't like when someone hurts you. Even though I know you can handle it yourself, I'll probably blunder in without thinking."

"I know." Pink flushes across her nose. "It's sweet. 'A bull trampling through a daisy field' sweet. But still."

Her smile is all cheek now.

Unable to help myself, I step closer. "Again with the sweet . . ."

"Pen," June says starkly, cutting through our moment. "I'm so sorry it came off so insulting. Honestly."

May hugs her knees and looks at Pen earnestly. "Me too. I was just upset and hurt that you hadn't told us anything."

"I know." Our linked hands are sweaty now, nerves and temper making us both overheated. But she hasn't tried to pull away. I ease a shade closer, using my body to steady her.

"Look," June says, in the tense silence. "I don't care about the money! That's your business. But something is going on. And don't you dare try to sell us on it being private or whatever. You two got engaged out of the blue! We deserve an answer!"

May nods as if to punctuate the demand.

With a sigh, I let go of Pen's hand in favor of wrapping an arm around her shoulders and giving her a slight squeeze of solidarity. "All right. It's like this."

I tell the truth, not sparing myself for adding how I begged Pen to help me. At this, she attempts to protest. But I shake my head. "I begged," I say with a wry smile, then look at my gaping sisters. "And I all but pushed the money on her."

"It's just a temporary thing," Pen says tightly. "I'm going to find a way to pay for this house on my own."

"You totally will," June says with feeling. "You're very smart."

Pen manages a weak smile. "Thank you."

May sits back with a huff. "So it's all a . . . a ruse?"

"You're mad at that?" June asks with a lift of her brows.

"Of course I am!" May cries. "For a hot moment I thought August would officially make Pen our sister! I wanted it to be true!"

EIGHTEEN

AUGUST

I WANTED IT to be true!

May's plaintive wail runs through my head on repeat. It pushes through the music I turn up as I make a midnight smoothie in the kitchen. I'm strangely bereft, like I've lost something, done something wrong. I can't focus.

The blender stops. I grab a tall glass from the cabinet when my phone pings a warning that the front gate has opened. Alarmed, I set the glass down and pull up the security app. Cameras show a Mercedes SUV rolling up the drive. It's either a wealthy thief, total nutter, or someone I know. I keep an eye on my phone, and the emergency call button for my security company, as I head for the front door. I can take most guys, sure. But my contract says I gotta protect the arm. And I'm not trying to get hurt playing hero when I have a house set up for all manner of protection.

The SUV pulls up to the front. From the safety of my phone screen, I see the passenger get out. A curse rips free. Setting the phone on the hall table, I whip open the door.

"How the hell did you get past my gate?"

January smirks. "You use the same damn password for everything, little brother." He opens the back door of his SUV and hauls out a travel bag. "You gotta stop doing that."

Balderdash! That's my word—complete with exclamation

mark; because obviously it's needed. And, yeah, it's not the smartest idea to keep using the same code. Especially in this family.

"At least it's not Taco Tuesday," I mutter.

Jan halts and grins. "I swear, sometimes I forget you and March aren't twins. You're both equally boneheaded."

I let that slide and open the door further so he can come in. I haven't seen him in person since my draft day. He looks good; his arm no longer wrapped, his weight back up instead of edging toward gaunt. He's dressed like a '50s film star headed for the Riviera—camel-colored wool slacks and an ivory silk knit polo. Knowing my brother, the whole outfit is bespoke, the brown loafers on his feet handmade in Italy. The man always looks effortlessly sharp.

In so many ways, he's been my hero. Except right now. *Right now*, he's on my shit list.

"Speaking of twins." I lock up behind me. "I can't believe you sicced the Terrible Twosome on me and Pen."

"Better you than me. They were screeching and wailing so bad, I'd have sent them to Hawaii if they'd asked. As it is, you totally deserved their company."

"Yeah, well, there's a little thing called brotherly solidarity."

"Don't complain." Jan sets his duffel by the stairs and looks around as if taking the lay of the land. "Mom and Dad wanted to come too."

"At this point, I might have preferred that."

When Jan wings a brow at me, I shrug.

"I'll talk them down easily. I'm their favorite."

His deep laugh booms in the vastness that is my house. "Good one, Augie. We all know I'm the favorite."

I flip him the bird and go to the kitchen where my smoothie waits. Unfortunately, January follows. Out of all of us boys, he's the biggest. Five years older than me, he's also two inches taller and a tad wider in the shoulders than March. With his build, you'd think Jan would have gone for tight end or tackle. But no, he's a quarterback like me. *The* quarterback, a legend in the making, with three Super Bowl titles and four rides to the show under his belt by age twenty-seven.

Then the accident happened. Last winter, my legend of a brother was riding passenger with his fiancée when a drunk driver crashed into them. They both survived, but my brother's throwing arm was broken in two places, his elbow shattered. The world mourned and prayed for a miracle comeback. But Jan has been adamant. He'll never be what he was, so he's done with playing, and trying to work on his future.

One that doesn't hold a fiancée. I'm not certain what happened with Laura. Jan remains tight-lipped about it, only muttering once that they weren't in similar places emotionally anymore. From his expression, it was clear that no more information would be forthcoming.

The whole incident both depresses and scares me. I want to make it better for my brother but know I can't. The reminder has me softening enough to pour him out a portion of my smoothie and pass it his way.

"Thanks." He takes a sip, then looks round again. "So . . . this is . . . a place."

"You can just say you hate it." I take a drink. "I'm immune."

"To personal style? Yes. Yes, you are."

When I pull out a stool, the sound echoes around the house. "I liked it at the time."

"You liked your real estate agent a whole lot better."

I flip him off with more feeling. He responds with an easy laugh.

"Is this where you and the future Mrs. Luck will reside?"

"Cut it out." The response lacks heat.

Jan grins like an evil bastard. "Maybe she can put some life into the place. Add a few throw pillows."

"Sexist ass." I drink my smoothie, peanut butter and banana

with flax seed. It's a new recipe I'm testing. Pretty good, all in all. Next time, I'll add more honey. "Besides, Mom already tried that. Didn't help."

"Damn."

We sit in relative silence, one arm resting on the counter, drinks in the other hand. Our movements are eerily in sync. The press often remarks on how alike the Luck brothers are in both looks and talent. Trade one for the other, it's all good. They know nothing.

"It's a lie."

Jan sets down his glass at my quiet confession. "That Mom decorated?"

The lightness of his tone tells me he knows exactly what I'm talking about and has decided to give me a chance to regroup. I run a hand over my head and sigh.

"The engagement with Penelope. Hell, the whole relationship. I made it up in an effort to look respectable in the face of my recent bad behavior."

"I figured."

At that, I turn his way. "It's not that big of a stretch."

The corner of his mouth curls wryly. "You move fast when you want to, little brother. But not that fast. Besides, Pen is Pen. It's not likely she'd up and get engaged in the space of a week."

Well, sure. But he doesn't have to look at me with amused pity.

"Please. For all you know, we might have been keeping our love a secret. Oh, fine. Fuck it. Of course she wouldn't." My shoulders hunch as I glare down into my glass. "She thought it was a crazy plan."

"Pen's very sensible."

I grunt in agreement.

"You're usually sensible too," he adds magnanimously.

I give him the stink eye.

He grins wide. "Well, you used to be."

Family. I swear to God . . .

Around us the house is still and cool. And dark. I haven't turned on any lights except for the kitchen. The reflection of us wavers in the thin glass partition wall that separates the kitchen from the great room. To look at us, you'd think we hadn't a care in the world.

"So you lied." Jan's tone is thoughtful. "The question is, do you want it to be true?"

I jolt, my head jerking up. January half turns in his seat to face me. His expression is stern; the Luck eyes like glacial ice. A dozen answers spin around my head. But he narrows his gaze, cutting ahead of the bullshit.

"This is me you're talking to, August. I'm asking you straight. Do you want it to be true?"

My big brother, famous for his dogged determination, waits patiently.

On the cold counter, my hand curls into a fist. May's wailing lament returns inside my head.

I wanted it to be true!

PEN

"YOU'RE DRAGGING YOUR feet."

At August's proclamation, I scowl at the phone. "I am not."

Apparently, our united front in the face of his sisters' wrath cleared away most of the awkward tension our denied practice kiss created. I still get flashes of want and don't know how to make that go away. Baby steps.

"You could have cleared that room of yours out in a couple of hours," he says dispassionately. "Yet you're over there once again, picking through your stuff."

"It's been three days since she kicked me out. Stop rushing me."

"Penelope, we both know you're stalling."

"I am not *stalling*." I might be stalling. Just a teeny bit. With a huff, I pack up another bag. "Need I remind you that I have to transport things via my bike?"

"No, you need not remind me, Ms. Granny."

Granny. Ha!

"My sisters are visiting you," he goes on, "*with* a rental car. Why aren't they helping?"

"They suckered Jan into taking them to Disney Land for the day."

"Why didn't you go with them?"

Because my first game day is tomorrow, and I'm suddenly nervous as hell. "Because I have to pack up my things. See? *Not* dragging my feet."

"Then why didn't you let me help you move everything when I offered yesterday?"

"I don't know why this bothers you so much." I toss an old playbill in the "Maybe" pile. "Unless this has to do with your ranidaphobia?"

He makes a sound of baffled amusement. "Rani-da-what?"

"Fear of frogs."

He scoffs with dry humor. "Edward and I are cool. And maybe we should talk about *your* phobia of accepting this very good change in your life. Got a clinical name for *that*?"

It's a well-known fact among the Lucks that I keep an ongoing list of phobia names. Not for any reason other than I like learning them.

"Metathesiophobia," I mutter. "And I don't suffer from that!"

"Thank God," he intones. "Because it was a mouthful."

Despite myself, a soft laugh escapes. "Okay, fine. I'm dragging my feet."

"I'm marking this day down in my calendar. Penelope admits that I am right."

"About this one thing!"

"Details."

Our accord lasts about as long as a smile. August proceeds to tell me—make that order me—to have everything packed up by noon because he's coming to move my things. I maintain that I can do it myself and he doesn't have to help; I know how busy he is. August finds this insulting, stating that he most certainly has time for me.

We bicker it out for a bit, but the same stubborn drive that made him the top draft pick rears its head, and I concede, fearing that I just might have a bit of a phobia over big changes. He gives me points for accepting defeat with such grace. His sarcasm is not amusing. Sadly, he can't see me sticking my tongue out through the phone. But I have a feeling he knows anyway.

At twelve on the dot, he knocks and I answer. A wall of man flesh stands in the threshold.

"Pen," Augusts says by way of greeting. "Meet your movers, Trent Gellis, aka Jelly, tight end. And Roderick Rhodes, wide receiver. He goes by Rhodes." He cants his head toward me with a smile. "Gentlemen, my dear sweet Penelope."

God. If I'm not beet red it's a miracle.

"Miss Pen." The tight end Jelly tips an imaginary hat as he gives me a friendly smile. About two inches taller than August, he appears to have naturally pale skin that's gone ruddy and freckled in the sun. The ends of his spiky light brown hair are bleached almost white, as are his lashes, which makes his brown eyes seem stark. But they hold good humor and warmth.

Feeling awkward, I give him what I hope is a good smile—not too much teeth, damn that August. "Hey."

Rhodes steps in with him. Rhodes's copper-brown skin glows with good health. He's shortest of the three at around six feet, but incredibly built. Muscles on top of muscles, but moving with such graceful swagger, I just know he's more limber than I'll ever be. With curled lashes framing shining brown eyes and a deep dimple in his right cheek, he has a sweetness that belies his size. "Good to meet you, Penelope."

Yes, I'm most definitely blushing. I shake his offered hand and return the greeting.

August fights a smile as he guides his friends farther into the living room, like he knows how disarmed I am and thinks it's cute. "You ready, Sweets?"

"Yes, but it's not that much." I look at his friends. "You didn't have to take time out of your day for this."

"Of course we did," Jelly insists. He glances around in interest, then his gaze returns to me. "I was looking forward to meeting you."

I bet.

Rhodes gives me a lopsided smile. "It's nothing. Happy to help, darlin'."

He's so pretty, I don't know how to answer.

August clears his throat and gives me the beady eye. "Want to show us the way?"

Still a little miffed at his high-handedness, I sniff and am about to head for the bedroom when Sarah comes out.

"Penny, I wanted to ask if—" She stumbles to a halt, her eyes going round as moons as she sees the guys standing in her living room. "I . . ."

That's all she gets out. She gapes as though struck senseless. The silence stretches.

"Ma'am." Jelly's greeting is a little less personal than the one he gave me but polite nonetheless. As is Rhodes's brief, "Hey."

Sarah gurgles like she's choking on her spit.

At my shoulder, August leans close and murmurs, "Rhodes is a Super Bowl MVP. Team picked him up as a free agent this season."

"Ah."

Sarah whimpers, mouth agape, eyes wide and darting between Rhodes and Jelly.

"And Jelly," August continues, "is the best tight end in the league."

"Hmm." I slide August a look. And find him smugly content. Shaking my head ruefully, I show the guys my room, and they stride past a frozen Sarah to begin grabbing boxes.

There aren't many, and it's soon apparent they won't need multiple trips. Rhodes alone grabs almost half of them in one go. I stand back and let them work, knowing I'll only get in the way otherwise. August lingers behind as his boys head out, leaving a paltry box for him to take.

I watch them go, then watch Sarah gurgle out a weak "oh, my God," before trailing behind them like a lost puppy.

"You picked them on purpose, didn't you?" I say to August, knowing this was a little tweak on Sarah's nose before I left.

"I might have done." He grins but then his gaze narrows coolly. "Besides, they wanted to help after hearing how you got abruptly booted."

"You told them about that?"

He shakes his head in mild reproach. "Pen, I talk about you all the time."

"Oh. Right. I guess you'd have to if we were engaged."

"Sure that's why," he says smoothly.

Sarah comes back, clearly giddy but also wavering as though she might need a lie-down. "Oh, wow! I mean, Trent Jelly Legs Gellis and Roderick Rhodes in my living room!"

August straightens, becoming all polite business. "We're going to get out of your hair now. Penelope, you got everything you need?"

"Ah, sure." I put on my sneakers and grab my purse, and he picks up the last box.

When I set my keys on the hall table, I feel nothing but relief that it's done and the rising anticipation of moving on.

"Well, Sarah." August shuffles the box under one arm. "It's been an experience I doubt either Pen or I will forget. While I'll miss coming here, I am glad Penelope was able to move on to new lodgings so quickly."

Sarah goes bright red. "Erm, yes. Well, that was good."

"Hate to think what would have happened to her otherwise. But, luckily, she has a team behind her now." He gives her his on-camera smile. "I have a little parting gift for you. From me and Pen."

Smooth as silk, August pulls a small bag from the inside of his loosely zipped leather jacket and holds it out to her. Fingers trembling, she takes the bag with the delicacy of one handling a bomb.

As soon as she does, August clasps my hand. "Ready?" he asks me.

I nod, but my attention is on Sarah and the bag.

Gingerly, she reaches in and pulls out an envelope. I already know what's in it, but her gasp still has me smiling. The woman lights up like Broadway as she fans out not one but four passes.

"Game's tomorrow tonight," August tells her. "Hope you can make it."

Gently, he tugs me toward the door.

"Bye, Sarah," I say as I go. She nods absently, eyes glued to her tickets.

We're almost to the landing of the stairs when she calls out.

"Wait!" Huffing, she runs up to me and holds out two familiar mugs. "Lucy and Ricky. For your new place. I know you liked using them, and they should be together—with you."

I take them with my free hand. "Thanks."

She nods. "I'm . . . sorry for how I handled things. I hope you're really happy with . . . everything."

"Thank you," I say again, with more feeling. "I will be."

August leads the way down the stairs and out to the sunny street below. "That was good how you left things."

Carefully, I tuck the mugs into the box he holds out for me. Wind coming down the wide boulevard whips the ends of his hair up in a mad mess. He's impossibly beautiful and peering at me with kind eyes that shine bright. It's all I can do not to hug him tight.

"August, that was all you."

NINETEEN

AUGUST

AFTER WE FINISH helping Penelope move in, she takes me aside.

"Invite them to stay for dinner," she says.

"They don't need that. They were happy to help."

She gives me a look as though I'm a bit slow on the uptake. "It's in my DNA to feed a guest. And they're your colleagues. It's good to bond with them. In fact, you should put out a call to all of your teammates to come."

Pen isn't wrong. I have been remiss in hanging out with my teammates just for fun. In college, it was different. We were in each other's pockets all the time. By default, we basically had to be. Now it's a job and more is on the line. But the premise remains the same: A team that bonds is a team that wins. As QB, I am the one who needs to lead that team. We're doing all right now, but there's always room for improvement.

I hesitate, if only because it's Pen's house and a lot to ask. Jan and the girls are still at Disney Land; Pen could be relaxing, not cooking for a bunch of hungry guys. But she's looking at me expectantly. "All right. But I'm helping you cook."

"Obviously." She grins. "And I'm always more appreciative of those who clean afterward. That would be you I'm referring to."

"Obviously. If anyone is getting the fruits of your appreciation, it's going to be me."

"Uh-huh. Make the offer, Pickle."

I invite them over. Not everyone takes me up on the offer. But plenty do.

Falling back on college experiences, I assign them items to bring. Cooking at Pen's place is encouraged. All too soon, the open kitchen is filled with laughing football players trying their hand at different dishes. Though the top of Pen's head barely reaches most of their shoulders, she holds court like a queen, easily maneuvering between hulking linemen to taste something on the stove or, in one instance, watch Carter explain the nuances of his grandmama's baked macaroni. Apparently, the secret is evaporated milk. I leave them to it.

We open the doors to outside, and a couple of us man the grill. Because we're, as Pen tartly pointed out, well-paid athletes, we go for quality as well as quantity. Thick, marbled steaks, free-range chicken, and even a couple slabs of salmon line the grill top. And *because* we're competitive athletes there is much discussion on what method is best. For the moment, we're deferring to Jelly. Mainly because the bastard got to the grill spatula first.

Pulling together the two outdoor tables, we all manage to squeeze in and eat by the pool. Pen sits at the head of the table. Rhodes had taken her arm in his and seated her there earlier, insisting it was her spot. Happy and relaxed, her skin glows warmly in the candlelight as she laughs at something Jelly says.

It physically pains me at this point not to touch her. If only to give my hands something constructive to do, I pass along a platter of avocado salad. It's mixed with cucumbers, chilies, and lime. I know Pen made it; she likes adding some sort of "brain" food into her meals. The fact that I recognize both her food and her thought process has an unexpected pulse of tenderness swelling in my chest.

When I meet her smiling gaze from across the table, that tenderness pushes a little deeper. I find myself rubbing the area over my heart to ease the ache. Jelly promptly asks me if I have indigestion.

After dinner, none of them want to go home, but linger around the kitchen, helping to clean up. Pen is so pleased by the way things are going, she pulls out the entire stock of ice cream she has stored. It's cute that she thinks six pints will suffice for these guys and her eyes go wide when it disappears in about 3.5 seconds.

"I'll restock it," I tell her as the guys head for the den to see what's what on TV.

"It's okay. I didn't mind." Her smile is wry. "It's just that I keep forgetting how much you all eat. It's kind of like locusts swarming a field. Fascinating to watch."

The curve of her jaw feels delicate when I stroke it with the tip of my finger. "Thanks for tonight, Penelope. It was a good idea."

Velvet brown eyes lift to mine. "You don't have to thank me."

I know she's thinking it's part of our arrangement. Being trapped in a device of my own making is a humbling experience. The only thing I've ever had to work hard for is football. Even that isn't a proper comparison because that was more like maintenance. If I put in the effort, concentrated on what I needed to do, I knew I'd succeed. The end goal was already there, waiting.

Here, with Pen, nothing is clear. I can misstep and lose her. I can do everything right and still lose her. Football is simple. Personal relationships are anything but.

From the depths of the den, comes Jelly's drawling voice. "You gonna fool around in that kitchen all night, son?"

Pen startles as if caught doing something naughty. Her gaze darts to the den, then back to me. When I simply grin, she lifts a brow as if to say, *Well, answer him already.* I hold her gaze.

"I wish," I call back lightly.

With a wink, I grab my glass of iced tea, take Pen's hand, and lead her toward the den. "I know it's going to be difficult, but try to keep your touches at least a little respectable in there, Sweets."

She snorts eloquently. "It'll be a struggle, but I'll restrain myself, Pickle."

They've left a spot on the long sofa facing the TV open for us, which is a surprise. Usually, I have to fight my way in. I'm guessing it's more in deference to Pen.

She takes the corner, and I plop down next to her.

"What are we watching?" I ask.

"Nothing yet." Rhodes has the remote and is channel surfing with typical speed.

"John Wick!" Pen perks up. "Stop there!"

Rhodes obeys, and I look at Pen.

"You like that movie?" This is unexpected for a variety of reasons.

"I love all of them." Her expression goes dreamy, and it isn't hard to guess that she's thinking of Keanu. Every woman I know, and a fair amount of guys too, get that expression when speaking of Keanu.

"Honestly, Sweets, I didn't think you watched any movies made after the year 2000."

Pen flips me the bird, but does it with class, pretending her finger is a lipstick that she then uses to paint her lips.

Chuckling, I settle into the couch. It's too fun needling her sometimes. "Wick is pretty violent. You used to leave the room whenever March put on *The Walking Dead*."

"Because zombies are *gross*." Her mouth twists in distaste. "All that rotting? Ack."

With a shake of my head, I give her a reproachful look. "You flat out refused to continue watching *Predator* because it was, and I quote, 'too violent.'"

Her eyes narrow, but her lips twitch. "You think you just won something, don't you?"

"I do."

We stare each other down, both of us fighting a smile; to do so first would concede defeat. I don't make the rules. I simply obey them. But then Pen makes a dismissive motion with her hand.

"Eh, John Wick is basically a beautifully shot live-action tactical RPG, which is ironic because they then created an actual game due to the popularity of the film, which is all very meta, but I digress. He's basically on a quest, and because none of the people he kills seem real, the violence doesn't bother me."

"Damn, that was sexy." When everyone turns his way, Carter shrugs. "Where's the lie?"

I point my finger at him in warning. But he's right. It was sexy.

"Gotta love a girl who loves gaming," Jelly says with a nod.

"Your girl hates gaming," I point out.

"I'm working on it."

I turn to Pen. "Let me get this straight. John can stab someone in the *eye* and that's fine. Yet you'll squeal like a terrified piglet when Predator rips out someone's spine?"

"I resent the piglet simile."

"Piglets are adorable, but fine. Consider 'piglet' rescinded."

Pen dips her chin in a queenly gesture of beneficence. "I really don't see what's so difficult to understand here, August."

"God!" I blink up at the ceiling. "Where to begin?"

"Hold up." Rhodes leans in, his gaze darting between me and Pen. "How long have you two known each other?"

"Forever," we say in unison, which makes me full-on grin.

Pen's cheeks pink, as if our like-mindedness is somehow embarrassing. She shrugs lightly. "We grew up together, but I was really more his sisters' friend."

My smile dies. Shot dead through the heart. Technically, it's the truth. But hearing her say it bothers me more than it should. The guys can't see that, though. Not when we're supposed to be a newly engaged, completely in love couple. Attempting casual ease, I rest my arm on the back of the sofa, close enough to Pen that my fingers touch the ends of her hair.

"Our moms are best friends. Whenever our parents got together for events, we kids inevitably ended up watching movies together." I stroke a lock of Pen's hair between my thumb and forefinger. The act might appear deliberate, but in truth it's born of sheer impulse. "Pen mostly loves classic movies."

She sits very still, clearly feeling my touch but choosing not to acknowledge it, either by moving away or leaning in. She's doing a good job of pretending my touches are her normal, but the idea that I might be unsettling her has me pulling my arm back in the pretense of grabbing my drink.

I want to touch her. I want to kiss her. This need is not easing or evening out. It's getting worse.

"I'm majoring in film history, so that goes with the territory," she tells the guys. "But I love movies in general."

God, she's cute. I'm so fucked.

Pen settles down and watches the first *John Wick* with the vocal vigor of a fan. She exchanges smack talk with the guys and clenches her fists when John's assassin friend gets murdered. I have more fun watching her than the movie.

JELLY IS THE last to leave. I escort him out, he clasps my shoulder. "Nice night here, son."

"Thanks, Pop," I deadpan.

His teeth flash white in the evening light. "It's a good thing you're marrying that sweet girl."

Guilt hits hard but perverse curiosity has me asking, "Oh? And why is that."

"Because, son, you are clearly head over heels gone on her."

He leaves me standing at the end of the drive, watching his taillights fade to small red dots as the olive trees rustle in the breeze.

TWENTY

PEN

JAN TAKES US to the first game I'll attend for August. I haven't seen Jan in years, and when he steps out of his rental to open the door for us, I move to hug him. Unlike the Lucks, I'm not particularly prone to hugging, but seeing him alive and healthy has a lump rising in my throat. The world had almost lost him. I feel that keenly as he gives a tiny start of surprise and then wraps me up in his big arms. A faint woody citrus scent clings to his clothes. To me, January will always be the big brother I never had but would have created if I had a choice: solid, dependable, wise.

"Hey, there, Penny Lane." His voice is gruff against the top of my head.

"Janus," I return, using an old nickname. "I should have come to see you."

He stiffens a little then relaxes. I know he understands I meant when he was in the hospital. "You were in Italy. And I was shit company at the time."

I'd been doing an art semester in Italy and couldn't leave. But the guilt lingers. Though we were never close as friends, he's still important to me.

"Your card was perfect," he adds lightly.

I hug him closer. "I'm just so . . . glad you—"

I can't say more without being weepy, but I suspect he knows that too. With a final squeeze, he leans back and looks me over. I do the same, and take in his face. Like the other Lucks, he's beautiful, same sculpted jaw and winged brows of his brothers. His features are more blunt than August's, eyes hold a tinge more frosty blue. But they're so close in appearance, it's a bit unnerving. Even so, I don't get weak-kneed when I'm around him.

A smile lingers in the crinkled corners of his eyes as he gives my arm a gentle pat. "You look good, oh soon-to-be sister."

I know August told him everything, so I purse my lips and snort. "Ha."

He flashes a quick grin. "Little Penny . . . Imagine my surprise. It's always the quiet ones."

June and May skip out of the house and scramble to get in the back of the SUV, but they catch his comment.

May snickers. "He'd know."

"Yeah," June adds. "That Jan, a mile a minute with him. Can't get a word in edgewise."

"Brats," he says fondly while holding the door for me. "We discerning conversationalists will just have to stick together, eh, Pen?"

Primly, I gather myself, putting on my seat belt as he jogs around the front and gets in. As soon as he does, May's leaning forward.

"Maybe you should wait to see how she's with August before you say that, Jan."

I shoot her a repressive look, and ignore the speculation in Jan's eyes, as he murmurs, "I guess I'll do that."

We arrive early, much more so than one usually would. But as it's been planned by Jan and August, I don't question. A deal's a deal, and if he wants me here now, I'll be here.

Maybe it's because we're with Jan, who is an established god of the sport, but we enter through an all but hidden door that leads us directly to the bowels of the stadium. Staff bustles around doing God knows what but looking very focused. I feel completely in the way, but Jan strides at my side with easy confidence.

Every few paces, he's greeted and fawned over like royalty. A casual acquaintance might think he's perfectly happy, but flickers of strain appear whenever a well-wisher walks off.

When we reach an elevator bay, June, May, and I cluster near a wall to stay out of the way, while Jan pulls out his phone. "I'm going to be taking the girls up to the suite," he says to me, still looking down at his phone. "But August . . . ah, there."

I glance over my shoulder and find August coming toward us. He's not in uniform but wearing a thin gray T that clings to his chest and loose-fitting blue athletic shorts with the team logo emblazoned on one thigh. His gaze locks onto mine.

Damn, but he makes me flutter.

He doesn't break that easy, graceful gait until he's right before me. He stops and simply smiles. That smile goes right through my clothes and heats up my skin.

"Penelope."

"August."

His grin grows broad. "Penelope."

"Back to this, are we?"

A warm chuckle escapes him. "Guess we are."

"Shouldn't you be in uniform?"

"It's a while yet until game time, and once that kit goes on, it ain't easily coming off. I'm in warm-up gear now." A quick wink. "Were you wanting to see me in my uniform, Pen?"

"You could put your helmet on. Cover that smug smile."

"Cutting me deep, Sweets."

"You'll live, Pickle."

"Told you," says May from the sidelines.

I'd forgotten about them. Damn it. Their presence somehow manages to thrust me right back to being a teenager, peering at August from the corners. I find myself wanting to squirm.

Jan watches with interest. "Curiouser and curiouser."

August ignores everyone in favor of looking at me as if I'm some mirage that might soon dissipate.

Jan says something about coming back for me, but I'm too drawn in by August's regard to fully answer. All too soon we're alone—well, as alone as we can be standing off to the side of a busy pregame corridor.

August breaks the silence. "You came."

"Of course. I'm looking forward to it."

"Are you?" He sounds so quietly surprised, I snap out of my shyness.

"This is my first time attending an NFL game. And it's you."

That gets him. He draws in a quick breath.

"Pen." He says it sweetly, like a sigh after a long climb. As if pulled by a string, his hand lifts, and he traces the curve of my jaw. "You're good for me, you know that?"

"I don't . . ." My train of thought derails. I don't know how anyone is expected to keep their head when August Luck looks at them with that soft, happy smile.

I'm in serious danger of flinging myself right onto his body and taking a big bite. Empathy for Sarah's earlier zombie state rises.

"It's good to see January," I blurt out.

He glances at the elevators where Jan and the girls had left from. "Part of me wishes he was playing instead of watching."

"How is he taking it?"

"I don't know, honestly." August sighs and rubs the back of his neck. "He's been cagey about discussing it."

"That's understandable."

Absently, he nods, but his focus is still on the elevator doors. "When I thought about going pro, I always assumed we'd be battling it out in a way, the two Luck quarterbacks competing for the ring."

August's expression flickers. "Of course I had a lot of catching up to do. But I thought he'd be there. Now . . . it's different. It's like I'm chasing a ghost in some ways."

He's chasing a legacy instead of competing with a brother.

"August," I say in the heavy silence. Instantly, I have his attention back. Complete focus. The sensation is heady. My fingers thread through his and I hold firm. "It occurs to me that the solution to your problem isn't me—"

"I don't know about that." He gives me a lopsided smile.

"Be serious for a second. I mean it. I think what you really need to do is to win."

"Pen . . ." he huffs, amused. "Of course I need to win. I've been trying my best to do precisely that."

"No, I'm not explaining it right." I push my hair back from my face and think. "What I'm saying is that it's you, August. You can win because that's what you do, it's who you are."

He's staring at me like I've sprouted a second head, but I forge on.

"Pops used to bet on basketball games."

It's clear he thinks I've lost the plot but he's kind enough to humor me. "I didn't know that."

"He almost always won too. I would tease him about being psychic. He'd say it wasn't precognition but the ability to read body language. 'Pen,' he'd say, 'at the pro level, the talent pool is elite, even when you include superstars, your playing field is basically even. What truly decides the game is a soul-deep belief in the player that they're going to win.'

"He'd tell me it wasn't enough to *think* you're going to win, you had to *know* it. That unfailing belief would show in the body language of the players. Other players, whether they knew it or not, would pick up on it too."

For a moment, I think I've lost him, but August looks off, his brows knitting. "I remember he loved Jordan."

"Yes," I exclaim. "Because Jordan didn't care who he faced or what the supposed odds were, he was going to win because that's what he did." I give August's hand a tug. "That's what you do too."

The words seem to settle over us, and August swallows thickly.

"You really see me that way?" There's a tone in his voice, stronger now. But also curious.

"It's one of the few things I know with absolute certainty."

His eyes close for a second, then he stares down at me with such intensity that I nearly quaver.

My voice is unsteady as I ask, "The real question is, do *you* see yourself that way?"

The long lines of his body practically vibrate with some withheld emotion. But he answers me clearly. "Yes, I fucking do."

"Well, then, there you go. You don't have to chase your brother's legacy, or anyone else's. You just be you, and your team will follow."

A chin jerk is all the confirmation I get. He's still focused on me with those hot eyes that have my insides fluttering.

"Pen?"

God, that voice of his. Dark and rich with just a touch of dry humor. Something about the look in his eye has a thread of anticipation unfurling within.

"Yes, August?"

"It's game day." Finely sculpted lips curl with impish glee.

I'd told him only on game day. Sweat blooms under my shirt, my heart beating overtime.

I swallow hard. "Yes, it is."

He steps closer. "We're in public."

"We are?" I'd forgotten everything but him.

His head dips, as his hands rise to cup my face. The second he touches me, I nearly fall into him. I clasp his wrists to keep steady.

"I'm going to kiss you."

My inner voice squeaks in alarm. August is going to kiss me. I won't be able to play this off. Objectivity has flown the coop.

I lick my dry lips. "I got that."

Carefully, he lowers his lips to mine, watching me the whole time, as if to say *It's okay, I got you.* And I believe him, even if my heart is trying to beat its way out of my chest. Almost lazily, his lids lower, and I follow suit, lifting up on my toes to meet him. The first touch has my breath hitching. Or maybe it's his. They intermingle and catch.

And then he does it again, brushes my lips so gently like they're made of spun sugar. I feel it everywhere, radiating outward in little pings of pleasure. I want more but all I can think of is him and how strange it all is that we're here now. And where do I put my hands? How much do I give him?

Perhaps he knows how nervous I am, that I have no idea what to do, for he murmurs a sound of reassurance and goes slowly, softly, learning my lips with little touches and tastes while teaching me his. And it feels so very good, that my head goes light as my body grows heavy and languid.

Those long, talented fingers of his cradle my face while he nuzzles my mouth nipping and caressing. I feel the tension in those hands, in the quickening of his breath. But he holds himself still. For me.

The knowledge of his care has me making a little sound of need, moving closer. August angles his head going deeper, lingering longer, one hand gliding down my neck, along my back to gather me up. I rise higher on my toes, my arms wrapping around his neck to hold on, or keep him close. I don't know anymore. I simply want. He could kiss me like this forever, and I would love it. And I haven't even tasted his tongue.

I should do that. I should open my mouth, invite him inside. Lick him up like ice cream. My breath comes in pants. And he grunts in response, his mouth firmer, greedy. Oh, but it's perfect. I had no idea . . .

"You two about done?"

January's question, though delivered with bland inference, snaps along my spine like a whip. I startle with a muffled squeak and rear back. Not too far; August doesn't let me go but lifts his head to glare at his brother.

Jan gives August a once-over, then raises a brow. "Came to bring Pen upstairs."

"Get your own girl," August retorts but steps back. His glossy hair is mussed and his lips look a bit fuller.

Swollen. From kissing me. I die. Honestly. Just die. Never in my wildest imaginings . . . Okay, maybe I did imagine somewhat. But the reality is much, much better.

August gives me a soft smile and gently smooths my hair. "Thanks for the good-luck kiss, Sweets."

Was that what it was?

Clearing my throat, I straighten and find my voice. "Go be you, Pickle."

His smile is a flash of light and promise. "On it."

TWENTY-ONE

PEN

THE LUXURY BOX suite is like a mini apartment with a wall view of the stadium. Rectangular in shape, there's a private full bathroom—according to Jan—at the back and then an intimate living room area with a long tan suede sofa, matching armchairs placed in conversation groups. Deco-style table lamps with cream-colored shades give the space a warm glow. Flat screens hang on each wall so that one might watch the game from there—although I have no idea why someone would come to a game and watch it from a TV.

In the middle of the space is a wood-paneled section dedicated to a kitchenette and long granite-topped bar. Here, one can help themselves to food, or eat at the island, and still see the action.

But the money section is definitely the theater-style rows of plush leather seats that face the field. A high-top bar runs along the back of the seats for eating and drinking as well.

In short, every comfort for the ultimate viewing experience has been thought of. I'm more than a little awed. It's relatively empty at the moment, with a few staff checking on the buffet and manning the drinks bar, but I spot June and May immediately. As soon as they see me, they hustle over with wide eyes.

"Oh, my fucking God," May whispers, clutching my hand like a vise. "You will never—"

The soft, muffled woosh of a toilet flushing has her biting her lip.

"What is it?" I whisper back.

June shakes her head as if to forestall the conversation. And just in time. The bathroom door opens, and a woman walks out. A swoop of shock has me shooting quick looks at my friends. I know they're mentally nodding along as if to say, *I know!*

It isn't every day Monica Reyes, Oscar winner and massive star, walks out of a bathroom and into a luxury stadium suite. Or maybe it is. I'm way out of my depth there.

She spots us almost as quickly as we'd spotted her. She falters only a tiny bit, but she puts on a wide smile and strolls forward. "August's siblings I recognized immediately by their eyes, which means you must be the fiancée, Penelope?"

On-screen, she shines—light brown skin, a tumble of glossy black hair, full lips and symmetrical features that can play good or evil with equal conviction. In person, she's just as stunning, but more real. There's a constellation of tiny freckles by her temple. Laugh lines fan the corners of her eyes. She's wearing jeans and a team jersey with the number 87.

It helps, but I'm still starstruck.

"Pen," I offer, holding out a hand that's shaking a tinge. "I desperately want to play this cool and act unfazed and continental here, but I know I'd only end up failing spectacularly at that. So I'll get it out now. I'm a huge fan and kind of want to pee my pants."

While June and May utter half-hidden groans of despair, Monica laughs. It's a low and easy rolling sound as she shakes my hand and appraises me with smiling eyes.

"Honesty is always best. Please don't pee yourself. We've got a good bathroom here."

"I'd never live it down, so I'll control that."

She grins wider, red lipstick against snow-white teeth. "We're cool. As long as you don't stare at me the whole time and drool."

"I can absolutely guarantee I don't drool, outside of sleep."

"And the staring?"

"I'm sure that will fade."

With another laugh, she gives me a friendly pat on the arm. "I can see why the boys like you. Trent's my man," she adds in exclamation.

Only then do I remember that her boyfriend was one of the guys who had helped move my things. "Jelly—*Trent* was very kind to help. I hope I can repay him in some way soon."

"He told me you made them all dinner." Her hazel eyes dance. "I think that makes you even in his book."

"Eh. The guys all helped. And it was nothing, really. I have enough Italian in me to feel bereft at missing the chance to feed someone who enters my house."

"I'm Hispanic, but it's the same for me," she says warmly.

The door opens and, from that point on, guests pour in. It shouldn't be a surprise that they include more actors, pop stars, rappers, and various athletes from other sports—the seven footer I know plays for the Lakers—but I find myself drifting close to the wall and just taking it in.

Although they'd squeed over Monica, May and June have been in this life long enough to be far more comfortable with the fame-filled room. They make their way around, talking to whomever about whatever.

"Sometimes, we Lucks tend to forget you don't like mingling," Jan says, suddenly at my side. His size and presence acts as a protective wall between me and the room.

"But I do like watching."

"This isn't so different from what you grew up with."

"Jan." I shake my head, smiling wryly. "I grew up in the audience, or waiting at home for my parents to return. Not all this."

He searches my face and gives me a look of reassurance. "At the end of the day, they're just people underneath the gloss."

"Oh, I know."

I don't fool him. He inclines his head my way, keeping his voice low. "And yet you look like you're two seconds away from bolting."

I huff out a breath. "I'm fine. I just . . . Sometimes I forget that this is your world. August's world."

"Only a small part of it. August's true world is down there." He nods toward the stadium that's slowly filling up. "And here, with us. Family and football. That's what matters."

The gentle admonishment, as though I should have known better, chafes. I take a long drink of the cocktail the bartender made for me. I have no idea what's in it, only that it tastes fresh and fruity and is creamy blue. He'd called it the house specialty.

The base of the glass makes a light clink when I set it down on a nearby bar top. "You and I both know I won't be here long enough to get used to it."

Glacial blue eyes hold mine. "I have a feeling, Penny Lane, that you'll be around for quite some time."

"You know this isn't real."

"Do I?" Suddenly he grins, wide and bright. It reminds me so much of August, my breath catches. "Keep protesting, Pen. I'm a competitive guy and like the challenge."

"Said just like a Luck," I mutter darkly.

"Exactly."

Jan offers his arm and, when I take it, leads me down to the plush seats. A rapper whose name eludes me is talking to Monica. But when he spots Jan heading their way, he jumps up to shake his hand. It's a neat trick how Jan manages to exchange friendly conversation while steering me into the very seat the guy vacated.

"It's the best," he says to me when I balk, before clapping the rapper on the shoulder and telling him to enjoy the game.

Caught between the seat and Jan's bulk, I choose to sit. Monica gives me a sly look as she leans back, a massive tub of popcorn in her hands.

"Those Luck boys," she says. "Smooth as cream and sweet as honey."

"I was thinking more like steamrollers with smiles."

"We're both." Jan plops down in the empty seat on my other side. Dark brows waggle once. "I have excellent hearing."

"Then I won't have to raise my voice when I tell you to bite me."

A laugh bursts out of him.

"Attagirl," he says, mussing my hair with his huge paw.

I swat him away but can't help but smile. Charming is what they are. The whole lot of them.

Content, Jan surveys the field. He's managed to procure a fresh beer without having to take a step. I swear the staff must pop up before he can even think to ask for something.

Monica, who's been watching our interplay, appears entertained. "August mentioned that you all grew up together. It shows."

Jan wraps a muscled arm around my shoulders and gives me an affectionate squeeze, much like a two-year-old would with his favorite woobie. "And now she'll be our real-life sister."

I swear I'm going to kill him. I expected this of March, but January? He's supposed to be the reserved one. The elder statesman. Then again, he's had it so rough this year, his good humor and sly teasing are to be celebrated. If I can keep him smiling, I will.

"I'm already composing my Christmas list," I tell him. "Prepare your wallet."

"Isn't that August's job?"

"Oh, he'll get his. But as my new big brother, I'm owed years of back presents."

Jan chuckles and drinks his beer.

"I'm glad you came," Monica says. "It's usually the same old boring crowd."

"Thank you for inviting me."

Monica does a double take. "The box is August's."

"He bought it?"

"Was tied into his contract as a benefit." Jan takes a handful of offered popcorn. "I told him he'd come to appreciate it, given the size of our family."

"It was a good idea," Monica says. "Rhodes has one. It's always filled to the brim with his people. Trent never bothered." She turns my way. "He didn't have me when he started, and he's an orphan."

"I didn't know that."

"Football pulled him through and was his ticket out." Setting the popcorn tub down, she wipes her fingers with a napkin. "I was looking to purchase a box, but there wasn't any to be had—our boys are a hot ticket now. So August offered co-ownership of his. Trent insists he'll be the one to buy in. Said it was his games I had to go see—that's some hardship—and so he's the one to spend the money."

"And you let him have his way," I say knowingly.

Crimson lips curl in a small smile. "Choose your battles, you know?"

Jan takes a pull on his beer and then huffs a laugh. "You women scare me, the way you effortlessly manage us."

"Take notes, Big Boy," Monica says. "Compromise goes both ways. You'll be a lot happier once you figure that out."

"Oh, I'm sure."

It occurs to me that Jan and his fiancée broke up soon after their accident, and that he might be a little salty about women and relationships at the moment.

"Anyway," Monica drawls with a gleam in her eye. "Now that you're here, Pen, we can go about decorating it a little more to our tastes and choosing menus together."

"Oh, I . . ." Hell. Despite Jan's taunting, I'm not actually "here" for any real length of time. "Wait, you have to decorate this?"

Jan looks at me like a professor having to work with a beginner student. "Having a box is like buying a condo. It's up to the box owner to furnish it and pay for food, drinks, and staff—all provided in house, of course."

"The house always wins," Monica says dryly.

"I honestly thought we'd be sitting out in the regular seats."

"August wanted you comfortable," Jan says idly.

Something in the way his gaze stays firmly on the field has me wondering if that really translates into August was worried about my safety.

"Besides." Monica nudges my shoulder. "As soon as I heard our boy Luck was getting married, I wanted to meet you."

It's sweet how much of a mother hen Monica is.

"Unfortunately, I'm not able to sit out in crowds for very long." She doesn't sound upset about it, more pragmatic than anything. "So it's box viewing for me."

Taking a handful of the popcorn she offers, I munch on it before speaking. "I also had this vision of sitting with the rest of the players' families."

"They're scattered about, mostly." She sees my expression and explains. "WAGs have to fend for themselves."

"WAGs?"

"Wives and girlfriends," Jan puts in.

"Oh." I let out a half laugh. "For some reason, I thought of dogs."

Monica cackles. "Girl, same. I don't know who came up with the acronym, or if it was on purpose, but, having heard some other sport's terms for women, I'm guessing the implied 'bitches' wasn't entirely out of mind."

My nose wrinkles. "WAGs and families have to buy their own seats?"

"Yep. Billionaire owners fret about profit margins and squeeze every dollar they can."

About ten minutes before kickoff, May and June file into seats around us, happily chatting now with Monica. Sarah arrives soon after, Daniel, Priti, and her ex-husband, Harry, in tow.

She's vibrating with happiness as she makes her way over. I'd say she only had eyes for me, but her gaze keeps darting to January in awe. Monica might as well be a seat; I think it amuses her.

"Isn't this the greatest?" Sarah asks, stopping in the aisle by our row. "I'm so happy! They let Edward in!"

At this, she pulls Edward from a glittering yellow-and-white-sequined purse shaped like a ram's head. "Look!"

My heart squeezes in tenderness, then seems to swell within my breast. There upon his froggy head and poised at a no-nonsense game day angle, is a tiny team ball cap.

He gave it to her anyway. Because he knew she'd love it. Because he wanted to make a fan happy.

"And it's signed! He signed Edward's hat!"

Sure enough, a small "AL" scrawled in black ink graces the bill.

Monica coos and exclaims over Edward.

As for myself, I focus on the brilliant green grass before me. A hundred yards. Fifty each way. Two sets of shining yellow uprights. With my whole heart, I want August to win.

Because he loves it. Because it will make him happy. And just maybe he needs someone to look after his happiness too.

AUGUST

"THE PROPER TEMPERATURE to roast a chicken is four-fifty for the first fifteen minutes to crisp the skin and seal in the juices. Then lower it to three-fifty for the remainder cooking time so it doesn't dry out."

Down on the sidelines isn't all football, kids.

I bite my lip to keep from smiling as Carter and Williams discuss the best way to make chicken. So far, Carter appears to have the method down pat. Williams takes mental notes. We lost the coin toss and our defense will start. Now, however, we're on a commercial break.

Guys deal with the adrenaline-filled nerves of waiting in different ways. Some talk smack. Others?

"You're saying a cast-iron pan is better than a roasting pan?"

"My mama uses cast iron, so I use cast iron."

"Valid."

Jelly snorts as he walks past. He's keyed up, striding back and forth to keep loose. "Just make the damn chicken and invite me over to eat it."

I do practice throws with my arm to keep it warmed up and limber. Inside, however, I'm struggling to find that focus Penelope urged me to remember. Ironically, the fault lies with her. I kissed Penelope Morrow. The thought rolls round and round like those records her roommate favors. I kissed her, something I'd imagined far too many times. I've had dreams about that sweet bud of a mouth, wondered how she'd feel, how she'd sound, how she'd taste.

I still don't know that last question. Not really. Because even though I'd finally got my mouth on hers, it had been for show. And I'd be damned if I'd invade her mouth with the kind of kiss I really crave under false pretenses. But it had been a very near thing. Multiple times during that soft, sweet kiss, I'd almost slipped, almost grabbed on and simply gorged.

A quiet shiver dances over my skin. Having fought off a hard-on since the moment I got my hands on her, I can't let it rise here of all places. Frowning, I pull my head—both of them—away from thoughts of Pen and her succulent mouth.

"Did you know there's a fungus that turns ants into zombies?" I ask no one in particular.

"Say what now?" Carter leans forward, intrigued.

"The ant is infected by the fungus and the fungus then compels the ant to latch onto the underside of a leaf until the ant dies. The fungus grows within its host and eventually shoots spores out of the dead ant's head to propagate."

"Get the fuck out," Jelly exclaims.

"It's true," Rhodes puts in. "Heard it on NPR."

"You listening to NPR?" Carter finds this amusing.

"Helps me relax on the way home."

"Put your ass right to sleep on the road, is what it'll do." Carter smirks.

Jelly makes a sound of wonder. "And here I thought *The Last of Us* would never happen."

"Better watch yourself. If they can come for the ants . . ."

On that note, Carter shivers. "Man, I hate all this zombie shit. Talk about something else."

"All right," I say easily. "We're going to win."

I do another mock throw. The commercial break is done, and our defense is lining up.

Rhodes quirks a brow. "You psychic or something?"

"No. Pen told me." I roll my neck. "Pen thinks her grandfather might have been psychic, though."

"Her grandfather told her we'd win?"

"Pay attention, Rhodes. Her Pops is dead. Pen says we'll win. I agree."

Rhodes runs a hand over his head in beleaguered fashion, then sets his eyes on me. "Is *she* psychic?"

I flash a grin. "Not that I know of."

"Bro, stop playing."

"I'm not playing. I'm clearing your mind of all the useless chatter. We're going to win. Pen knows it. I know it." I punctuate my words with a focused look at the whole of them. "Because that's what we do."

The tone of my voice, the look in my eyes, or maybe even the way I stand—something there must transmit because a change stirs through my offensive line. It starts with the group of guys closest to me, then spreads out like a ripple in a pond.

Winning.

Pen was right. It's all in the mind. A mind-fuck, really. Because you gotta feel it, know it, but not be owned by worrying about it. I'd understood this for years. But it took her words to remind me. My head's been in my ass for too long, worrying about things I can't control.

Here, I can control.

Our time is up. The defense has done a good job at keeping the other team contained. Now it's our turn to run up the scoreboard.

I grab my helmet and put it on, as the defense jog back to the sidelines. The field spreads before me, a vast sea of vibrant green, the sides of the stadium rising up around us like a cresting wave. Sound rushes down those seated sides and crashes into us.

People sometimes ask me if I feel small stepping out on the field, with all that noise and those eyes watching. Never. Out here, everything is huge—the guys moving around, the yellow uprights taunting us from beyond. A wall of guys surrounds me, faces dark and sweat-slicked behind the grill of their big helmets.

They look to me to lead. Focus. Win.

Anticipation pulls tight at my gut, prickles along my skin. Fucking heady sensation. I can hear the blood pumping through my veins, my heart thumping strong and steady in my chest. Arousal, not unlike sex, but slightly different, more aggressive, something dark and primal, has me twitching. I know my guys feel it too. Battle ready.

The game plan runs through my head. My coach's voice a presence inside my helmet. It's all there. Everything I need. Inside, I slow it down, focus. Outside, I ramp up, flex my muscles, remember the power in my body, in my arm. The talent.

Jelly saunters up, taking front and center in the circle we create. "How we do, Rocket Man?"

"We do it right," I bark.

"We do it hard," Carter adds.

They're bouncing now, adrenaline and anticipation surging.

I catch every eye, let them see the focus, then give them the play name, and end with a sharp "No fear."

My hands come together in a thunderclap, and we flow to the line.

Game on.

TWENTY-TWO

PEN

WITH ALL OF the Lucks now in the know, I realize I can't put off the inevitable, so I bite the bullet and call my mom on Monday morning. By now, pictures of me sitting next to Monica *freaking* Reyes while cheering for August have circulated. Mom's bound to be twitching with irate curiosity. I can't exactly blame her there.

We've opted to tell our parents the truth; the risk of our family members exposing us is nil. Even so, the call with my mom goes about as expected with her lecturing me on being inconsiderate, implying that I didn't tell her because I was still salty about her not helping me with the house—I didn't inform her that I was getting help from August—and then her insistence that she somehow knew our engagement couldn't have been real.

Given that it *isn't* real, I can't object to her conclusions. It's her reasoning as to why that irks. In her words, *You and August live in such different worlds. The idea that they would suddenly collide, much less mesh, is fantastical.*

I'd hung up as soon as I could without hanging up on her. But my mood remains low and *squicky*. There's a wriggling nest of disgruntlement in my belly that I can't evict. Thanks for that, Mom. But I'm not going to let her get to me. She didn't mean it to be insulting, even though it was.

My self-imposed lecture goes in circles as I make my way

down the sunlit hall from the bedroom to the kitchen. Doesn't matter my mood, being here never fails to fill me with a sense of awe and thankfulness. Living in a place of grace and beauty will do that. Everyone should have the pleasure. The irony being that architects like Cliff May designed houses like this with that thought in mind. Beautifully functional homes for the average American. And now it's so freaking expensive, only the wealthy can live in them.

"What's that scowl for?" May asks from her seat at the wide marble island counter. Sunlight streams down from the skylights set on either side of the center barn beam and gleams in her inky hair like stars.

"The state of the world. My mother. The fact that I haven't yet had my morning coffee." I shrug and grab a mug from the cabinet. "Take your pick."

"Your mom give you a lot of shit?" she asks in sympathy.

"Not so much as implying that the idea of me being with someone like August was laughable." Fragrant coffee fills my mug and clears my head. I reach into the fridge for some half-and-half. "Which left me with the very mature urge to yell back, 'I could so be with him!' When, obviously, I'm not so . . ."

I end my tirade by making a face and fixing my coffee how I like it: tan and creamy.

May lifts a foot onto the rung of her stool and stabs what looks like a bowl of yogurt and blueberries with her fork. "Well, you absolutely could be with him. If you so chose."

When I give her a "get real" look, she raises a perfectly arched brow. "Don't tell me you agree with your mom? Because we're going to have words if you do."

"May Day, I have a healthy relationship with my appearance in that I know what I look like and am mostly fine with it. That also means I'm not delusional. In no way do I remotely resemble the type of women August usually goes out with."

"Studied his sex life, have you?"

Walked right into that one. With a huff, I lean against the

counter and clutch my warm mug. "It's not like I go looking for information. August, March, and Jan are in the news, as are the people they date."

"I'll give you that."

"So look me in the eye and tell me I'm wrong about the type of women he usually favors."

Her shoulders slump. "Okay, you're not wrong. But! That doesn't mean the idea of him dating *you* is laughable."

I bite my bottom lip and stare at my feet. I really need to have my toes painted. Something cheerful like pale yellow or hot pink. "It just pricks, you know? Because there's a hint of truth in it, and here I am having to pretend that he's so in love with me that he proposed marriage." The taste of coffee on my tongue turns extra bitter. "It's awkward."

"Hey," May soothes. "I get it. I'm only in the press a little, a comment here or there when they talk about our family. And I hate it. I can't imagine being picked apart by lookie-loos who think they're entitled to know everything about August, not to mention your own mother."

"The mother thing . . ." My heart pinches, and I bat the pain away with a wave of my hand. "As for the rest, it's what I agreed to. And I'm not sorry about that. I'll shrug it off after breakfast."

"Yes, you will. And, hey, it's not as bad as you assume. I was looking at those pics of you and Augie eating on the Pier—"

"Ugh. That." I shake my head. "We knew they'd taken pictures, but it was still the first shot. Freaked me out a little."

"You two look adorable!" Her phone rests on the counter by her bowl, and she flips it over to scroll. "Here. I mean, I totally bought the love thing."

With great reluctance, I drag myself over to her and peer at the pictures. At first, I only see August. He's beautiful. Just perfectly formed. A Michelangelo with those sweeping brows, strong nose, and sculpted jaw. And he's smiling. It lifts the sharp, clear angles of his face, fills him with light, and creates a little dimple at the corner of his firm lips. *Sigh.*

Seriously, I'm in real trouble here because he just does it for me.

Then I see myself. It's not terrible. But if August sees this picture and doesn't notice my moony expression, it will be a miracle. My cheeks are plump with the smile, all my "nice" teeth on display. The shot was taken at a side angle, and well, that's not great.

Groaning, I rub my temple. "Ah, man, I loved that shirt."

"What's wrong with the *Murder She Wrote* shirt?" May's gaze wings from me to the phone and back again. "I love that show. So cozy. Although you just know Jessica is doing those murders and blaming it on everyone else. You just *know*."

"Serial killer or not, I'd run for my life whenever she rolled in to town— Argh. I'm talking about the fit." I point to the photo. "I look like a marshmallow skewered by toothpicks."

Her lips twitch. "It's not that bad."

I raise a brow.

"Okay, maybe a little. But photos lie! You absolutely do not look like a marshmallow in that shirt. I've seen you wear it."

"But I do there." I tap the screen. "And that's what people see. What they comment on."

May wisely tucks the phone away. "You're right. We, as a society, are a bunch of judgy shits." We share a look, then she straightens with a determined look. "If people are going to be sneaking pics of you from all angles, then a proper fit is key. You've got those sexy big boobs that I'd kill for. But they require care."

I almost laugh. "God, I've been hanging around August too much. All I can think of is sex jokes."

"If he's making sex jokes that often it must be on his mind."

"Moving on."

She presses her palms on the counter, a gleam of anticipation in her eyes. "I think it's time for a makeover!"

"Uh . . ."

June shuffles into the kitchen, inky hair snarled around her pale face. "Ugh. I think I had too many cocktails yesterday."

"You're the one who kept pouring them," I point out with asperity. But I quickly prepare her a coffee.

She accepts it with a grunt, takes a sip, then eyes us with suspicion. "Why are the two of you up so early, anyway?"

"It's ten fifteen," I drawl.

"I repeat. Why are you two up so early?"

May gives her twin a dry look. "I had to get up. You snore."

"Lies!"

May affects a loud, dramatically rattling snore.

With a sniff, June gathers her dignity. "Never happened."

"Then I guess tiny invisible dwarves were drilling for dragon gold in your nose."

Coughing back a laugh, I step in between their line of sight before they really get going. "This house has five bedrooms, why are you sharing?"

May and June pause as one and look at me with twin expressions of befuddlement. "We always share when we travel."

As if this is perfectly obvious and I'm a fool for even asking. I shrug and head for the stove.

"I'm making a frittata," I tell them, as June takes a seat next to May and the two of them lean into each other like kittens. "Anyone want some?"

Both immediately give me hungry puppy eyes, proceeding to tell me I'm the absolute best and could I please cook for them every day? Very sweet. But they're not getting away with sitting and watching.

"Cut up some avocados and tomatoes," I tell them as I pull out a pan.

"Look at you living the high life with your pricey avocados," May teases.

We'll ignore the fact that I'm currently living in a dream house. Details. I reply blandly, "There's avocado trees on the property."

"Maybe you should set up a stand. Sell those bad boys to pay the taxes."

"Maybe I should."

June opens the fridge and finds the eggs. "What were you

two talking about when I came in? Pen looked like she was two breaths away from panic."

"Oh!" May yips, spinning to grin at her sister. "We're giving Pen a makeover today!"

"Now, hold on—"

"Yes!" June holds her fists under her chin as she dances in place. "Oh, I so know how we should do her hair!"

"Right?" May says, as if June has already given a full description. "And then clothes! I have plans. Big plans!"

Hours of shopping-related, "thrust into the center of attention" torture loom before me. "Don't I get a say?"

"No!" From both of them.

"We're going home tomorrow," June says. "Let's have this day of fun. Besides, I think you need a little relaxation after all this August related PR."

Slumping in defeat, I begin to crack my eggs. "Avocado riches aside, I'm not sure I can afford a full makeover."

"We're paying for the hair," May says firmly. "Consider it an early birthday present."

"My birthday is months from now."

"As for the clothes," June adds. "We know how to shop for bargains that will still look both hot and classy. It's really a matter of adding good pieces to what you already have."

"Absolutely." May nods. "We got you, boo."

I try not to laugh. Or sigh. No wonder August was terrified of facing these two. The Luck brothers might be a veritable wall of physical strength, but the Luck sisters have persuasive skills bordering on hypnotic. I already feel myself being pulled under.

June wraps her arm around my shoulders and gives me an affectionate squeeze. "Don't look so glum, Penny. We're going to take good care of you."

"That's what I'm afraid of," I mutter darkly.

"You'll survive." She kisses my cheek. "Sometimes you've got to let yourself enjoy a little pampering."

Thing is? She's right. I don't do enough self-care. Hadn't I been lecturing myself on getting better clothes? On crawling out of this shell I've constructed around myself? I can't be the me I've always wanted to be if I don't try. And if there was ever a time when I needed to put myself in their capable hands, it's now.

A long breath leaves me, and I rest my head on June's shoulder. "All right. Have at me."

They both squeal. I'm enveloped in a group hug of joy. And it feels good to let go. Really good.

AUGUST

IT'S LATE WHEN I finally head out. Hours of training, followed by footage reviews and QB meetings have left my body drained and my eyes sore. I just want to kick back with a cold drink in one hand and Pen in the other.

The thought bursts through the fog like a lightning strike, and I halt a step. I shouldn't be surprised; she's on my mind more often than not. And I knew that having her in my life would change everything.

But the fact that she's my first choice of reward after a long day truly sinks in. I've never had a person I looked forward to seeing in this way. Women: mother, sisters, aunts, grandmothers, play a huge factor in my life, and I love each and every one of them. I'd like to think they've made me a better person, shown me what it is to truly love and be loved.

When it comes to sexual release and romance, women have basically been interchangeable and not exactly necessary in my life. Truth is, I've felt no desire to get close to any of them. As for sex? That I've gone through a dry period since the last week of the draft—a time I do not want to think about—doesn't faze me.

What does faze me is that one woman I want—no, *need*—to be near is the one I've convinced to fake it with me.

The thought makes my steps heavy as I head for the Grouch. Press have gathered at the visitors' entrance for shots of players and quick sound bites. We have an important big game this week, so we'll be peppered with the usual nonsense questions and given the usual stock answers. There are times when I'm answering that I imagine myself pulling a folksy Ted Lasso or, even better, a Roy Fucking Kent and letting loose. But reality is much less permissive of going off script. Last thing I need is to further tarnish my image by not being a "team player."

Luckily, no one has yet spotted me. I exited a rarely used janitorial door in the hopes of evasion. It's now a matter of casually strolling to my vehicle without them noticing.

The sun is doing an easy slide toward the western horizon, leaving a swath of gilded tangerine and bruised purple in its wake. Idle breezes dance over the warm concrete and rustle in the giant palms overhead. California is beautiful like that. Volatile at times but gorgeous all the same.

A gust of wind rushes past, lifting the ends of my hair and cooling me off. Sighing, I raise my head.

And spot her.

The sight goes through me in a thump of emotion—a punch to the heart, the solar plexus, everywhere. Again, my stride stutters to a halt.

She's sitting on the hood of the Grouch, her booted heels resting on the chrome bumper. Her smile is lopsided, straining a little at the edges as I stand there staring back at her. The same wind that stroked me, tousles the gorgeous cloud of her shining brown hair, whipping it over her face, and she struggles to hold the mass back.

Happiness swells over me. In a crescendo it rises, vibrating in my bones. The smile on her face starts to turn uncertain, wobbling as though about to fall. Can't have that. Not when her smile is the best thing I've seen all day. I grin back at her, full out so she can see what she does to me.

The answer is a light in her eyes, a slow, shy curl of her lips. She's so fucking pretty. My feet move before I even think about it, pounding the pavement. It isn't a run, but it's close.

"Hey!" she says in greeting when I get to her.

My duffel hits the ground. I step between her legs, wrap my arms around her, and nuzzle the curve of her neck.

"Hey." She smells so good. Sugar, spice, and everything nice.

It's clear I surprised Pen with the hug. Her hands hover around me for a moment before she rests them on my shoulders. I almost sigh. An actual fucking sigh of contentment. As it is, I draw in another deep breath and let the feel of her sink into my bones.

"What are you doing here?" I ask her neck. *Would she flinch if I kissed it?*

Pen huffs out a nervous laugh. "I don't know. I was just . . . nowhere near your neighborhood."

The response filters through my contentment, and I lift my head. The bridge of her nose and the crests of her cheeks are flushed. I cup the side of her face to feel all that silken warmth. She's so delicately small boned, my hand nearly engulfs her. I want to touch her all the time. And once I start, I find it difficult to stop.

Smiling softly, I run my thumb along her cheek. "That was a movie quote, wasn't it?"

Pen blinks for a second. "It was."

She sounds both impressed and happy at the catch. When she moves to speak, I cut in.

"Wait, don't tell me. I know this. We watched it once for movie night."

The corners of her eyes crinkle. "You . . . you remember that?"

"Uh-huh." *I remember everything.* I close my eyes to concentrate. "Bunch of people living in a Seattle apartment building . . . Coffee and flannel. There's a guy who wants to make a super commuter train and mentally converses with basketball stars to prevent orgasm—"

"Figures you'd remember *that*."

My eyes pop open in triumph. "*Singles*! Right?"

Pen beams, sunset in her hair, eyes like stars. "You got it!"

"I'm so fucking happy to see you, Penny." It comes out without forethought. But I'm not sorry. It's the absolute truth.

Even so, she frowns a little in shock. "You called me Penny."

Not what I thought she would address. "Everyone in my family calls you Penny."

"You never did." It's not delivered as an accusation, more an observation.

And what can I say to that? *I didn't want to call you what everyone else did; I was already too much in the background of your world.*

Her gaze darts over my face, waiting for an answer, starting to wonder. I slide my fingers into the satiny mass of her hair. "I saw you sitting here, so pretty and shiny like a new penny."

"You're making me blush," she murmurs, averting her eyes.

"I know. It's cute." I brush a kiss over the tip of her nose. And she blushes some more.

Pen leans back with a stern look. "I hate blushing. Damn my pale skin."

I can only grin. "Aside from me being extremely glad to see you, what are you really doing here? Is everything okay?"

"The girls and I went shopping today. We finished with hair appointments—"

"They got their hair done?"

There's a pause, in which she gives me a long, bland look. And I know I've stepped in it. Badly. I glance at her hair. It's shorter, isn't it?

"You got your hair done," I amend, regrouping.

"Yes. Doesn't matter."

Yes, it fucking does.

"I didn't notice before because—" *I only saw you* "—the wind." I make a swirling motion with my free hand. I'm still cupping her head, and she hasn't pulled away. So I'm staying put.

Now that I have a chance, I truly look at her. Her hair is definitely shorter, better framing her heart-shaped face, which makes her eyes look bigger. She's wearing a pale yellow sundress that hugs her breasts like a lover and emphasizes the smallness of her waist. The skirt puddles between her parted thighs to reveal the pale caps of her knees. The dark brown cowboy boots she has on are well-worn and clearly well loved.

She catches me looking at them. "They were Pegs's. I found them in the mudroom."

"They look good." Sexy as hell, in all honesty. "You look fantastic."

"Anyway," she says with a small hitch of breath. "When you texted that you'd be leaving soon, the girls dropped me off. I thought here I am getting fixed up to play the part, I might as well greet you after practice like a smitten fiancée."

And here I thought nothing would deflate my mood. I fight a grimace. She doesn't need to see that. But my act doesn't appear to fool her.

Pen wraps her hand around my wrist. Dark eyes search mine. "I'm glad to see you too, August." The mix of utter sincerity and mild surprise in her voice has me tipping my forehead to hers. I want to kiss her. I want it so badly my hands tremble.

She breathes quick and light, as though she's as affected as I am. "I've been wanting to tell you about my day."

"And I want to hear it." My lips brush the shell of her ear. *Just one little kiss. I'll be good.* "After we take care of this. Are they looking now?"

In the distance are the faint sounds of rapid-fire questions and friendly laughter. Most of my teammates will have come streaming out of the front exit by now. That doesn't mean the press hasn't noticed me.

A small movement of Pen's head, and then she answers conspiratorially. "The pack appears to be stirring in this direction."

Softly, I chuckle. A pack indeed. Then I catch her gaze with mine.

"I'm going to kiss you now."

Nerves flutter over her in little beats. I feel it against my fingertips where our skin meets. Ducking my head to hold her darting gaze, I make my voice as gentle as possible. "Okay?"

She licks her plush lips. "Okay."

I force myself to keep it slow. Respectful. Just a little taste.

Her lips soften beneath mine like butter in the sun. She trembles, a small hitch in her breath gusting over my skin. My gut tightens with hot, insistent lust. I want to open her mouth and delve deep, drown in her flavor. I've kissed her twice now and still don't know her taste. It's a travesty. But to kiss her that way would be too real. And she expects an act.

Keeping my head in the game, I kiss her softly. Once. Twice. Gentle as I can be.

God, but it hurts not doing more. With sheer force of will, I pull back. Because while I'm willing to play this game for the media, that's all they're going to get of us. If I'm ever given the chance to truly kiss her with all the lustful greed in my heart, it isn't going to be in public.

A spark of satisfaction ignites in my chest when I find Pen a bit dazed, her lips parted and lush. Without thought, my mouth gravitates toward hers, and I kiss her a few more times. Softly. *Softly.* She's just so . . . Nope. I pull back, my movements a touch jerky when I help her off the hood and then bend down for my bag.

"All right, Sweets. Let's go."

"Do you think they got a good shot of us?" The hopeful question has my smile wavering.

While I'm fantasizing about making Pen blush and sigh with pleasure, she's focused on our agreement. Like everything in her life, she tackles the assignment wholeheartedly. I admire her dedication. Truly. If only it wasn't homed on keeping to a pretend relationship I never wanted in the first place. Irony, oh, how you suck.

"If they haven't, then they're not doing their jobs very well." I have stopped giving a great fuck what the public thinks of my private life. I have an urge to flip the press off, hide Pen away from their prying eyes—my self-righteous inner rant ends with a swift kick to the gut; the entire situation has been manufactured by *me*.

What's really doing my head in is wondering how it would have gone if I'd simply asked Pen out that day at the airport.

Now you'll never know, fucko.

Tight-lipped and grim, I hold the passenger door for her like my mamma taught me, and when she's securely inside, I stalk around to the driver's seat. Once inside, I start the Grouch, and it comes to life with a satisfying grumble.

"Well," she asks me, intent. "What do you think?"

Nonplussed, I blink. "What do I think?"

So many things I could tell her.

She huffs and gives me an admonishing look. "About the girls' idea. Did you not hear a word I said?"

No, I was mentally pouting and kicking myself in the balls. Welcome to my hell.

"I must have drifted. Sorry, Pen. Long day."

She sits back, resting against the door. "That's okay. I was saying that the girls keep track of all your schedules, and they say you have a bye week in November that coincides with Thanksgiving. But March has a game that day and can't get home. Since Jan's house is close to March's university, they thought it might be nice if we all stay there for the week and celebrate Thanksgiving break together."

I know the drill. The Luck family hasn't had a quiet home Thanksgiving schedule in, well, ever. First it was my dad playing, then it was we boys throughout college. In college you're doomed to play that day, chomping down on a meal when it's done. Not every NFL team plays on Thanksgiving, so one day, schedules willing, once March is drafted maybe we'll have one.

Until then, we make do.

"You'd want to go?" I ask Pen. It's a nice idea, and I miss the hell out of my brother.

She frowns, a small moue of worry. "Unless you don't want me to?"

"Pen. That is *not* what I'm saying. Of course I want you there. Jesus."

"No need to get testy."

"Then stop thinking you don't belong." *With me.*

Pen turns and looks out the window, giving me a view of the long, pale arc of her neck. Outside the mountainside is a blur of wavering dusty brown grasses.

"I was only asking because I thought you might want to be with your mom," I put in to fill the silence.

"You forgot, didn't you?"

"No!" *Yes.* Fuck. "Uh, remind me again?"

She shakes her head but smiles as if in exasperation. "Your parents and my mom are going on a murder mystery cruise that week. They've been planning it forever."

Right. Some sort of *Death on the Nile* reenactment. In *Egypt.* "Sure, I remember."

"Uh-huh. Anyway, I'd like to see March. I hate to think of him alone during the holiday."

March. She wants to see him? Since when? In all the years of college, I never had a visit from Pen. I doubt she gave two thoughts about my existence. Now she's *worried* about March's tender feelings?

Just stop right there, asshole.

Being jealous is not normal for me. Being jealous of *my brother* is repugnant—both as point of personal pride and because he is the closest person in my life. Parents aren't supposed to have favorites. But siblings are another matter. I have no qualms about it: March is my favorite sibling.

Worse? This isn't the first time the ugly green fuck-face, jealousy, has sprung up with regard to March and Pen. I'm spiraling here. I need clarity. Unfortunately, that's going to require some space from the temptation of Pen. Fuck, but it's going to hurt.

Taking a breath, I compel myself to relax, pull up my usual easy tone. "It's a good idea. Let's do it."

I need to figure this the fuck out. Until I do, I've got to keep as much emotional distance from Pen as I can.

TWENTY-THREE

JuneBug: We're taking off soon. I'll miss you, Penny Lane!

Penny: Me too. I wish you didn't have to go. I love having you guys with me. Safe flight.

MayDay: I hate that we have to go back to class! WHYYYYY???? Love you, Pennywise! Give our bro a big ol' kiss will you?

PennyWise: uh-huh

MayDay: Srsly. Kiss him! Bet he melts into a puddle of jock-goo

PennyWise: That sounds disgusting

JuneBug: I agree; kissing August is disgusting.

MayDay: Yeah, but someone has to do it. Might as well be Pen

PennyWise: I'm not kissing August

JuneBug: What never?

MayDay: Or hardly ever?

PennyWise: BYE!

MayDay: Mwah!

Augie: Safe flight, brats

MayDay: Good game, noob

JuneBug: Take care of our Penny

Augie: Of course

MayDay: I swear to G, Aug, if you don't tap that and wrap it up in a bow, I'm gonna be pissed at you forever

Augie: March? Did you steal Thing 2's phone?

MayDay: So even our goober brother agrees? Should tell you something, bro-ho

Augie: Bro-ho? Simmer down there, mini March

JuneBug: May's colorful suggestion aside, be careful, Aug. It's Penny. She's special

Augie: I know

PEN

THE GIRLS GO home. Weeks pass. October rushes toward November. I attend August's games, and we go out for dinners so the press can take pictures. But August has become increasingly busy. It isn't a surprise; he warned me his schedule was nonstop. And, really, we aren't a real couple. What personal time he has should be spent with his actual friends.

The thought hurts. More than is safe. Somewhere along the way, I'd convinced myself we were real friends.

"No, we are," I mutter, pacing my empty kitchen. "We *are*."

But I find that I'm . . . lonely. In a way I haven't been in a long time. I want friendship. Unfortunately, I haven't taken the time or made the effort to cultivate any. That's on me. But, I have to believe a person can change their patterns if that's truly what they want. To quote the late, great Heath Ledger in *A Knight's Tale*, "A man can change his stars." I don't have to remain cosseted away, afraid to fully soak up life. I've been doing that for far too long. All that is required is action.

In that vein, I take a big breath and decide to invite Monica over. Okay, sure, she's a world-famous movie star and I'm a college student with a somewhat famous fake boyfriend. Details. We've sat beside each other for a few games now, and she gave me her number, said we should hang out. I'm going to take her at her word. Besides, I *like* her.

This is what I lecture myself on, while inside I'm a shaking anxiety ball as I text her. My existential crisis eases a fraction when Monica answers almost immediately to say yes. I give her directions, then promptly go on a tear throughout the house, picking up discarded clothes, a mug in the den—not that I see us going in there—and then clean up the kitchen. There isn't much. I'm one woman in a big house. An empty house.

It never bothered me before. But hanging out with August is changing me too. I find myself wanting to talk, to share thoughts that pop into my head, hear someone else's too. Okay, mostly I want this with *him*.

Nothing about our interactions feels fake or forced. I know this. Only, he's pulled back a bit. Not in any obvious way: He still texts and calls whenever he can. He still teases and flirts. But sometimes it feels . . . *cautious*, is the only word I can think of. As though he's catching himself when he's being *too* friendly or too familiar. As though he's mentally pacing himself in some way known only to him.

"Ridiculous." I toss the cleaning rag into the sink and set my hands on my hips to survey my now spotless kitchen. "I'm being paranoid and ridiculous. And talking to myself!"

Thankfully, the gate bell rings, pulling me away from a full-blown *rantus-paranoius.*

"She's here!" I do a little panic dance and then hit the open button on the security app. My fingers tremble, besieged with "new friend" nerves. I haven't tried for one in years. "Changing stars. Changing stars."

Speaking of stars. Monica knocks on my door. I jump like a horse out of the gate and go to answer.

Worry recedes when I open the door and greet Monica. I'm enveloped in her slim arms and a fragrant cloud of Baccarat Rouge 540.

"I brought my bikini," she says, pulling back. "And cocktail fixings!" She holds up a big black cooler tote with a smile.

"Excellent." I step aside to make way. "Come on in."

"You said you just moved in, so I figured you might not have much in the way of liquor." She stops in the hall and looks at me with wide eyes. "Do you drink? I didn't think to ask."

Maybe Monica is a little nervous too. The idea calms me even more.

"I drink. And you're right, I have nothing here but a few bottles of wine."

"Not even beer?" She steps in and looks around in interest. "I'd have thought August would take care of that."

Hell. August probably *would* have stocked up on beers if he spent a lot of time here. If he was my actual fiancé, I'm guessing we'd spend every night we could together. I know I'd want that. With my fiancé, that is. When I truly have one.

The bottles within the cooler clank as I take the bag from her. "He doesn't drink much during the season." God, I hope that's true. I *think* he said so once. I can't remember. "We ran out."

I'm explaining myself way too much. The first sign of a liar. My insides roil. I don't want to lie to Monica. But it's not my place to tell her. August trusts me to play this part.

Worry pulls at my steps as I lead her farther into the house. I'm trying to make friends with a woman I'm ultimately deceiving. What is wrong with me?

Thankfully oblivious to my turmoil, Monica slows to peer at the framed picture gallery that runs along both walls in the front hallway. She halts before an old black and white in an ebony frame, and her mouth falls open. "Is that . . . That's Rita Hayworth!"

"With my Great-grandmother Lola. She wrote a few pictures Hayworth starred in."

"I love how you call movies 'pictures.'"

"It's what they were back then."

"You look like her. Your G-G Lola."

"Hmm. Funny, it just hit me that you look a little like Hayworth."

"Thank you for that." The glossy curtain of Monica's hair puddles on her shoulder as she tilts her head, considering the photo. "I've been approached about doing a biopic on Rita. Maybe . . ."

She steps to the next photo. "Get the fuck out, that's Cary Grant!"

"With Cole Porter, Fred Astaire," I point them out as I go. "And my great-grandfather, Linus." The men are hamming it up, crowding around a piano, laughing and smoking cigarettes, as I'm convinced everyone over the age of twelve did back them. Strange times.

"I repeat, Cary Grant is sitting . . ." She gasps and weakly gestures to the grand piano just visible in the corner of the living room. "He was sitting right there!"

"The whole wall is filled with snapshots of parties over the years."

It was way before my time, but there are moments I hear the ghosts of those days, a lilting laugh, a few bars of music, the clink of glasses.

Entranced, Monica strolls along. "I don't usually get starstruck, but this is Hollywood royalty. The originals, you know? Hold up!" She frowns at a color photo toward the end of the hall.

I know this one well: It's of Pops, Pegs, my mother, and me at six cuddled in her lap.

Monica slowly turns, one brow lifting eloquently. "Your mother is Anne Morrow?"

"You know her?"

"Pen, I'm an *actress*. She's a multiple Tony winner." The exasperation is clear.

"Yes, true. But not many people outside of New York follow the theater. Not like they do film actors."

"*Act-tress*," she enunciates, poking herself in the chest for emphasis.

I throw up a hand in resignation. "Fair point."

"You have her last name."

"Mom changed my name to hers after the divorce— My father is Douglas Merriweather. He treaded the boards as well. But his career fizzled after he ran off with my nanny."

"Karma," Monica says succinctly. "Were you okay with your mom changing your name like that?"

"I wasn't asked. At any rate, I didn't mind. My father left us. Mom wanted to be a united family of two after that. Felt reasonable."

"But this was his parents' house?" She follows me through the living room and past the breakfast porch.

"They left it to me. He's a bit of a shit."

"His loss. I'd rather have my daughter's love."

Me too.

We enter the kitchen, and Monica does a slow spin, taking in the spreading wings of the house and the pool courtyard. "It's beautiful, this house. Really beautiful."

"Thank you." I heft the bag on top of the island. "I can't take any credit for it, though. My grandmother updated and redecorated the whole place a few years back."

"She did a great job. It's so restful." Monica opens the bag and starts pulling out bottles. Gold bangles chime musically on her slim brown wrists. "I just had my place done. Hired a designer to do everything. Asked for Boho cottage core. Though I think it's giving more eccentric cat lady. Which is cool. Only I don't own a cat. Anyway, I can't pretend that I had much to do with the process either."

There's something mesmerizing about the way she moves about like a dancer, chattering with cheerful self-deprecation.

"I can tell just by the way you put yourself together that you have great taste."

She's wearing scuffed black motto boots with brown linen bubble shorts and a draping pale pink T with Chanel printed across the chest in bold black. It's not something I could pull off if I tried. But she looks great.

Monica, however, snorts. "Girl, I have a stylist to pick my clothes too." With a shrug, she deftly sorts through her supplies. "I'm a manufactured image. It goes with the territory."

"Do you like it," I ask her quietly. "The life? The job?"

She looks up, her face familiar and yet still startling to see in my kitchen.

"I do." Her tension eases with a real smile, her trademark scarlet lips pulling wide. "I really fucking do."

"Well, that's good, then."

"Yes, it is. I didn't bring glasses."

"Oh, I have a ton of those." I show her the butler's pantry off the kitchen. It's a long room, surrounded on three sides by glass-fronted cabinetry displaying china, serving ware and glassware of various styles and ages. The whole room is cream white with pale marble counters and a copper bowl sink for prep.

"Damn," Monica murmurs. "People like me hire designers to attempt to re-create spaces like this, and here's the real deal."

"Oh, I don't know." I open a cabinet and pull down two Deco-era martini glasses. "My grandmother was a set designer. Her job was to help people like you re-create fantasy spaces." I glance around. "She liked white in the house because it was restful to the eye. But for some reason, I see it painted a glossy lipstick red so the china patterns pop."

"Oh, I like that idea. Sexy-cool. You should do it."

Change things? Here? A flicker of disloyalty dances at the edges of my mind, but it's pushed back by a barrage of little tweaks and fixes I picture every time I think of the house.

"Maybe I will." Slowly, I run a hand over an upper cabinet door, imagining it cool and smooth with lacquer. "Be a hell of a job."

"I can almost see the wheels turning," Monica says. "You ever think of following her footsteps?"

"I inherited her love of design and the appreciation of beautiful spaces, but I'm not sure about the talent."

"Won't know unless you try."

I make a noncommittal sound. "I really do wish I had your emphatic drive to do something. Whatever that might be. I envy those who know exactly what they want to do."

We take the glasses back to the kitchen.

"I'd say both sides have their pitfalls." Monica opens a cocktail shaker. "People like me, my man and yours? Sure, we know what we want. But on the heels of that is a relentless drive to be the best at our chosen profession and the utter terror that it might not happen."

"Sometimes I think—" I bite my lip and grimace.

"Oh, no," she says with a laugh. "You can't leave that hanging."

"It's not anything big. I just realized it might sound disloyal to August."

Her eyes light with approval. "Loyalty is a good thing. Now spill."

Laughing, I slide onto a stool. "I wondered if that's what had August climbing onto a table and making an ass of himself. Because he's not like that usually."

"I'm going to go out on a limb and say you're right. Trent worries about him because he knows all too well how much pressure they're under. And your man?" Glossy black hair tumbles around her shoulders as she tuts. "He's the number one pick. People are either desperate for him to give them everything or waiting for him to fail. Or maybe both."

Despite all this pressure, August still makes time for his fans, for charities, for me. He's on the road right now. And I miss him madly. When he's not working, he texts or calls. It only makes me sink deeper. I spent twenty-two years of my life without him, and I find myself wondering how I managed.

"Come on, then," she says briskly. "Into our suits, then I'll shake us up some liquid libation."

"I'll do snacks."

"I like my snacks like I like my men. Salty and a little bit nutty."

Fifteen minutes later, Monica and I float side by side on two white pool chaises. A floating tray connects us and holds our drinks and an assortment of nuts. It's autumn, but here in LA the weather is warm and sunny.

A breeze stirs, catching the vibrant purple blooms of the jacaranda trees, making them rustle with a gentle shushing sound. Trumpet-shaped petals fall like soft rain.

One lands on my belly. Idly, I pick up the bloom and swirl it. A subtle honey-grape scent releases.

"I need a pool." Monica sighs in contentment. "The previous owner wasn't a swimmer, but if you have the means and the room, how you gonna live in LA and not have a pool?"

"I have to see this house of yours."

She turns my way, and the mirrored aviators she has on reflect tiny images of me. "You really do. I still think you should consider adding some courses on design."

"Maybe." If she knew I sketched interiors to relax, she'd really be on me.

"A good designer makes a shit ton of money in this town," she sing-songs. "I should know. I just paid one."

Her laughter is husky and free. I find myself smiling.

"I'm guessing the competition is cutthroat fierce."

"Isn't everything?" She shrugs a shoulder, then brushes a petal off her white bandeau bikini top. "Besides, you'll have a leg up in the form of your fabulously rich and well-connected friend."

When I raise a brow, she grins. "That would be me."

"I would never ask you to hook me up that way."

"I know. That's your problem."

"Refusing to take advantage of you is a problem?"

Monica pushes the sunglasses up on her head and gives me a level look. "Your problem is in thinking that accepting help from people is taking advantage. There's nothing wrong with networking when it comes from a place of mutual trust."

"Let's just say I witnessed a lot of networking disguised as friendship thrown my parents' way while growing up. I never want to be like that."

"Fair. But the key point here is intention. A person in my position becomes very good at spotting fakes. You're not one. If I know of a situation where you might benefit, it gives me pleasure to see it come to fruition."

"You sound like August." I trail my fingers through the cool water and watch it ripple. "He wants to outright pay the taxes on this place, and I keep telling him no."

"I gather he's made it clear it's not a burden to him and he wants to help because he cares for you."

"Well, yes. But accepting his help is a stopgap, not a solution. Taxes come up every year. And wouldn't feel right—no, more than that, it wouldn't feel like my place if he was the one paying for it."

She hums thoughtfully, and we fall silent. Sunlight hits the glass in Monica's hand and the pink cocktail glows. She licks an errant drip along the rim before taking a long drink. Settling back with a sigh, she turns her attention my way.

"It occurs to me that you're thinking about this whole money thing the wrong way."

"How so?"

Holding up an elegantly manicured finger, she takes another sip. "Damn that's good. I'll tell you how. You *are* wealthy. You just don't seem to realize it."

"Please don't tell me August's wealth is my wealth," I say with a sigh. "It's just . . . not."

Monica snorts. "The good state of California begs to differ. When you marry him, you'll get half. However," she adds with another raised finger, "that's not what I'm talking about. Look, I hear you. Having your own money is important. But you're so worked up about not taking anything from August that you don't see what's right in front of your face."

"What?"

"This!" She waves her hand around at the grounds.

"But I don't want to sell it."

"You don't have to." She adjusts her pose to face me. "Doesn't matter. You still hold ten million in equity in your hands. You don't have to sell the house to utilize some of it. You just have to think smarter."

Her words swell within me, and I sit back with an unsteady breath. I haven't been thinking smart. Flutters of anticipation and anxiety war within my belly.

"You're right."

"I know I am." Her teeth flash white against the red of her lipstick. "Your grandparents gave you a wonderful gift. Generational wealth. People love to sneer at it, as though those who benefit from it are unworthy. And God knows there are assholes who *are* completely undeserving. But isn't generational wealth the dream?"

"It is?"

A strand of her wet hair slides when she shrugs. "Work hard, make money, and build a life that leaves your children in a better place than when you started? That's what we're told to strive for, and yet when we get there, suddenly it's wrong? What the hell is that? It's like society is setting us up to either fail or be sorry we didn't."

With a flick of the wrist, she pops a cashew into her mouth and chases it with her drink. "I don't even want to contemplate the shit I've had to put up with to get where I am. But I'm here. When I have children, you better believe they'll have the best of everything. Anyone who wants to talk smack about that can get fucked."

Laughing I take a drink, then look down into the clear water. Opaline glass tiles lining the pool catch the sunlight and glimmer softly. "I keep feeling guilty for wanting to keep this place."

"Because you're buying into the bullshit." Her expression turns stern. "Your great-grandparents, they came to LA with nothing and made a name for themselves in Hollywood as screenwriters, didn't they?"

"They did."

"And your grandparents?"

"Pops put himself through medical school. Pegs had a leg up with her parents in the business, but she didn't go into screenwriting. She became a set designer."

"And their good fortune grew. Now you have the fruits of their labor. They could have sold this place. Your great-grandparents could have sold it. But they wanted you to have it. So don't feel bad. Just think smarter."

We fall silent. The sun warms my skin and sparkles on the surface of the water. I can almost hear the echoes of the past, the laughter of parties my great-grandparents and grandparents threw. The kids who played here. I learned to swim here, cut my knee open tripping on the rough limestone patio one day when I ran too fast. And Pegs sat me on her lap in one of the wrought iron chairs, cuddling me close as I cried.

"Monica?"

Quietly sipping at her cocktail, she looks my way.

"You're a great motivational speaker."

Her chuckle is low and satisfied. "So my man keeps telling me."

"Well, listen to him. He knows of what he speaks." My cheeks warm as I open myself up just a little bit more to the world. "You're also a good friend."

She looks at me thoughtfully. "I know how shy you are, and it's difficult for you to open up. So what you say means that much more to me."

God, my cheeks must be red. They burn hot, but I don't lower my gaze. And she grins. "That's the way. You're a good friend too, Pen."

"Well, then. Here's to thinking smarter."

"And while you're doing that, consider giving your man a little break. I know he blunders in his zeal to fix things for you, but it's obvious that boy is so in love with you he's not thinking clearly."

An unpleasant jolt hits my heart. He cares, but he doesn't love me. The lies August and I are weaving tighten just a bit more. I want to brush them off like cobwebs, yet they're too sticky. But this play between us isn't forever. That doesn't mean I can't become more of who I want to be.

The last dregs of cocktail go down sticky sweet.

"I definitely want to see your house," I tell Monica.

Likely she knows I'm desperate to change the subject away from August.

And she's kind enough to let me. "Can you come over this weekend?"

"I can."

Her smile is easy, and somehow just a little different than the ones I've seen her give in multiple performances. "You know, Pen, I just bought a beach house in Santa Barbara that's in desperate need of some personality."

Nice work if you can get it.

Setting my glass securely in the tray, I take off my sunglasses and sit forward. "Maybe we should go there too."

"Oh, we will."

With a grin, I slide off the lounger and slip into the cool clear water, letting it rise over my head.

AUGUST

WIN, THAT'S WHAT she told me. That's what I do. One step at a time. Every game is a new opportunity. Every play is another push forward to the ultimate goal. It ain't easy, but nothing worth having ever is. I swear I heard that line in a movie—most likely one of Penelope's picks. She always chooses the ones that have lines to remember.

Winning at pro football, I'm beginning to learn, is more than a mind-fuck. I'm not in control of every player's performance. Not possible. Defense has to deliver, and there's shit-all I can do about them. But my men? The offensive line, the backfield, and the receiving core. Eleven of us are united in one main objective: forward momentum, score. It's that simple. And that difficult.

On any given play, we can fuck up, including me. The trick is to mitigate those errors. First by playing without fear, hesitation, or flaw. And if I do fuck up? Pull it back together, and show my team that it's all good, we still got this. My job is part actor faking out the defense, part director leading my guys downfield, and part performer getting that ball into the right hands by brilliant handoffs or perfectly timed and aimed throws.

We're in a sweet spot now, a smoothly running machine. It's a heady sensation. A drug-free high. Defense picks up on it as well, shutting down teams and dominating with vigor. We're now the ones to beat. Which means everyone is gunning for us.

Though I'm well protected, when I do get hit, I fucking feel it. God, do I feel it.

My body thrums like one big bruise as I gingerly get onto my hotel bed and rest against the pillows. I've done my postgame ice soak, been stretched and rubbed down by my excellent PT. And I've been fed, a nice dinner of chicken, rice, and veggies. Everything a growing QB needs.

I miss Penelope's food. She claims she's no chef, but whatever she makes me is delicious. Maybe because it's her cooking.

I miss seeing her eyes light up when I get her to smile. It feels like a gift every time. I collect mental snapshots of her smiles, hoarding them like a dragon would gold coins.

Alone in my darkened hotel room with *The Hobbit: The Desolation of Smaug* playing quietly in the background, I feel something I haven't in years—lonely.

I've tried to put a bit of distance from Pen when we weren't making a public appearance. I can't go on interacting with her as I have with this agreement hanging between us as it is. It isn't fair to either of us. Maintaining distance, however, has proven more difficult than expected.

"Fuck it." I pull up Pen's number.

She answers on the third ring. "You won!"

Pleasure and pride mix in a cocktail of warmth, and I smile. "You saw that?"

"I did. Monica and I watched it at her house. She has a theater room. An actual one with a concession stand."

"I have one of those too," I tell her, adjusting to ease an ache in my lower back. "When I get home, you should come over and we'll watch one of your old Hollywood flicks. *Casablanca*, *Notorious*, or something."

"Those are both Ingrid Bergman movies," Pen points out, clearly pleased I even know of them. Of course I do. She loves classic movies. So I watch them when I can.

"She's hot."

In truth, however, I empathize with the heroes who had to sit back and stoically watch the women they love drift farther and farther out of their reach while they pretend it isn't destroying their soul.

Clearing my throat, I pull a light tone. "So you're hanging out with Monica?"

The girls have gone back home, and from what I can tell Pen doesn't have any other friends here.

"She's great. I don't know what I expected at first, but she's fun and just . . . normal."

Having met my fair share of famous people at this point, they usually fall into two categories: assholes or awesome. I'm happy that Monica is the latter, both for my teammate Jelly and for my girl.

Though she might not see it that way, Pen *is* my girl. I can't think of her any other way.

"I'm glad you two clicked," I tell her. Pen has always been a bit of a loner, but before college, she had my sisters. I don't like the thought of her all alone.

She hesitates, and I can feel a push of tension through the line. But before I can ask why, she's talking again. "It looks like you're clicking with your team as well."

I don't think that's what she was initially going to say, but her pleased tone distracts me. "That I am."

"You took a few hard hits."

I rub a hand along my flat belly. There's a bruise blooming along the side. Ugly fucker. But what can you do? "I got up. That's always a plus."

"Yes," she agrees dryly. "There's that." She pauses, then says with clear hesitation, "It's hard to watch, sometimes."

"It probably looks worse than it feels." Probably. "I'm well padded."

"That one guy who slammed into you after the play? I wanted to punch his dick."

A shocked laugh bursts free, and though my body does not approve of the sudden jostle, my mood lifts. The fuck-face defensive tackle's late hit was most definitely personal. He didn't like our winning streak very much. I made sure to point out the scoreboard to him with a one finger salute at the end of the game. Fucko.

"I would have loved to see that," I tell Pen, still grinning.

"He wouldn't have seen it coming. I'm small but speedy. And I got good aim. I've been practicing my Bruce Lee one-inch punch."

Another chuckle escapes. "Oh, you have? Remind me not to piss you off."

God. I miss her.

"August," she sounds reproachful. "I would never hit you."

"No?"

"No, my violence is reserved for bullies." She pauses a beat, and her voice turns sly. "And we both know you're far too sweet."

This girl. She's pure endorphins to my system. Before now, only football accomplished that. And yet, this high I feel with her is different. At the end of the day, football is only a game. One day I won't be able to play. But Penelope?

I need her.

"Now, Penelope," I chide, loving our game, "I thought we discussed this whole 'calling me sweet' thing."

Only then does it occur to me that last time we "discussed" this topic, it ended up with Pen on her back and me being seconds away from claiming her soft mouth. And she'd balked.

Hell.

I can't do this anymore. Not with Pen. Eventually, she'll pick up on my duplicity. I might lose her. Either way I flip it, I might lose her. The thought has my blood running cold.

This is where I tell her the truth: that I'd like to renegotiate. That I want her. Just her. No game day kisses, unless they're real. I want the real.

"Pen—" In the background comes the sound of a woman laughing. I pause, recognizing the voice. "You're still with Monica?"

"We're going to get dinner. It's early here."

Which means I can't talk to her about this now.

"West Coast. Right. I can't remember where I am half the time."

Sympathy laces her voice. "Get some sleep."

Not likely.

TWENTY-FOUR

AUGUST

"AND YOU, WHAT, just hung up?" March's disappointment comes through loud and clear.

"Yes," I grit out, doing a set of quick push-ups. My phone rests on the weight bench at my side. It's bad enough having this conversation. I might as well be active lest I bust out of my own skin.

"Sigh."

"You don't say 'sigh,'" I tell him, grunting through another round. "You just sigh, for fuck's sake."

"Doesn't have the same impact over the phone. And I need my sigh to be impactful, bonehead."

"I don't know why I keep calling you."

"You desperately need my help. Obviously."

He's not wrong. Are my feelings for her that transparent? And if so, how does Pen not see it? Or does she and it makes her uncomfortable?

Whatever the case, I can't go on interacting with her as I have with this agreement hanging between us. It isn't fair to either of us. I need to get my head in the game and stop fucking around. It's always been my way—before her.

I finish the final round and flop back onto the floor, panting slightly. My body aches with a nice burn. But not enough. "I don't know what the fuck is wrong with me. I never hesitate like this."

"True. You always take action. As to what's wrong with you, where to begin?"

I flip him off, knowing he can't see it but also knowing he'll *know* that I am. I can all but feel the smarmy grin on his side of the phone.

"You know what's wrong," he says levelly. "It's Pen."

Sighing, I jump to my feet and grab a towel to wipe my face. "I fucked myself here, LB." *LB: little bro.* It still shames me that I've had flashes of jealousy toward him. That particular tidbit, I will not be sharing.

"Sounds about right, BB." *Big bro.* His voice turns dry. "When who you really should be fucking—"

"Funny."

"It's really not," he deadpans. "Sexual repression is no laughing matter."

"I swear, I'm about to hang up."

"But you won't. Not when you need to talk it out."

I strap a set of weighted bands around my ankles and start with high steps. "I should have called Jan."

March makes a scandalized noise of horror. "He'd just kick your ass. You know he thinks of Penny as his kid sister."

"For the love of football, can you not twist it that way? I'm fucked in the head enough over this as it is."

"Sorry. Sorry." March adopts his business tone. "Look, neither of us have done much by way of pursuing women. We're Virgin Pursuers, if you will."

I give the phone, and March, the stink eye. "Never use that term again."

"Eh, I kind of like it. Regardless, I gotta imagine it's humbling not having Pen fall at your feet by this point in time. And, let's be honest here, it's been a *long* time."

"One day, LB, you're going to be humbled. And I will sit back and enjoy the show."

"Sure, sure." He doesn't sound remotely concerned. "My

point is, that as a VP, you're not thinking clearly. Your virginal ignorance in the art of pursuit—"

"I swear to God—"

"—has you overlooking one very important thing."

"What? And I warn you now, if you go on about popping pursuit cherries, I will fly out there and literally kick your ass."

"So warned." He clears his throat, and I know—*just fucking know*—he's laughing up his sleeve. But he's suddenly serious. "You're forgetting that Pen is shy."

My moving feet come to a stop as his words sink in. Frowning, I stare out at the skyline just beyond my house. Pen *is* shy. I know this. But I've started to see her differently, haven't I? She doesn't act shy with me. For most things. But when it comes to romantic relationships? Maybe . . .

"Huh," I say thoughtfully.

"Right," March says. "Shy in that she doesn't see herself properly. She thinks she's second fiddle when she's first chair."

Little known fact: March played violin in the school orchestra from first grade to high school graduation.

"Not only that," he goes on. "She tends to overthink things—like someone else I know. Which means she's not going to view your sad attempts at flirting as anything other than you just playing around."

I'll ignore the "sad attempts" for now. Grabbing an energy drink, I sit on the bench and think. Because March is right on one big point: I haven't been considering Pen's lack of belief in her own appeal. She always laughs it off, as though I'm joking, when I say she turns me on.

"You've got to be crystal clear with her," March says in the silence. "Tell her you've been a shortsighted, sexually confused—"

"That's not how you use that term."

"—horn-bro who has no interest in being a fake-ass fiancé. That what you really want to do is be her devoted love god."

"Poetic," I deadpan.

"It's true. I slay."

Outside, the sky is starting to yellow, the cradle of mountains on either side of me dimming to dark brown.

"March." I lean forward, resting my elbows on my knees.

"Yeah."

"It's Pen."

He waits a beat.

"I know. Ain't no coming back from that."

"Yeah."

There's nothing more to say. Only action counts now.

PEN

Pickle: You doing anything?

The message comes in just as I finish up my cinematography paper discussing the utterly gorgeous use of light and shadow in the 1932 film, *Shanghai Express*, starring Marlene Dietrich. I'd been curled up in the den watching the black-and-white film, while writing down my thoughts.

Pen: sitting here wondering why I didn't go into cinematography

This film, for me, is all about beauty—the actors, the shadows and light. I'm keyed up with an urge to create something—anything—as beautiful as the artfully lit glory that is Dietrich and Anna May Wong in that film. Unfortunately, I got nothing. And, despite my quip to August, I don't really want to go into the business.

Pickle: Watching old movies again

It's not framed as a question. A smile teases my lips. Classic movies are from a world outdated and wrong in many ways. For good or ill, they're also windows to the past. I focus on the artistic beauty of them, the stunning clothes, and fabulous interiors. The dialog is always snappy and quick, and the storylines, once you get past the slower bygone pacing, are often better than we have now.

> **Pen:** maybe

Pickle: You are

> **Pen:** shows what you know. I just finished

Pickle: There you go being pedantic again.

Grinning now, I pack up my laptop and put away my bag before stretching out on my back. My day has been going pretty well, but now? This man turns a light on inside me and I find myself glowing.

My heart does a happy dance—the cha-cha or something equally ridiculous. I tell myself to be cool as I text him.

> **Pen:** are you texting just to bust my chops or do you have an ulterior motive?

Pickle: When you pull out the grandma talk, I'm going to assume you want me in the worst way.

I roll my eyes. But he isn't entirely wrong. I think I'll always want August Luck. It's a problem. Not that he needs to know this.

> **Pen:** you know what they say about assuming

Pickle: Only do it with a friend?

(. . .)

Pickle: Heh. No? Ok I was trying to ask if you wanted to hang out

Was he? Glancing back at our texts, I flush as I read them. I'd answered him literally. God, I really am a pedantic grandma. But he's still here, and he seems to like my ways just fine.

I had always wondered what it would be like for August to be fully aware of me, but never in my imagining had I expected it to feel this good. Not just good but easy. It's as though there are now two worlds: the outside one, and the society of Us. And though I may enjoy venturing outside from time to time, when I'm with him, my world is complete.

The realization makes me slightly breathless and afraid, like I'm teetering on the high crest of a roller coaster, about to plummet. If being with August can make me feel this good, how bad will I feel if he's not in my life?

I don't want to think about that. But I must.

We act like a loving couple for the public, sharing a few kisses for show, smiling for the cameras. In private, however, we're good friends. *Affectionate* friends. But there's a definite line. I should know; I was very clear about putting it there. And August has no problem maintaining that line.

Oh, he flirts. He's an expert at it, and when he does, I drink it down like fine wine. Being with August is like going on a dream vacation. Everything is beautiful. Vivid, fun, exhilarating. I'm more relaxed but also more present in the moment than I've ever been.

But like a vacation, this has an end date. And I'm not sure I can keep up with the act. Not when we're alone, at any rate. I have to tell him how I feel. If only for my own mental well-being. It makes my heart hurt. Physically *hurt*.

My hand trembles so hard it's difficult to text.

> **Pen:** Come over. I'll make you dinner

> **Pickle:** Srsly? You're my favorite girl, Pen

The sentiment has my lower lip wobbling. Why am I doing this? I don't have to. I can keep going as we have been.

And become totally miserable.

Since August has some sort of freaky precognition when it comes to my text moods, I go flirty instead. Because if he asks what's wrong now, I'll lose it.

> **Pen:** Men. Offer them food and they're all smiles.

> **Pickle:** See what happens if you add dessert onto that, Sweets. 😊

Oh, he's so cute.

"Sooo cute," I whisper, a bit weepy. I doubt most people realize that about him. What if I never get these kinds of texts again? The thought is intolerable.

> **Pen:** Give me about an hour

> **Pickle:** See you soon

"Shit." I run a hand through my hair and sigh.

> **PennyWise:** I think I liked it better when I didn't have a pretend boyfriend

> **JuneBug:** Trouble in paradise already?!? Say it ain't so!

MayDay: if there is, it's Augie's fault

JuneBug: Obvs

MayDay: Because our Pen would never!

PennyWise: It's NOT August's fault. He's fine. Great. Too great

PennyWise: I'm the problem.

MayDay: Problem= U want 2 ride him like a see-saw. Up. Down. Up. Down.

JuneBug: Gak. NO

PennyWise: She's not wrong

MayDay: I knew it!!!!

PennyWise: Ugh. That was too much. I'm sorry. He's your brother. I shouldn't be talking to you two about this

JuneBug: Don't you dare! You're our bestie. Of course you talk about it to us. We'll just mentally put someone else's face on his while discussing.

MayDay: I vote Killian James

JuneBug: Ooh! Good one!

MayDay: He's so hot and moody. Like liquid sex

PennyWise: We're not going to impose a famous rock star's face over August's

MayDay:):-|

JuneBug: She's a salty one

MayDay: What's the problem, Pen?

PennyWise: Acting like it's real makes it feel real. Then I'll remember it's not, and nothing feels real.

MayDay: (o_O)

JuneBug: That actually makes sense to me. How do you know what's true when you're lying to everyone?

MayDay: Harsh

PennyWise: June's right. It's like that line in *A Room with a View*, when Mr. Emerson says to Lucy, "Why should they [trust you]? When you've deceived everyone, including yourself?"

MayDay: Juney, she's quoting old movies. She's in a bad way

PennyWise: It's a costume drama, not an old movie

MayDay: and when was it made, professor?

PennyWise: 1985 is not THAT old

MayDay: >_<

PennyWise: >:-P

JuneBug: Anyway! How do you know it isn't real? I get that Augie asked you to "fake" it with him. But he's not exactly the faking type. IDT he has it in him to pretend. If he isn't into something he just checks out. If he is? He's all in.

MayDay: this is true. Sure he's got his public "game face" but in private? It's pretty clear exactly where you stand with him

PennyWise: That's what I thought—before he did a 180 on me! He went from mild politeness our whole lives to giving me his complete flirtatious attention.

JuneBug: it happens like that sometimes. See someone again . . . Boom! Wham! Helloooo, gorgeous!

PennyWise: No, no. He said he knew I was a safe pick for this . . . charade because I wouldn't fall for him! Then he said he'd never fall for me because football is all that matters to him. What am I supposed to think with that hanging over my head?

MayDay: Ok. He's an idiot

JuneBug: Deluded at best. Careless at worst

PennyWise: No, he's great

JuneBug: PENNY!

PennyWise: Sigh

(. . .)

PennyWise: He's coming over for dinner. I'm going to tell him

MayDay: WHAT R U TELLING HIM???

PennyWise: That I can't do this anymore

MayDay: O.O

JuneBug: If you're asking for advice, and I think you are since you texted, I'll tell you this. The truth is always best. However! August puts on a good front but he's incredibly sensitive. If you don't want him to go into full retreat, tread lightly, my friend.

PennyWise: I know. That's what's scaring me. What if he goes back to cold politeness?

JuneBug: Then he isn't worth it. IDC if he's my brother. If he'd do that, he's not worth it.

MayDay: ^ths

JuneBug: Bro

MadMarch: Sis

JuneBug: What's going on with August?

MayDay: If he hurts our Penny we'll kill him

MadMarch: What RU clowns on about?

JuneBug: Don't B cute. We know he talks to you

MadMarch: Which would B private

MayDay: Spill it, DB!

MadMarch: DB???

MayDay: Dirtbag

MadMarch: I don't think I like your tone. BYE

JuneBug: MARCH! This is serious

MayDay: IKR?

MadMarch: Why R U asking?

JuneBug: Penny *might* really like Augie, you nob!

MadMarch: duh

MayDay: And Augie obvs REALLY likes Pen!

MadMarch: DUH

JuneBug: MARCH!

MadMarch: Ok, ok. Geez. Don't worry, I already talked to him. Gave him great advice

MayDay: GASP! Noooo!

JuneBug: WHAT DID YOU DO!

MadMarch: Jay-zus. Would you two calm down!

JuneBug: What did we say about telling women to calm down?

MadMarch: Uh. To not to?

JuneBug: Now be a good bro and tell us what you said

MadMarch: Easy. Tell the truth

MayDay: o.o

JuneBug: Good. That's good.

MadMarch: Obvs. Where's the trust?

JuneBug: March, it's Pen and Augie

MadMarch: I know

MayDay: There's no coming back from that

MadMarch: I KNOW

JuneBug: Sigh

MadMarch: Welp. I've enjoyed our time together. Don't text again until Thanksgiving.

JuneBug: We love you too, broheem

MadMarch: Back at you, witches

MadMarch: Bro Don't fuck this up

BestLuck: What?!!

MadMarch: just sayin

BestLuck: I'm about to leave. WHY are you telling me this now!

MadMarch: Brotherly support

BestLuck: Go look up support in the dictionary

MadMarch: Remember to think before you speak.

(. . .)

MadMarch: And make good eye contact. Girls like that

BestLuck: I'm blocking you like that safety did to you on fourth & goal

MadMarch: Hey! BS call. I was over the line! What kind of brother are you!

BestLuck: The supportive kind. See what I did there?

MadMarch: ha ha. And you are so NOT the "best Luck"

BestLuck: Scoreboard, fuckface

MadMarch: While UR begging for Pen to luurv you I'm changing our group names to KingLuck and DelusiBro

BestLuck: I'm okay with being the king

MadMarch: I'm the king!

MadMarch: Hello?

MadMarch: Best Luck my ass

TWENTY-FIVE

PEN

BY THE TIME August is set to arrive, I am a nervous wreck. I showered, blew my hair out, changed. Changed again. Fiddled with my makeup—too much? Not enough? Dabbed on perfume, then scrubbed at the spot, terrified it would be obvious.

I paced, considered changing again. Did my probably too-tight red polo T and flowing white midi-skirt look weird? Not dressy enough? God! Told myself to stop it. Then went and made spaghetti carbonara. It's quick, filling, and fuck it, I cannot be relied upon to cook something more involved, or I'll end up burning the house down.

When the doorbell rings, I literally jump in place, the wooden spoon in my hand almost flying free. With a breath, I turn off the heat on the stove and head for the door. My palms are clammy. Has the route to the door ever taken this long? Or been this short. Briefly, I consider turning heel and running for it.

Gritting my teeth, I open the door. August stands on the threshold, big, tall, and utterly beautiful. Faded jeans hug his thighs with loving care. He's wearing an old black Boston Museum of Fine Arts T that's probably a size too small and likely from when he lived back East. But it doesn't matter. He looks so good. Delicious. All I want to do is press myself up against his long strong length and devour him.

And clearly, I've stared too long because he frowns and shifts his weight, as his gaze darts over my face. "Penelope?"

"August."

A slow smile unfurls, taking his features from beautiful to extraordinary.

For a moment, I'm struck by the reverse in our placements. How long ago it feels since he'd opened the door for me and our relationship utterly changed. Would it do so again? Or fizzle out into nothing.

I resist the urge to press my hands to my chest and simply weep. *Pretend for just a little longer. Then it will be out in the open and over. Just like ripping off a bandage.*

"Sorry." I open the door wider. "Come in."

He does, stepping over the threshold and into my space so that I crane my neck to meet his eyes. Amusement and something softer light his. "For a second," he says, "I thought we'd be playing the name game again."

He's too close. The heat of him warming my skin and making my heart strum.

"Once was weird enough," I tell him thickly.

August's lids lower with a slow smile. "Oh, I don't know. I have fond memories of that moment."

Does he?

His head tilts as he regards me. "You look gorgeous, Pen."

"Eh," is my smooth reply.

"Every time I see you again, it's like I forget just how pretty you are, and I'm caught off guard by it."

Why does he say these things? As a lover would. But then gives me a cheeky smile like he's only being sweet and not to put too much into it.

When I don't answer, he glances toward the kitchen. "Something smells good."

Food. Yes. We can eat and I'll tell him . . . I might truly be sick. I swallow hard and hold a neutral face.

"I made carbonara."

His happy expression makes my knees weak. "Can I keep you?" he asks. "Like forever?"

He can't keep saying sweet things and not mean them. It isn't right. Suddenly, I want to rip that bandage off swiftly. I brace myself against the door, then, remembering it's still open, close it firmly behind me. Sweeping past him, I go to the kitchen and start serving up our bowls.

"You want to take this outside?" I ask August, who's come in behind me.

"Sure." A small furrow gathers between his brows, but he takes the bowls without further comment and heads out, leaving me to bring utensils and napkins.

By the time I catch up, he's lighting the gas fire in the stone hearth set into the wall of the pool veranda. Built against the back wall of a guesthouse, the veranda faces the end of the pool and looks toward the main house. A beam-covered roof supported by two stacked stone columns provides protection from the elements.

When my grandparents were alive, they often used this space as an outside living room. The gas fireplace and two heat lamps tucked under the eaves offer warmth when the hills grow chilly at night. Iron torchiere lamps, procured from a studio backlot, have been here since the late '40s and still stand like somber sentinels on either side of the fireplace, giving an amber glow.

Because of the solid roof overhead and the fact that it rarely rains with any ferocity in LA, the veranda boasts two deep and plush couches that face each other. August sits at one, waiting.

I hesitate. It would be safer to sit on the opposite couch with the big, petrified wood coffee table between us. It might also appear standoffish. I don't want that. Not with what I have to say.

If he notices my dawdling, it doesn't show. In truth, he's staring at the flickering flames with a small frown gathering on his brow. Maybe my anxiety is catching. Or he too is wondering what the hell we're really doing here. I can't take not knowing.

I sit on the couch next to him. "August?"

"Hmm?" He stirs and looks my way, his expression softening. "Right. Let's eat."

He's left the bowls on the coffee table, and I set the forks there too. But neither of us moves to take them. Awkward silence descends, thick and heavy, between us.

He's hunched over, forearms on his knees, staring down at his clenched hands. I think he might be struggling too. I don't want him to speak first and risk hearing that it would be better for us to regroup, to see a little less of each other.

"Pen—"

"I don't think I can pretend anymore," I blurt.

He flinches back as though slapped. "I . . . ah . . . Why?"

"You, me. We spend so much time together and . . . it's proving difficult to navigate . . . I don't want to upset you, but . . ."

I trail off, confidence leaving me when his brows snap together in dark slashes, and he leans in.

"Pen, don't you dare worry about my feelings. You can tell me anything. I'd rather call it quits than see you unhappy."

His firm assurance has me faltering.

"You'd end it?" I ask. "Just like that?"

"Yes." The line of his profile goes hard, and he swallows thickly before facing me. "But I'd like to know . . . Shit, Pen, I thought—" He clears his throat and shoves to his feet to pace in the narrow space between the couches and the hearth. "You seemed to enjoy my company. Was I wrong? You know what, forget that. I'm not going to be the guy who guilts a girl into keeping him in her life."

I watch him pace, my mouth open, then I scramble to sit on my heels, gripping the back of the couch so I don't grab him just to make him stay. "August. Stop. Hold on. I'm shit at this."

He wings around. "I don't think there's any good way to tell someone you don't want to hang out with them anymore."

"I do! I like being with you. Too much, August. It messes with my head when we pretend to kiss and cuddle in public.

And then we come back here and it's so great . . . I can be your pretend girlfriend. And I can be your friend. But I don't think I can be both. Not without losing something of myself."

Lips parted, he stares at me for a long moment. Then, as if his strings are cut, he flops down on the couch next to me. Given that I'm kneeling, we're evenly face-to-face. August's gaze darts over mine like he's replaying what I've said and still trying to figure it all out.

"I'm sorry," I tell him in the resounding silence. "I thought I could handle it but—"

His big hand engulfs my clenched fist. "Pen, I was sitting out here trying to come up with the nerve to talk to you about all this. First, I want one thing clear. If you're not in the same place as I am, it's okay. I'll always be in your life, if you want me there."

"Of course I do." The idea of him not being in my life as he's been lately fills me with panic.

Inky strands of hair fall over his brow as he ducks his head and smiles faintly. He gives himself a shake and then focuses on me with unnerving intensity. "You're right. We can't go on like this."

Oh.

"This *pazzo* plan of mine was doomed from the start. I think I knew that even when I was forming it in my head." Softly, he tucks a lock of hair back from my cheek. "Thing is, Penelope, I looked at you, standing there in my parents' doorway and . . ."

He trails off, drawing in a breath before letting it out slowly. "You know what I think when I look at you?"

Oh, God, I'm almost afraid to ask. But those quicksilver eyes hold so much emotion. Eyes I've been wanting to look my way for so long I've lost count.

I lick my lips, find my voice. "What, then?"

"That you're so beautiful it makes my heart hurt. That I want to touch you so badly my hands shake. But that you're Penelope Morrow, and I'm not supposed to want you this way."

Oh, God.

A fine tremble starts low in my belly and begins to spread outward. He wants me. Me, Penelope Morrow. But wait . . .

"Says who?"

His brow furrows. "Says who?"

"Who says you're not supposed to want me?"

That gives him pause. "Well, hell."

"Have I told you no?"

His lips twitch, a light entering his eyes. "No."

"Do you want to touch me, August?"

The wry humor dies. Instantly he's serious. Intent. "Yes. Fuck yes."

"Then ask *me*."

His nostrils flare, and his voice dips low and strong. "Penelope. May I—"

"Yes. Fuck yes."

That's all he needs. His mouth is hot on mine in the next breath.

TWENTY-SIX

AUGUST

SHE TASTES LIKE honey. I've waited for so long—so fucking long—to know. And she's delicious. I eat at her mouth, a man consumed by hunger. I didn't know I could be this hungry. My fingers slide into the thick mass of her hair, gripping it as I angle in for a deeper taste. It will never be enough.

She's just as frantic, fisting my shirt, cupping my cheek like she's afraid I'll disappear. Never going to happen. Little gasps puff from her mouth as we feast on each other. Groaning, I lift her onto my lap and lean back as she presses against me. Lust makes me lightheaded, clumsy. My tongue slides over hers, slick and hot and perfect. I could lose myself in this. Just kissing. I nip her lower lip, slide my hand up under her shirt to feel her silky skin. I want to touch those tits. They've starred in too many dreams. My hands are shaking with that want.

But suddenly she pulls back, our kiss breaking with an audible wet sound. Her hair is mussed, breasts heaving with panting breaths. "Wait. Hold on."

The command knocks the wind out of me. It's such a shift that my head pounds before I can find my voice. "What's wrong?"

If she's changed her mind I'm going to cry. Big football player tears.

My fear increases as she slides off my lap and curls up at

the edge of the sofa. Her velvety eyes are huge in the oval of her face as she bites the edge of her thumb. Fuck. What did I do? Was I coming on too strong. Probably. I'd never been that relieved or that needy from hearing a simple "yes." I'll have to explain; I can be gentle. I *can*.

"Pen—"

"I have to tell you something." She lowers her thumb then nibbles on it again. "But I . . . well, honestly, I should have said this before."

The way her gaze keeps darting away makes me sit up fully. "What is it? You're scaring me with that expression. Just tell me, Sweets."

"I will, I'm just . . . God. I'm so embarrassed. I can physically feel little flames of it on my skin." She waves her hands as if trying to beat off that embarrassment. It's cute. Or would be if she hadn't just slammed the breaks on us. She's also clearly uncomfortable, which is the last thing I want her to be.

"Sweetheart, nothing you could say could possibly be—" She shoots me a repressive glare, and I hold up my hands. "Okay, okay. Just . . . take your time. I'm here."

"I know. You're so great. I want you so much—"

"Well, that's good to hear. Fucking great to hear, honestly. I want you so badly, sweet Pen. More than you know."

She pinches the bridge of her nose. "Okay. Just let me say this. I can say this . . ."

Really worried now, I take her hand in mine and find it clammy. "Baby. Just say it."

"I'm a virgin."

Oh. *Oh*.

"Okay." I frown. "Really?"

"Yes, really."

"But you're—"

"Twenty-two, yes, I'm aware."

She looks so cutely disgruntled; I bite back a smile.

"I was going to say, 'so hot.'"

"Oh." Her cheeks pink as though the idea of me calling her hot is a shock. Honestly, this girl.

"How have you gone this long without anyone trying?"

Pen's eyes narrow. "I didn't say no one tried. I just never accepted."

"Right." I swallow, stare down at our clenched hands, then meet her defensive gaze. "Is it . . . didn't you want to?"

She wrenches her hand away. "Oh, for fuck's sake. This is why I was afraid to tell you."

"Penelope." I take her hand back and squeeze it gently. "I'm only trying to understand why you're embarrassed."

"I'm not. Okay, I am, but I don't *want to be*. It's more I feel like maybe people will think I'm a freak or I don't know . . ." She sighs and straightens like she's facing a tribunal. "It's like this. I don't make new relationships easily. It's hard to let someone in. And it's not that I think virginity is some sort of precious commodity that I must save for marriage.

"But sex is, for me at least, an act of trust. I'm letting someone touch my body, *into* my body, for fuck's sake. That's big for me. So it was never going to be a drunken fumble on someone's couch—"

Inwardly, I wince a bit because that's exactly what my first time was.

"—I wanted to wait for someone I really liked. Then the whole awful pandemic happened, and I'm not risking a kiss for nothing, never mind going all the way—"

"Hold on." I lean forward, peering at her glassy eyes. "A kiss?"

She flushes rose red. "Ah, yes. I mean, kissing hasn't been . . . That is to say, if I'd liked someone enough to kiss them, I probably would have liked them enough to have sex with them, I guess."

A certain sort of horror blooms in my gut as I figure things out. "You never kissed anyone?"

"Why would I?" She shrugs. "I didn't date, didn't have a boyfriend . . ."

The horror grows. "Your first kiss was—"

"With you in the stadium," she finishes with a nod.

I can see it now. How nervous she was, how she'd been stiff at first and let me lead, not only because it was a manufactured show but because she'd never done it before.

"Oh, no." I run a shaking hand through my hair. "No, no, no..."

Pen's brows snap together, her nostrils flaring. "Are you upset that I'm so inexperienced?"

"I'm upset because your first kiss was done under false pretenses," I exclaim, wanting to kick my own ass. "That's on me. Shit."

Pen glares hotly. "I thought it was good. I mean, yes, it was supposed to be fake, but I liked it. I liked all of our kisses."

"Baby." I cup her face with hands that aren't too steady. "Fake kisses or not, you nearly brought me to my knees with them. But your first kiss should have been real both in action and thought."

"Funny thing is, it felt real."

"Maybe because I've been wanting to kiss you forever. It was real to me."

"So why are you upset?"

"Because, in the back of our minds, we were thinking it was for show. That's not right." I brush a kiss over the tip of her nose. "Not when I should have told you what I wanted all along."

Pen takes hold of my wrists and strokes my pulse as she searches my face. "So you don't think it's weird? The virgin thing?"

I kiss the corner of her mouth. Then the other corner. "I mean, I do wonder how you didn't burst with horniness at some point."

With a huff she wrinkles her nose. "I can get myself off perfectly well, thank you."

"Killing me here."

"August."

I smile at the note of warning in her voice. "Sweets. No, it's not weird. And you shouldn't be embarrassed. You stayed true to yourself. If you never found anyone you wanted to do this with, then you didn't." My thumb brushes the elegant curve of her jaw. "That you want to with me is humbling, and a huge turn-on, if I'm honest."

The glossy tumble of her hair sways over her shoulder as she dips her head shyly. "I do. Want you, that is."

"Sweets," I whisper and pepper soft kisses along her cheeks, the corners of her eyes. "I do too. So fucking much."

"Good." She trembles and scoots closer. "But I don't know what I'm doing. You're going to have to take the lead."

The plea affects me so much I take a minute to just breathe, resting my head against hers. The idea of leading her into sex, of being her first . . . I don't give a shit if it's base man-thinking, I fucking love it. I love that she trusts me that much, that I'll be the one she remembers forever as her first. Because I *will* make it good. It's the most important job I've ever been given.

Breathing in deep, I straighten and hold her hands.

"We need to talk protection."

"Okay." Her expression turns serious, and even that makes me want to smile; I'm so gone on her.

"Okay," I repeat. "I didn't bring anything because I honestly hadn't thought I'd be given this gift tonight."

Her smile is small but sweet. "Shows what you know."

"Yeah." I kiss her again. "That'll teach me."

A soft laugh vibrates my lips. And I pull back to meet her eyes. "I'll go and get some condoms."

She nibbles her bottom lip before saying, "I'm on the pill."

Stilling, I cup her cheeks as my heartbeat kicks into overtime. "Are you saying—"

"I don't want to wait for you to go buy a condom." She draws back. "Unless you're uncomfortable with not using one, which is totally cool. Well, that, and if you have an STI we're going to wait until it's cleared up."

A laugh bursts out of me. It honestly feels so good, I keep grinning. I love how bluntly forthright she gets in certain situations. Even now, she simply looks at me with a quirked brow as though waiting for confirmation.

"I'm good to go," I say, getting myself under control. "I've been checked and haven't been with anyone since then."

"Well, okay," she says, pleased. But then narrows her eyes. "And you're all right with foregoing the condom?"

Am I okay with it?

I fist my hands and press them into the couch to keep from hauling her onto my lap and simply taking. "More than okay. In the spirit of honesty, I've never gone without. It's a matter of trust too."

"Because someone might not be honest about protection."

"It happens." The first lecture my dad hammered into me with "the talk" was that I needed to protect myself as well as any partner I might have.

Pen rests her hand on my thigh. "And you're willing to take that risk with me?"

"Penelope, there is no risk with you."

Her smile is shy but glowing.

"This means something to me too," I tell her. Because she needs to know how safe she is with me.

She tightens her grip on my thigh. "I'm so glad it's you."

Simple words. They punch into me with the force of a linebacker.

"Come here," I whisper, gathering her up in my arms and rising.

She holds on tight, as I shut off the fire and kill the lights with my free hand. "Where are we going?"

"Bedroom." I kiss the plump of her cheek. "We're going to need a lot of room to maneuver. And your first time isn't going to be on a couch."

SHE'S LEFT THE lamp on her bedside table lit. I set her on the bed in the circle of that glow, then close the drapes and turn on another lamp. I want to see everything, and I'm guessing my expression says as much because she arches a brow and gives me a knowing look. Grinning, I toe off my shoes, then reach for her house slippers, tossing them out of the way. Her skirt goes next. I'm gentle as I can be, drawing it down her legs to bare them. I love her legs. She reminds me of those vintage pinup posters her roommate, Sarah, had on her walls.

"You're just going to strip us," Pen asks, amused.

"Not yet." I climb on the bed, resting my back against the headboard, and haul her onto my lap, enjoying the way she yelps and laughs. "We get naked too soon and it's all over."

"Oh, really?" She smiles at me, setting her hands on my chest. The touch is a bit shy but also proprietary. After waiting for so long for those touches, my body all but strains toward her.

This isn't some quick hookup to scratch a horny itch. This is Penelope. Every time she puts her hands or mouth on me I fucking melt. Imagine that.

"Why are you smiling," she asks softly.

"I got you on my lap."

She laughs. Then tugs my shirt. "I get the 'not yet naked' thing. But . . . take this off. I want to see you."

"Yes, ma'am." I reach behind me, grab the collar, and yank the offending shirt away. It flies to the corner of the room.

"Oh, my." Her expression turns covetous.

Soft hands slide over my chest, along my arms. I clutch her hips and let her play, shivering with each pass.

"I've wanted to touch you like this," she confesses, her attention on my body.

That's it. I clasp the back of her neck and draw her near. Her mouth is soft and lush. And I find myself making a noise of pure want, licking into her slick warmth, sucking the full curve of her bottom lip.

I imagined kissing Penelope Morrow countless times. For years. The reality of being able to sink into her mouth, kiss her at my leisure releases something deep inside me. I want her more than I want to breathe, but I'm good with staying right here, learning her mouth, the sounds she makes, the way she moves and grasps at my shoulders like she needs to hang on.

The room is warm and quiet as we learn each other. I grow heavy and tight with want. She leans fully on me as we make out, our kisses growing deeper, wilder. I suck on her tongue, and she whimpers, angling her head to get in more. Then she does the same to me. It feels so good, I'm groaning, gripping her tight. Holding her hips, I slide my leg between hers and rock her back and forth over the length of my thigh. Letting her ride. She grinds on my leg with little jerking rocks that I don't think she's fully aware of.

I lose time. There's just her mouth, her body, *her*.

I don't know how long we go on. I can't seem to stop kissing her. Sweat breaks out on my skin, hers blooms hot and damp. The need to feel more of it has me easing her shirt up and over her head. The glossy dark cloud of her hair settles over delicate shoulders. I take my first look and almost swallow my tongue.

Her bra is candy apple–red lace and holding two round creamy breasts that nearly spill out into my panting face. Jesus. I run a shaking hand along her tiny waist, up to those perfect, sweet tits.

"You're staring," she says.

"I'll probably be doing that a lot," I rasp. My hands aren't steady as I cup her there.

We both make a sound of pleasure. She's firm but soft, and I'm in heaven. I didn't even know I was a boob man until now. I think it's her. Nature made the perfect pair just for me.

Pen lets me fondle her with an amused but flushed expression. Unable to help myself, I groan and lean forward to kiss the deep swelling valley those pretty tits make. I kiss each one with reverence. Pen makes a needy little sound, squirming on my lap. My hard-on pulses beneath her peachy ass.

She's so sensitive. Little goose bumps break out on her skin as I nuzzle along the edges of her bra. She smells like honey.

"You like this?" I murmur.

"Yes." It comes out in breathless wonder.

Well, then. I'll have to give her more attention. Reaching around to her back, my fingers find the clasp of her bra and flick it open. She shrugs a shoulder, letting the straps fall. I watch rapt, mouth open—most likely panting. Red lace slides down ivory skin, stopping like a taunt on the tips. Pen's smile is a siren's as she slowly lowers the bra and reveals herself.

I whimper, an actual whimper. They're perfect, soft and round, the color of cream. Tight little nipples like honest-to-god rosebuds.

"Fuck." I need a moment. I can't . . . My hands cup her and lift those sweet buds to my waiting mouth. I lick one nipple, then the other. Each time she gasps, arches up to get more. And I'm lost. I suck one into my mouth as deep as it can get. My fingers pluck at the other nipple, caress and fondle those plush tits. Lick and suck. Loving how she moans and writhes, holding my head to her, demanding I pay proper homage.

I am converted. The most ardent acolyte.

"August?"

Dimly, I hear the faint whisper. I cup a breast in my hand and lash the rosy nipple with my tongue. "Yes."

"August?"

"Present." I could feast here for hours. But her touch on my cheek has me lifting my head to meet her wry gaze. Her cheeks are flushed, lids lowered over dark eyes glossy with desire.

"August, I've waited this long, you can fuck me now."

Those words. It snaps me out of my fog and takes my breath.

"Sweets, Jesus, you're going to undo me." My lips ghost over hers because I can't be this close and not kiss her. But I need to focus. This time is all about her. And I can't be distracted.

"I am absolutely going to fuck you. A lot. As much and as

often as you'll let me. But you told me this was an act of trust for you. Will you trust me now? To take the lead here and make it good for you? I promise I won't let you down."

"Okay."

That's all I need to hear. I ease her back onto the bed, and she lies on her side, watching with interest while I rip off my jeans—I'm too fucking hot to keep them on now. Taking her in my arms, I kiss her until she's melting against me once more. My hands roam back to her breasts that tickle my chest, down the soft curve of her belly. All the while, my mouth moves with hers. Kisses that soothe, kisses that cajole, that tell her how fucking much I worship her.

She trembles when my hand slips under the band of her panties. And then I'm the one trembling. Because she's so wet. Slick and swollen. God, I want to see her pussy. Spread those plush thighs and drink her in. But she's never been touched here. Never been exposed that way. If it kills me, I'm going to take it slow.

With as much care as I can, I find the pearl of her clit and run a finger along its plump rise. Pen groans long and low, pressing herself against the pillows as her hips rise to meet me. It's fucking beautiful.

"Oh, God! That's sooo . . ." She pants, rocking her hips.

"You like that?" I don't recognize my voice, it's so guttural. I work her in small circles, adding more fingers.

She tosses her head, sweat-slicked hair sticking to her cheeks. "Yes. So much. I feel it . . ."

"Where?" I dip a finger just inside. Sweet mercy, she's tight. Pulsing with heat. I almost lose it. I slide back out to find her clit again. "Here? Do you feel it here in this slick little button?"

"Hmm." It's a whimpered affirmative.

"And here?" I sink into her again, a little deeper, and her snug canal clenches tight.

"God, there. August!" She grips my arms, eyes wide. "More."

I'll give her everything I have. I find her slack mouth, suckle her bottom lip, my fingers playing. "Everything, Penelope."

PEN

THERE ARE THINGS about sex that I never fully understood. Such as how the sight of my own nakedness, dewy and flushed with perspiration and sprawled out on the bed with August's hand pushed down my panties would turn me on. I feel wanton, swollen full of lust and need. Every movement seems exaggerated, my skin more sensitive. The breaths he takes gust over the tight buds of my nipples, and I shiver. Yet I'm so very hot, like I might soon melt into the bedding.

His open mouth brushes wetly against my nipple once more, and I groan, arching up into the touch, wiggling slightly to get more, *more*.

God, the way his fingers slip-slide over my throbbing clit—my thighs clench tightly, trapping his hand, urging him on, begging for relief—and I shudder, so close.

As if he knows I'm about to break, his touch turns light, teasing, as his lips coast along my neck toward my panting mouth.

"Bastard," I say weakly before touching my lips to his. "You're doing that on purpose."

His answering chuckle is rich butterscotch, decadent and dark. He kisses me softly, deeply, and not enough. "It's better when you're desperate for it."

Hazy with desire, I manage to open my eyes and meet his gaze. His is equally foggy with need, but he keeps hold of his control. It costs him—I can see it in the tremors along his arms and the way he keeps swallowing quick and hard. But he's managing it, just.

"I'm going to return the favor one day," I warn him with a rasping whisper.

He smiles tightly. "Oh, honey, I'm counting on that." With gentle movements, he pulls his hand from my panties and then eases them down my legs. I'm too needy to even feel a moment's embarrassment.

When I'm fully naked, August stops and simply stares. "Penelope," he breathes. "You are a dream made real."

Exposed to him, I don't feel vulnerable. I feel beautiful, sexy. And needy. My legs move restlessly.

"You're wearing too much," I point out and trace a line along his chest. He has a smattering of hair across his pecs, and when I touch him, his tan nipples bead tight.

August captures my roving hand, holding it against his chest. "You want to see me, Pen?"

His hard cock strains the limits of the blue boxer briefs he still has on, pulling the fabric away from his tight abs. I try not to look too hungry as I nod. But I don't think I fool him. His grin widens. "Greedy girl. I'll let you have anything you want."

I want it all.

"Pants off," I say, earning a laugh.

Hooking his thumbs in the waistband, August tugs off his boxers with a swift move. In a blink they're across the room. I don't see them land; my attention is on him. He's so hard it appears almost angry, flushed ruddy and pulsing. And very thick. I've seen dicks before. But not in real life. And not *his*. For a second, it hits me that August Luck is sprawled out next to me utterly naked and clearly very turned on. The idea makes me a little dizzy.

I snuggle closer, pressing my chest against his, and he grunts low in his throat, his big hand settling on my hip. He's warm and solid. I love the feel of his skin against mine. The topography of his body is a revelation: smooth, hard, hot, alive. The smattering of hair on his chest, the tight beads of his nipples . . . so many textures. All of it mine to touch. Between us, his dick moves as if waving for attention.

"Can I touch it?" I'm whispering, though I'm not sure why. It simply feels momentous.

"I'm going to have to insist," he says with a small, pained smile.

I notice again how much it's costing him to go slow. He's fairly shaking now. Wanting to soothe, I run my hand down his chest then head downwards. His breath hitches as I brush my fingers over the smooth crown of him.

My gaze darts between his eyes and his cock.

"It's so soft."

He lifts a brow.

"The skin, I mean. Silky. And warm." I wrap my hand around him and stroke lightly, loving how his hips jerk and twitch.

When he manages to speak, it comes out in a ragged rasp. "Feels pretty hot to me, Sweets."

"I like this." I pump his hard flesh. "I like your cock."

"Good. He likes you too. A lot." He's starting to pant now, his head falling weakly to the side as he watches me play. Hot spots of color rise on his cheeks.

"I'll be sure to give him lots of attention."

"What you're doing is a good start." He licks his lips, his hips jerking again. "Yes, just like that."

I can feel the blood pulse just beneath the surface. He's rock-hard and yet so alive. "It's getting harder."

"You're very affectionate. He's gonna show his appreciation." August sucks in a breath and shivers. "Ah, Christ." He grasps my wrist, halting my movements and looks at me a bit wildly.

"No good?" I ask, worried. I might have gotten carried away. I had no idea how much I'd like touching his dick. It's lovely— although he probably wouldn't want to be called that. Strong and hot. Touching him turns me on too.

August shakes his head, all flushed and agitated. "No, it's perfect. God. Just . . . Too much right now."

"I thought desperate was good."

"For you," he says, rolling over me to find my mouth with hot, searching kisses. "For me, it's over before we really start."

I make a dubious hum, but he's kissing me again and it scatters all thoughts of arguing. These kisses are different too. The way his lips coax mine, playing and searching. It's as though he's telling me a story, showing me how much he wants me. His tongue is slick and when it slides along mine, delves into my mouth, I feel it everywhere. I love it. I love how he tilts his head to get deeper, the soft gravelly noises he makes in his throat. I love the taste of his mouth and the silkiness of his lips.

Half sprawled over my chest, August kisses me like it's his passion, what he was made for. His fingers toy with my hair, trace along my neck. When I run out of breath, he meets my gaze with soft tender eyes, then ducks his head to taste me again. It feels like I'm floating and the only thing that grounds me is him.

The world falls away as he maps the dips and curves of my body with his mouth and hands. So gentle. But also hungry, each touch becoming a little *more*. I reach out, smoothing my hand down the hard arc of his side, but he's moving down, trailing open-mouthed kisses over my belly. Big hands ease my thighs apart. For a second, I hesitate, peering at him. He rests his chin on my hip and looks up at me with a tender expression.

"You're going to like this part," he says. Long fingers stroke my skin, coaxing. "I promise."

"I like everything you do."

That pleases him. He kisses the spot just above my mound. "Only if you want to, baby."

"I do. But what if . . ." I lick my lips. "What if it isn't attractive?"

Augusts pauses for a moment as if absorbing what I said, then a smile unfurls. "Oh, sweet Pen, that isn't possible." Holding my gaze, he spreads me wide. My chest rises and falls with light, agitated breaths, while down below, my sex feels swollen, hot, and oh so ready for his attention.

When he lowers his gaze, his expression turns rapt. "Oh, honey. You are so fucking pretty." Hot breath gusts over my sensitized skin. "A glistening rose of perfection."

I almost giggle. Only he kisses said rose just then.

"Oh!" I clench the sheets as he does it again. And again. He could do this forever. Nothing has felt better. The flat of his tongue licks along my labia, and I groan, closing my eyes to soak in the sensation. The crafty devil hums in appreciation, the vibration moving through me.

"I guess she likes it," he murmurs against my flesh.

I grab his head and hold him there. Even that feels like sin. A warm chuckle rumbles between my legs. And then he commits the whole of his talent to the task, licking, kissing, sucking. I feel it everywhere, slippery, slick, white-hot lust. Heat washes over my skin, plucks at my nipples, bites along my thighs. I'm babbling, pulling at his hair, losing my mind. A long, thick finger sinks into me and crooks, rubbing a spot that has me jolting as though touched by a live wire.

"There it is." Slowly, he eases his finger in and out. Adds another. "That's it. So beautiful. Take, Sweets. Open for me. You're doing so well."

He presses a kiss on my clit. Then sucks it. A choked cry gets caught in my throat as I writhe and the orgasm rolls in like a great wave—something I'd read about but never fully believed.

I'm a believer now.

And all I can do is whimper, reach for him as he brings me round with tender kisses, whispering what a good girl I am, how good I taste.

His expression is one of satisfaction as he makes his way back up, sliding his long body over mine. Weakly, I wrap my arms around his neck and pull him down. I taste myself on him as I show my appreciation with a hungry kiss. "I want more." The words come out feverish, my hands roving along the hard caps of his shoulders. I'm stuck on pure need now. "I want *you*, August. Only you."

He tenses for a moment, then eats at my mouth the way he ate at my sex. We're frantic with it. Hands coast over skin. Legs intertwine. He rests more of his weight on me. Suddenly he's there, between my thighs, his dick pressed against my wet, needy sex. The feel of it has us both pausing. Inky strands of hair fall over his brow as he stares down at me with wide eyes. I stare back, my heart pounding.

It's time. I'm nervous, excited, breathless.

Panting, he touches his forehead to mine. "All good?"

"So good." My hands move to his waist. His skin is fever flushed and damp. He trembles with restraint as his hips slowly move, sliding that hot brand up and down, teasing me. And I ache, deep inside, an empty ache that needs to be filled, pushed, claimed . . . *I never knew* . . .

Soft lips touch mine. "You want this, Penelope?"

The way he says my name, reverently, darkly. I swallow thickly, my pulse fluttering, my body trembling. "Yes. Please, August. I need . . ."

A groan tears from him, and he flexes his hips until the wide round crown of him notches into my opening. It feels huge and just *there*. It's all I can think about.

A gentle nudge pushes him just a bit more. He hasn't breached me yet, and I'm beginning to worry he won't be able to. But he holds the course, working himself slowly in. His head dips until our cheeks touch.

"You can do this," he whispers. "You can do this."

"Are you talking to me? Because I believe you."

I feel him smile against my cheek. "That was for me. Call it a motivational speech."

"You need a motivational speech?" I squirm, widen my thighs. And he swallows convulsively before lifting his head. His eyes are dark, his expression pained.

"Penny love, feel here." He sets my palm on the center of his chest where the beating of his heart races fast and hard. "I'm strong of will but really fucking weak of flesh right now. I want you so badly. And, frankly, the reality of you is so much better than any fantasies I've had."

I grin wide enough to feel it in my cheeks. "You've had fantasies about me?"

"So many." He kisses my mouth. "Now, pay attention."

Desire becomes buoyant. "Yes, August."

"It's your first time. Finesse is called for here, and I'm afraid I might lose it and just plow the fuck out of you."

"Honestly, both those scenarios sound good."

A low groan vibrates in his throat. "Pen . . . I'm trying to be good, and you're killing my resolve."

A giggle bubbles out of me, soft and warm. I love this. Love that, even now, we can talk, that he can make me feel safe and joyful. I trace his brow with the tip of my finger. "August?"

"Yes, Penelope?"

"I want you so much."

A whimpering moan tears from him, and he rests his cheek against mine. "Never thought I'd hear you say that."

"Then you weren't thinking very clearly." I kiss the corner of his mouth. He's breathing erratically now. My own breath hitches. "Stop worrying and fuck me— Ah . . . Oh, that's . . ."

He pushes, the invasion thick and wide. I feel it all the way down my thighs. I feel it in my core, my belly. It's . . . He pulls back, then pushes in deeper.

God. I had *no* idea.

He does it again, and again, slowly working himself in and out. The wet sounds of us joining, the way every breach and retreat fills and empties me, the movement of his body against mine, it's overwhelming, and yet I need it more and more. My legs wrap around his hips, and he sinks ever deeper, groaning as though in pain as I cling to his shoulders.

Our breath syncs, our gazes colliding. I never . . . He's in me, I'm taking him. It's . . . everything. I moan, start to move, my hips rising to meet his.

"That's it," he says, panting. "Like that."

A whimper escapes. I clutch him tight, urging him harder, faster. It doesn't feel strange anymore. It feels necessary.

"August."

"I'm here." His mouth moves over mine, not quite a kiss now; we're too focused on other things. "I'm here, baby. You're so perfect. So good."

I find the crook of his neck, kiss and lick the spot where his pulse races. And he whispers words of encouragement and adulation. Cool waves wash over me followed by intense heat. I shiver, fevered with it. Everything is twisting tighter and tighter. My breasts sway against his chest, nipples tight and sensitive. Pleasure *hurts* now. A good, clenching pain that makes me writhe. I'm panting, babbling, I don't know.

But he has me. Big hands cup my head, cradle me close as he pumps faster, almost frantic now, his hips circling, grinding my swollen clit.

"Baby." His eyes find mine. "Tell me what you need."

"I don't know." I feel heavy with pleasure but also like I'm flying. It's so *good.* "I . . ."

He dips his head, hot mouth finding my nipple. I arch, a groan tearing out of me as he sucks, opening his mouth wide to pull as much of me in as he can and thrusts his dick at an angle that hits some spot . . . Lightning-hot lust streaks along my breast, down into my sex. Pleasure explodes outward. A supernova.

I lose myself. I lose him. There is only here and now. Feeling.

I swell outward and then break apart. A thousand stars.

And then so does he.

I feel the power of him as he comes undone. It feeds me. I come again, screaming my pleasure.

Looking into his eyes, I see the amazed shock, same as mine. As though he's thinking the same thing.

I never knew.

TWENTY-SEVEN

PEN

BECAUSE WE HAVE a hard time keeping our hands off each other, and August's schedule is so tight, I try swimming with August at his house for my workout. *Workout* is probably somewhat of a loose term for me, as I avoid doing certain exercises like the plague, i.e. running or any type of class I'm expected to join in. I tend to go for low-key things—the occasional yoga session from my home app, light weights now and then, or a long hike when it's nice out—and hope it's enough to keep me healthy. Swimming, as far as I'm concerned, is a relaxing and easy way to get moving and tone my body.

Not like August does it. While I'm content with an even, turtle-slow breaststroke, he swims freestyle, cutting up the water like a scythe through butter. With his powerful build, and long-ass limbs, he easily outpaces me, doing two laps for my one. I don't mind. It's a beautiful thing to see. Inspiring even.

I'm done long before him and sit back on the little rest shelf built along one side of the pool to watch him move. It's all flashes of lean muscled arms, brown and gleaming wetly in the sun, the round caps of his shoulders, and the gorgeous slope of his back moving in perfect harmony. He never breaks pace or falters.

Endurance.

A delicious shudder goes through me. I know very well how

excellent August Luck's endurance is. Even now, when he's busy honing that fine body, I want him. But I can wait. It isn't easy, but I *can*.

I'm patiently sipping lemonade when he finishes, gliding up to the side of the pool to pop up. Water runs in glistening rivulets along the dips and valleys of his body. I bite my lip and look my fill as he gulps down the tumbler of water he left on the pool deck.

God, he's delicious. Broad chest, tight waist, thick thighs. In deference to his workout, he wears body-hugging swim shorts that hide nothing. I've seen everything multiple times now, and it never fails to stir me. His body is art. But something about his particular art stirs my soul like no other.

With a satisfied sigh, he sets the tumbler down and then spots me looking. A gleam flickers in his silver eyes. He's on me in the next breath, tugging me off the ledge and maneuvering me back against the pool wall. His mouth hot and slick, lips cool in comparison.

Gripping those strong shoulders, I kiss him back, greedily and deeply, loving the way he holds my cheek like I'm precious but ploughs my mouth like he's fucking it.

Dirty but sweet. My August.

The kiss ends on a breath, mine quick and agitated, his deep and hard. Desire tightens his jaw as he looks me over with the satisfaction of a man who knows exactly how much he affects me, but that's all right because I affect him just the same.

"Good workout." His voice is gravelly with tempered heat. August, I've learned, loves to seduce me. As much as I love letting him.

"I enjoyed watching it."

A brilliant grin flashes. "Did you now?"

He eases closer. A big hand hooks under my knee and guides my leg around his waist.

"Mmm." With the edge of my thumb, I wipe a trailing bead of water from his brow. "You look real pretty swimming, Pickle."

Distracted, he trails his fingers along my collarbone, then leans in to press a lingering kiss there. Soft kisses meander along my neck, and over to my shoulder.

He pauses at the bathing suit strap, and his finger hooks under it, running up and down it as though contemplating. Watching the movement, he tells me almost offhandedly, "I don't think you should wear this suit anymore."

"Oh?" My voice turns breathy; he's kissing the corner of my mouth . . . the spot right before my ear . . . "And why is that?"

The strap eases over my shoulder. Helpful-like.

"Too constricting, for one." He pauses in his work and gives me a reproachful look. "What if you damage these beauties?"

Amusement bubbles through my veins. "Somehow I doubt that."

"But why risk it?" He shakes his head, tutting. The other strap slides down. "No, I think, either forego suits altogether, which would be my pick if you're asking—"

"Which I'm not."

He sighs tragically. "Then let it be a bikini." Oh so gently, he eases my arms out of the straps. "Much easier to take off, you know?"

"You seem to be doing fine with this one."

Slowly, the top lowers, over the crests of my breasts, pausing at the hard peaks of my nipples. He watches his progress with rapt attention, biting his lower lip in anticipation. I arch my back in impatience, and August, in a charitable mood, gives the top one final tug.

"Ah, there they are." His smile would be tender—if it weren't for the covetous look in his eyes. "Hello, babies. Daddy's home."

A shocked gurgle escapes me. "Daddy?"

"No?" he asks, cupping my breasts in his big hands.

I suppose I should mind. Societal norms and all that. Oddly, though?

"I'll let you know."

His grin turns downright lascivious. The blunt edges of his

thumbs brush over my nipples. Such a simple action shouldn't send pulses of heat straight to my sex. But it does. I resist the impulse to squirm or press myself against him. Not just yet. Besides, August is too busy having fun.

He leans in and kisses me just above my left nipple. His breath is warm, gusting over my skin on a sigh. "Oh, fuck, I love your tits, Pen. They're so pretty."

I know this. Any chance he can get his hands or mouth on them, he'll take.

Of course, *he* doesn't have to live with them on his body. I look down at them dispassionately. "They're huge."

"I know." He grins up at me. "Isn't it great?"

"Maybe for you. For me, it's a pain in the butt to find clothes that fit over them."

"Now, Pen, I won't have you disparaging my girls."

"*Your* girls?"

"*Mine.*" Tenderly, he peppers kisses over them, his voice becoming drowsy. "Besides, look how nicely they fit in my hands."

"That's because your hands are huge." I can honestly say I never imagined my boobs looking small, but August's wide palms and long fingers easily span their rounded weight.

"It's like they were made for each other." August beams, smug and triumphant.

Happiness floods my system. I cup his strong jaw and kiss him, pouring that joy into it. He makes a faint noise of surprise, and then sinks into the kiss, his hungry mouth giving me the luscious tastes I crave.

Cool water laps against my skin. Quiet descends around us, amplifying the sound of our increasingly agitated breaths. The slick of his tongue slides over mine. I open my mouth wider, desperate to get more of him. His big body is hot and tight as it presses against mine, making my breasts ache. I arch my back, trying to ease that swollen heat, and he dips his head down to draw a stiff nipple into his mouth.

A whine of need escapes me as he sucks. My fingers tangle in his wet hair.

August makes his way back up my neck, open lips gliding along my skin, while his hand slips below to pull my suit down my hips. It flutters along my legs and floats away. Clever fingers move between my thighs, finding where I pulse with need.

"Pen," he says, stroking my clit just enough to make me squirm and grind into him.

"What? Yes?" I tug on his suit, dragging down over that fine ass so I can grab it.

A dark chuckle huffs against my neck. His hand moves to cup my butt with equal greed as he pushes himself between my legs. The hard length of his cock slides over my slippery sex like a taunt.

"You ever fuck in a pool?" Rhetorical question given he's my first and only. But I appreciate the sentiment.

A smile dances on my lips as I brush them against his. "No. You?" It comes out breathless and weak. I'm too distracted by the way he rocks his hips, the fat crown of his dick nudging at my opening.

"Nope." He pushes just enough to breach me then holds steady. "Want to try it?"

My eyes flutter. I catch his earlobe with my teeth. He shivers, and holds me tighter, as I wiggle my hips, trying to get him inside me where I'm empty and aching. But he won't let me get my way. Not yet.

He presses firm kisses along the curve of my neck, sending shivers down my skin. "You didn't answer the question, sweet Pen."

I find his mouth, kiss him with messy need. "Yes, please."

"So polite." He grins against my lips. "Now, be a good girl and wrap those legs around me. That's it. Just like that."

With a dirty grunt, he moves those powerful hips and thrusts in slow and deep. I am filled. And there's no more talking.

TWENTY-EIGHT

MadMarch: Question. If Plankton is serving chum, and Mr. Krabs is serving krabby patties, & we ALL know it's ground up crabs. Does that make the populace of Bikini Bottom a bunch of cannibals?

BestLuck: Back in my day, I studied during midterms

MadMarch: Your "day" was last year, broho & why do you think I'm watching SpongeBob? My brain needs a break

BestLuck: Needs more than that

Penny: If Bikini Bottom was created from the fallout of Bikini Island being destroyed by a nuclear bomb, then it would fit that the inhabitants might be a little . . . different.

JuneBug: They're talking sea creatures. Obvs they're different

ONLY ON GAMEDAY 289

MayDay: WHY is Pearl almost the same size as Mr. Krabs? She's a WHALE

BestLuck: SpongeBob has been on boats. That SINK. Underwater. They have campfires on the beach. Underwater. Suspend your disbelief, MayDay. It's the only way

(. . .)

BestLuck: And shouldn't you ALL be studying?

MadMarch: We're having philosophical discussions here, old man. Go throw some balls or something

BestLuck: How about I throw you?

MayDay: I'm gonna start calling you Dad, Augie

Penny: Pls don't. He's my boyfriend. I can't cross the streams

JuneBug: WHA?

MayDay: Like for reals???

MadMarch: knew it

Penny: Um

BestLuck: ;-)

PEN

THOUGH WE HAVEN'T formally discussed things, August comes over every night he's not out of town. I guess we're living together in a way, but it's more like we can't seem to be apart and make the effort for that not to happen. And I like it. I *really* like it that he comes home to me.

The thought enters my mind again when I hear the front door open and August call out, "Where's my girl?"

A happy smile forms as I shout back that I'm in the kitchen.

It's evening now. Golden light sits heavily on the trees and glitters on the pool's surface. I've spent the day studying and writing papers—despite August's chiding—and then vacuumed the house, which is my least favorite chore. Now I'm relaxing by listening to Goldfrapp and cleaning off the vegetables I harvested from the garden earlier. It isn't something I ever thought I'd enjoy but here we are. These tomatoes are thriving because I tended to them, and I find it satisfying. Besides, they taste damn good.

A pair of big hands settle on my hips, as soft lips find the exposed column of my neck. "Hey."

Smiling, I reach back to cup his cheek. "Hello."

His mouth roams over my sensitive skin. "Whatcha doing?"

"Prepping dinner. I hope you're ready to eat."

"As it happens . . ." With a deft move, he spins me around and sets me on the counter. A grin flashes before he kisses me. Soft, deep, luscious. I melt into it with a gasp, my hands wrapping around his neck to keep him close.

I haven't fully disclosed everything to August regarding sex. He doesn't know that I never got involved with anyone else because I only wanted him. Confessing that might sound stalkerish. And, in all honesty, I didn't *want* to be so hung up on August that all others left me cold. I'd found myself annoyed by my body's stubborn resistance to alternate lovers, and its equally stubborn insistence on having *him*. It's an awful thing to crave someone who never looks your way.

Now that's changed. And there are times—many times lately—that I feel as if I'm navigating a dream. He wants me as much as I want him. There's a heady joy in that. But it's not like the pretty fantasies I had as a teenager. Sex is messy, sweaty, tiring, addicting. Freaking perfect.

Had I known what I was missing, I just might have—as August suggested—burst long ago. I'm glad I didn't know. I'm exceptionally glad I found out with him.

Clever fingers trail up my hips and snag the waistband of my panties. He pulls them down with a dark chuckle as I make a small sound of shock.

"August . . ."

My panties fly across the kitchen, and he sinks to his knees and eases my thighs apart. Now eye level with my pussy, August hums in satisfaction. The sound sends a hot thrill through my core.

"What are you—"

He tugs me forward and presses his mouth against the plump swell of my clit. "Eating," he says with a proprietary lick.

And it feels so good. There's nothing like it . . .

A groan tears out of me as he feasts. Weakly, I grasp the silky strands of his hair and hold on, hold him closer. The kitchen fills with the lewd sounds of his mouth on my slick flesh and my needy cries.

We don't speak for a long while. Not when I finally come, gasping and trembling. Not when he eventually stands and unzips to free his hard length to sink it into me. Not until the sun sinks behind the trees and we're both breathless and shaking from our exertions.

And all I can think is: *Don't let this end. I don't ever want this to end.*

LONG BOUTS OF sex, I've also come to realize, can leave you starving.

While August mops up the bathroom floor—we got a little

too frisky in the shower after our kitchen activities—I cook up a quick chicken Milanese. When the thinly cut, breaded chicken is golden and crisp, I set it on a caprese salad of ruby-red tomatoes, bursting with sweetness, and bright green leaves of herbaceous basil fresh from the garden. Creamy pillows of buffalo mozzarella, rich olive oil, and inky ribbons of balsamic vinegar finish it off.

I must say, I'm proud of my efforts. Cooking isn't something I've done much of over the years. But I've been taught how, and being able to do it here in this kitchen makes me happy.

We eat on the wide porch facing the pool. The night is cool but not cold enough to go inside. August has two huge helpings, moaning and groaning as though I'd delivered him heaven on a plate. While it was easier to make than it looks or tastes, his appreciation is satisfying.

I drag a piece of mozzarella through some olive oil and pop it into my mouth. August watches me, the corners of his eyes crinkling.

"So," he says.

"So," I repeat. He's clearly in a good mood and wants to talk about why.

"Boyfriend, huh?"

And there it is. My text confession. Warmth wiggles under my skin. "Um. Yes? Unless you don't want to—"

"I like it very much." He sets his napkin on his empty plate. The strong lines of his face go soft with a tender expression. "I like that you claimed me in front of my siblings."

"Is that what I did?" Standing, I collect the plates.

August follows, grabbing our glasses and the serving platters. "You regret it?"

"No." In the kitchen, I set the plates in the sink. "I prefer it, actually. They should know we're together now."

He comes up next to me and follows my lead. "Then why the little frown wrinkle between your brows?"

Instantly, I widen my eyes, self-conscious of the supposed

wrinkle. He chuckles and smooths a thumb between my brows. "You do it every time you worry."

He reads me too well.

"Our family knows the truth," I say, opening the dishwasher to load it. "But Monica keeps asking what style of wedding dress I like and what sort of wedding I had in mind."

"Ah." Leaning a hip against the counter, he reaches out and gently grasps my wrist to turn me around and face him. His expression is solemn. "That upsets you."

It isn't a question. But I answer it anyway.

"Of course it does." I glance down at the ring on my finger. It's beautiful, something I find myself looking at far too much. And it isn't really mine. "We're lying to our friends. I don't like that."

"What can we do? We're together now."

"But not really engaged. Maybe you should take this back."

He looks at my hand as though I'm offering up a bomb instead. "If you don't wear the ring, it will look like we're having problems when we're not. Then they'll wonder why you took it off if we aren't breaking up."

"Shit. I know. I know! But, eventually, they're going to wonder why there isn't any wedding happening."

"Some people take years to plan a wedding."

This is offered so half-heartedly that I smile before shaking my head. "I don't think we're a couple who would take years."

The corner of his mouth lifts. "You're contradicting yourself."

"Well, this is complicated!"

"You're telling me."

"Not helping." With a huff, I run a hand over my forehead. "There has to be some way out of this web."

His amused expression drops. "This is my fault. I'm sorry, Pen."

"I'm not upset. Just feeling guilty."

"Leave the guilt to me. I earned it."

"No, no. We agreed to be partners in this. That means we share any blame."

"Okay, but as partners who now have lots of sex—"

"Lots?"

"Tons. A phenomenal amount." He reaches out and draws me against him. "Record worthy."

A kiss to the crest of my cheek has my eyes fluttering closed. I rest my hand on his firm chest and tilt my head to give him better access. "That much, huh?"

"Yes." He nibbles on my earlobe. "I'm calling an audible."

"Football talk. Sexy."

He hums, warm breath tickling my skin. "Can I interest you in some ball handling?"

"Less sexy."

"Damn it."

Undeterred, he kisses the curve of my neck, his big hands roaming over my back, down to cup my bottom. He's had me three times since coming home. And still, I want him. My body sways against his as heat and need wash along my skin.

He palms my breast, making a pleased sound when he finds me braless. The blunt tip of his thumb worries my nipple. Lust leaves me floating and weak.

"What were we talking about again?" I murmur, nipping at the column of his neck.

"I forgot." He hauls me up and carries me into the bedroom.

And so it goes. We insulate ourselves in a blissful bubble of sex and happiness. When we're together, the outside world goes away. It's not a situation I'm familiar with, and yet it feels exactly as it should.

Only there's a small voice in the back of my head that likes to remind me that there's a vast difference between playing house and seeing things through for the long haul.

I tell that voice to shut it.

TWENTY-NINE

Pickle: Hey. I'm going to be finishing up pretty late. Sorry about that.

Pen: Not your fault. It's okay. I'm writing a paper now. Boo. Oh! I painted the den tobacco brown. Here's a pic.

Pickle: You did awesome. I admit, I thought brown would look off. But this is great. I like the monochromatic darkness.

Pen: your assessment makes me smile.

Pickle: I did major in art history. My sense of color is now highly educated

Pen: Oh, is it? You can give your opinion on the shade of blue I'm going to paint the pantry then

Pickle: Okay. But if this is some girl trap, I'm going on record now that it's not my fault if you hate it later.

> **Pen:** Shows what you know. If I hate it, I'll pick the other color

> **Pickle:** If you say so

> (. . .)

> **Pickle:** I'll miss you tonight

> **Pen:** Why? Won't you see me later?

> **Pickle:** I didn't want to wake you

> **Pen:** oh. If you don't want to come over that's fine

> **Pickle:** PEN. I'm trying to play it cool. If you want to know the truth, I'd rather be with you whatever the time

> **Pen:** Good. Then get your hot ass over here ASAP

> **Pickle:** God, you're romantic

> **Pen:** I've got more where that came from, baby

> **Pickle:** Sweet talker

PEN

I DRIFT UP from layers of deep sleep to find his firm body pressed up against my back, his arm around my waist, wide palm gently rubbing my bare belly.

Little shivers of pleasure skip along my skin as he softly kisses my neck, the curve of my shoulder, then back again. I lean further into him, letting my body meld with his. His hand eases upward to cup my breast. He gives it a squeeze. White cotton sheets rustle as I turn in his arms to face him. The low glow from the bedside light I left on for him spills over the bed, warm and butter yellow and make his eyes appear pewter.

"Sweets," he whispers in greeting.

"Pickle." I kiss him with sleepy languor, running my fingers through his silky hair, along the strong column of his neck where his pulse beats strong and sure.

When we break apart, he smiles softly. "Best welcome I've ever had."

"There's more where that came from."

His chest rumbles with a chuckle. "Does that mean I have permission to sneak into your house at all hours and wake you up in any devious way I see fit?"

"Describe these devious ways. I'm intrigued."

He laughs again and hauls me up so I'm resting on his long length. He's so much bigger than me, my toes brush his shins. Gentle fingers thread through my hair, pushing it away from my face.

"My little pervert," he says fondly. "I love how much you love fucking."

"Now, who's the pervert?" I rest my chin on my hands and gaze down at him. He's utterly beautiful like this, dark hair mussed and his strong body at total ease. "I do, though."

"Do what?" He's distracted by touching my cheek, and then the shell of my ear again. The man loves touching me. All the time.

"Love fucking you."

August bursts out laughing, his body shaking beneath mine. "God, I've created an addict."

"Your addict."

He pauses at that, eyes alight with something that looks like joy, and his voice lowers. "Are you?"

The way he asks, as if he can't believe it might be true. It amazes me. I'm the one constantly wondering if I'm in a dream. Craning forward, I brush a kiss over his soft mouth.

"I'm yours, August." I've been his for as long as I can remember. One day I'll tell him. One day, I'll have the courage.

This day, however, August merely hums thoughtfully and pulls me forward to kiss me again. "And if I want to keep you?"

His low murmur takes my breath. It gusts from my mouth and into his. He must feel how he's shocked me, how he's stolen my heart. August eases back to meet my gaze, but he doesn't stop touching me, gentle quests of his hands over my body.

Before I can answer him, he kisses the far edge of my brow where I have an old scar. He kisses that place a lot, though I'm not sure he knows I've noticed.

"I remember when you got that," he says, touching it with the tip of his thumb.

"You do?"

His lip curls wryly. "Pen, come on. I was there."

This isn't the conversation I want to have, laid out half-naked on top of him. My emotions feel too . . . thin. Without breaking contact, I slide to the side and tug him to face me. He goes easily, tucking a hand under the pillow while his free arm drapes over my waist. It hits me that he's giving me an out on the question of keeping me. His quiet care never fails to undo me.

My voice is thick when I speak. "It was so long ago, I didn't think you'd remember."

August searches my face for a moment, then traces the scar with a delicate touch. "I was ten. You were nine. All of us kids were outside playing around my backyard."

"You, Jan, and May were climbing trees," I fill in.

"And you, June, and March were hitting baseballs." His attention flits to my scar. "March threw you a fastball, the dumbass."

"I didn't even see it coming." A small laugh escapes. "Just lights exploding in front of my eyes."

"Little twerp could have killed you." August sounds as mad today as he was then.

"He was nine. What did he know?"

He makes a noise of dissent but then strokes my hair. "God, there was so much blood. And you were sobbing. It terrified me."

That makes me smile. "You didn't show it. You ran over, tore off your shirt, and bunched it against the wound."

"Yeah, well, we were accident prone, so we all knew how to deal with those things."

I shake my head. "Only the rest of them, except for you and Jan, just stared in horror." As soon as he'd seen August taking care of me, Jan had run off to get our parents.

There are memories of my childhood that have already begun to fade away. But not this one. August had sat behind me, his already long legs wrapped around mine, his arm tight over my shoulder as he held the shirt against my head and told me I'd be okay, that my mom would be there soon.

It was the most he'd ever paid attention to me. Even then, I'd noted the difference. And, despite my pain, I'd felt safe with him.

"I knew it would be okay," I tell him now. "Because you said so. And you never lied."

Something in his eyes dim, and his hand drifts down to my waist. Long fingers grip my waist as he searches my face, almost as if he wants to say something but doesn't know how. Then his lips tilt in a half smile. "I wasn't totally correct. You had to get your forehead taped back together."

"Details." I wave it away with an idle hand, and grin. "You made me feel safe and didn't yell at me for doing something stupid like my dad did later."

He scowls. "Well, he's an asshole."

"True." I lean in and kiss the tip of his nose. "August Luck, however, was my hero."

August's eyes narrow. "So long as you don't call me sweet."

"Well, it was really—"

"Pen . . ."

"Fine, you were a total badass. Satisfied?"

"Were?"

A giggle, easy and languid, leaves me. "Always. You slay. In all things."

"Better." But he grins and kisses me. It deepens, goes slower, a bit greedy.

My body melts into his, as I eat at his lush mouth, taking my fill. He doesn't take it further, content right now to kiss me and kiss me. I slide a hand to the warm column of his neck.

"Pickle?"

"Hmm." He nibbles my lower lip, touches his tongue to the sensitive corner.

"You don't have to ask to come over every night. Or keep going home to get clothes."

August pauses and meets my eyes. "I do look good naked. But eventually—"

"I meant, well, you don't like your house. And we mostly stay here. You could bring your stuff over if—"

The careful expression erupts into a wide smile, and he grabs my hand to press it against his chest. "Penny love, are you asking me to move in with you?"

"Umm . . ."

Brows knit as he gives me a stern look. "Don't mess with my heart here, Sweets. Tell me that's what you're saying."

Beneath my palm, his heart beats a rapid tattoo. And I know this means as much to him as it does to me. I exhale deeply and press my hand more firmly against him. "Yes, that's what I'm saying. I miss you when you leave, and I don't sleep as well. I don't care if it sounds clingy."

His eyes light up. "Cling all you want, Penny love. I can take it."

Before I can say another word, he rolls me over, bracketing my head with his arms, and kisses me until I'm weak and dazed. "I was going to ask the same, you know," he says against my lips.

It takes me a moment to focus. "Really?"

"I'm gone so much, when I'm home, I want *home* to be where you are."

"Oh, my."

"I know." He gives me a cheeky look. "I would have won major points. But you've gone and messed it up by asking me first." His head shake is dramatically aggrieved.

I brush back his hair. "Somehow I think you'll survive."

August answers by kissing me again. Soft, luscious kisses. Like I'm priceless, precious, *his*.

"We're going to be so happy here," he says.

"Just remember who asked first."

THIRTY

PEN

"NO, I THINK you should use that shot." Monica's glossy red nail points to the picture I'd taken of the guesthouse from an angle that shows the whole bottom floor bathed in golden November light. "Then these of the pool."

When we first hung out, she told me to think smarter and use what I have. More easily said than done, but I finally have an idea.

We're putting together an information packet in my new venture to pull in some extra cash. Last week, August filmed a commercial for a cellular service company and had offhandedly mentioned that they rented a huge house up the coast by the hour for the shot.

I did a little research and was shocked to see how much locations charged—and earned—for a couple hours' rental. Seeing as I have an idyllic location myself, I'm going to offer the same. Not all over the house, but the grounds and guesthouse are up for rent on a limited schedule. Just enough to cover taxes.

August heard of my plan and offered up his place as well. "Might as well. I'm never there anymore."

"But it's your house," I'd argued.

He'd merely shrugged. "You do the legwork, find the bookings and whatnot. And we'll split the fee fifty-fifty."

While I think I'm getting the better part of the deal, Monica had agreed with August that it was not only fair, but it was also a great idea. His house will earn more than enough to keep me in the black.

If I can get the word out there and book both places with good consistency.

"This is great," Monica says, peering over my shoulder. "I'm about to throw a lot of bookings your way."

I rest my head on her shoulder briefly. "You're the best, you know?"

Her teeth flash behind crimson lips. "I do."

When I pull up another picture, she gives me a happy kiss on the head. "This is good. But I still think you should keep up with the design ideas."

I'd been giving her ideas for her beach house, and it's been an interesting experience. So many times in my life, I've felt an antsy kind of urge deep in my belly. The need to create but no outlet for it. I filled it with watching movies, reading books, sketching interiors every once in a while. It never helped.

Working with Monica felt different. All that twitchiness inside eased a little more.

"I'm looking into taking some design courses."

"That's great!" She wraps an arm around my shoulders and squeezes. "But you're still helping me with my house, right?"

"Just don't blame me if you don't like it, okay?"

"Ha! I'll just have us start all over again."

"Pazzo."

"Loca."

Laughter erupts but then my phone reminder chimes.

"The game." I set aside the laptop and grab the remote.

"You have it scheduled on your phone? I'm impressed."

"I'll forget otherwise. Is that bad? Should I have them memorized?"

With an eloquent snort, she waves a hand. "Girl, please. You're watching, aren't you? It's not like you *have* to do that."

"So you don't have their schedule memorized?"

She fiddles with the fringe on her leather wrap skirt. "Eh."

"Oh, my God, you do!"

"Well . . . yeah." Her nose wrinkles in embarrassment. "This is my first long-term relationship. The others lasted a few months tops and then . . . poof! Done. I'm trying to be supportive."

I've purposely tried to keep from reading about Monica or her life before we became friends. I don't want to think of her as a huge movie star who walks the red carpet and wins Oscars. I'm afraid I'll get weird or starstruck, and I don't want that.

"I actually like football," I tell her.

Her gaze darts to mine, and then she huffs a light laugh. "Nothing wrong with that. You make it sound like a shameful secret."

"Not shameful or a secret, really. It's just that August, and the rest of his family, assumed I never watched or was into it."

"And that assumption pissed you off," she says with a nod of understanding.

"Not pissed so much as I found myself not bothering to correct it."

"They boxed you into a category. You were pissed."

I blow out a soft, amused breath. "Maybe a little."

"And he still doesn't know?"

"Still haven't told him." I cross my legs in front of me on the deep couch. "But he knows I watch now."

"All supportive-like."

"Precisely."

We watch for a while, and then I get up to get us some refreshments. It's only in the relative quiet of the kitchen that I think about how I'm keeping things from August. Important pieces of me. Guarding them like a trembling little mouse for fear of . . . what? Why can't I tell him my secrets? Would it be so bad?

We're so into each other right now. When we're alone together, we're the air the other breathes. I know August's heart: it is good and tender. He would never hurt me. But when I imagine laying my soul utterly bare to him, something inside grows hard and thick, bottling everything up like a stopper. I don't know how to pull that plug. But if I want this to last, I have to.

My hands shake only a little as I pick up the cocktails I've made and head back to the den and the game.

Monica sits on the edge of the chaise. Lines run between her brows as she leans forward, gripping her knees. The game has taken a downturn, and our guys are falling behind. I hand Monica her drink. Then sit and watch for a while in silence.

At second down on the thirty, August executes a beautiful *tough throw* to Jelly, who catches it with the grace of a dancer. And is instantly tackled by a linebacker with the force of a truck. Jelly slams into the ground, head bouncing, legs flopping.

"Oh, shit, that was hard." Monica bites her knuckle, eyes on the TV. She isn't wrong. It's difficult watching them get pummeled like this. Worse, when it's your man.

"He got up and is walking okay." I place a hand on her back. "That's what August always says, anyway."

Monica sips her drink and gives me a wry look. "Trent says the same. Still sucks watching."

"It really does."

"He's off tonight."

I know she means her man. Poor Jelly isn't on his game. He's fumbled twice, missed two passes. August looks pissed one second then rallies the next. Each time they regroup, he's giving them pats on the shoulder, bending close and talking to them.

On-screen, a shiny-toothed commentator in a bulky-fitting checked suit ponders the current plight of Trent "Jelly" Gellis. It's of his expert opinion that Jelly just isn't in the game anymore. That he has his mind on "other things."

"Aw, man." Monica grimaces. "I felt that."

Anger surges hot in my belly. "He's full of shit."

Even as I speak, the co-commentator chuckles meaningfully. "What are you trying to say, Brad?"

Brad holds up his hands. "I'm just sayin' when A and B lead to C . . ."

"Give dickhead a gold star," I mutter to the screen. "He can say the alphabet."

Monica pushes a grim smile that ends with a wobble. "If I hear this, you better believe Trent will too."

"And he'll tell you the same thing I did. It's. Bull. Shit."

A wave of glossy dark hair falls over her cheek. "I know . . ."

"You don't look convinced." When Monica doesn't answer, I lean in and take her hand. "Hey, it is not your fault."

She inhales sharply and lifts her chin. Anger crackles in her eyes. "Why is it that whenever an athlete has a famous girlfriend, it's always the girlfriend's fault if his performance slips?"

"Blatant sexism?"

"Right? Because it's never the guy's fault. It's his dastardly, vain girlfriend ruining his life, taking up all his time. And they never blame a famous boyfriend when a female athlete is in trouble. No, that's still on her."

"The siren situation," I say with a nod.

"Sounds like the name of a band or old mystery." She surges to her feet, assuming a fighting stance in front of the two chuckleheads still going on about Jelly's troubles. "We're damned if we do and damned if we don't."

From the screen comes the groan of good ol' Brad. "Gellis for another fumble. I don't know what it is, folks, but the guy can't hold on to a ball today."

"Trent Butterfingers."

With a snarl, she flips the screen the bird. "*Pendejo!*"

It's said with such verve, I fight a smile. Because it isn't funny. To most people, the men on the field are viewed through the lens of the game. They might be heroes or enemies. They'll be the best thing in the world when they make the play. And the biggest dumbasses alive when they mess up. I get it. There's a gloss of unreality about it. They aren't quite human out there in those uniforms.

Unless you happen to be in love with one of them. It hurts to see them fail. I don't know what I'd feel if I was publicly blamed for August's bad playing. Maybe one day I will. But I imagine it would be a kick to the heart and soul.

"Do you want me to turn it off," I ask Monica quietly.

She's staring at the screen as if in a trance. The camera focuses on Jelly, hunched over on a bench, helmet in his hands. Sweat runs down the ruddy planes of his face. But it's the stark pain in his eyes that really tells the story.

"I don't know what's going on with Gellis," the other commentator says. "But he's clearly going through some things right now."

"Maybe it's more a matter of what he's doing off the field than on it."

Monica's chest lifts on a ragged breath.

"Hey." I touch her arm and find it cold. "You okay?"

She snaps to attention and gives me an overbright smile. "Of course." Her humorless laugh crackles between us. "It isn't nearly the first time I've been picked apart by the public. Not even the most subtle way."

"Why don't we turn this off and go for a swim?"

"No, no." She shakes out her hands, then visibly relaxes her frame. "I'd feel disloyal."

I would too. But I'd do it for her.

"Well, there's one thing we can solve." I pick up the remote and hit Mute. "Take that, fuckos."

"Fuckos?" Monica repeats with a delighted laugh.

"It's an August word. *Fucko*." Smiling, I set the remote down. "He uses it so much, I don't think he's even aware of it half the time."

"Trent just loves the good old-fashioned *fuck*." She waggles her brows. "And how."

With that, she bursts out crying.

"Oh, hey! No . . ." Rushing over, I hug her to my shoulder and rub her back as she sobs. "I'm sorry," I say. "I'm so sorry."

My heart squeezes with every sob that wracks her body. But it isn't for long. Monica must either be used to letting go and getting it out fast or is holding it in with sheer force of will. She gathers herself with dignity and looks about, pressing the back of her hand against her running nose.

Quickly, I get her a box of tissues from the hall bath and then sit back as she blows her nose and dries her eyes.

"I'm a mess." It comes out as an accusation.

I half smile. "But you always clean up real nice."

Her eyes water again as she chuckles. "Fuck you, don't make me cry again."

We share a grin of perfect understanding, then hers fades. "I'm going to wash up and fix my face." She grabs her purse and heads out.

Once she's gone, I turn back to the game. Frustration rides high on the men. It shows in their expressions and body language. August's, however, never exposes what he's thinking. He never gives the outside world much. Already he's able to internalize like a seasoned pro.

"Where's that cocktail?" Refreshed, Monica strolls in, tossing her purse on the far chair.

I hand it to her and take a sip of my own as we silently watch the screen. "They might still win."

"Yeah," she says. "But it won't be on account of Trent. That's your man's doing. He's reining them in."

Despite the somber mood, pride swells within my chest. He absolutely is. I know August is pulling them together and holding on to this game by sheer will and determination. It's incredibly hard to do. No one will be questioning his commitment or "wild" behavior now.

He doesn't need me to be his fiancée anymore. I doubt he ever really did. He just needed the chance to settle in.

"Trent was at the top of his game before he met me." Monica sips her cocktail and watches the game dispassionately. "Best of the best, is what they called him. A fucking football god."

"He still is. One game does not make a career."

Her gaze slides to mine with quiet worry. "He's been off for four games. *Four.* That's a pattern." The limoncello spritz sloshes in her glass as she uses it to point toward the TV. "The people who run this business are all about patterns."

"*Is* something on his mind?"

Monica shrugs. "Won't tell me. Says he's fine. But I know he isn't."

"Well, we both know it's not you."

"I don't help either." Gold hoop earrings flash as she shakes her head. "Everywhere we go we're watched, commented upon."

The "Monica effect" as the press calls it, is a phenomenon I never fully grasped until I was drawn into it.

At every game we attend, whenever there's a big play or even discussion of August or Jelly, a multitude of telephoto lenses unerringly swing toward our box. Mainly, they want shots of Monica reacting, Monica smiling, dancing up and down in celebration, whatever they can get. As I'm invariably next to her, and the apparent fiancée of golden boy Luck, I get a fair amount of attention too.

Why anyone would care or need to see our reactions every other damn play is beyond me. I figure they'll get bored. Eventually.

Monica used to be more pragmatic about it. *I sell seats*, she'd told me one game when the cameras, yet again, pointed our way. *They figure, show me, and others will follow.*

It's fine. Whatever. I hate it. But I love Monica. And August . . . well, every day with him is a gift as far as I'm concerned. Now, however, I'm seeing that buildup of attention crushing my friend's heart. We can tell ourselves the pain is worth the gain but actually living through it takes its toll.

As the game plays on, Monica worries her lip with her teeth. "I'm taking a role in England. Starts up in two months, but maybe I should head over early, get settled in, and let all this . . ." She waves a hand at the screen. "Settle down."

"You want to leave now? Won't that make it look like these assholes are right?"

"Maybe I need a little distance. Maybe I want easy."

"Okay."

"Relationships are hard enough as it is. Add fucking fame to it and suddenly the world has front row seats." She scowls at the TV. "Penny, my friend. Think long and hard about this life. Because it's never going to be easy and it's never going to be normal."

I'm not nor ever will be famous like Monica. But August is. Hell, his smiling face pops up during a commercial break as he uses all that Luck charm to sell a sports drink. It's followed by another one of him throwing a sub like a football. Jelly catches it and takes a huge bite. Together, they tell us it's better to eat fresh.

I'll always share him with football, with the public.

"What's normal anyway?" I say half to myself. "And why are we all trying to be it?"

Monica eyes me for a long moment. Perhaps she understands I need convincing as well. The shadows clear from her eyes as she nudges my shoulder. "Beats me."

The woman is a good actress but not that good.

"Look," I say carefully. "I've heard everything you said. You have to follow your heart here. But, before you do anything, I think you should talk to Trent about this. Don't leave him without telling him how you feel."

She ducks her head and studies the carpet. When she looks back, her expression is resolute. "You give good advice, Pen. Are you going to take it for yourself?"

This shocks me enough to set me back on my heels. For all Monica knows, August and I are a newly engaged couple. Why would I need to confess feelings?

She makes a soft noise of annoyance. "I wouldn't be a very good actress if I couldn't see it in others. Or read body language. I don't know what's going on between you and August. You're obviously crazy about each other. You've been engaged for months, and yet when I ask about the wedding you act like you've been caught stealing. Half the time I expect you to bolt from the room. Not the actions of a woman who wants to get married."

What can I say? I'm stuck in a web of my own making. If I want out, I'll have to confess all. Not just to our friends but to August too. He hasn't said he loves me, but he's obviously deeply into me. Do words of love really matter? If they don't, then why is it so hard to say them?

"It's complicated," I say to Monica.

She snorts without rancor, but instead sounds sad. "Isn't it just?"

AUGUST

LOSING IS NOT as fun as winning. Obviously. But there are different ways to lose. There's total annihilation in which everything falls apart and the other team kicks your ass up and down the field. Demoralizing as fuck. There's loss of confidence, like a slowly deflating balloon and you go from being far ahead to just . . . not. There's the "what the fuck, that was a shit call and now we've lost by mere points and what the fuck, where's the justice?" Or perhaps the good old, "we just didn't bring our game to the field and got our lazy asses served to us."

So many ways with the same outcome: defeat.

Over the years, I contemplated which type of loss is worse—aside from annihilation, of course, because that's always going to be the king of all loss. Regardless, I've never been able to swallow defeat easily.

Today's loss should be a mild sort of pain. We did well, it was by inches, and my personal performance was on point. But in a strange way, it cuts deeper. Because we *should* have won.

The game was ours. Until Jelly began to fall apart. Not in a subtle way but an all-out fucking mess. It hurt to see, and it was frustrating as hell as a teammate.

The truth of this shows in the dark, irritable looks the guys send him as we shower and get dressed in veritable silence. Grumbles abound.

One of the TVs set high on the wall of the dressing area plays back our not-so-greatest hits while a talking head implies that Jelly's performance might be due to his personal relationship.

Jelly's neck tightens but he doesn't look up from buttoning up his shirt.

The man appears so broken, I flinch.

"Turn that off, will you?" I say to one of the staff aids near the TV controls.

Rhodes huffs under his breath. "Truth hurts, huh?"

I raise a mild brow. "Everyone in this room could fill a reel of fuckups. Or did I imagine last year's playoff game you starred in?"

Rhodes's head jerks up, his nostrils flaring. We stare each other down.

"I can get on this bench and do a chicken dance right now," I threaten.

His lips press together, then he snorts. "Man . . . You're right." He grabs a bottle of his cologne and begins spritzing. "Then again, that was off the field."

"Bro, let it go," Carter says, shutting his locker. "That shit helps no one."

Rhodes shrugs, still sullen.

"And chill with the perfume. It's like a scent bomb up in here. Gives me a fucking headache."

A chorus of "amens" ring out.

Irate, Rhodes glares around. "It's cologne, not perfume. And ya'll salty because you have no class."

"The difference between cologne and perfume," I tell him, "is simply the amount of fragrance oil included in the mix. Cologne has about two to four percent, whereas perfume can go anywhere from ten to forty-five percent in concentration." I glance at the bottle he's set on his locker shelf. "That, my friend, is perfume. But call it cologne if it makes you feel more manly."

They all stare at me.

I shrug. "Twin sisters and a mom. All of them love perfume. And I pay attention, fuckos."

Carter gives me a bland look. "They gave you shit for calling it cologne too, didn't they?"

"Fuck yes, they did." I grin at the memory. "Then hid my body spray after the first use, on account of it being a 'biohazard.'"

Rhodes starts laughing.

"I don't care what it's called," Carter grumps. "Too much is too much. Reminds me of my freshman roommate. Bitch sprayed that shit all over himself like it'd grant wishes. Made me high half the time."

"My roommate too," says Jenkins, a defensive end. "Stink lasted forever. Control, brother. *Control.*"

"It's a fucking epidemic," Mario Christiane, a tackle, adds. "Bombing dorm rooms around the country."

Williams runs a brush over his hair. "They say 'cologne' is the new vape."

"Truth."

"The cheap stuff is the worst. Sticks around like my mama's memory."

"I know y'all ain't calling my *perfume* cheap."

"We *are*," shouts everyone.

Rhodes retaliates by spraying some more on himself—to much groaning. "Clowns. Women always ask me what I'm wearing because it smells so good."

"They probably asking what you're wearing so they know what to avoid," Mario says.

Williams nods. "Too polite to up and say, 'What is that dead flower funk?'"

Still razzing each other, the team begins to trickle out of

the locker room. I linger behind because Jelly hasn't moved. And, frankly, I'm not looking forward to the presser. I have no problem saying my cliché lines when we lose. But I don't want to talk ill of Jelly, and I know they'll try their best to get me to point the finger at him. Why this makes for good copy, I don't know. I never find those interviews, whether it's for a loss or a win, informative.

"You didn't have to speak up for me," he says, breaking the silence. He's still staring off, head slightly down and away. "I can take it."

"I know you can. But you're my teammate. We have each other's backs."

"I didn't have y'all's backs today. Or the last few games."

"Well, no." I rub my stiff neck. "Got yourself into a bit of bad mojo is all."

A heaving sigh breaks free, and he sits hard on the bench, resting his head in his hands. "I'm sorry."

I take a seat next to him. "Not long ago, you told me all we can do is try our hardest."

"That's just it." Despair colors his voice. "I don't know if I can."

Glancing at the dark TV, I wonder if there's some truth in the speculation. Because this feels personal. "What's going on, Jells?"

He swallows thickly with a clicking sound. "My high school coach is dying. He practically raised me. Got me out, held me up."

"Hell."

Jelly clenches his fists. "And there's nothing I can do. Can't even be with him. Gotta play, you know? Game goes on."

Every one of us knows this. It's what we're taught, from the moment we picked up a ball as little tykes. Every single one of us has missed key moments in our loved ones' lives because of the game. It sucks, but it's also so engrained in us that we stuff regret and sorrow down deep.

When Jan crashed, I remember being grateful that my season

was done. Because it meant I could be there with him. It's all kinds of fucked-up.

"I'm sorry, Jells."

Dully he acknowledges this with a chin dip. Tears gloss over his eyes and he blinks rapidly. "I need to suck it up, I know this. But it's been . . . hard. He's my family. I ain't got no one else . . ." He blows out a sharp breath but slumps forward, bracing his arms on his knees.

"I don't want to make light of that bond, but I want you to hear me when I say, you got me too." I lean into him until our sides touch.

"Means a lot to me, Rook."

"And you got Monica."

Jelly closes his eyes and fists his hands tightly. "I'm thinking of taking a break with Monica."

That brings me up short. "T, no. Why the hell would you do that?"

"She doesn't need this heat. Hell, they're already blaming her for my fuckups."

"And you'll just prove those assholes right if you do this. She loves you. Don't break her heart and yours."

He opens his eyes and looks at me from over his shoulder. "How would you feel if it was your girl they sat around blaming? If you saw her hiding tears? Still want to subject her to that?"

It would kill me. But the thought of letting Penelope go? No. No way. That would most definitely kill me.

You'd keep her even if this life made her miserable?

Gritting my teeth, I work through the surprising burst of rage the hypotheticals create inside me. This life I've chosen, it has highs that feel like the best drug on earth. And lows that can break you. It's every player's job to find a balance. Peace.

Penelope is my peace.

"I think . . ." I say slowly, "if you love this woman, really love her, you've got to talk this out with her and let her choose."

We're silent for a long moment. Then Jelly speaks, his voice sandy with emotion. "Maybe that's the problem. What if she chooses to go?"

And there it is: The problem we both have. The one I don't have an answer to. Because what if?

THIRTY-ONE

PEN

AFTER OUR GUYS lost—by one stinking point via field goal—Monica had left, subdued and agitated. The game had ended late on the East Coast, and I hadn't gotten a chance to talk to August aside from a text he sent, telling me he'd be back tonight.

I go to class and find myself in the fishbowl of attention. The loss seems to have the effect of amplifying the usual stares. *It's just a small part of being his girl.* I repeat this to myself as I walk across campus and am subjected to the occasional catcall or stares. I can handle it. I've spent my whole life building walls around myself and being content as a party of one. Whenever it feels like too much, I simply recede into my imagination. It's as easy as breathing.

It's a bright and clear autumn day, something to appreciate. I drift in my own little world where I contemplate the lecture I just heard in class, what I want to make for dinner, the way August's toned belly bunches just so when I nibble on his . . .

"Penelope!" A finger taps at my shoulder just hard enough to really feel.

I blink out of my fog and see Jessica from one of my classes. "Sorry?"

She makes a face but pushes a smile. "I'd been calling your name forever."

"I was drifting."

"Clearly."

We walk together for a few paces before she speaks again. "You done with classes for the day?"

"Yes."

"You're on your way home?" She leaves the question sort of dangling in the air.

I realize I have to catch on here, but I'm fairly terrible at knowing how to act when people pop up without warning.

"That's the plan . . . Did you need something?"

Her golden hair sways as she shakes her head. I can see the exasperation in her eyes. But it's equally clear she doesn't want it to show. "I was wondering if you wanted to go over to Ackerman and get something to eat?"

Oh. She wants to be friends.

Discomfort wars with soft, floating hope. I find I like having friends. But I'm also wary. If Jessica hadn't brought up August when we first met or questioned how he was in bed, I might be a little less cagey. But now I can't help worrying if this is about getting to know me, or August. After all, we've been in classes together for going on four years and have never spoken. But maybe she's shy like me and . . .

"Penelope?" She frowns, and it's obvious I've taken too long to respond. "I mean, it's cool if you have to go. If I had August Luck waiting for me at home, I'd be booking it too."

"He isn't waiting at home. He's at an away game."

She brightens. "That's right, he is. Tough loss. How is it? Having to share him with the public?"

I don't want to talk about August. We're almost at my bike. It's just around the next corner. If I can get there, it will be easy to ride away—

The blow hits me with the force of a punch on my lower right shoulder. It's so hard and fast, I stumble forward, a guttural cry tearing from me as I fall. My knees hit the pavement with bone-jarring pain, hands slapping on the rough surface to brace myself.

Dimly, I hear Jessica's shout, but my ears are ringing, my body throbbing with a sort of muffled horror. I've been hit. Something hit me. I don't even know what. My shoulder pulses in pain.

Jessica is at my side, blue eyes wide and shocked. "Oh, my God, are you okay?"

"What . . ." I lick my dry lips. They're trembling so badly I can't coordinate them enough to form words.

"Some dickhead threw a sub at you." She's awkwardly petting my other shoulder, her gaze darting from me to just behind.

What?

I'm shaking now, hard, then soft, like my body can't decide what to do. My hair hangs over my face, obscuring my vision. But then my focus comes back online, and I see the slimy remnants of what looks like a cold-cut sub scattered on the ground and, just underneath, the wrapper of the sandwich shop August promoted in a commercial last night. A slab of limp pickle rests near my knee. The ignominious sight tears a sob from deep within my chest.

Shaking, I press a hand to my mouth, and Jessica gingerly helps me up. A crowd has gathered, not many but enough. People look around confused or stare with pity.

Someone's asking who did it. Others are baffled. Jessica says something about it coming out of nowhere. No one saw anything but me fall.

Slowly I straighten and then wince as the pain in my shoulder throbs. The violence of it. The ugliness. Bits of sandwich, mayo, and lettuce cling to my hair. I feel sick.

"You should file a report." Jessica bends down and picks up something from the debris. It's a hand-size slab of greasy granite. "They put a fucking rock in it!"

I swallow with difficulty. "Just get me to my bike."

"Sure." She's surprisingly gentle now, holding my helmet for me as I grab my pack.

It takes effort but I keep my head high and focus straight ahead. A few phones are out and pointed my way. Fuck them.

I'll get to my bike, get home. I don't know if I can ride. My shoulder hurts. I have my leather riding jacket on, which padded some of the blow. How bad would it have been if I hadn't?

My questions scatter like leaves when we round the corner and I spot my bike.

"Oh, no." Jessica's horrified whisper has the clarity of crystal.

Shock has me halting. My body locks up, skin prickling, heart squeezing so hard it hurts. The nausea I've been holding in surges thick and oily up my throat.

In the shadows near the hedge wall where I'd left it parked is my bike, lying on its side like a corpse. It's trashed. Tires punctured and flat, leather seat slashed with the stuffing coming out in yellow white clumps. Glass glitters on the ground, remnants from the smashed instrument panel and headlight. The fenders and tailpipe are dented.

But what really gets my attention. What makes the blood drain from my face and has me weaving with the urge to collapse and cry, is the message scrawled across the fuel tank cover in ugly neon spray paint: Luck Sucks!

THIRTY-TWO

AUGUST

AFTER THE TALK with Jelly, I'd been subdued and low on the trip home. Oddly, though, as soon as I see the glittering sea of LA spreading out in the darkness from the plane window my mood begins to lift. I'm tired, aching, and a bit hungry, but I'm home.

Coming home from a game has never made me downright giddy before. But I swear, I'm grinning as I head down the drive and see the glowing lights of the house. Just the sight of it makes me feel good. Everything relaxes. I'm home. I can shut away the world and just be.

It isn't the house that makes me feel this way. It's who's in it. Penelope is my home. And I'm so fucking happy to be back, I don't bother with the garage but pull up to the front door and park. Grabbing my gear, I'm practically skipping up the steps—yes, skipping. Look at me now, a total goner.

The house smells of the vanilla peach candles Pen likes to burn at night, and something warm and savory.

"Sweets? Where you at?" The kitchen is empty, but there's a big pot on the stove. A quick look under the lid tells me it's some sort of stew. Would it be bad to take a taste? Food denial has never been my strong point. I grab a spoon, sneak a bite, and groan.

Beef stew. Rich, dark, tender stew. My girl can cook. Speaking of...

"Pen?"

The lamps are lit about the house, spreading pools of warm light around the space. Ella Fitzgerald's butter-sweet voice croons about thinking of her love night and day. If it weren't for the fact that the music is coming from strategically placed house speakers, I might as well have stepped back in time.

But I don't see Pen. She's not in the bedroom. I leave my gear by the hall that leads to the closet and go in search of my girl.

I find her in the laundry room. She's in one of the loose sleep Ts she likes to wear at home, made of a soft fabric that flows over her curves like milk and flutters around her thighs. Hunched over the work counter, she balances on one leg in tree pose—my girl, I've come to find out, does yoga—and scrubs at something with frowning focus.

"There you are." My heart says the same thing: *There you are.*

She's so pretty it hurts. Glossy nut-brown hair tumbles and sways around her shoulders. The faint scent of shampoo lingers in the air, and I know she's just had a shower. Next time, I'll join her.

But she still hasn't acknowledged me.

"Penny love." I touch her shoulder.

And she explodes, yelping and swatting out like I'm an evil fly intent on mayhem. It startles me as well, and I jump back.

"Whoa. Pen!"

She halts, catching sight of me and her fear deflates on a gasp. "Jesus." She presses a hand to her heart. "August, you scared the hell out of me."

"Got that." Smiling, I pull her close. "Sorry, baby."

She expels a shaking breath and leans against me, laughing weakly. "Shit." Her nose nuzzles my neck. "What the hell, Luck? You can't go sneaking up on me."

Gently, I run a hand over her hair. "I called your name. Right behind you."

"Oh."

"Hey, but if I was a killer fly, you'd have got me good."

"Shut up." She punches my ribs lightly before snuggling close and wrapping her arms around my waist. A small sigh, and then her body softens against mine, warm and curved. Tenderness squeezes in my chest. I cup her head to my shoulder and breathe her in. It's what I've been waiting for.

"You have a good day?" I ask.

It's as if the question ripples through her and she stiffens on the impact. Before I can wonder why, she answers. "Sure."

"Sure" feels a little forced. I pull back enough to meet her eyes, but she steps out of my hold and smiles up at me. "Good flight?"

"Uh. Yeah. It was okay."

Something's off. But I can't place what.

"You made stew," I say for a lack of anything better.

"I made it last week. Heated it up for tonight."

"Well, I appreciate it."

"Sure."

Hmm. Two "sures."

"You okay?" I ask, glancing around. "What were you cleaning?"

A dark garment of some kind lies crumpled on the counter, half draped into the wash sink.

"Clothes." Briskly, she rubs her hands on her thighs and moves past me, heading for the bedroom. "You want to eat now? Or wait until after you shower?"

I stroll after her, hands shoved in my jeans pockets. "I can wait."

She's fluttering around, picking up a pair of socks from the floor, then heading for my bag as if she might soon put it away. Frowning, I ease myself between her and the bag.

"Pen. What's wrong?"

The winged curves of her brows draw together. "Why, does something have to be wrong?"

Having some experience living with my mom and sisters, I feel like this might be a trap. That, or some kind of test that I'm failing. Because something's definitely off, and she's not telling me. Shifting my feet I debate the answer.

"No," I say carefully. "I'm just really fucking happy to be home."

"I'm happy you're here too." She says this as she deftly rolls the socks into a ball and chucks them toward the closets.

"Yeah, see, you don't exactly appear happy right now."

For a second, I swear her lower lip wobbles. But her chin wings up and she meets my gaze with those big dark eyes that usually shine but now look dull.

"Because not everyone expresses happiness the same way. In fact, not everyone has it in them to be happy at all times. Some of us have down times."

"Some of us?" It comes out a choked laugh. What the fuck? Seriously, what is going on? I've never seen this side of her.

Maybe she's hormonal. I immediately swat that idea aside. If she is, asking will get my balls crushed. That much I know.

"Are you suggesting I don't have bad moods?" I say instead.

"No, yes." She waves a hand in the air. "You know what pisses me off?"

"Not right now, no." Hand to God, I'm fucking baffled at this point.

"You're so happy!" It explodes out of her like an accusation.

I blink down at her, rooted to the spot by confusion. "My happiness pisses you off?"

"No! Yes! Argh!" Again she flings out her arms, and then starts to pace. "For twenty-odd years, I thought I knew who you were. But that August Luck was even-tempered and well-focused on his sport. He did not go around all happy-go-lucky. He didn't smile at the drop of a hat!" At this she halts, putting the bed between us, and points a finger in my direction like I'm exhibit A. "So I have to conclude that I never truly saw you."

She stands there, arms crossed, chest heaving. Sparks shine

in her eyes, and I swear, even that turns me on. Or it would if I didn't feel like I've just been blindsided and left on the proverbial ground.

I have no idea why she's saying all this now, but it hurts. More than that, it pisses me off. "Boy, when you're wrong, you just go all-out wrong, don't you?"

"What?" Her shocked tone almost makes me laugh.

Almost.

"Let me see if I've got this straight." I hold up a hand to count my so-called transgressions. "You've always viewed me a certain way, and it didn't include this 'happy' me, and because of that, it's your *conclusion* that I've been . . . What, hiding myself from you before? Is that it?"

"Well . . . I . . ." Her gaze darts away then back as if she's valiantly trying to hold on to her moral ground. Not happening.

"Did it ever fucking occur to you that the reason you see me so happy now, the reason I smile, as you say, at the drop of a hat, is because of you!"

The shout echoes between us, and she flinches. And I don't want to feel bad about that. Not now when anger and hurt pummel my gut.

"Seriously, Pen? Is this denial or delusion? Either way, you're now pissing *me* off!" I run my hands through my hair. "How the hell can't you see it?"

She frowns. Confused and flustered.

I throw out an imploring hand. "I fucking light up whenever you're near. My 'happiness' is tied directly to you, and you refuse to see it!"

Her brows snap together. "Stop air quoting my words back to me!"

"That's all you have to say?"

Pen has the grace to flush. "I'm thinking."

"Oh, now she thinks."

Glaring, she looks away. "Your sarcasm sucks."

"Yeah? Well . . ." I got nothing. I'm drained.

"August?"

"What?" It comes out waspish. Last thing I want to do is answer any more of her accusations.

She reaches me in three quick paces, plastering herself against me and wrapping her arms around my waist. "I'm sorry." She hugs me tight. "I'm so sorry, August."

It takes me a second because she's quick, and I didn't expect this. My heart turns over in my chest, and all the lingering fight falls away. I rest my cheek on the top of her head and hold on.

"It's okay," I tell her.

"No, it's really not. I shouldn't have said those things. I'm really messed up—" She cuts herself off and kisses the center of my chest. "You make me happy too."

Well, good. That's good. Because I need her happiness.

She kisses me again, softly, before pressing her cheek to my sternum. Her voice grows small and muffled. "Part of me doesn't like it."

She leans back, and her brown eyes are glossy with remorse. "If you have the power to make me this happy, then you also have the power to make me miserable."

It shouldn't make me feel better, but it does. Maybe we're both messed up. Sighing, I lean my forehead against hers.

"It goes both ways, Penny love. You can level me without half trying."

A fine shudder works over her frame. "I really am sorry."

"No, don't. Sweets . . ." I kiss her cheek, the damp heat of her temple. "It's over. Okay?"

Her answer is a small shake of the head. For a long moment, we're still. Pen smooths my chest with soft pets like she's trying to soothe me. I let her do it, because it feels good. My eyes close, and I stroke her hair, letting the silk of it run over my fingers.

"We had a fight." She says this in wonder.

"Yeah."

"I don't like fighting with you."

"Can't say I'm a fan of it either." I lean back to meet her eyes.

"But it'll happen again." When she frowns, I can't help a smile. "People sometimes fight. It's human nature."

"Yes, but this time is worse because it's my fault."

Her pout is adorable. I nip her earlobe, loving the way she shivers.

"I hear the making-up part can be good. Hot, even, if done right."

She quirks a brow. "Is that so?"

"I'm almost certain it'll lean toward hot if you put real effort into it."

"Hmm . . ." Her gaze narrows but humor lights her eyes. "Well, it is my turn to make it up to you."

"Oh, well, if you insist."

Her soft lips curl into a real smile, and I feel it in my chest. The feeling grows when she cups my face with her smooth hands and rises to her toes. Her mouth is sweet and full, and she kisses me like I'm a treat she's been waiting to have.

Total goner.

With a groan, I grasp a handful of her hair and grip it as I feast on her mouth. I've missed it. Missed her. And she tastes so fucking good. She kisses me back like I'm her air, pressing her perfect, plump breasts against my chest with a little whimper that has my dick perking right the fuck up.

Starving now, I wrap my free arm around her back, intent on hauling her even closer. But she instantly flinches as though in pain and gasps. I know enough about injuries to understand she has one. Immediately, I step back.

Guilt tightens her features. Guilt?

"Penny?" I search her face. "You're hurt?"

"I . . ." She chokes up, her eyes glossing over with tears.

"Jesus. Baby, where are you hurt?"

"It's nothing." She shies away. "I'm fine."

But things are clicking in my head now. The way she jumped. Her weird tension. The wash sink . . . I glance that way. "That was your leather jacket." There'd been a massive stain on the back.

My head goes light.

"Penelope." I clasp her arms as gentle as I can, given my panic. "Did you have an accident on the bike?"

Wrong thing to ask. Her eyes well up and spill over. Another breath and she starts to cry. Not the pretty, streaming tears thing but heaving sobs that rip my heart in two.

"Christ." I hold her like she's glass and bring her as close as possible. My heart beats too fast. I could have lost her. "Baby. Are you all right?"

"I'm okay." She grasps my roaming hand because I can't stop petting her, looking for the hurt. "August, it's just a bruise."

"Let me see." I know it's on her back. I felt her flinch. Beside myself, I turn her round and lift her shirt, while she protests that it's nothing.

It's not fucking *nothing*.

"Fucking hell." She's got a black-and-blue bruise the size of a football on her right shoulder blade, and a bit on her spine. "Fuck, baby. Penny love."

I've had worse bruises. But it's on her. Not me. Shaking, I lean down and kiss her skin.

Pen sighs, then steps out of my grasp. Her creamy cheeks are blotchy with tears. "August." She rubs a fist over her eyes. "It wasn't an accident."

"What?"

"I didn't crash my bike. I— Shit." Her hands clench at her sides. "It's so stupid. Fucking assholes . . ."

Assholes? Something ice-cold and dark starts to spread in my gut. Something like rage but more violent.

"Pen," I get out through numb lips. "What happened?"

She shifts on her feet, her fingers playing with the hem of her shirt. "Someone ah . . . someone threw a sub at me."

Icy-hot rage claws at my throat. There's a buzzing in my ears, and I'm worried I misheard. "A sub?"

Pen's cheeks go bright red. "As in a big sandwich. I think it was an Italian cold-cut."

Someone pinged a fucking sub at my girl. A fucking sandwich. At Pen.

"There was a rock in it," she confesses in a small voice. Like it's her fucking fault. Like she thinks I don't believe it.

Then I focus on the pertinent part: a rock. An anguished sound escapes me. I sway a little before blowing out a breath. "Who?"

Because I'm going to— I suck in a calming breath before I punch a wall.

Woodenly, Pen shakes her head. "I don't know. It was on campus. I didn't see. I was walking to my bike and it just . . ." She swallows with a clicking sound. It's too much.

Cursing softly, I gather her up and sit on the bed, gently settling her on my lap. I kiss her damp cheeks, her swollen mouth, and smooth back her mussed hair. "Baby. I'm so sorry."

She nods as if by rote. I can't stand it. She shouldn't be hurt. Ever. And I wasn't there to protect her. With a grunt, I rest my head against hers.

Pen sets her hand over mine and clutches it. "There's more."

"More?" Dread returns full force. The way she looks at me, as though trying to defuse a bomb. My free hand trembles as I brush her hair back and try my best to look calm and reassuring. "Tell me, honey. Just get it out."

Pen lowers her gaze to our hands. And tells me about her bike. I listen quietly, while the blood drains from my head and my heart slams against my chest.

She was attacked. Because of me.

"August?" Cool hands touch my hot face. "Baby?"

I don't . . . I can't . . . A lump rises in my throat. With a strangled breath, I lean my forehead against hers.

"Pen . . ." It comes out thready.

"I didn't want to tell you," she whispers, stroking my temple. "I didn't want to see that look on your face."

"It's my fault," I rasp. "I'm sorry. I'm so sorry."

"Stop." She presses her palms to my cheeks, making me meet

her eyes. They're clear now, determined. "I knew you'd blame yourself, and I don't want you to carry this burden."

"It's my burden to carry. If it wasn't for being with me—"

"No. Not even a little. The blame lies on the grotty little shit, or shits, who did this. The cowardly *fuckos* who don't have anything better to do than hurt other people. Not you. Never you."

"Jesus, Pen. If they did this after one loss . . ." I feel sick just thinking about it. In that moment I hate the game, hate that my place in it put her in danger.

The tip of her finger skims along my jaw. "We don't know if that's why. It could be a fan of some other team or some bored loser."

"The next one could be some sick fuck who hurts you to get to me."

"I could walk outside and die a thousand different ways."

"Christ. That's not helping."

"My point is that this—" she gestures between us "—is the only thing we can control. Right here and now. And I'd just really like it if you'd kiss me now, let me feel something good."

"I can do that." I find her rosy sweet mouth with mine. Pen kisses like a dream. Soft at first but then greedy like she just discovered chocolate and has to have more. It gets me every time. With an impatient noise, she lifts her sleep shirt overhead and tosses it aside.

In the low lamplight her skin glows like a pearl, the full teardrops of her breasts swaying as she moves. I think we'll be eighty and the sight of her will still make me slack-jawed with base lust. Instantly, I fill my hands with them, loving their firm weight, the round softness. Those deep rose nipples stiffen, pointing up at me like a taunt.

Her skin is smooth silk under my lips. I glide along her neck, over her shoulders. Down to those perky little nipples begging for attention. I kiss each of them in turn, lovingly because they deserve it.

As much as I want to linger, I can't get the sight of her injury out of my mind. Gently, I turn her around. She hesitates for a second, clearly not wanting me to look there again. A soft kiss at the base of her neck has her relenting. She ducks her chin, arching the long line of her back against my mouth as I move my way down to the bruise.

It's deep and splotchy, the colors of pain I'm familiar with. But not on her.

"Pen . . ." I kiss around the area as light as I can. "I hate this."

She looks at me from over her shoulder. "I'm so pale, any bruise I get looks worse than it is."

"It looks pretty fucking bad. It breaks my heart, Pen."

She turns, blocking my view of it, her expression fierce. "Don't let them do that to you, or me. Now that I told you, I feel better—safe. I always feel so good when I'm with you."

I can't hold on to my outrage in the face of that. She melts my resolve with such ease, I should be worried. But I'm not. I'm fucking grateful she feels the same.

Softly, I rub her arms. "I had this idea that it would be easy to be with you." I swallow thickly. "And it *is*. But it's also fucking hard. Because everything is at the surface. Your hurt makes me hurt. I've never had that before."

"You think it's different for me?" Her lips curve wryly. "I watch you take hits that would break normal people. I listen to them pick you apart in the media. It hurts because I care. I'm okay with that. Are you?"

"Yes." I touch her cheek. "I'm really okay with that."

"Good." She kisses me lightly. "You promised me a few hours of forgetting the world. I'm holding you to it."

"You can have all the time you want."

"I just want you."

Suddenly, she's the one taking the lead, pulling off my shirt, exploring my chest with her mouth and hands. It feels so good, I lean back and let her have at it, my heartbeat kicking up as my gut tightens. Her fingers tug at the button of my jeans. I help her out, unzipping and lifting my hips to slide them free.

My dick slaps back against my belly, hard and wanting. And she wraps her fingers around it with a sound of delight. I shudder at the touch and cup her cheek, bringing her mouth back to mine. Our kiss deepens, gets messy, but then she's moving away, licking the column of my neck, peppering hard, greedy kisses over my chest.

I hold her head in my hand, wanting to bring her back up to me, but she slides farther down, her tongue tracing the line between my abs.

The tiny hairs on my skin rise as pleasure ripples over me. But when she brushes a kiss over the tip of my cock, I stop her with a hand to her shoulder.

"Pen, baby, no. Not like this. It should be me who serves you tonight." My dick is yelling at me to shut it, but my brain and heart overrule the fucker.

"But I want to. Especially tonight." She rests a hand on my thigh. "Don't you see? When I'm with you like this, everything else falls away. I'd really like to forget about today. And I love touching you here. I love the way you shiver and bite your lower lip like you're trying your hardest to be patient, but like you also want to draw it out because you love it too."

"I do. Oh, fuck, I do."

"You're gorgeous, August. I want you constantly. Your pleasure is mine, isn't that what you say? Give me this pleasure. I've been wanting to suck you."

"Christ." I'm shivering now. Hard pulses of lust punching into my gut.

"I want to know if you'll taste as delicious as you look."

"Baby . . ."

"Let me have you like this, August."

"You have me. Any way you like. Anytime." I stroke her hair. "Pen, you have me."

Her answering smile is impish but when she gazes down it turns covetous. And then those luscious lips part. She runs them over the swollen tip of my cock, humming in satisfaction. I feel it in my balls, in the sweat-slicked base of my back. A groan tears out of me as she sucks me deep and pulls back out slowly.

Weak now, I brace myself on my elbows to watch. She doesn't appear to have a plan but simply explores with her mouth and hands, stroking my length, kissing it, then sucking me. Her hands cradle my balls gently, fondling there in an almost lewd way.

I fucking love it.

My abs tighten to the point of pain, my breath coming in pants. "Like that," I rasp when she starts to bob up and down on my cock. "Suck me like that . . . Jesus!"

With a moan, I tip my head to the side, my eyes struggling to stay open. I want to see her do this—the delicate curve of her jaw stretched open to accommodate my girth, the sway of her tits as she moves, how her eyes flutter closed like she's taking just as much pleasure as she's giving.

She's a novice at this, and yet nothing has ever undone me more. My hand falls to the crown of her head, holding her there gently as my hips begin to pump—just a little, just enough to take the edge off. Heat ripples over my skin, and I grit my teeth to keep from coming. I don't want it to end.

Pen glances up at me, dark chocolate eyes, candy pink lips wet and full. She gives the sensitive tip of my crown a saucy little lick, and I just about float out of my skin.

"Penelope . . ."

I want to tell her that I adore her, that she is my everything. I want to tell her how utterly precious she is to me, and the knowledge that she'd been assaulted, that something she loved was destroyed out of petty violence, is abhorrent to me. That I have this need to cuddle her up and protect her from the world. I want to tell her so many things that it gets jumbled and caught in my throat. And all I manage to say is her name. Over and over. Like it's a prayer. Benediction. Salvation. Mine.

THIRTY-THREE

PEN

AUGUST TRIES HIS best not to be upset about my assault and bike. But in some ways, I know it haunts him more than it does me. While I'm mostly angry when I think about it, he's afraid for me and guilt ridden. The guilt intensifies when I tell him I'm going to finish off the semester with remote learning.

"It's your last month in college," he says, visibly distressed. "You should be able to enjoy it to the fullest."

"August, you need to believe me when I say I'm not in the least upset about not going to class. Not everyone has the same college experience. For you, it was a whirlwind of football, parties, and fun—"

"Not all fun," he mutters, pulling me onto his lap like he needs the physical contact. "A lot of it was stressful as hell."

"You're right. I shouldn't have implied it wasn't."

"No." He huffs out a dry laugh. "It was a pretty accurate assessment, all in all."

"I only meant that, for me, college has always felt more like a job. I went to class, did the work, and that's about it. I never joined teams or clubs, never really partied."

August frowns, tracing the curve of my neck in concern. "Did you want to?"

"I don't know. I think if I did, I would have. It just wasn't me. Not really." I rub his broad chest with slow strokes; turns out I constantly need to touch him too. "I don't have regrets. I am who I am."

"I like who you are too," he whispers against the crown of my head. "I like it so much, Penelope."

Those words sink into my heart and grab hold. I find myself taking his hand and placing a kiss in the center of his wide palm. My heart squeezes harder when he makes a fist as though clutching that kiss close.

"There's only a few weeks left," I whisper back. "I won't miss anything by going remotely."

Four days after the incident, August surprised me with my bike, completely restored and a custom riding jacket with armor that's also light, breathable, and fits my curves like a glove.

I'll sleep easier knowing my girl is protected when she rides, he'd told me when I tackled him with kisses.

MayDay: So who's ready to par-tay on the big boat besides me?

MadMarch: Is that Speed 2. God. No. May. Why? Just why?

JuneBug: I thought we agreed that movie didn't happen! Annie sped off with Keanu into the LA sunset! END OF STORY!!!

MayDay: You two wouldn't know good cinema if it bit you on the ass

No1Luck: your taste is dubious at best, MayDay. And my boat is not big enough for a party

MadMarch: that's what she said

No1Luck: Keep talking, Michael Scott. See what happens.

MayDay: Ooh, what happens? I wanna see!

RcktMan: Will it be like the time Jan made March slap himself? Cuz that was awesome

MadMarch: shut it you! Remember the FROG?

RcktMan: Right. Jan's a dick. And who the fuck named me in this chat? MARCH!

MadMarch: Why you coming after me? I want to give the person a beer for that one

RcktMan: fuckos

LuckyPenny: I did what I had to! Believe me, it was better than SoulBroChickn they workshopped earlier.

RcktMan: Penelope? How could you!

LuckyPenny: I repeat, they wanted to call you SoulBroChickn! Suck it up, RcktMan

JuneBug: Our girl has teeth. Heh.

No1Luck: She's one of us now.

MadMarch: I for one welcome our new evil overlord, Lucky Penny

LuckyPenny: Thank you, thank you. I want you to carry on with the dreary normal things you normal people do. Let's just have fun with this!

JuneBug: Calm down there, Megamind

LuckyPenny: :D And I was supposed to be PennyWise!

MayDay: NO CLOWNS!!!

RcktMan: My girl is too cute to be a murder clown

LuckyPenny: D'awww

MayDay: I think I prefer the clown

No1Luck: FFs keep it holstered, SOULChicken

RcktMan: You can't see it, but I'm flipping you all off.

No1Luck: Can't wait til you're all here. No, really. What time do you arrive? I'll schedule the next plane out

MadMarch: We have a key, bro

RcktMan: We'll make ourselves nice and comfortable

No1Luck: Fuck

LuckyPenny: He loves you guys SOO much!

MayDay: IKR?!?

No1Luck: see you chuckleheads on Mon

PEN

I FIND IT a relief to get out of town the weekend before Thanksgiving. I think August does too. And so now we're in Texas, driving up the long, private road to January's house for a mini vacation. We'd met May and June at the airport and driven in together.

"You'll love Jan's house," June tells me from the back seat of our rental. "It faces the lake."

We'd been catching glittering glimpses of the massive lake as we drove. I crane my neck to see as August turns the corner, and the house comes into view. It's a Texas modern ranch house—cut stone, charcoal-colored board-and-batten siding, and big industrial windows. The wide wraparound porch is screened in on both wings but open at the center.

Jan walks out, his body limned in the light of the doorway. He jogs over and hugs his sisters as soon as they get out of the car—picking them off their feet to twirl around until they laugh and demand to be put down.

I smile at their antics, but squawk in surprise as I'm soon treated to the same. Jan chuckles as he sets me down, then kisses my cheek.

"Better get used to it, Penny. You're one of us now."

"One of us!" May leaps onto my back, pushing me further into Jan's hold. He laughs and adjusts his grip to tuck both of us under each arm. With a gentle squeeze, he walks May and me up the stairs.

"Get the bags, little bro," he calls over his shoulder.

"Asshole," August says with good humor.

I'd always been welcome and a close family friend, but this change feels significant. As though they're doing their best to make it clear I'm a Luck now. It feels both wonderful and terrifying. As an only child, there's a certain yearning in me for all their boisterous warmth, the laughter and company. It touches me deeply that they accept me so fully. And yet, August and I aren't really engaged. Yes, we're together now. But they're treating me like we're a done deal, a sure thing.

Having been left behind by my father—someone who should have cherished me unconditionally—letting myself sink completely into the Luck family feels fraught. I want it so badly. I want August so badly. Forever and always. But these things haven't been said.

I should take that leap of faith. But a small part of me, the little girl who was left behind, stubbornly waits to hear it from him first. She *needs* it.

Maybe my father fucked me up more than I want to admit.

Shaking off dark thoughts, I follow Jan inside. June was right, I love the space. Old, weathered cypress boards over a foot-wide creak. Much like my house, it's a ranch with old beams overhead and wings branching out from a center hall. But where I have smooth stucco walls, Jan's place has a lot of stacked stone and more board-and-batten walls. The furniture is substantial, deep gray velvet couches, camel-colored leather chairs, heavy oak tables and chairs. It's cozy but not stuffy.

A fire crackles in the hearth, and the lamps glow warmly. Jan heads for a long walnut-topped bar that faces a wall of glass doors and the silvery lake beyond. June, May, and I take a seat on the barstools as he plays bartender, fixing up apple cider old-fashioneds.

"Where do you want us?" August calls from the hall. He's laden with bags, the bulk of them May and June's, but they don't appear to weigh him down in the least. Ah, to be that strong. I'd probably toss logs for fun.

"The girls have the blue room. You're in plaid."

"Plaid," I question, as Jan slides a drink before me. "Thanks."

The corners of his glacial-blue eyes crinkle. "They honestly look the same except one has a dark blue throw on the end of the bed and the other has a plaid one. Let's see if he can figure it out."

Laughing, I raise my glass to Jan and take a sip. Who am I to get in the way of brotherly shenanigans?

"Asshole," August repeats, striding in a few minutes later. "Think I don't know what you're doing?"

Jan chuckles and hands him a cocktail. "I let you off easy this time."

Remembering the story about the frog, I grin up at August, sliding my arm around his waist. He reads me well and raises a brow in mock warning. "Don't you go getting on his side. You're my girl, not this dirtbag's."

He places a soft kiss on my smiling mouth as if to remind me.

June and May instantly make gagging sounds. Mature-like.

Over my shoulder, August flips them off and kisses me again. "You taste like apples."

"Ugh." May wrinkles her nose. "I'm never going to get used to August being mushy. It isn't right. It's like someone took over his body."

"And replaced it with a tub of goo," June deadpans. "Remind me again why we were happy these two made it official?"

"We're not really official," I burst out.

A pregnant pause fills the room. Heat prickles my cheeks as I feel August stiffen beside me. But he keeps his warm hand light and easy on the back of my neck. I glance around and find his siblings trying their best not to make eye contact.

The flush grows. "I mean, official as in engaged. Obviously, we're together. Not fake together but really together. I mean, you know the whole tasting like apples thing and all the sex we've been—"

"Here." June pushes over a bowl. "Have a nut. They're delicious."

Giving her the stink eye, I take a cashew and eat it.

August breaks the silence by chuckling. It's warm and slightly rough, and the sound eases into me. He strokes my back in solidarity then kisses my cheek. "She stopped you at the good part. I want to hear more about all the sex we—"

He ducks as his siblings ping him with cashews. "Assholes."

THIRTY-FOUR

PEN

"YOU'RE BEATING IT too hard."

"I'll have you know my beating technique is honed over years of experience."

"I'm sure you like to think so, but there's always room for improvement."

"Would you'd like to take over here, Sweets? Because I'm not against witnessing your beating skills."

"Nice try, buddy. Just don't come crying to me when your cream comes out too thick."

At this, August bursts out laughing. He'd been holding it in admirably while we pretended to bicker. So had I, but the damn has broken. I join him, doubling up against the counter where we've been trying to make dessert.

Jan, March, and the girls are out picking up barbecue for dinner; I've been promised a veritable feast of ribs and brisket. When I'd asked about sides, I got a long, suffering look from the boys. But after a lecture from March about how sides were superfluous in the presence of good barbecue, I was promised there would be some—if I so chose to fill up on needless carbs.

I'd offered to make dessert: fresh whipped cream piled on top of syrupy baked apples and a butter cookie crumble.

That was the idea, anyway. I'd tasked August with whipping the cream. In hindsight, a bit of a mistake.

His laugh rolls full and deep as tears of amusement make his eyes shine. In his hand is a whisk with cream sitting upon it like a fluffy white hat. The tip of it trembles as he snickers.

"Oh, sweet Penelope," he sings with mirth. "Won't you taste my cream?"

"Get out of here," I say through actual giggles, and push the whisk threatening to coat my lips with his *cream* away. "Pervert."

"I didn't used to be. This must be a new *you* thing."

Bare footed, dressed in a blue college T that stretches nicely over his chest and low-slung faded jeans, he looks happy and relaxed. The sliding glass doors facing the kitchen are cracked open to the crisp evening air and the piney scent of fall drifts in. Just beyond, the still waters of the lake shine silver in the moonlight.

"Give me that." I take his whisk and the bowl. "We will not be having cream wars in your brother's kitchen, thank you very much."

Without warning, he clasps my waist and lifts me onto the counter. I land with a surprised squeak, and he chuckles, stepping in between my thighs to cup my cheek. In the warm glow of the kitchen, his eyes gleam like polished pewter. "Now, Penelope, where's your sense of adventure?"

"It got kicked to the side by my sense of decorum."

Even as I say it, my lips coast along his skin. I love the strong column of his neck, how it's sandy with his beard just under his jaw, then becomes silky and hot by his pulse. I love how he shivers every time I kiss him there, and how he'll inevitably tilt his head just enough to give me more access.

He does it now, his big hands kneading my hips as I kiss along that smooth, hot skin and lick his sensitive points. "Guess a little cream landed here," I lie, licking him again.

August grunts, dipping his head to return the favor. His mouth opens over the curve of my neck. Gently, he sucks there. I feel it in shivering licks of sensation along my thighs, in my core.

"Pickle," I warn, weakly.

"Hmm?" He nibbles his way back up my neck toward my ear. And I lean back to let him, my hand clutching the whisk tightly.

"Brother's house . . ." It's the saddest attempt at behaving ever. August cups my breast with a big, warm hand, fondling me in that way of his that makes me weak.

"Live dangerously, Sweets." A husky plea as his head lowers to my collar, looking for a way in. He finds the first button and pops it free.

Oh, how I want him. I want that clever mouth to find all my swollen and eager places. But he's seducing me too easily.

"August," I say again, leaning in just a little, because, damn it, he's tweaking my nipple now.

"Yes, Pen." He doesn't appear to really care what I'm saying at the moment. He's got his hands full, after all.

I ease back just enough to break contact. He meets my gaze, his slumberous and carnal. I give him a long look over. "You got a spot . . ."

"A spot?" He frowns, slow-moving due to lust. I empathize. However . . .

"A spot," I confirm. "Right . . . there!"

I dot his nose with the whipped cream–topped whisk, then, with a squeal, hop down and run for it.

"Just head right for the bedroom," he calls from behind me. "We're going to be a while."

Giddy and laughing, I race that way, August hot on my heels. His deep laughter vibrates along my skin. I feel his breath on my neck, the nip of his fingers at my waist. But he doesn't catch me. No, he's herding me along, moving us exactly where we want to be.

Our route takes us right by the front hall. It's a surprise, however, when the doorbell rings. My steps falter.

"Ignore it," August says at my back. He's got me now, swinging me up into his arms to kiss me swift and deep. The bell rings again.

"It's Jan's house," I say against his lips. "We can't leave it."

"Jan isn't even here," he grumps.

But I've already slipped free, my sense of politeness prompting me to answer. In retrospect, the ringing bell should have been our first hint of disaster. After all, as with our houses, there's a nice big gate to keep strangers out of January's as well. It stands to reason that whoever is ringing the actual doorbell at the very least has the code to get through the first barrier.

None of this occurs to me. And the very last thing I expect is to see my mother and his standing on the stoop and wearing twin expressions of impatience.

August comes skidding up behind me, his hand wrapping around my waist and pulling me back against his chest, then sliding under my shirt to palm my belly.

"Wait for me," he chides with a laugh, burrowing his face in my hair. "God, you're slippery." He suddenly catches sight of our parents and freezes.

"August," Margo says. "Penelope."

"Babies!" my mother exclaims happily.

With a dramatic shudder, August looks around at the air above him as though searching for something. He notices us staring and gives himself a little shake. "Sorry, I could have sworn I heard the *Psycho* music playing just now."

Biting my lip, I turn my head to avoid meeting anyone's eye.

Margo's droll voice is unmistakable. "You see what I deal with, Anne? I raised five kids, and every one of them a smart-ass."

My mom shakes her head in sympathy.

August, however, decides to poke the bear and places a hand over his heart with a wounded expression. "But, Ma, it's what you told us to do!"

"Oh, *I* told you?"

He gives her an angelic smile. "You were always saying, don't be a dumbass. Ergo it stands to reason . . ." Smile growing, he spreads his arms as if to say, *and here we are.*

There's a small beat, one in which I fear for August's life, but then Margo barks out a laugh, and shakes her head. "And every one of you got your father's charm. Damn it."

She steps in, and August ducks his head to give her cheek a kiss. "But I got the most, didn't I, Ma?"

"Sure, honey." She pulls him close and gives him a long hug before mussing his head. "Smart-ass."

"Just like you taught me."

"Hmm. You have whipped cream on the tip of your nose."

I have the pleasure of seeing August blush bright red.

"Oh, dear," Mom murmurs. The wicked gleam in her eyes tells me she's enjoying the hell out of it.

August grimaces, and I burst out laughing. He gives me a look that promises creative payback, and in return, I grin with glee. That is until my mother's droll tone breaks through my high humor with all the dryness of desert sand.

"Your blouse is unbuttoned, Penny Lane."

Shit.

AUGUST

"AND AS USUAL," says my father from the drive, "I've got the bags."

I empathize.

Pen, however, utters a mortified gasp and quickly turns toward me to button up her shirt, as Dad trudges up the stairs. She flashes me a death glare that promises retribution. But I can only grin. I'm not the one who started a cream war.

All right, so I am the one who started taking off her shirt. Maybe I do deserve the glare. I kiss the crown of her head in penitence.

"You're a big strong man," my mother is deadpanning to my father. "A few bags won't kill you."

"Woman, I've the knees of an eighty-year-old."

"I'll remember that later, when you—"

"Hey, Pop," I cut in quickly. "Let me get those." Anything not to hear about "later."

He gives me a smug look and tosses all three bags my way. With a grunt, I accept my fate, adjusting my grip, then stepping aside to let them in.

"Caught them fooling around, did you?" he says to Mom and Anne with a grin that is way too familiar.

If anyone ever wants to know how I'll age in thirty-odd years, they need only take a look at my father. I've got no complaints. He's fit and strong—despite his whining. His once dark hair is now steel colored but thick and full. All of us boys look like him. Sure, there are some differences, but overall the gene pool is potent on the Luck side.

Pen turns a lovely shade of pink and refuses to meet anyone's gaze.

While her mother scoffs. "I thought this engagement thing was supposed to be a charade."

"It is," Pen hisses, still put out from being half undressed. "At least the engagement part."

She's been very insistent on clarifying that lately. And can I blame her? There is a huge difference between being engaged and being . . . whatever it is we are. What are we, exactly? I like to say she's mine and I'm hers. Period. And I don't really think she's angling for marriage or upset that there isn't one forthcoming. No, it's that damn lie that brought us together still haunting us in subtle ways.

I find myself shifting on my feet, unaccountably uncomfortable. Worse, Mom is peering at me with interest. The woman can see through walls, I swear to God. No one is going to convince me otherwise. And I do not want her looking too closely at me, because I'm fairly certain she can read minds as well.

"Jan and the rest are out getting barbecue," I tell them for no other reason than to fill the silence. It feels awkward and fraught—like a couple of busybody parents will soon start probing with endless questions.

Turning on my heel, I take their things into the side hall where it leads to the bedrooms. There's only two rooms left, so I leave the bags by those doors. When I get back, everyone has retreated to the kitchen and settled around to watch Pen pack away the cream for later. The elegant line of her neck is tense as she moves, the lobes of her ears bright pink. I know she's thinking of that cream and what we might have done with it. And that our parents are too.

Again, a pulse of aching tenderness hits me. It does that a lot now, at least once a day. I might have been concerned, except I know exactly what it is.

Moving to Pen's side, I press my cheek to the crown of her head in comfort, and lower my voice so only she can hear. "Let me do this."

"I got it," she says just as softly. But she leans into me for a moment to acknowledge the offer.

Swiftly, I kiss her head, then turn back to three sets of very interested eyes. It's clear they are completely disarmed by seeing Pen and I together. "How about some drinks. Mom, Anne, you want some white wine, tequila maybe?"

It snaps them out of it a little. Mom rises from her perch on the island stool. "I'll get the wine."

"Want a beer, Dad?"

"I'll probably need more than that," he mutters but then heads for the bar. "Guessing you need one too, son?"

God, yes, I do. "Sure."

Anne slides up next to me. "Since I don't know where anything is, why don't you help me put together something to tide us over. Does January have cheese and crackers, or something?"

"Let's see what we got."

Anne pats my arm in solidarity. She's a beautiful woman, but aside from their coloring, Pen and her mother don't look very much alike. Whereas Pen is soft curves and delicate features, Anne is bold and vivid, her jaw more squared and sharper, her nose a strong slash down her face. Features well suited to the stage. As is her voice with crystal-clear diction and warm resonance.

When I was a kid, I used to hear that voice booming up from our downstairs to vibrate around my bedroom. And every time it would set off a small flutter of anticipation in my gut because it meant Penelope Morrow might be there as well. Later, when Pen stopped coming over with her mom, I still felt that flutter, that strange ache, because even though Pen wasn't there, Anne could be counted on to tell stories of her daughter's life. It was through Anne that I'd learn where Pen was, what she might be doing.

And they never had a clue. All of them thought I didn't like Pen. *That's why they stare. They can't figure it out.*

The realization is disquieting. I feel like I've done Pen some wrong, dishonored her somehow.

My movements grow sluggish as I help Anne set up platters of cheese, cold cuts, and bread, and by that, I mean I show her where things are, and she arranges everything like art. It reminds me of the way Pen presents food; it's not enough for it to taste good, it has to look good as well.

She sets everything on the round conversation table by the kitchen fireplace. And soon, we're all tucked into the wicker armchairs that surround it. Dad lights the fire and settles down with a sigh. "Christ, I'm tired of traveling."

"Be glad it wasn't to Egypt," Mom chides.

"Yeah, about that. Aren't you all supposed to be sailing down the Nile right now?" Pen has the seat next to mine, a glass of wine in her hand. She's composed now, and I'm gratified to notice, is leaning toward me in an unconscious manner of ease.

Anne heaves a long, artful sigh and selects a sliver of cheese. "The boat caught on fire and they had to cancel last minute."

Her once dark brown hair has been colored to pale honey, and she flips a length of it back in apparent annoyance. "Two years of coordinating our schedules for the right trip and some ass-munch ruins it by deciding to smoke in bed."

"The bastard," Pen puts in, lips pursed in a smile.

"You betcha!" Anne's eyes flash dark sparks. "Never get involved with a smoker, Pen. They stink."

Pen shakes her head, laughing as if to say her mother is being dramatic. But she says nothing more about the subject of potential future involvements with other men. I find myself clutching my beer bottle tighter as I take a long pull. Cold beer slides down my dry throat.

From across the table, I catch my dad's eye. There's a speculative glint in his that I want to ignore. But I find myself staring back. *Yeah, Dad, it's like that. And isn't it the damndest thing?*

Empathy flickers in his gaze as he gives the slightest nod of acknowledgment.

"So, we figured," Mom is saying with a laugh, "that we'd drop in on our kids—"

"Given that they're all together for the first time in years," Anne adds, reproach coloring her tone.

"And have Thanksgiving together," Mom finishes with a happy clap.

Pen and I do *not* share a look. We have more restraint than that. But I feel it along my side where she sits. And I know she's thinking similar thoughts.

Now, I love my parents. I love "Auntie" Anne. But the idea of all of them underfoot when I can barely keep my hands off Penelope is rough. Never mind the fact that all of them seem hell-bent on reminding Pen that our budding relationship is unfathomable to them. Which fucking irks.

Thankfully, I am spared having to say a word because Jan, March, May, and June come walking in just then, Jan's and March's arms loaded with fragrant tin platters of food.

March halts mid-stride and looks about at the ceiling. My lips twitch.

"Why are you looking around like that?" May squawks. "Did you let a fly in!"

March shakes his head. "Sorry, no. It's just I could have sworn I heard the *Psycho* music playing."

THIRTY-FIVE

AUGUST

AFTER DINNER, WHILE the women claim the living room couches and a new bottle of wine, the Luck men head for the outdoors. This division isn't the norm. But this is the first time Jan, Dad, March, and I have been together since both my draft and Jan's accident. It feels necessary to be together alone to talk over football and our lives in the cold quiet of the night.

In the backyard, close to the placid gray waters of the lake, there's a circular stone patio centered around a large round firepit. Jan sets up a couple logs and then starts a fire. Flickering orange light dances off his features as he stares down at the flames and gives the fire a poke with tongs. The logs settle with an impatient hiss and crackle.

March and I watch alongside him the way men are compelled to do whenever any sort of fire is involved, but as soon as he sets aside his tongs and sinks into an Adirondack chair, we follow suit.

The night is crisp and cold with enough bite of frost to fog our breaths. But the fire does its job, spreading a blanket of warmth over our legs and faces.

For a long moment, we sit silently. Well-fed brothers with nothing to do but watch the stars. The sound of footsteps has us turning. Dad carries a tray of beers lined up like frosty soldiers.

"Boys."

We each take a beer, and he keeps one for himself, setting the tray aside and taking the chair on the other side of Jan.

"Nice night," Jan comments, sipping his beer.

"Good company," Dad says.

We clink bottles and fall silent again. The fire crackles and settles. Light from the full moon turns the lake water silver and limns the edges of the dark and murky tree line that slope toward the water.

"I'm thinking of selling the place," Jan says idly.

Dad pointedly says nothing. But March and I exchange a glance.

"Why?" I'm slightly surprised. "This is a great setup. I envy it, honestly."

Jan's mouth curls but he keeps his eyes on the fire. "The only reason you never liked your spot is that, in your heart, you wanted to live in Pen's house."

"What?" It comes out in a startled half laugh.

He quirks a brow. "Oh, come on, brother. Who are you kidding? You've been wanting to be in that house for a good long while. Longer than you think, I'm guessing."

"Oh, my God." March exhales. "He's fucking right!"

Holy shit, he *is* right.

On some level, the desire to be there and only there with her had bloomed long ago.

Dad leans forward so he can catch my eyes. His brow furrows. "I thought the engagement was fake."

"Dad," this from both my brothers. Both of them quietly exasperated.

Dad's gaze darts over us. "What am I missing?"

"A clue," March says under his breath.

He's saved from being heard when Jan says louder, "Not fake if Augie has his way, Pops."

I busy myself with taking a long drink of cold beer.

"Huh," Dad says thoughtfully.

Manfully, I do not squirm. I do however keep my tone neutral. "We were talking about you selling and why."

Jan makes a noise of amusement but then shrugs. "My time here is done, and I'd rather not stick around the area I used to play in."

Our shared silence at that takes on weight.

Jan plows through it. "I was thinking of moving to LA."

"Really?" Again, I'm surprised.

"March is graduating and will likely move on to somewhere else. You and Pen are there. The weather is good. A lot of opportunities for me." He shrugs. "Got to start over somewhere."

Silence stretches, as every Luck man except for Jan tries their best to look properly supportive instead of sorrowful. A fact that is painfully obvious to all.

Jan sighs expansively and shoots us a repressive glare. "Stop acting like I'm Job."

"Who?" from March.

"The biblical guy who had it all and then lost everything—you know what? Never mind. Just don't feel sorry for me."

Dad gives him a hard look. "It isn't pity, son. When you hurt, I hurt. That's just how it goes when you love someone. And I know a part of you is hurting."

Jan picks at the label on his bottle.

I swallow thickly, feeling compelled to explain. "I don't—fine, I do a little. I can't help it. It's like Dad said, I know you're going through some things, and it hurts me that you hurt."

Jan sighs. "Well, that's okay, I guess."

March raises his hand and Jan narrows his eyes. March grins in response. "Okay, I'm the asshole because I absolutely felt sorry for you."

"Little shit."

"But I won't anymore!" He puts a hand over his heart. "Swear!"

I swat March on the head. Sadly, his reflexes are already pro, and he easily evades, giving me the finger.

Jan huffs like he's trying to laugh but can't quite manage it. "The truth? I don't know . . . maybe I'm in denial or mentally numbed by shock, but what I mainly feel is a strange kind of freedom. It's like a weight I never knew I carried has been lifted. The burden of all this *expectation*, the drive to always be perfect, always win is just . . . poof! Gone. Now that it is, I feel lighter."

My beer is empty, and I set the bottle at my feet. "That's healthy."

Dad rests his wrists on his knees. The flickering firelight dances over his sharp features in flashes of gold and black. "I dreaded retirement. But when I got there? Son, I felt exactly the same."

"Damn," March whispers at my side.

It's clear he only wants me to hear it. And the truth is, knowing that both Jan and Dad felt relief over no longer playing the game we've all professed to love with our whole hearts *is* a little unsettling. Fate willing, March and I have years of play ahead of us. Will it wear down on us too? Hell, isn't it already? And if that's the case, why go on?

Frowning, I run a hand over my mouth and watch the flames. For the past half a year I've felt at a crossroads at a time when I thought I'd be gunning to live the hell out of my life. Football, Pen, neither of them feel completely settled.

"What I'm trying to say," Jan continues, "is that I understand the pressures you're under, August. I lived them. But, where we differ, and what I hate, is how you've been forced to live under my shadow. The press, all those talking dickheads, they can't help but compare us and hold you up to my record. It's life. But it's also shit and unfair."

"I didn't know you'd thought about that."

"Of course I did. Fucking pissed me off. I didn't want that for you. Then again, they held me up to Dad, and March's performance will be compared to ours as well. That's what comes of being in a football family dynasty."

"Damn my excellent genes," Dad deadpans. Then shrugs. "He's right. It's a hell of a thing, but no escaping any of that mess."

Thoughtfully, I nod. But then look around at them slowly. "I wouldn't change it even if I could. I love you knuckleheads."

Jan laughs shortly. "I love you all too. Probably don't say it enough, but I truly do. If it helps to chase my record, puts a fire in your belly, then use it. If it doesn't? Then fucking ignore it. There's no clear way here."

At his side, Dad slings an arm over Jan and gives him a rough squeeze before kissing him on the temple. I know Jan's accident and all that came after has been hard on him. Dad is a fixer.

I don't want to add to his worries, or pile guilt on Jan, but it's already out there anyway, and honesty feels like a balm in this quiet spot by the lake.

Linking my hands over my stomach, I take a breath and confess, "I think I've been fucking up because your shadow hovered over me."

Jan waits a beat. "I think so too."

"It's not the fear of failing so much as the need to do right by your legacy."

"It is a pretty awesome legacy."

Though he sounds smug, I give him the credit he's due. "Yeah, it is. But now that I can fully look it in the face, I'm going to use it. Not chase it, but hold what we are, all that awesomeness, close. I'm going to win and lead because I can."

"Fucking right, you can."

"That's my boys," Dad says proudly, earning a couple of eye rolls. He merely beams with happiness before turning serious. "If you want to move to LA, Jan, then do it. No point wavering."

Jan nods then winces, his gaze moving back to the flames. "One more thing . . . It's going to come out soon anyway. There's an unauthorized tell-all article coming out about my accident."

A horrible ringing sounds in my ears. Jan's whole life was upended in that crash, and now someone is going to profit off it? I swallow convulsively. Several times.

"Is it Laura?" March grinds out.

"No," Jan huffs without mirth. "Her boyfriend is singing his song for a buck."

I jerk upright. "Boyfriend?"

He gives his beer a sour look and sets it down. "As in the asshole she was fucking while supposedly being in love with me."

I slump back, deflated.

Jan shrugs with an unaffected air, when I know he's anything but. "We were arguing about it. That night in the car. She'd decided to tell me then."

"Fucking hell," March says.

"Eh. I had it coming." Jan surges upward and grabs the fire tongs to poke at the dwindling logs. His long body looms stiff and bunched against the night. "I was never around. Always traveling, practicing, doing something for football."

"Bullshit," Dad snaps.

"Dad, it's true. She was always on me for more attention. I didn't have it in me to give it. My head was on the game, only the game. Laura just faded. And the thing is? I didn't much care."

His profile is stark as he stares at the flames. "That night . . . she picked me up from the airport, and I realized that I didn't want to be with her anymore. It was too hard and too much. So, like a colossal asshole, I blurted out the truth, and she shot back that she already had someone who appreciated her. We got into a huge fight. When that drunk weaved into our lane, neither of us saw him coming."

A scathing laugh breaks free. "It's my fault, when you think about it. If I had waited to tell her when we got home, she wouldn't have been distracted and—"

Dad stands and pulls Jan into a hug. "No more of that."

Jan wavers then clutches him like a lifeline. "It's my fault."

"It's life." Dad holds him close, rubbing Jan's back as though willing the pain to leave his son. He squeezes Jan hard, then cups the sides of his face. Jan is now an inch taller than him but, in that moment, he seems smaller. Dad meets his gaze with a look of resolve. "Just life, son."

Blinking rapidly, Jan nods once, stiffly, and Dad gives him a fierce kiss on the forehead before rubbing him on the head, mussing Jan's hair. They both step back, gathering themselves.

March rises slowly, his mouth a thin, pinched line, but he quickly puts on an expression of ease. "My ass is cold. Come and show me how to work these high-tech showerheads you got installed here, Jan-Jan, because I need a hot shower."

Jan takes the escape route offered, and they're soon walking back up to the house, leaving me and my dad alone by the dying fire.

Dad waits until they're gone before turning my way. Firelight is supposed to soften hard edges, but he looks older, deep grooves winging out from the corners of his eyes and bracketing his mouth. Fatigue, worry, or both—I can't decide. But the expression in his eyes seems almost gentle.

"I can see you thinking over there, August. Thoughts going a mile a minute."

He's not entirely wrong.

"Dad—"

"You're not your bother," he says. "Your life's your own."

Dully, I nod, wrung out by everything. He starts to pass me, but pauses, laying a heavy hand on my shoulder.

"At the end of the day, football is a highly personal thing. What you feel about it will never be exactly the same as anyone else does." He laughs wryly. "Kind of like with women. There will always be that one.

"You should know, when it's real and true, you're never going to go looking somewhere else for something more. Because you've already found it."

With that, he gives me a squeeze and walks off, leaving me alone in the dark. And I can't bring myself to call him back and explain what I've known for most of my life. That I found the real thing years ago, and it isn't the finding that matters; it's the keeping. And that's the part I have zero control over.

PEN

WITH A SIGH, I flop back on the deep cushy sectional couch in Jan's den. "God, I can't take it anymore. I'm literally stuffed with meat."

"Penny, Penny, Penny." March tuts from the doorway. "When are you going to remember that you can't go around saying things like that in this family?"

Laughing is too painful, so I wave my hand weakly in his direction. "Sorry. I'm too full of meat to think properly."

His gaze narrows. "You said that on purpose."

"He's quick," I tell the ceiling. "Very quick."

"Brat," March says fondly while strolling into the room. He plops heavily on the couch next to me. It's enough to send me rocking.

I groan, holding my stomach. "Bastard."

His hair is damp and carries the fresh scent of shower. "It's a good thing I'm heading back to campus on Monday. I can't eat like this again until *after* the Thanksgiving game."

"Ugh. Don't mention food. I beg you."

"Poor Penny," March croons with an evil grin. When I give him the stink eye, his smile grows. "Don't kill me yet. Look what I brought you."

With an enticing little shimmy, he holds up an icy can of ginger beer.

The sight of stomach-soothing soda has me crab-crawling back up to a somewhat sitting position. "Gimme!"

He chuckles and hands me the can. The snick of it opening has anticipation surging through me. I take a long, cool drink and sigh. Right before an oh so elegant burb erupts.

March bursts out laughing. I'm so full, I don't even care.

"Thank you," I say. "I needed that."

"No, no . . ." Pale jade eyes crinkle with mirth. "Thank you for the entertainment."

Humming, I lean back and cradle my *food* baby protectively. "Where is everyone?"

By "everyone" I mainly mean August. I lost track somewhere between finishing dinner and hanging out with the girls. They've since dispersed to their respective rooms to sweat out their own food babies, but the Luck men had gone out to sit by the lake. We'd let them be, understanding they might want a moment alone with Jan. Apparently, none of them have spent any amount of quality time with him since the accident; he wouldn't let them.

March sits next to me. "Jan's gone to bed. I left Dad and Augie out by the lake. They'll probably be up soon."

Though he's good at hiding it, I know March well enough to notice the strain around his eyes and mouth. "Something wrong?"

He takes sudden interest in the textured weave of the couch cushions, tracing one with the blunt edge of his fingernail. "I'm only telling because I know August will do the same when he gets the chance."

"You don't have to," I assure. "I'm not going to pry."

"That's why I don't mind." Brow furrowed, he runs a hand through his hair in a gesture so like August's that he might as well be his twin just now. "It's Jan . . ."

I listen quietly as March tells me about the accident, Jan's ex-fiancée, and their breakup.

"It's just a shock, you know?" he concludes, unhappily. "I thought my big bro had it all together. The girl he loved since college, the top of his game—for fuck's sake, he's a three-time Super Bowl winner and he isn't even thirty." Wide eyes implore me to understand. "You know how fucking cool that is?"

"I do."

"And here he's telling us that it's a relief to be free of it. All of it." March shakes his head softly as though to clear it. "August and I looked at each other like, *What the fuck?* He's what we've strived to be. And now he's telling us that wasn't what he wanted!"

His words settle over us in a heavy blanket of quiet. Gently, I reach out and hold his hand. He takes it immediately, which tells me he's more than flustered: he's upended.

"It just does my head in," he whispers. "Makes me wonder what's the point in dreaming."

It hurts to see happy-go-lucky March, the sweet boy who never left me out of anything, distressed like this. After all these years, I never fully accepted that he's my friend too. Just as much as June and May. January too. They're my family. Not by blood but by love.

I grip him more firmly, and our fingers thread. "Does that mean you'll quit football?"

"No!"

The immediate and emphatic answer has my lips curling upward. "Even though Jan found it a burden?"

March scowls down at his jean-clad thighs. "I'm beginning to think Jan took too many knocks to the head. How the hell could football be a burden?"

"Well, that takes care of that." I squeeze his hand, then let it go. "I know Jan has been your hero, and I think he still is. Thing with heroes, though. We tend to forget how human they are under all those feats of greatness."

March worries his lip then blows out a hard breath. "You're right. I know you're right. Hell, I shared a bathroom with that fucker for years. If anyone knows he's human, it's me."

"Well, that's an image."

He flashes a quick grin. "The things I could tell you, kid."

"Let's not."

March hums thoughtfully, but his smile lingers.

"That only leaves relationships," I say. "You in one we don't know about?"

"God, no." This too is emphatic. And not exactly flattering to those in current relationships. March's scowl returns. "That's one road I'm sticking clear of. Jan was right there. Football takes so much out of you. What's left for someone else? I don't know what he was thinking getting engaged—"

A look of embarrassed horror breaks out. "Shit, Pen. I didn't mean—"

"To imply that August and I are stupid to get involved?" I supply blandly. He isn't saying anything I haven't worried about myself. August warned me not to fall in love with him because of football. The problem is, it's useless to warn someone of the danger when you've already fallen.

March shifts to turn more my way. His expression is a little wild as though he's worried his words might make me do something rash. "No, Pen. It's different with you two."

"How so?" I'm genuinely curious. "Jan was with Laura since sophomore year. That's far longer than August and I have been . . . involved."

March huffs. "Laura and Jan latched on to each other because Jan was the hot ticket and Laura was hot. Every time I visited them, they seemed more interested in who they were around than being together. It's like they were together because it was the expected thing to do."

"August and I got together because he needed a fake fiancée."

March makes a face. "Pen, come on."

"It's true! And you know it. Okay, we're together for real now. But our relationship started on less than Jan and Laura's."

Sighing, March ducks his head, sending inky strands of hair over his brow. When he lifts his gaze to mine, his is troubled. "I know we all make jokes about you having a crush on me when you were younger."

"And I laugh every time. Internally."

"Because it's hilarious."

"Hilariously overstated, if we're being honest."

"I think we're the only ones who realize that."

Before I can ask him to explain that more, he grows solemn and says, "The true question people should be asking is why I never went after you."

"Was that ever a question?"

"It should have been. Because, Pen, you're totally hot in that subdued librarian sort of way."

Flushing, I glance away. God, I don't want to hear this. I have never disliked my looks. There are days I feel downright pretty. But being told that I'm "totally hot" feels like putting on an ill-fitting overcoat.

Deflection, however, comes easy. "I don't know why people always assume librarians are subdued. In my experience, they're a fairly wild bunch."

"Sure, sure. Let's just go with the cliché, all right?"

"Okay, but it's a tired cliché."

March gives my hand a tug. "Stick with me here, Penny."

"Fine."

"Right. Back to the sexy librarian." He grins as I grimace. "I was attracted, Penny."

"What?" I don't know whether to laugh or gape. "No."

"Yep."

"Oh, lord, just no."

He frowns. "You don't have to look disgusted."

"This is the look of utter shock."

March laughs. "More like horror, which isn't doing my ego any favors."

"Your ego doesn't need favors."

"True." He waves a hand. "Regardless. I would have made a play."

At this, I do gape, trying to picture the scenario and failing. March was never meant to be anything other than a good friend to me. If he'd tried to hit on me way back when, it would have ended in disaster. Mainly because I would have accepted his offer out of sheer shock, a tinge of curiosity, and a good dose of flattered ego. And I would have been miserable because he was the wrong Luck.

"If you were any other girl," he amends.

Wait, what?

"Any *other* girl?" I ask, baffled.

"If you were any other girl but August's."

That sets me back against the cushions. I grab a throw pillow and hold it against my overfull tummy. "I'm . . . Did we experience an alternate childhood universe? I was never August's girl."

March's expression is one of quiet reproach. "Pen, you were always August's girl. You just never realized it."

"You're talking crazy."

"No, I'm not." He says this as though it's entirely reasonable. "You were his."

My head spins, so I focus on the least important issue. "That makes it sound like he owned me or something."

"That's not what being 'his girl' means, and you know it." March leans forward, resting his forearm on the couch between us. "You're his girl because whenever you walk into a room, he knows it. Whenever you are around, he becomes more present."

"Maybe now . . ."

"Always."

"I . . . I don't—hell, I don't know . . . *What?*"

"Flustered you good, haven't I?"

"Yes! How can you say that? August acted like I was a . . . a disease he needed to avoid contracting."

"He acted that way because you flustered *him* good. Which, again, is why you were always his girl." March lifts a nonchalant shoulder. "He might not have known it. But I did. I knew it would hurt August if I made a play for you. And I'd never hurt my brother."

"Well." It comes out more of a helpless huff than a statement.

"Well, indeed." He points a long finger at me. "So you can squawk about 'August never did this or that' but the fact remains he's always been into you, Pen. He's just been utter crap at showing it properly."

Slowly, I shake my head but then stop and give him a sharp look. "Why are you saying this now?"

"Because you're worrying over there, thinking he'll do you dirty like Jan did his girl. Or she did him . . . they're pretty square in that department, I guess."

"March. Focus."

"Right." He straightens and meets my eyes. "August is never going to let you down. You and him? That was always going to be. You two are inevitable. Like Thanos."

A laugh bubbles up and I lean into him. "You're ridiculous." I muss his hair. "But I love you anyway."

He chuckles. "I know. I'm very lovable."

And that's how August finds us, grinning at each other, me having just told March that I loved him. He stands just inside the doorway, an inscrutable expression on his face. The urge to squirm, like I've done something wrong, rises. But I squash it down. He must know that I love all of his family like my own. I won't apologize for that.

But you haven't said those words to him.

He hasn't said them either.

We stare at each other for a beat, but it feels longer. Then he turns his attention to March.

"March," he says blandly. "Get your own girl."

March rolls away then hops to his feet. "I don't want one."

"Then get your own guy."

"Don't want one of them either." He grins broadly. "I'm a solo act."

August breaks a faint smile. "One day, little bro."

"Stop trying to curse me." March saunters across the room, heading for the door. He stops abreast of August. "All good?"

August pauses, then nods. "Jan?"

"Went to bed. Seemed okay."

They both exchange a long look, then August gives the back of March's neck a quick squeeze before shoving him out the door. I say "shove" when really it's more of a mutual scuffle with the both of them snickering and batting at heads as they often do; no one is involuntarily moving either Luck brother without considerable force.

As soon as March leaves, August turns back to me. His expression shifts from a brotherly smirk to soft tenderness that I feel deep in my chest. Warmth blooms over my skin. Any doubts or worries I have dissolve in the wake of the honey sweetness of his smile.

His tone is quiet and easy. "You ready for bed?"

Here, in this moment, is what I need to focus on: the perfect contentment and rightness I feel when I'm with him. Maybe we were inevitable.

"Yes. But I'm so full, I don't think I can move." I lift my arms in supplication. "You may have to carry me."

I was mostly joking. I can walk. But August is at my side in two long-legged steps. He scoops me up with shocking ease and cuddles me close. Warm lips touch mine. A promise. A claim. Maybe both. But it's soft and lovely, and I relax into him with a happy sigh.

August nuzzles my mouth with his. "I'll carry you anywhere, Penelope."

"Take me to bed, August."

And so he does. Unfortunately, that's all he does; I'm still too full for anything other than cuddling under the covers.

"Don't let me eat this much ever again," I tell August as he slides into bed next to me. "I mean it. Just slap that rib out of my hand and yell 'Be gone, Satan!'"

He snickers. "Yeah, I can see that going over real well."

"Why would I be upset? I'm asking you to do this saintly service."

"Uh-huh." He settles on his side, tucking an arm under his

pillow. "Have you forgotten I grew up with two sisters? You'll either forget this convo or don't really mean it."

"Right now, I mean it." With a groan, I frown up at the ceiling. "No one should eat that much meat."

His grin flashes in the moonlight. "You sure were cute snarfing down those ribs, though."

"The soda March brought me helped."

"Good."

He says it quietly, and I look over at him. He appears relaxed but a little withdrawn. Again, I find myself wondering over what March told me. I don't want to ask, and yet . . .

"Pickle, when you came into the den, March—"

"I know what you're going to say," he cuts in. "And you don't have to worry."

I don't think he has a clue what I was going to say. But I find my courage failing. He sees me frowning and winces.

"All right. I confess. I've had a few . . . instances in which I've been jealous of you and March."

He says it formally, as though dragged from the depths of him, but he doesn't blink or look away from me. Shock prickles my skin. I think about the scene he walked in on.

"You know you don't have to be, right?"

His expression goes soft. "I do. You're mine and I'm yours. I don't doubt that at all."

I rest my head in the crook of his arm.

"It wasn't logical," he admits. "And I hated feeling that about March. He's my best friend and brother. So I let it go. When I saw you two just now, I was happy. I realized how close you two are. I like knowing he'll be there for you when I can't."

Smiling, I take his hand and set it over my belly. It's a comforting weight, and he flashes me a quick grin at the action, but doesn't move away.

"But why were you in the first place?" I ask him. "Is it that stupid crush rumor?"

"You mean the fact—not rumor—that you had a crush on him in high school, yes, that's part of it. But more so that your mom and my family seem to be shocked we're together and assumed you'd fall for him."

"Ugh. First of all. That 'crush' lasted a few days at most. And it's only because he danced with me that one cookout we had, when no one else would, and I thought it was—"

"Do not say sweet. That's my word."

Oh, *now* he wants to claim *sweet*? I fight a grin.

"—kind of him," I offer instead. "Second, March has never, ever made me weak at the knees."

"And I do." It's cute the way his eyes light up and his mouth dimples with a grin.

"Pickle, you only have to be you—all pretty-like—and I'm flustered."

He stares at me for a moment as though he's thinking things through, almost absently rubbing my belly. "I feel like I've been waiting forever to hear you say that."

Has he? God, was March telling me the truth? He must have been. They're so close; March would know. I don't doubt him, and yet, I still struggle to believe it. *All* these years? It can't be true. My heart leaps about in my chest like a startled rabbit at the idea.

"I'm surprised you're letting me hold you this way." At his quiet comment, I snap out of my musing and gently touch the hair hanging over his brow.

"What?"

His gaze roams over my face. "You're letting me rub this cute little belly you have going. Most girls hate having a guy touch them there."

My nose wrinkles in the darkness. "August, if you're trying to make sweet word-love to me, this ain't it."

He chuckles from deep within his chest and the sound reverberates through me. "You're right. I'll shut up now." Gently, he smooths a small circle on my stomach. "Forget I said anything."

"Too late," I say darkly. "Now I'm thinking about all the beds you've been in besides mine." Not really, I'm very good at shutting that part out. He's with me now. That's all that matters. Still . . . I frown some more.

"Penelope?"

At his soft query, I turn my head.

When I meet his gaze it's serious and clear. "You're the only one."

"Pfft . . ."

"I'm serious." He nudges me with the arm tucked under my pillow. "There haven't been any other girls in my bed. We're more alike than you think. It's hard for me to trust too."

At that, I roll onto my side to face him. "That's why I let you rub my food baby, Pickle. Because I feel comfortable with you. I trust you."

August's long fingers curl over the crest of my hip. In the dark, he's mainly shadows, except for his eyes. They shine in the moonlight slanting across our pillow, and I see the emotion in them.

"I trust you too," he says.

It sounds like something else. Something more.

We fall silent and eventually sleep. But deep in the dark of night, when the house is still, I wake and think about how August told me nothing of Jan's confession. And how, when we'd been drifting off, he hadn't snuggled me close as he always does, but had turned over and fallen straight to sleep in a huddle beneath the covers.

THIRTY-SIX

PEN

WHEN MORNING COMES, I don't ask August about his strange mood the night before. It might be cowardly, but all our family is here. I'd rather leave it for now. At any rate, he's his normal self when we wake. By that, I mean I'm woken with slow, searching kisses, his large hand gently cupping my cheek, stroking my neck and shoulder as if he can't believe he's found me here in his bed.

His voice, gravelly with sleep and soft with tenderness, tickles my ear. "Do you know how beautiful you are?" Kisses pepper my temple, the crest of my cheek. "Do you have any idea?"

I shiver, snuggling into him. "Not a clue. Tell me more."

An easy chuckle vibrates against my neck as he nuzzles it. "How about I show you?"

Those talented hands of his sneak beneath the down quilt to find the hem of my nightshirt.

"I don't know," I whisper at his ear. "Our parents are here." I suck the tender lobe, knowing he'll shudder in pleasure.

"I can be quiet." Gently he eases my shirt upward, slides his hand under my panties. "Can you?"

My breath hitches. He's too good at this, circling and stroking just enough to make me hot. Not enough to get me off. The perfect tease. Liquid pleasure flows like molten gold through my veins. Shivery rivers of desire run along my skin.

August's mouth finds mine. We kiss soft, slow, hard, deep, exchanging breaths that become more agitated and needy. All the while he slowly fingers my clit, his movements hampered by the tightness of my panties. Whimpering, I lift my hips in entreaty. I feel him smile against my lips.

"You want it," he whispers.

"Yes." There's no hesitation now.

A nip on my lower lip. "You gonna be a good girl and stay silent?"

I'm panting now, breasts swollen and hot, rubbing against the shirt bunched around me, rubbing against his hard chest. Washes of balmy heat flow over me.

"I'll be the best girl," I plead, clutching his neck, pulling him closer.

August grunts, dragging my panties down with rough uncoordinated moves. When they're around my ankles, I kick them away, and he rolls in between my spread thighs. His mouth captures mine with quiet desperation, then he's yanking my shirt free. Our struggles are silent but for the rustling of the covers and the panting of our breath. He dips down, sucks an aching nipple in deep. I bite my lip, my hands tangling in his damp hair.

His gaze finds mine as his cock sinks into me. I feel it with my whole body. Every time. The thick, stiff invasion that seems to push so deep I *must* bear down, push back. Every time. When I whimper and writhe, he gentles me with kisses, sweet murmurs as he begins to thrust that big dick I love so much. In. Out.

"There you go," he whispers, working me. "You're doing so good, being so quiet for me."

The low encouragement makes me clench with deep pulses of heat. Here, in this moment, I'll do whatever he asks of me and beg for more. Our gazes lock as we take each other. The look in his eyes, molten silver beneath lowered lids, as if he's burning for me. As if I'm his world. My belly clenches so tightly it's almost painful.

August. I mouth his name, unable to speak. But he hears it.

As if weak with lust, his head dips, our mouths brushing, exchanging air as his thrusts go harder, deeper. "Pen." He shivers, rotates his hips in that small urgent circle that makes me whine with need.

"I'm not going to last." Breath catches in my throat. "You're so . . ."

"You're taking me so well." He adjusts his angle, finding a spot that feels so good, I sob into his panting mouth.

"Shhhh . . ." he says.

Thick slabs of muscle tremble along his back. I slide my hands down to the hard rise of his ass and squeeze. It's his turn to moan, tilting his head so he can bury it in the curve of my neck. We're torturing each other now, and I love it. His teeth sink oh so gently into the meat of my neck, and his hand moves to cup my breast. I'm close, so close. I know he is too. He's becoming messy with it, using short, brutal thrusts. I love this part.

And when he finds my nipple and plucks it, I break apart.

He holds me there, letting me shake and come, my lips pressed to his shoulder to keep it in. A moment later, he follows me, and it's my turn to hold him close.

We stay like that for a while. Until the sounds of the house waking, our family talking and fixing breakfast, makes us stir.

Slowly, as if he's lost all strength, August eases to the side, slipping free. He gathers me close and sets my head on his damp shoulder where his heart thrums against his chest. Gentle hands stroke my hair.

When he speaks, it almost sounds overloud in the contented quiet. "I had every intention of taking my time with you. But you were too soft and delicious. And my will is weak."

"Hmm." I nuzzle the small oval of his nipple. "We'll just have to try again later."

August clutches the mass of my hair and turns toward me. "I vote for now."

"There's that stamina I love so much."

He pauses, gaze colliding with mine. His expression is strange, piercing but also hesitant. "Do you?"

The intensity of his tone catches me off guard, but before I can answer, March's voice booms from the other side of door. "Oi! Are you two up?"

With a noise of annoyance, August glares at the door. "If we weren't, that would do it."

"Good. We got pancakes up in ten!"

"March!" comes his mother's aggravated voice. "Leave them alone."

"I left them alone all morning!"

August groans and flops back on the bed. "It's eight thirty, asshole!" he yells to the celling.

"Language, August," his mom calls back, her voice muted by distance.

I bite my lip and fight a laugh. "Do you think they heard?"

"No," August says empathically, and reaches for me again.

"Yes," March says, clearly against the door.

Embarrassment bursts hotly over my body and I duck beneath the covers, as August wings a pillow at the door and tells his brother to get lost. March leaves with gleeful chuckles.

"He's just messing with us," August says.

I take in his sex-flushed skin and messy hair that sticks up at all angles. He's relaxed against the pillows, a lascivious glint in his eye. I return it with a look of warning.

"Nope. Not again until we're home." With a yelp, I jump out of bed and high-step it to the bathroom before he can grab me. "I mean it, Pickle."

Again, August groans and drops back against the bed dramatically. "I'm gonna kill him."

"We can get March together," I tell him from the safety of the bathroom doorway. "It can be one of those couples' activities advice columns are always going on about doing."

A brilliant grin lights up August's face. "Penelope Morrow, I fucking adore you."

"I CAN'T BELIEVE you stood at their door and harassed them to get up." June stabs a sausage and shakes her head. "You're such a brat."

"Hey!" March gives his best "innocent yet outraged at the accusation" face. Not that anyone buys it.

May narrows her eyes. "Ma, are you certain March isn't the baby in the family? I have doubts."

Margo chuckles and sips her coffee—a pointed gesture of refusing to answer that has March scowling. But there's humor in his eyes as he looks at her before addressing his sisters.

"Every family vacation we've had, this—" he points his fork at August "—assho—er, aspirational player, wakes me up at the butt crack of dawn to go jogging." He takes a bite of apple pancake. "Payback was in order."

"Just remember, *little* bro, one day it'll be you." August leans back in his seat. We've been at the table for all of ten minutes and his plate is already cleared. The man can eat after a workout, even if that workout is me. I unfortunately blush like one of the guilty. While August idly plays with the ends of my hair, unrepentant.

"You keep saying that like it will make it come true." March salutes him with a sausage. "Not gonna happen."

My mom laughs lightly and pats March's shoulder as she walks by on her way to the sink. She's wearing a fabulous scarlet silk muumuu embroidered with fireworks bursts of hot pink chrysanthemums. She pulls it off with effortless elegance. If I wore that, I'd look like a walking tea cozy.

"You haven't watched enough theater if you're saying those famous last words." She rinses her glass and sets it in the dishwasher. "August, dear, that green smoothie was lovely."

He made it for her when Mom announced she was off complex carbs for the duration of her upcoming play.

"I'll give you the recipe."

She rests a hip against the counter, clear Lucite bangles on her wrists clinking musically, and her attention homes in on August's fingers carding through my hair. A speculative light enters her eyes. "I can't quite get over seeing the two of you together. It never even occurred to me—"

"*Mom.*"

August's hand stills in my hair, then slips to my shoulder.

Mom gives me an innocent look. "I'm only trying to explain that it's a bit of a shock seeing you together."

As if we didn't know. Her continuous "shock" has moved from irritating to insulting. Temper rises like a geyser. August's warm hand curls over the back of my neck, the edge of his thumb stroking my pulse. He must feel it beating in agitation, for he strokes it again as if to soothe.

"I agree," Margo says, jumping to Mom's defense. "It's a trip to see. From adolescence on, they were barely in the same room together without one of them soon leaving it."

"Exactly! Frankly, I thought they hated each other. Pen, at the very least, professed total indifference—"

"And this," June announces sotto voce, "is the downside of your mothers being best friends."

"They'll just have to get used to it, won't they?" August says with deceptive ease. His gaze, however, is hard with warning.

His mother's expression softens as she reaches over the table to touch his arm. "We're looking forward to that, Augie."

"Hear! Hear!" my mom says, waving a hand as though she holds a scepter.

I'm still irked and feel massively exposed, but Neil comes into the kitchen with a troubled expression. Oddly, his gaze goes straight to me before winging to August and then his wife.

"I think you should come and see this," he says to the room. He glances at my mom and then me again. The concern in his face sets off my own. At my neck, August's hand clenches just once, and I know he's noticed as well.

Quietly, we rise and go into the great room where Jan is standing in front of the massive TV set on pause. Jan's gaze darts to mine and holds the same queer look his dad had. Without comment, he lifts the remote and hits the jump rewind button.

The program cues up to a group of reporters shoving phones and cameras in a man's face to get a sound bite. My insides lurch with a great heave.

It's strange seeing my father, even if it's on a television screen. I haven't laid eyes on him in years. He looks the same. A little grayer but the same. Hugh Grant in *Bridget Jones's Diary* level of smarm, gracefully aging boyish good looks. To this day, I can't watch those movies.

"Is it true you and your daughter are estranged?" someone asks.

Blood rushes in my ears as my body goes cold. Vaguely, I'm aware of August holding my hand tight. But I can't focus on anything other than my father, and the sound of his smug voice.

"I've reached out many times. Sadly, my daughter is more interested in fame than family."

A punch of hot rage has me swaying. I tighten my core and clench my jaw. My ears buzz so loudly now, I only hear snatches of the conversation.

"Marriage. Sure."

"You sound a bit dubious there. Care to explain?"

He makes a face like a doubtful duck. "My daughter and August Luck never even liked each other. Now they're in love?" A shake of the head. "She inherited an estate she can't afford the taxes on. Now she's marrying Luck and all the money that comes with him. Something to think about, is all I'm saying."

All the blood leaves my head, gushing toward my feet.

"Where is this estate?"

"Los Angeles, California. Where the stars are, and Luck plays. It used to be called Merry Place. Look it up."

On a breath, I close my eyes. I won't cry. I'm too angry.

I won't cry in anger either.

He doesn't deserve it.

The TV clicks off. Silence is a winter coat tossed on my head. I lick my dry lips, swallow thickly. I'm encased in ice. "Now they'll know where I live."

"*We* live." August's low but firm voice drifts over me. "I'm with you, Pen. You're not going to be alone in this."

In my mind's eye I keep replaying that small glimpse of my father. Of his cutting, snide words. He didn't care about me at all. He simply wanted to make me look bad.

God. He took it all away: my plans, my pride.

"I'm not sure renting will be feasible anymore," I say behind the dark safety of my closed eyes. If I don't open them, I don't have to make it truly real. "Security and all that. What if someone goes snooping? I'll have to be there—"

"Fuck the rentals. Pen, talk to me."

August's harsh reply has my eyes snapping open, and with it the floodgates. Rage rushes in. "Fuck them? I am counting on them to earn those taxes."

He flinches. "You know I'm not belittling that. Don't try to say differently. I'm only trying to help."

"Well, this isn't it."

Just beyond him, our families hover. They all saw. They all heard. All of it.

Oily humiliation slides down my skin. It's so thick and heavy, my shoulders sag. Every one of them is trying hard to convey sympathy but not pity. But it's there. How could it not be? My father, the one man who should by all rights love and protect his child, sold me out for a couple of pathetic minutes of attention.

August steps close, reaching out to take my hand. He's making it worse. He's making me the center of it all. I can't . . .

My feet stumble as I back up.

He frowns in confusion. "Pen—"

"No. Stop. I don't want to fight."

"I don't either."

"I need to calm down." I want away. *Away.* I can't be here, in this spotlight. I need to get away.

August lowers his hands as though facing a wild thing and swallows thickly. "Okay."

But he doesn't go. He just stands there. They're all just standing there. Watching me.

My skin crawls.

"Alone." I hold up a hand, warding him off. "I need to be alone for a while. Please, August. Just . . . go out or something."

"Or something." He blows out a hard breath. "Sure, Pen."

I can't stay another second. Biting my lip to keep from crying, I flee the room.

THIRTY-SEVEN

AUGUST

"YOU OKAY, MAN?" March peers at me from the stern of Jan's bass boat. We're currently drifting around in the middle of the lake. Pretending to fish. Because I'd been ordered out. Except neither of us really knows how or actually wants to fish at the moment.

"That was a hard hit," he adds with a frown.

No shit. A five-foot-six pissed-off woman knocked me flatter than any hulking linebacker ever could. I swallow thickly and flick at the tab of my coffee thermos. It's supposed to be temperate here, but the lake is freezing today.

"Pen had a hard time accepting my help from the get-go. She didn't want anyone to think she was taking handouts from me."

"She's got to know that you don't see it that way."

"I think she does. But too many people, including our sisters, assumed she was too."

"The hell they did." March glares back in the direction of Jan's house where, presumably, our sisters are. Somehow, I doubt Pen kicked everyone out of the house. Just me. "What the hell, August?"

Icy wind sweeps down over the tree line, rustling the leaves and rippling along the water. I hunker deeper into my parka. "They didn't put her down for it, just assumed our association came with financial benefits for Penelope. We set them straight, but the fact is I *am* helping her."

With a sigh, I make a point *not* to look back at the house. "It chafes her regardless, but all of that was relatively private. Until her fucko father put it out to the world."

"Fucking bastard." March tosses his gloves on the seat by him and roots through our snack pack. He rips open a bag of chips with a vengeance. "The guy always was a colossal dick bag."

We clink coffee thermoses in agreement.

"Point is, what was once a sore spot is now an open wound." And she won't let me help her heal. That hurts the worst. Not that she needs some time alone, but that she ordered me to go away. As though I was part of the problem.

"I'm part of the problem," I say aloud. Yep, sucks just saying it.

"Oh, bullshit." March gives me an irate look. "Are you kidding me?"

"No, I'm all over this. Doesn't matter if my intention wasn't to hurt her. She's still hurt."

"By her selfish dick-weasel dad! Not you."

March's immediate and wholehearted defense of me is gratifying. But it also makes me feel worse. Because he doesn't know the whole picture. No one does.

"If it wasn't for me, she wouldn't have this particular hurt going on." For the first time, I truly understand Jelly's desire to put some distance between himself and his girl, if only to ease the fodder their relationship gives the public. But, no, it's worse. Pen was assaulted too. All because of me.

Absently, I rub the aching hollow behind my breastbone.

March, however, continues to scowl. "If it wasn't this, it would be something else. Like it or not, we're famous. Someone is always going to dig up some shit to drag out and flap in the wind. I *know* Penny understands this."

I thought so too. But does it even matter? She's been repeatedly hurt. Because of *me*.

I don't know how to fix this. I don't know what she's thinking about now. And it's quietly killing me. Worse? She doesn't have all the facts. I've been keeping something from her and it's a big thing. I don't want to lie to her anymore.

I could lose her. Even now.

The hollow in my chest gets deeper, colder. Clearing my throat doesn't help.

"There's something I have to tell Pen, and I don't know how."

March pinches the bridge of his nose. "Please, please, *please*, don't tell me you're dumping her for the game because I will fucking kill you where you sit."

"What? No. Dump her? As if I could." *But maybe you should . . . No! No.* "Why would you even—"

"Sorry. What with Jan and all the utter shit piled on him that we're just hearing about . . ." He shakes himself like a dog. "Fuck. It's got me twisted."

"Okay, I have shit timing."

"Well, I wasn't going to say it."

"You basically did."

"Fine. Lay it on me, brother, because my balls are freezing off and I want to go inside."

I want that too. Not just for my balls, although I *am* worried they'll soon be frozen to the boat seat. Mainly, I just want to be back with Pen.

But I can't until I have a game plan. So I tell March the awkward truth. When I finish, I don't feel lighter. If anything, the hollowness has spread to my guts. Silence rings out, broken only by the occasional cry of a red-tailed hawk migrating south and the slight lap of lake water against the side of the boat.

Forearms resting on his knees, March stares at me a long moment, then rubs a hand over his mouth before speaking. "Look, I'm not gonna say it, but we both know I'm thinking it."

I nod. March's disappointment in me couldn't be any clearer.

"Right," March says briskly. "I mean, I guess your bone-headed thought process can be excused given that you lose you damn mind when it comes to Penelope Morrow."

"I though you weren't going to say it."

"I lied," he drawls, then looks out over the lake in contemplation. We're both quiet for a minute. Both of us thinking things through. And even though there's pictures to prove we were born over a year apart, at times like this, I swear we shared the womb.

March clasps his hands and addresses the problem. "Maybe there's another way. Maybe you could—"

"That wouldn't work."

"Okay, but have you considered—"

"You think I'd ask for help if I hadn't?"

"No, no. Of course you had. I'm all out of ideas, then."

"Terrific."

"Oh! Remember that time? With the nuts?"

"Could work."

"Agree on three?"

"You know I hate 'on three' it's so—"

"You and your odd number fear. Fine. On four, though it seems superfluous."

"We could always go with two."

"Not enough momentum."

"What was I thinking?"

"I'll never know."

PEN

I AM ALLOWED roughly one hour to myself. Then my mother barges into the room, looking me over with a critical eye at where I lay curled up at the head of the bed under the covers and surrounded by plump pillows.

She raises a brow. "Made a comfort fort, did you?"

With a scowl, I snuggle a pillow closer. "So what if I did?"

Yes, I make forts when I'm upset. Always have. Never underestimate the power of a good pillow or warm blanket. *You could be surrounded by August's warmth instead, you noodle.*

No, I can't. Not when August is part of the problem. To be clear, I'm not upset with him; well, not much. Irritation lingers from the way he pushed aside my concerns over the house being exposed, but I know he didn't mean it that way. Regardless, no matter how I tilt it, he's in the picture. And in that moment, with our family watching us, I needed to get away from him and everyone else.

"Well," my mom says pragmatically, "it's time to crawl out."

I glare at her. But it doesn't work. Mom is immune to such puny threats. She hovers by the doorway, looking vaguely amused but also sadly sympathetic. "Your father is an asshat."

It startles a laugh out of me.

"Now get up." With that, she pulls a two-foot-long dowel-shaped pasta roller out from behind her. "We've got work to do."

"Where the hell did you get a *mattarello*?"

"I asked Neil to pick one up in Austin." She weighs the wooden roller in hand. "It's not as fine as Nona's but it will do."

"You want me to help you make pasta?" Why can't she leave me be? I want to wallow.

"*Tortellini in brodo.* Much more comforting than a pillow fort." Mom uses her "theater" voice: clear, commanding, and brooking no argument. "Now up you get, Penny Lane."

With a groan, I flop into a cloud of pillows and sigh. She'll never let up until I comply. I roll over and head for the kitchen, after her.

Margo is already at the stove, attending to a big pot of broth. At the other end of the counter sits a stand mixer. They move in perfect tandem, handing over a hunk of parmigiano to grate into the blended pork filling, offering up a spoon to taste the broth. A bit more pepper is suggested.

When they were younger, they spent several holidays with

my *nona*—who is actually my great-grandmother—in Bologna, learning how to cook, and, let's be honest, drinking copious amounts of good wine.

I'd done much the same throughout my childhood—well, not that much with the wine until recently. "We should have started the broth and filling yesterday," I mutter, still grumpy about being pulled from my cave, though less so now that the scents of rich broth fill the air.

"Yes, well," Mom says. "We'll just have to muddle through."

"We've got a good starter," Margo adds. "I left a few batches of broth with Jan when I was last here. I thought he might like to make soup for himself, but he hasn't touched it." Her voice is softer than usual, and she doesn't quite look my way. I know she's tiptoeing around my feelings. I'm horrified to wonder if she'll think less of me after seeing me all but boot August out of sight. But she gives me a small, encouraging smile.

I return it, feeling as thin and brittle as an eggshell. "I'll start on the dough."

"Neil picked up a pasta board too," Margo says over her shoulder. "It's on the counter."

"That was nice of him."

Margo flashes a quick smile. "He'll do whatever it takes for homemade pasta."

I'd thank him, but he's nowhere to be found. Neither is Jan. I know March pulled August out of the house—and the guilt twinges. Not just guilt; even though I asked for space, I still miss him. I still want him near.

What a mess I am.

"Neil, Jan, and the girls went out for some more wine," she adds diffidently, as though we both don't know she's alleviating my curiosity. "They should be home in a bit. And when August and March come back from fishing, we'll have a feast."

Fishing. When the weather has taken an unexpected dip and no one else wants to go out there.

My throat closes on a swallow. He's on the cold lake avoiding me because I made him leave. Part of me wants to text him and say: *come home now; I need you.* But I still don't know what I want to say to him.

With dogged determination, I scrub the board and dry it thoroughly before setting it on the long dining table just off the kitchen. The height of it works best for me.

A fire crackles in the stacked stone hearth at the far end of the table, giving off the scent of charred wood. In the kitchen, Mom and Margo chat, their familiar voices creating a soothing cadence that takes me back to childhood.

Quietly, I make a flour well and crack eggs into the center. My mom laughs at some old joke as I whisk the eggs and start bringing the flour into them. When the eggs are incorporated, I use my scraper and work on creating a ball to knead.

Kneading dough is deceptively hard work. There isn't room for pausing. But the repetitive action feels good. Muscles snap to life, growing warm, as I go at it for at least fifteen minutes, maybe more, until the once sticky ball is smooth and elastic.

While I let it rest, I help myself to coffee, watch the moms finish up the filling, and then drift back to the table to my work.

Rolling out the *sfoglia* is my favorite part of the process. It isn't easy, but the pride I felt when my *nona* announced in her short, stern way that I'd done it well remains. Grabbing the roller, I lightly dust the board with flour, shape my dough into a disk, then begin.

Roll up, turn, roll up, watch it spread. Control the movements, left, right, roll it over the *mattarello*, drape half over the edge of the board . . .

It becomes apparent that my mom's pasta making plan is diabolical in its simplicity. I don't have time to think or brood while working the dough. My mind empties out. Muscle memory kicks in. The familiarity of the process soothes.

The rhythmic *kah-kunk, kah-kunk* of the *mattarello* moving over the wood, the rocking motion of my body as my hands glide along the dowel, finely gritted with flour, outward-in, back and forth.

The *sfoglia* grows bigger, thinner, smoother. My back and neck burn. Sweat gathers along my spine.

Mom and Margo drift in to watch. I don't mind. It's quiet work, and they respect the process. When I'm done, the dough is silky thin and translucent enough to see the shadow of my hand behind it. I sit to rest my aching back, and Mom takes over cutting the sheets into small squares. Margo brings in the filling and soon we all draw up a seat to create the tortellini.

Filling and shaping the delicate little pasta purses is a different type of labor. Repetitive work in which one can chat with ease while letting their fingers do the work.

"Now," Mom says as she pinches together the tips on one tortellini. "Talk to us."

It's so unexpected, I don't have time to brace or evade. "I hate that I hate my father."

"He doesn't make it easy to love him."

"True." I flick a filled pasta to the growing pile and start another. "I hate that he doesn't love me."

That one hurts to say. Rapidly I blink down at the table.

Mom's quiet for a moment. "He doesn't have it in him to love. That's on him. Not you."

"I know."

Warm brown eyes, the color of mine, find me. "You are loved, *cara*. So very much."

"Ma . . ." I don't want to cry all over these tortellini.

"She's right," Margo puts in quietly. "We all love you too."

For a second, I concentrate on my task. "I shouldn't have kicked August out. I hurt his feelings."

"He'll get over it." Margo dots more of the ground pork filling along the cut squares of pasta dough.

"Maybe. But I shouldn't have been so . . . reactionary."

"You bottle too much up," Mom says.

"I took it out on him. I sent him away."

"Why did you?" Margo asks. There's no judgment. I have the feeling she's trying to let me work it out myself.

"I don't know . . . I find myself always wanting to lean on him or turn to him for comfort."

"What's wrong with that?" Margo asks. "A benefit of being in a relationship is having that comfort."

"But I should be able to comfort myself. Work out my own problems."

Sighing, I roll my stiff neck. It doesn't help. Everything feels like it's clamping down. I think about Monica crying over being blamed for Jelly's performance, me being hit with a freaking sandwich, my trashed bike, August's face when Dad sneered about us. It's a kaleidoscope of panic. Shouldn't this be easy?

"I don't know . . . maybe I'm making things hard on myself. I want everything now and I want it for forever."

"That's called ambition, Penny dearest. It's a good thing to have."

"But when it causes all this . . . *emotion*." I press a fist to my aching heart. "Maybe I'm asking for too much too fast." In the space of a few months, I've gotten everything I ever wanted. What if it's taken away? People leave. The ones who are supposed to love you can *stop*.

"I'm only in my twenties," I rush on, frantic now. "They say committing to someone too early isn't really a good thing."

"Oh?" Mom sounds amused. "And why is that?"

"Because you need time to grow into yourself, figure out life. If you don't do that first you inevitably drift apart."

"Bullshit."

"Excuse me? What?"

"You heard me fine." Mom shakes her head ruefully. "As a person who is not in her twenties and most definitely had plenty of time to figure things out, I say that is absolute bullshit. It's an excuse people tell themselves to feel better. And if it makes them happy to believe it, fine.

"We're always growing into ourselves. You think you hit some magic age and boom! it's all figured out? That you're somehow going to be a different person? I hate to break it to you, but, no. We are who we are. We can mature in our outlook or change opinions on things, but we'll be doing that for our whole lives. We're a constant work in progress. That's life."

"Well—"

"If you love someone," Margo says, "truly love them, and they make you happy, embrace it. Don't worry about tomorrow or some nebulous future. Be happy now. Because now is where life is."

God, they're right. And it leaves me with the inevitable truth. That, aside from this current shit show with my dad, I am happy. More than I've ever been in my life. And it's because of one person.

"I'm afraid."

"I know you are, honey. And you aren't alone. Opening yourself up to being with another person is a risk. That's terrifying."

"You and Neil are the ideal. But . . . My dad—"

"You think August would do to you what Doug did to me?" Mom asks softly.

"No." I exhale weakly. "No, he's not like that. But it's just . . . scary how much I want it to work."

Margo dusts her hands on a towel and then gets three glasses from the bar and pulls out a bottle of Chardonnay from the wine fridge. She glances at the ring on my finger. It's quick, but assessing. A smile plays around the corners of her lips. "If I know my son, I'm going to guess he's scared for the same reasons."

She hands a glass of wine to Mom before pouring mine. I don't have it in me to tell her what I really fear. That my depth of feeling might be more. That, despite my claims of growing apart, I know I'll never not want August. But I'll only know for certain he feels the same if I ask. And *that* is scary as hell.

Mom takes a sip of wine, then looks at me from over the rim of her glass.

"Fear is what stops people from truly living. You gotta learn to push past it. You might have to do it again and again because, as I said, we're all a work in progress."

"Great."

Her smile is cheeky. "Isn't it, though?"

"Not really."

"But it is." She pets my hand. "Because you're alive. And that's a fucking gift. Oh, relax, Margo. *Fuck* is a great word. Use it more."

A laugh breaks from me, sounding more like a sob. But I love the way Mom can set everyone straight without falter.

The front door opens with a clatter, bringing in a gust of cold air and happy laughter. Neil, Jan, May, March, and June clamber inside, all noise and life.

And on their heels, walking with a somber, almost reluctant gait as though he's not sure he'll be welcome, is August. Our eyes meet across the expanse of chatting family. My heart turns over and my pulse kicks in.

Those impossibly beautiful eyes of his are uncharacteristically reserved, but I don't miss the way he homes in on me, or how a small smile hovers at the edges of his fine lips. Like he's so happy to see me but won't let himself fully show it until I give him a signal.

Tenderness swells so hard and fast it hurts my chest. My lips lift in return before wobbling. August steps forward, moving past his siblings. Apparently, seeing me on the verge of crying is his hard limit for staying away.

"Just in time," Margo announces to her brood. "You all can help finish assembling the tortellini."

Groans fill the air. I rise and, holding August's gaze, glance toward our room before heading that way. Mom squeezes my hand as I leave the table.

THIRTY-EIGHT

PEN

WE DON'T SAY anything until we're shut in our room. I head to the center of the space before turning to face him. He studies me a moment, the dark slashes of his brows lowering over cool eyes.

"Are you okay?"

The sound of his voice has my heart leaping. I press a hand to my chest and hope he can see the sincerity in my eyes. "I'm all right. August, I'm sorry I told you to go—"

"Can I hold you?" His expression tightens, and he takes a step forward. "We don't have to talk. I just want to hold you."

My lower lip wobbles before I bite it hard and nod. I don't know who moves first but I walk into his arms, and he cuddles me close, pressing his lips to the top of my head. Still carrying a hint of frost, he smells of lake water and coffee. I snuggle closer, wrapping my arms around his waist.

"I'm sorry," I say. And then start to cry.

"Penelope." He cups the back of my head in his big hand and strokes my back with the other.

"I'm sorry." I sob, burrowing my face into the wall of his chest. "So sorry."

He stills, realizing that I'm talking about more than just us, then he adjusts his hold so I'm somehow closer. "I know it hurts. It's okay. I got you. I got you."

When I sob harder, he dips down, kisses my damp temple. "He's a pathetic asshole. You're the very best of him, and he'll never get it."

Shuddering, I settle, letting the feel of August rocking me slowly sink into my tense limbs.

"I know that's not enough," he says in the quiet. "And I fucking hate that I can't make it better."

"But you do." My voice crackles with tears, and I lick my swollen lips before leaning back to meet his eyes. "You always do, Pickle. You walk into a room, and I feel it. Know it. And I'm . . . better."

August's eyes close as though he's taken a blow. He rests his forehead against mine and cups my cheeks with his hands. "You don't know how good it is to hear that."

I hug him tighter. "I *am* sorry I sent you away. I was freaking out and I just needed a moment."

"You can have that anytime." He rubs my wet cheeks with his thumbs. "I shouldn't have pressed you when you weren't ready."

"No, you can. I like that you care. It's just my dad—" My voice breaks, and I take a deep breath. I don't want to cry over him anymore.

"Come here." Grabbing a box of tissues by the bed, he takes my hand. Gently, he leads me to the big armchair by the window and sits down before pulling me into the shelter of his lap. I lean against him, and he palms my hip as I blow my nose and settle.

We sit quietly, watching the gray skies roil outside the window. Ripples spread over the lake as strong gusts come down the hills. Slowly, steadily, I relax into August. He's warm now, solid and comforting beneath me. When I'm calm, I sit up and place a hand on his chest to feel the familiar rhythm of his heartbeat.

He looks at me with worry in his eyes. "All right, Sweets?"

"Yeah." I ease off his lap. "I'm going to go wash my face."

When I come back from the bathroom, August is carrying

in a tray with two bowls of *tortellini in brodo* on it. He toes the door closed behind him and sets the tray on the little end table between the bed and the chair. I perch on the side of the bed and take a bowl.

We eat in relative silence, me still raw and he still restrained. But the hot savory broth with floating pillows of tender pasta fill me up and warm my bones.

"This is fantastic," August says, looking at me with awe. "I can't believe you made this."

"I only made the pasta dough. Our mothers did the rest."

"The pasta is the hardest part," he points out, finishing up his bowl.

"I've been doing it so long, it feels more like meditation than work."

Setting his bowl aside, August leans back in the chair and surveys me as though putting small pieces together. "It's hard for you to accept praise, isn't it?"

"Isn't it for everyone?" I stack the empty bowls.

"I live in a family of overachieving showboats." A corner of his mouth wings up dryly. "We have to fight for every piece of attention we get."

He's overstating. I've seen the Lucks praise and fawn over each other without prompting. They love lifting each other up. For them, everyone in the family is a star, no matter what they've done in life. And maybe that's the difference.

"Mom is a star of the stage. She walks into a room and holds it. Even with you all. It's as natural as breathing to her. And Dad, well . . ." I shrug him off. "Seeking attention in the face of Dad's abandonment and Mom's exuberance is as uncomfortable as wearing underwear that's too tight."

"That bad, huh?"

"Yes." Leaning forward, I rest my hands on my knees and tell him earnestly, "I don't need it, August. As long as I'm appreciated and not ignored, I'm happy. Being in the spotlight? No. I never wanted it."

He frowns and glances out the window, giving me his coin-crisp profile. "You're stuck in it when you're with me."

Am I? I suppose a little. But he'll always be the main focus when it comes to the outside world. I'm okay with that. More so, I like that.

"But I'm there *with* you," I tell him.

His attention snaps back to me, puzzled.

"When I'm with you, August, I feel like I'm the person I'm supposed to be. Like I was . . . waiting for you all along."

His shoulders drop, and he blinks down at the floor as if unseeing. Fear snakes along my spine as I watch him clench his fists and struggle for air.

"Ah, Pen . . ." August blows out a hard breath. "You have no idea—"

He doesn't say anything else, and that niggle of worry worms its way farther into my chest. Because he looks so stricken. Was it so wrong of me to want him this much? My fingers turn cold.

The line of his jaw bunches as he finally speaks in a short tone. "I don't want to do this anymore."

"What?" I can't feel my face.

"Shit. That came out wrong." He rubs his palms against his thighs in agitation. "I meant lying. I've been lying to you, Pen. I don't want to do that anymore."

Okay. That's a little better. I guess. Wait, lying?

I swallow a few times before I find my voice. "How have you been lying?"

"I . . . shit. Okay, let me say it all before you decide to kill me, all right?"

Numbly, I nod.

"Right." He runs a hand over his hair, making the ends stick up wildly. "Okay. Well. It's like this. My team didn't demand I get engaged."

"They . . . didn't?"

"No. They didn't even ask for me to be in a relationship.

It was more broad strokes, clean up your act and stop being a clown."

"But, why—"

"Because I opened a door, and there you were. Penelope Morrow. The one I've always wanted."

"Wait. *Wait!* What?"

"And for once, *for fucking once*, you weren't looking at me with your cute little nose wrinkling in distaste. For once, you talked to me, flirted with me. Christ, Pen. Do you understand what that did to me? Fucking poleaxed. Made my head spin."

He's at the edge of his chair now, his big body straining toward mine as he confesses in a rough voice. "Not only that, but, once you really started talking, I *loved it*. I always suspected we'd have fun together, given the chance. But to actually know it? To witness you giving as good as you got? Pen, it was like being deprived of air and suddenly breathing."

I understand, because I'd felt the same.

"I didn't want to be parted from you. Not after only a few hours. And, yes, I should have just been honest and asked you out, I know this. But after a lifetime of disdain, I couldn't risk it. So I made up a lie and hoped it would give me more time to be with you.

"Only, a lie, once uttered becomes a tangled web, doesn't it? I had you, but not for real. Even when I could finally admit how much I wanted you, I couldn't admit the full truth. Because I might lose you."

With this, he slumps back in the chair and eyes me with a mix of trepidation and a bit of defiance as though he's sorry about the lies but not the fear of losing me.

And for a heavy moment, I can only stare back.

"You did all this—" I wave a hand in the air to encompass the whole of his deception "—because you wanted to spend more time with me?"

"Yes." The confession is tight, his jaw bunched as though

bracing for impact, while, as for me, the worry and fear slides from my shoulders. Something else replaces it. Light, fizzy. My head feels like it's floating. He's shocked me well and good. And my brain seems to be shorting out.

"March said that you'd been into me for a while. I didn't believe him because, well, you're you and I'm me. Now you're telling me it's true."

August shakes his head with a huff. "Sweets, it truly amazes me how you don't want to believe this."

"Excuse me, but I've only had . . . oh, a lifetime of thinking something entirely different. It takes me a bit to do a one-eighty."

"I get it," he says with a tinge of irony.

"I'm not sure you do. August, I like who I am. I know my worth. Which means I know, without hyperbole or subterfuge that, when it comes to the outside world, you and I couldn't be more different. With or without football, you are a star. People draw close as though you're their center of gravity. I don't begrudge you that. In truth, I love that about you. But me? I like to observe. I like the sidelines. I'm not the heroine who goes on adventures. I'm the side character who blends into the background. The idea that you even saw me . . . well, it's a surprise, is all."

"I told you before, you never see yourself the way I do." He leans in, a fierce look in his eyes. "You say you're a side character in everyone else's story. In my story, Pen, you are the main character. You always will be."

I breathe out a soft "Oh!"

"Yes, *oh*," he snaps gently. "You stubborn woman."

"I'm stubborn. That's rich."

His lips twitch, humor lighting his eyes. "Fine. How about fairly clueless?"

I should be insulted. But the fact is I have been clueless. I'm amazed about how much. Besides, he keeps looking at me with that tender gaze, as if, even in annoyance, I'm precious to him. It squeezes at my heart and makes me all fluttery.

"I've never been able to think clearly when it comes to you," I confess.

At this, he smiles, a slow unfurling that pulls wide. "All right, then. Let me be crystal clear. No more lies or evasions. Just the truth."

Slowly, he rises from his chair to sit at my side and take my hand. "Penelope Morrow, I have been in love with you since I was ten years old."

My world flips over on its axis. "*What?*"

He gives me a pained grimace. "I don't claim to understand it fully, but that day you cut your brow open and I held on to you while Jan ran to get help, I knew with bone-deep conviction that you were mine to love. Back then, it was the innocent love of a child.

"But it never faded. I was always aware of you. It was like some superpower, a built-in Penelope radar. The mere mention of your name grabbed my complete attention. Whenever you were around, I'd light up. And you never saw."

The darks slashes of his brows snap together as he looks at me in bafflement. "How could you not see that? Honestly, it pissed me off some days. But then I realized, you weren't ever going to see me when you never bothered to even look. You'd just run, and it broke my heart every time."

August huffs out a half laugh full of self-deprecation. "I tried to get over it, over you. But I couldn't. The heart knows what the heart knows."

So great is my surprise, it takes a bit for his words to truly sink in, for me to really hear him. When I do, however, it's as though I'm champagne uncorked. Giddy, effervescent joy bubbles up and overflows. And I start to laugh. Really laugh. I can't help it.

Unfortunately, August takes it the wrong way. He rears back as though struck. "You're laughing?"

"Yes. I'm sorry. It's nerves. Irony. Both." Weakly, I reach out and catch hold of his hand, squeezing it. "You loved me the whole time? I can't believe . . . August Luck, I have been in love with *you* since I was nine years old and you cuddled me close while I bled all over your shirt. You were my hero. You've always been. It's *always* been you."

My words seem to bounce around in the following silence as he simply looks at me blankly. Then, as if snapping out of it, his brows lift in clear shock. "How . . ." He frowns and narrows his eyes in annoyance. "You always looked at me like I was something foul the cat dragged in!"

And he talks of *me* not seeing things as they are.

"I looked at you the way a painfully shy girl does when facing the object of her affection and being totally overwhelmed with feeling."

"Damn it, Pen. I didn't have a clue." With a huff, he stands and grasps the back of his neck with both hands like he doesn't know what to do with this information.

"As you said, we never see ourselves the way others do." My smile is wry. "I guess I'm a better actress than I think. And anyway, why would I have a clue about your feelings? *You* never looked at me either."

At that, he drops his arms with a scowl. "Oh, I fucking looked. You simply never looked back."

"And none of the girls you hooked up with were remotely like me—"

"There's a reason why none of them were like you. Because if it couldn't be *you* then I was damned well not going to settle for a weak copy."

Heat prickles behind my lids. His words, the emotion in his expression . . . I want to hold him close. Soothe away all those past hurts. But he's on a tear now.

"Are you going to keep arguing with me on this, Pen? Or are you going to accept that I love you, just as you are, and always will?" He looks so good standing there, irate and flushed. Strong and tall and mine.

Giddiness returns. I'm floating with it. "No more arguing. I love you, August. So much."

It's as though I've winded him. He sinks to his knees before me. Eye to eye now, he searches my face. "Say it again, Penelope."

Now that I have, it's easy. Like breathing. "I love you. I love you."

His answering grin is like the sun, bright and hot. Then he kisses me with such quiet intensity, my insides go soft as warmed butter.

He's mine. He's mine.

Laughing, I tackle him. He takes my weight easily, holding on as I wrap myself around him like a monkey, then stands to set us both back on the bed, chuckling as he flops against me. I kiss that smiling mouth. August hums in pleasure and deepens the kiss, his hands gently touching my cheeks, trailing through my hair, finding the small of my back. Soft words of love flow from his lips.

Love. Loving him used to be so hard. I struggled to ignore it for so long. Now it's everything. A balm. A gift. I sigh in pleasure.

We do nothing more than kiss each other, touch like we can't believe this is real. The sun sinks low in the sky, and we're cuddled up on the bed, limbs intertwined.

Idly, August toys with the tips of my fingers. "I have one more confession, then I'm done."

"If you say so." I'm so happy now, he could tell me anything and I'd still be floating. *August loves me.*

"When we started this agreement, you asked me if there was any risk of me falling for you, and I said I'd already found my true love in football."

"I will never resent sharing you with football."

"I know that. But I was lying."

Lifting my head, I meet his gaze.

Silver eyes are soft with emotion. "I meant you. I loved you before football. And one day, when I can no longer play the game, I'll love you still."

"August Luck, you say things like that, and I can't think."

He chuckles, ducking his head to kiss me. "You're my everything. You're my reason."

"Gaahhh!"

His laughter deepens. Hauling me close, he rolls between my legs and braces himself above me. "I kind of like flustered Pen."

"Oh, that's good," I say with a breeziness I don't feel. "You keep talking like that and you'll see a lot more of her."

He's still grinning as I grasp the back of his neck and pepper kisses over his face. "You should know," I say, between kisses. "Wherever you go, however you choose to live your life, no one is going to love you as much as I do."

He closes his eyes and nuzzles my neck. "Still feels like a dream hearing you say that."

"For me too."

"You know," he says after a moment. "I almost hate to bring it up but you never really said anything about my fake fiancée plan."

"Oh, well, the whole 'I've loved you forever' dual confession side-tracked me."

He nips my earlobe. "You're not upset about what I did?"

"Should I be? I suppose . . . But when I think about you doing all that just so you could spend more time with me . . ." I shrug. "I don't feel upset. I think it's kind of—"

"Don't say it." The dark warning has me grinning.

"Hey. I thought you claimed *sweet* as 'your' word."

"Mine to veto at will."

"You only get two vetoes a year."

"A year? But I'm sweet way more than—"

"Aha! You admit it." I poke his side, loving the way he yelps, ticklish and laughing. "Now that I think about it, your pet name should be 'Sweets,' not mine."

"Penelope?" Quicksilver eyes twinkle.

"August."

"I love you so fucking much."

"I love you too . . . sweetie pie."

"Veto."

EPILOGUE

AUGUST

"SWEETS?" I CLOSE the front door, kick off my shoes, and set the car keys on the hall table. "Where you at?"

It's a common question. Sure, I can go hunt her down, but I like calling out the second I get home. The ritual of being able to ask that and knowing Pen will answer is highly satisfying.

Her soft voice carries from the back of the house, telling me she's in the bedroom. I head that way, mentally shedding off the layers of the outside world as I go. Here, in this space, it's just August and Penelope. Nothing else matters.

Sunlight streaming through the tall, windowed doors make the bedroom glow with golden light. One of the doors is open, letting in a soft breeze. But no Pen. The faint scent of paint lingers in the air.

"Pen?"

"Up here in the office."

I take the stairs two at a time and spot her immediately. She's perched on a ladder that's resting against the built-in bookshelves. A fresh coat of shiny raspberry-red paint gleams on the back walls of the shelves. She looks over her shoulder and smiles softly, those big eyes of hers lighting up.

It doesn't matter that it's only been a few hours since we woke up together, the sight of her never fails to affect me. It's as though she has her own power source, and whenever I draw near, my body jump-starts. She's so pretty. Delicate but strong. Clever eyes and smart mouth. And mine. God, I love that.

"Penelope," I say, strolling across the room.

"August."

I pause a few feet away, resting a hip against the desk. Pen turns on the ladder to fully face me, and I take a long, lingering look. She's a feast after a famine. Delicious. I know this now. The knowledge doesn't ease my hunger, only makes it more rampant. I find myself wanting her all the time.

"Penelope."

Candy-pink lips curl in a smile. "You realize that, unless you're using it as a greeting, you only call me Penelope now when you're in some sort of a mood."

"Oh, I'm definitely in a mood right now." Surprise, surprise. "Your full name is sexy."

Her nose wrinkles. "Hardly."

How little she understands her appeal. One day, she'll fully realize it. I've made it my job to educate her.

"I'm serious. There's something sexy about it, purposeful. All those syllables. You can't ignore it—Pen-el-o-pe. It rolls off the tongue with such intention."

She tilts her head, eyeing me thoughtfully. "And what is your intention now?"

"To get you to come closer."

Slowly, she climbs down from the ladder, a saucy look in her eyes as she takes a step in my direction. "Like here?"

"Closer."

The corners of her eyes crinkle as she takes a few more steps. "This good?"

Little temptress.

"A little more."

Holding my gaze, she strolls forward, hips swaying until she's inches away, then smiles up at me, clearly pleased with her teasing. I am too.

"Mmm. That's very good." I tuck my hands into my pockets. "Now kiss me, Penelope."

Rising to her toes, she wraps her arms around my neck and gives me a soft, lingering kiss hello. A sound of satisfaction rumbles in my chest, and I deepen the kiss until she stumbles against me, breathless and eyes shining.

I can't keep my hands to myself any longer. Without warning, I pluck her up in my arms like a bride and whirl her around. She yelps but wraps her arms around my neck and peppers kisses along my jaw. I love that she takes what she wants.

"I told you I'd help you paint when I got back," I say.

Pen has been redoing the upstairs office and making it hers. The curtains are no longer white but lime silk. She's mentioned a set of Billy Baldwin X-benches that she put on hold at an antique store. I have no idea what those are, but Pen was excited as hell about them.

It's taken a year, but she's redone the whole house to create a home that's entirely ours. A drafting table sits near the window now because Pen has started to do more designs. I love watching her blossom and find her place in the world.

"Eh. I got antsy." She busses a kiss over my cheek. "You can hang the art, and I'll tell you if it's crooked."

I glance at the framed movie posters stacked against the wall and imagine that particular task. "I'd rather have painted."

"But you're better at holding up the frames with those freaky long arms so I can take a look."

"Yeah, great." I nip her earlobe before putting her down. "And you'll have me holding them up ten different ways before making up your mind."

"So dramatic." She walks over to a paint can and puts the top on it. "How's Jelly doing?"

I had been over at his house for a couple of hours hanging out. Jelly was still getting over the death of his coach but he's back in playing form. He and Monica are now officially engaged.

After returning from Texas last Thanksgiving, we confessed all to them because we knew they'd keep it secret. They'd been surprisingly understanding; Monica especially, having shrugged and said that's Hollywood.

As for the rest of the world, we're having a long engagement. Not that I think many people care much anymore. They're hung up on my Super Bowl win right now. Mainly because I made history by becoming the first rookie quarterback to ever win. Some days it doesn't seem real. Other days, it doesn't really matter. The only game that counts is the one you're playing. The past is just that.

"Jelly's good." I leaf through the movie posters and pause at a familiar one. "*The Lord of the Rings*?"

"I consider that the Luck family movie."

I laugh, feeling nostalgic about it now. "True." Curious, I keep looking through the other ones. But it's not a movie poster that has my hand stilling. Heart in my throat, I lift my head. "What's this?"

But I know. I just can't believe . . .

Pen moves to my side and looks at the framed photo blown up poster size. It's of me backlit by the stadium lights, hair slick with sweat, arm upraised in victory and holding my helmet as I shout my joy at an equally joyous group of teammates.

"I love that photo." She leans against my arm with a soft smile.

"I didn't think you would be so into my games. But I love that you are now."

Shaking her head as though I'm being ridiculous, she then looks up at me. "Pickle?"

"Yeah?" My attention is divided between her and the photo.

"I've watched every game you ever played."

Though softly spoken, her words slam into me, and I'm left unsteady.

"What?"

Deep brown eyes hold mine calmly. "Every game. Ever."

"I . . . You . . . Really?"

At that, she walks to the desk and picks up her phone, thumbing the screen as she comes back to me. From over her shoulder, I peer at the phone as she finds a folder entitled "AugustGames."

"Here." She hands me the phone.

I'm clumsy with it, unable to get my fingers to work at first. But then I scroll through the images saved. And something inside me breaks open. Years of articles, pictures saved, stats. She has it all. Emotion wells up from deep in my chest.

"I kept these as well." She's holding a shoebox filled with papers.

My hands shake as I accept the box. I swear, I've got to sit down. But I hold it together and examine the contents. Shock bolts through my chest as I riffle through old ticket stubs from my middle and high school games. A program from homecoming. Little pieces of my career lovingly saved.

My gaze darts to Penelope.

"I told you." She shrugs with a small smile. "I've loved you all my life. Your games have always meant something to me."

Slowly but deliberately, I set down the phone and the box, then reach for her. I wrap her up tight and hold her as close as possible. For a long moment, I simply breathe her in. I don't know what to say. I've never felt this . . . loved.

"Pen," I finally manage. "You're going to make me cry."

She gives me a squeeze, then pats my chest. "It's okay, big guy."

It pulls a laugh from me. I haul her up and head for the stairs. I don't stop until we're both lying in bed. The oval of her face beams with happiness as she looks back at me. Again, comes that strange sensation of buoyancy.

"Sometimes it doesn't feel real." I take her hand. "Like maybe I'm in a coma somewhere, dreaming this all up."

The corners of her eyes crinkle. "You know, I had the same thought a couple of times since we got together. Either that or I'm in an alternate reality."

We laugh about it for a second, then fall into contented silence. But my mind is moving ahead again. I've been holding back for months now with increasing difficulty. After seeing the pieces of my life lovingly saved by her, I can't do it anymore.

The tip of my thumb catches the edge of the ring on Pen's slender finger and toys with it. "Looks good on you, Pen."

Inside, my heart is pounding hard and insistent. While she simply smiles fondly.

"You should have seen the way May and June gaped. They were convinced it was your grandmother's ring."

"Because it is."

Surprise has her gaze shooting to mine. "I wondered but I didn't think . . . How did you get it so fast?"

I shrug, pretending I'm calm. But I'm not. "I always had it."

"What?" It comes out in a squeak.

Ah, but the way she continues to be surprised by my love for her. One day she won't. I want all the days.

"That day, when you were hurt," I tell her. "After your mom took you to the doctor, I went to see Nanna Linda in the den. I told her what had happened, said with great authority that I wanted to marry you, but I needed a ring."

"*No* . . . Truly? What did she say?" Her rapt expression has me smiling, my mind sinking back into the memory of Nanna's indulgent look when I'd told her of my plan.

"She didn't laugh or tell me I was being foolish. She just nodded and said sometimes that's the way of it. That Grandpop Charles had pledged his love to her when they were thirteen. And since I appeared serious about the matter, she was going to give me her ring for you.

"Took it off that weekend. Said her knuckles were getting too big for it and she wanted to remove it before she couldn't. Put it in a safe and, when she died, left it for me in her will."

With a little noise of pleasure, Pen presses her lips to my neck and hugs me. Her breath is warm on my skin. "You floor me sometimes, Pickle. You really do."

"It doesn't freak you out?"

"Why would it, when I loved you just as long? It's more like . . . sometimes I wish I'd opened my eyes a little more and really seen you then."

"I think about that too, wishing I'd realized sooner that you actually liked me instead of the hate thing." I grin at her sour face. "But we're here now. That's all that matters in the end."

"You're right." Gently, she spreads her hand out over my heart and looks at the ring I claimed for her long ago. I never thought I'd be able to give it to her. In truth, I never actually tried until I opened that door one rainy night, and she finally looked at me.

Call it pride, or perhaps it was the fear of rejection. But I held myself back from Penelope for too long. No more. I'm all in. Come what may.

Pen's voice cracks with emotion when she finally speaks. "My whole life I was content with sitting back and watching others shine. I'd resigned myself to watching you too. Then you came along and pulled me right into the sun, made me feel beautiful and treasured. With your beautiful soul, immense talent, and tender heart. You're the best person I know."

Hell. I curl into her, holding her hand to my heart. I can't wait any longer.

"Penelope?"

"August."

I meet her eyes. "I don't want you to take the ring off."

She pauses, lips parting on a breath. A gleam enters her eyes. "You don't?"

"No." I stroke her wrist where her pulse beats as fast as mine. "I never did. But it's a delicate thing asking the girl you've loved forever to marry you when you've only been together for a little while."

Pen swallows thickly. "I can see that being something to consider."

I nod, looking down at the ring, then back at her. "So I've been waiting. Letting you get used to the idea of you and me."

"But you didn't need to get used to it?" She gives me a look of total understanding and growing impishness.

"No," I say easily. "I knew from the start. We were inevitable."

"Like Thanos." It comes out weepy but happy.

A smile pulls wide. I feel it to my toes. "Yeah. Only not evil."

"But perfect." She threads her fingers through my hair. "We were always going to be perfect together."

Our kiss is soft and reverent before I pull back. She's the most beautiful thing in my life. Always was. "So fucking perfect. Marry me, Penelope? For real and forever?"

Her smile blooms. "I love you, August. For real and forever. And I'm never taking this ring off."

"You've made my life, Sweets."

"That's good. You've made mine too, Pickle."

You see that guy? The one lying next to the most perfect woman in his world? The one smiling at him like he brought her the sun? When really, it's she who gave him everything he ever wanted? Yeah, that's me, lucky bastard that I am.

Am I entertained?

You bet your ass.

★ ★ ★ ★ ★

ACKNOWLEDGMENTS

It takes a village to raise a proper book. I'd like to thank all those who helped make this one: Kimberly Brower, my agent; Cat Clyne, my editor; the hardworking team at MIRA—Alexandra McCabe (marketing maven), as well as Stephanie Choo, Gina Macedo, and Taryn Ortolan (for production and copyedits); and Ann and the Milk & Cookies Marketing team, who pitch in when it's all done. And, of course, the readers, reviewers, and booklovers who give the book life once it's out in the world. Thank you!

PLAYLIST FOR ONLY ON GAMEDAY

A SELECTION OF SONGS THAT INSPIRED KRISTEN CALLIHAN IN WRITING THIS BOOK.

"Rocket Man," Elton John

"Teen Spirit," Nirvana

"Bad," U2

"Satisfaction," Rolling Stones

"Take a Chance on Me," ABBA

"Summer Samba," Astrud Gilberto

"L.A. Woman," The Doors

"Old Enough," The Raconteurs, featuring Ricky Skaggs and Ashley Monroe

"Night and Day," Ella Fitzgerald